DOPPELGÄNGER

Marc J. Seifer

Rudy Styne Quadrilogy
Book II

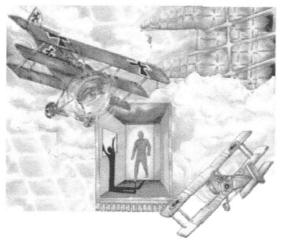

Lynn Sevigny

Doorway Press
Box 32, Kingston, RI 02881

DOPPELGÄNGER
Subtitle: The Dead Wringer
RUDY STYNE QUADRILOGY, Book II
© Copyright 2016 by Marc J. Seifer (b. 1948)

ISBN: 978-1-931261-22-7
LCCN: 2016912696

Printed in the United States of America
First printing: September 2016

10 9 8 7 6 5 4 3 2

For information: Doorway Press.

❖**DOORWAY PRESS**
Box 32, Kingston, RI 02881

Frontispiece: *Eli Helman*
Title page drawing: *Lynne Sevigny*
Cover design: *Devin Keithley*

mseifer@verizon.net
MarcSeifer.com

PRAISE FOR MARC SEIFER'S BOOKS

DOPPELGÄNGER

In *Doppelgänger,* Marc Seifer runs a story of the 20th century through German eyes together with a contemporary U.S. murder mystery set in the cyber-world. He masterfully ties the two stories together through Abe Maxwell (b. 1906) who is about 98 years old in the contemporary story. Seifer tied Abe to both Rudy Styne, the hero, from the U.S.A. to Rolf Linzman, Rudy's sometimes protagonist, of Germany.

Richard Vangermeersch, Professor Emeritus, University of Rhode Island

CRYSTAL NIGHT

I had to tell you how much I am enthralled with *Crystal Night!* You are an incredible chronicler, your knowledge is vast! You have woven such minute detail into the tapestry or rather web of the novel. It lives for me, that is the [Germany] and times I remember.

I rush through supper to get comfortable on the sofa with The Book. I just can't put it down.

Gloria McMurrough, Admissions Office, Roger Williams University

The overall presentation of the trials that faced a Jewish-German family, during the rise of Anti-Semitism after World War I, is stirring on how the triumph of faith and spirit, can overcome the suffering of a strong, resilient people during one of the darkest periods in modern history.

Edith Moraglia

DOPPELGÄNGER & CRYSTAL NIGHT

Dr. Seifer's novels **DOPPELGÄNGER & CRYSTAL NIGHT** contained some fascinating and well-researched details about World Wars I & II that added richness to the narrative. He displays admirable ambition and he crosses genres ably in his quest to tell a large-scale story in the second two novels of his **QUADRILOGY**. Using an impressive amount of research, the author paints a wide panorama which includes an inside look at Nazi Germany as a Jewish family struggles to maintain their small prestigious airline in an anti-Semitic environment. But these two books are not just rooted in the past. There is also a modern story, a search by the protagonist, news reporter Rudy Styne, to uncover a master hacker who is attempting to take over the internet as he is also moved to discover who is German double is and who his biological parents really are. Yes, there are a number of diverse paths in this complex tale, but Seifer deftly brings all threads together in a satisfying way that enriches, because the reader, not only gets to learn a lot about real history, namely how both world wars were conducted from the German perspective, but also experiences the complex emotional strain of a family doing their best to maintain their assets and survive in a hostile environment. Given the novel's breadth, the pace is quick, particularly considering the myriad topics covered and the large cast of characters. Overall, this is an imaginative, worthy and ambitious work. *Compilation of comments from New York City Editors.*

RASPUTIN'S NEPHEW

An espionage thriller, (a la Tom Clancy).… You write with great intelligence and authority. *Nicolette Phillips, New Vision.*

This is a terrifically original book, with elements of satire as well.
Dr. Stanley Krippner, author of *Song of the Siren*

Like a journey through the Major Arcana [of the Tarot], *Rasputin's Nephew* takes the reader into the bizarre and mind-boggling world of the paranormal. I enjoyed Marc Seifer's book thoroughly.
Uri Geller, Paranormalist Extraordinaire

FRAMED! MURDER, CORRUPTION &
A DEATH SENTENCE IN FLORIDA
with Stephen Rosati

A story that must be told! *Robert Leuci, "Prince of the City"*

A fascinating and exceptionally documented case study that reads like a best-seller. *Midwest Book Review*

Amazingly readable book - a true page-turner that had my complete attention from the first page to the last! *5 Star review Amazon.com*

WIZARD: THE LIFE & TIMES OF NIKOLA TESLA
BIOGRAPHY OF A GENIUS

Seifer's vivid, revelatory, exhaustively researched biography rescues pioneer inventor Nikola Tesla from cult status and restores him to his rightful place as a principal architect of the modern age.... Seifer provides the fullest account yet of Tesla as an entrepreneur, experimental physicist and inventor. *Boxed & Starred, Publisher's Weekly*

Seifer's biography rescues [Tesla] from oblivion, bringing back to life the amazingly creative intellect that gave us fluorescent lighting, wireless communication, cheap electrical power and the remote control. But Seifer also resurrects the wounded, self-destructive personality who never recovered from the loss of a favored older brother and who spiraled into weird obsessions, mental collapse and poverty as he watched other men use his inventions to win fame and riches. Seifer does an admirable job of explaining his subject's technical feats and analyzing his psychological idiosyncrasies. Tinged with pathos, this meticulously researched biography deserves attention from all who would understand the human tragedies played out in the shadows of our neon culture.
Bryce Christianson   Booklist

Marc Seifer is an excellent writer and scholar, who has produced a wonderfully readable and illuminating biography of one of the most intriguing men of this century.... mak[ing] us understand not only the man, but also the times in which he lived.... [a] masterpiece.
Nelson DeMille, New York Times best-selling author

Seifer paints a picture of Tesla that anyone familiar with the life of someone such as Orson Welles will recognize. Here was a man who peaked early, traveled in famous company.... and started believing his own press hype. That made him spend the rest of his life trying to score another universe-changing coup..... *Wizard* does a pretty good job of placing Tesla within the firmament of inventors, thinkers and futurists. With Seifer's scholarship to build on, anyone reconstructing those dizzy years of invention and litigation at the turn of the century would be foolish to try and leave out Nikola Tesla.   *Winston-Salem NC Journal*

I highly recommend this biography of a great technologist.
A.A. Mullin, US Army Space & Strategic Defense Command.

THE DEFINITIVE BOOK OF HANDWRITING ANALYSIS

Altogether this book rises like a lighthouse out of the morass of the other graphology publications in the USA. The author presents a great array of American handwritings on astoundingly high level. Although the author only had access to English sources, in spite of this, it is amazingly comprehensive. Maybe this book gets into the hands of one or another university professors and if so, it may help to break up his/her prejudices and this could lead to a raise in standards of academic psychology in the America.

Helmut Ploog, Ph.D., Editor-in-Chief of the German handwriting journal Angewandte Graphologie und Personlichkeits Diagnostik.

TRANSCENDING THE SPEED OF LIGHT
Consciousness, Quantum Physics & the Fifth Dimension

I highly recommend this book to any and all readers who are seriously interested in the puzzling problem of the nature of mind and consciousness.... Marc's epochal achievement will offer thoughts and areas of new thought to the reader for many decades to come.

Col. Tom Bearden (retired) Author of Excalibur Briefing

How is it possible for consciousness to exist in the physical universe? This is the classic mind-body problem that has eluded philosophers for many generations. Now, it appears that answers are within reach -- provided that one is willing to explore unorthodox approaches. This is exactly what author Marc Seifer has done. The depth of his scholarship and the clarity of his thinking make this book a worthwhile read for anyone interested in the frontiers of consciousness research.

Jeffrey Mishlove, Ph.D., Dean of Consciousness Studies, University of Philosophical Research

DOPPELGÄNGER

Rudy Styne Quadrilogy
Book II

Also by MARC SEIFER

Non-fiction
Wizard: The Life & Times of Nikola Tesla
The Definitive Book of Handwriting Analysis
Framed! Murder, Corruption & A Death Sentence In Florida
(with Stephen Rosati)
Transcending the Speed of Light: Quantum Physics & Consciousness
Nikola Tesla: The Man Who Harnessed Niagara Falls
Where Does Mind End?

Art Book
The Art & Life of Robert J. Adsit
(with Marta Waterman & Terrell Neuage)

Editor-in-chief
MetaScience: A New Age Journal on Consciousness, Vol's 1-3
Journal of American Society of Professional Graphologists, Vol's 1-5

Screenplays
Tesla: The Lost Wizard (Tim Eaton, co-author)
Hail to the Chief

Fiction
THE RUDY STYNE QUADRILOGY:
I Rasputin's Nephew
II Doppelgänger
III Crystal Night
IV Fate Line

A millennial belief in a Holy God may have the effect of deepening the soul, but it is also obviously archaic, and modern influences would presently bring me up to date and reveal how antiquated my origins were. To turn away from those origins, however, has always seemed to me an utter impossibility. It would be a treason to my first consciousness to un-Jew myself. One may be tempted to go behind the given and invent something better, to attempt to reenter life at a more advantageous point.... But the thought of such an attempt never entered my mind. Thus I may have been archaic, but I escaped the horrors of an identity crisis.

Saul Bellow, *New York Review of Books*, 10/27/2011

For my Parents & the Family Circle

DRAGONFLY — *Eli Helman*

RUDY & CHESSIE

"One minute, Chess. I'll be there in one minute" Rudy called into the bedroom as he tried to decode the coy message.

"Rudeee, you said that over an hour ago." Chessie sat in bed and clicked away on her laptop. "There's this neat website on strollers and car seats. You can't believe how many there are, kiddo," she continued excitedly. "You just have to see this."

"Okay, okay, just one more minute," Rudy shouted back from his office study. With a pencil in his ear, two computer screens lit up, several books opened, and a dozen newspaper articles and magazines scattered about, Rudy continued to communicate to his anonymous source.

As the writer's fingers flew across the keyboard of his Mac laptop, and his response to the codebreaker appeared on the screen, Rudy found he had gotten beyond the capacity of the computer, and so had to wait for the letters to filter in before he could type again.

He searched for the cursor, but couldn't find it. He jiggled his mouse, tapped it, flipped it over to see if it picked up any pebbles, swept the mouse pad, tried again, moved it back and forth more furiously, but he couldn't get a thing. Nada! His mouse would not respond, no matter what he did. Without his cursor, he not only felt frustrated, strangely alone, alienated from the so-called real world. He was isolated now, made inert by a glitch. He found himself staring at the screen immobilized.

"Hey, what's going on?" Chessie said. Rudy found his hair tousled and felt Chessie's warm breasts resting on the back of his neck. "C'mon, what's going on?"

"I lost my cursor."

"It's about time you cleaned up your act."

"Very funny, got any ideas?"

"Your computer froze." Chessie shifted her weight and flipped Rudy's chair to the ground.

"Be careful!" he said, completely startled.

Chess looked down at him and grinned.

"Come on, give me a hand." He reached up with his right arm.

As Chessie grabbed it, he gently tugged and brought his willing fiancé to the ground. "We don't want to hurt the bambino." Rudy hugged her on the rug and patted her belly.

Lying underneath, he gave her a kiss. "You gonna help me fix my computer?" As he spoke, he slipped his free hand into the back of her undies and cradled her tush.

"That's it," she declared, pulling his hand away. "You're just going to have to retype it anyway. Do it tomorrow. Let's get to bed."

Rudy stood up and pulled Chessie to her feet. She bent her midsection to him, wrapped her arms around his neck and stared into his eyes. He locked his gaze on the green irises. He looked in wonderment, once again at the crinkly outside corners and her slightly wrinkled eyelids. Lost in her eyes, the feelings of great love that he had for Chessie Barnsworth simply overtook him. "I love you," he thought.

"I know," her gaze returned.

Hand in hand, they ambled to the bedroom, gave each other a kiss, locked themselves into their pretzel embrace and tumbled into slumber.

The bloated General Secretary called Rudy into his chamber. Rudy could not understand why this man, so full of himself, resembled Hermann Göring, or why he had a Nazi insignia on his armsleeve. Chessie was waiting in the rotunda at the main section of the United Nations building. Rudy was concerned that he would miss her as he watched in amazement the Secretary General's hair burst into flame.

He wanted to tell the Secretary General that one of the greatest problems the modern world faced was the destruction of the integrity of the Internet by computer virus terrorists, but every time he tried to make this simple statement, the Secretary General would be interrupted by another delegate who would pour water on his head to try and cool it off.

Göring raised his eyebrows in a manner so as to say, "Let us get up." The Fat One swaggered down the hall, his hair still aflame, and Rudy followed after him.

"Come," Göring said, guiding Rudy into a computer game room. Computer screens and virtual reality images burst into his brain as alarm bells went off and the new day broke.

"Are you sure you want to go in?"

"I'm only into my fourth month and I want to work as long as I can. Once the baby is here Rude, my career is going to go into the toilet."

"On hold. It sounds better."

"Come on, we're going to miss the train." She bit off one more bite of the bagel, swirled a last hit of coffee, grabbed her valise and pocketbook and dashed out the door.

"Wait up." Rudy cantered after.

The 7:51 screeched to a halt and the commuters climbed aboard.

"Hey kids," Judy said. "I saved you seats. Judy Shea, a scraggily looking corporate attorney, patted the simulated leather beside and across from her.

"Eight hearts," Rudy shot, to the foursome playing bridge.

"Hey, Rudy," Fred, Norm, Terry and Paul, nodded back.

"Are you really going to bid on that crap?" Rudy kibitzed, as he feigned to study Fred's hand.

"Gedoutahere." Fred physically pushed Rudy away.

"Alright, alright. I can take a hint." Rudy took his seat across from Judy.

"Let's go, you're gonna bid or not?" Terry nudged.

"Fuck you, double," Norm said, and then he saw Chess. "Come on guys," and the foursome stood up and applauded.

Chessie's work at Taylor & Taylor's Auction House resulted in a spot on *Antiques Road Show* which had played over the weekend. Everyone had seen or heard about it.

"Nice bid," Chessie called back. "Come on, guys, go back to your game."

"Forget her autograph," Paul said kiddingly.

Smiling, Chessie said offhandedly, "So, Rude, is your computer still frozen?"

"Jeeze, I forgot." Rudy dropped back into his seat, pulled out his laptop and prayed. "It's dead," he said dismally.

"Motherboard's shot." Paul declared. "Redouble."

"You leave his mother out of this!" Norm bounced back. "And I pass."

"Did you press the start-up button?" Judy asked.

"Duh!"

"Rudy!" Chessie chastised. "How about resetting the PRAM."

"Man, I can't believe I didn't think of that. I did reset the slithy toves. Really, Chess, what am I going to do?"

"Reset the PRAM, like your wife said, schmuck," Norm called out.

Rudy looked questioningly at the other bridge players. Terry and Fred nodded in agreement, while Paul mouthed "Motherboard."

"All right, Chess, I'll bite," Rudy said. "What do I do?"

"Wait, let me look it up." Chessie opened up her iPhone and searched the Internet for resetting the parameters. "Here it is. Press the Power, Command and Option buttons at the same time you press the P and R."

"How many fingers do you think I have? Isn't there just a reset button."

"Do as she said, schmuck," Norm called out again.

Rudy looked over, and, once again, like bobblehead dolls, Sam, and Terry nodded agreement, while Paul continued to mouth "Motherboard." Stretching his fingers, after first smirking at Paul, Rudy complied. It started right up. He sat there amazed.

"You're welcome," Chessie said triumphantly.

"Thanks," Rudy replied. Breathing a sigh of relief, he logged on and then began searching his emails for the file he was working on the night before.

Turning her attention back to Judy, Chessie remarked, "I was on the Martha Stewart site last night."

"And?"

"Thought it would be a good place to check about menus for the wedding."

"Ahhh." Judy said.

"It was great. They had everything and then they asked...."

As their conversation continued, Rudy tried to bring up his lost e-mail to CodeBreaker Morant. "Shit, it's gone."

"But if I wanted to be on their list," Chessie continued, "then I would have to accept their cookie."

"So, which flavor did you get?" Judy asked.

"No, dummy. It's not food, it's a parasite they latch onto your computer to find more information about you."

"You're kidding."

"Does she look like she's kidding?" Rudy's fingers continued to click away in at attempt to reproduce from memory the gist of his conversation with Morant. Something about "attaining godlike status by," Rudy racked his brains and then typed, "controlling the destiny of men."

"So, tell me again. What's a cookie?" Judy asked.

"I can't believe you don't know this stuff, Judy. Corporate law and all that," Rudy chimed. Chessie flashed him a look.

"I'm not a computer person. That's what I have a secretary for," Judy said.

"What about Facebook. You mean you don't have a page?" Chessie asked.

"Hey, I just got friended by Stephen Colbert!" Norm shouted over.

"Good for you, shithead," Paul grumbled.

"No, I don't have a Facebook," Judy said, ignoring Norm and Paul. "I don't text message and I don't twitter. So shoot me," Judy continued, "but I do want to know more about this cookie shit. I think we got an invasion of privacy issue."

"They asked my permission," Chessie said.

"Yeah," Rudy said, "They did, but most don't. And who's to say some of these cookies are not Trojan horses."

"Trojan horses?" Judy asked.

"Yeah, plants that can do more than simply just monitor where you're going."

"We supposedly have a fire wall down at our office to stop Trojan horses." Fred, one of the bridge players and also an attorney, got up on his knees on his side of the seat and butted in. Judy looked clueless.

"A bridge to nowhere, one that can't be jumped."

"The only fire wall I know about," Chessie said, "is a computer not hooked up to the web."

"Well then, maybe that's what we have," Fred said.

"Can you download information from these computers to email?" Rudy asked.

"Yeah, I think we can, now that you mention it," Fred reflected. "Maybe it's a filter or one-way street or something."

"I wouldn't bet on it."

"I don't know," Fred conceded, returning to the game. "I passed, pass, pass. OK." Back to Rudy, "They need me over here."

"Hey," Norm yelled over, "If you were using a Trojan, then how come Chessie's pregnant."

The group continued their titter as the train rattled towards the city. "Penn Station!" the conductor cried. Everyone got ready to get up.

"But I've got nineteen points," Norm complained. "Can't we keep our cards and play this out tomorrow?"

"Sure, Normie" Terry said. "I'll carefully collect each pack and hand them out just as I got them tomorrow."

"Really, you'd do that?"

Didn't I just say I would?" Terry said as he gathered the cards, shuffled and put them in the pack. Just then, the train screeched to a halt, the commuters poured out of their seats and rushed into the station. Smiles adorned the faces of the bridge players and those kibitzers who followed their daily action. Chess grabbed Rudy's hand, yanked him out of the train, and took him to the subway that led to Grand Central. Following the masses, they scooted up the stairs and into the giant rotunda.

People moved in different directions as if on conveyor belts. Large bright colorful advertising placards emanated from the walls as if they were Andy Warhol paintings. The Off Track betting line, as always, was lazily snaking its way through the commuters at the near end of the corridor. Live music as if from the Andes Mountains pierced the rotunda with the sounds of a pan flute, bongo drums, tambourine and guitar. Rudy and Chess stood amazed for the brief time they had to watch and be seemingly teleported to a holy mountain village like Machu Pichu. With jet black hair braided into a tight ponytail trailing out the center of his hat, the flute player radiated a charismatic power that made him appear as an ancient Peruvian prince. Chessie looked over at Rudy with one of those looks.

"OK." Plunking down a $20 spot, he purchased a CD and handed it to her.

"How romantic." Chessie stuffed the little packet into her pocketbook, pecked him on the lips and then they parted.

"See you for dinner," he called after. Chess simply waved her hand without turning back.

Rudy traversed the long hall, made a right turn at the west end of the tunnel and turned north so as to exit four blocks uptown through the Roosevelt Hotel.

Emerging at Vanderbilt Avenue, he walked west along 46th Street. As he crossed Madison Avenue and thought back, as he often did, to the first time he had ever come to the city and how it kept metamorphasizing as the years rolled on. The use of glassed in atriums was one change Rudy particularly liked, and, another, of course, was the pooper scooper law which allowed the city streets to be transformed almost overnight from a place to avoid to one of outdoor cafes.

The Fifth Avenue office at Modern Times had been refurbished with wall to wall carpeting, a pleasant light-teal mottled design, and new work stations set up like a geometric maze in a series of rows spanning the entire 3rd floor. Rudy entered the labyrinth that led to his pod. He passed the metro desk headed by Mort's cell which was adorned with framed signed photo reproductions of Casey Stengel, Yogi Berra, Roger Maris, Mickey Mantle and a Victoria's Secret calendar with the September gal dressed in a bra and laced panties hanging near his computer. "Hi," Rudy said to Mort, who wrote a daily column on local politics.

No one could ever remember Mort wearing a jacket. Always a dark blue or brown denim short sleeve shirt with a rope-thin red, silver or yellow tie. Deep winter, rainstorm or Indian summer, didn't matter, same outfit. It was Mort's sex life that was the real mystery. A youthful fifty-two, give or take, it had been rumored that Mort had once been married, but no one ever had the courage to ask if the rumor was true, and no one knew a single thing about the guy's private life.

"That new?" Rudy pointed to an autographed photo of Sammy Sosa?"

"Yeah!"

"How'd you swing that?"

"Very funny Rudy. My nephew's got a pen pal from Santo Domingo, and he got it for me."

"So that's a real signature?"

"Duhhh."

"If you can get me a Willie Mays...."

"Yeah, yeah, I know, I'll FedEx it to your home." Well, at least Rudy now knew Mort had a nephew.

Kimberly Attison, the rookie photographer, had a new hair style. To everyone's surprise, she had cropped her thoroughbred ponytail, and replaced it with a Dorothy Hamil wedge. Today she wore a white suit with light green Charlie Chan style silk shirt, a laced scroll design with a Nehru collar, two pairs of gold earrings, corked platform shoes that increased her height by a good six inches and three gold bracelets on her right hand. The effect was topped with a thumb ring on her left hand with the neck and head of a swan, and small metallic green and white paintings of what looked like sailboats at sunset emblazoned on each fingernail.

"Hi Rudy," she said as he passed by. Boy, she was a looker. *Would she even know who Dorothy Hamil was?*

"Hi Sal," Rudy said to Sally-Ann. No longer the prettiest gal in the office, Sally-Ann had long ago stopped wearing dresses, and now had a butchy haircut to boot, and it appeared to become a bit more plastic each day. It seemed that some of the fight had been taken out of her, now that she was aging, and she hadn't quite readjusted. Sally-Ann had a simulated double window which was "open" and overlooked the wine country in Napa Sonoma. The fields of grapes spread through the valley with mountains in the distance all which gave the illusion of a great space in her compact office cell. Rudy had heard that she was on anti-depressants. He kind of hoped she wasn't, because if she was, they didn't seem to be doing much good.

"Oh, hi Rudy," she said, barely looking up.

"Why so glum, Sal?"

"I lost $240 last month and feel like an idiot."

"How'd you do that?" Rudy asked.

"You are not going to believe it, if I tell you," she whispered. "And you can't tell anyone else."

Rudy could see Sally-Ann really needed to unload, so he agreed.

"If Mort or Bill hears this, your ass will be grass."

"All right, Sal, all right." Rudy also talked as quietly as he could.

"It happened playing solitaire on line."

"What are you talking about?" Rudy said. "The card game?"

"Yeah, well it's kinda like Crazy Eights. And it wasn't my fault."

"I'm not following," Rudy said.

"It was all Cathy's fault. She's my mother's nurse's aid. She's a friend on BrainSpace."

"Yeah...." Rudy prompted.

"She's the one got me started on these computer games."

"I don't get it. How'd she get you started?"

"Well, that's the whole point. I was just minding my own business, going through my emails, and I get this one from Cathy saying, 'Join me on Diamond Head.' So I click the hyperlink which says 'accept' and it takes me to a series of computer games."

"And you started playing solitaire?" Rudy asked.

"Not right off. The first game was called Shoot'm Safari. It's a monkey with a gun shooting different colored grapes in a tree. So you play and you get points. I think I got about 9,000 points, but it tells you that the average player gets about 16,000 points, and if you get 35,000 points, you win $100, so it asks if you want to Level Up."

"Level Up?"

"Yeah. The monkey can get more ammunition if you ask your friend for help."

"What are you talking about?" Rudy just didn't get it.

"Your list of friends from BrainSpace come up and it asks you to choose one of them to help increase your odds."

"So, did you level up?" Rudy asked.

"No, that's how I got hooked. I wasn't going to bring someone else in. I'm not that dumb! So I clicked the exit button, but instead, a list of other games popped into my line of sight. Egyptian Solitaire looked intriguing, it said *A chance to win $1,000*, so, what the heck, I clicked, and out pops this Hieroglyphic-like Egyptian who deals out a set of about fifteen cards in different layers, and at the bottom of the screen you turn a card over and if it's next to one of the cards on the screen, it gives you the right to click them off."

"I'm still not quite there," Rudy said.

"Well, say, you can see a 7, 8, 3, Jack and King."

"OK," Rudy prompted.

"And you turn over a 6. This allows you to click on touching cards, so you can click on the 7 and then the 8, and they disappear, and if, say, you get a 9 and a 10, you can click those on and then that gets you to the Jack, and if a Queen appears, you can click on the King, and a bunch of replacement cards which you can see in the background come to the fore. And the goal is to get rid of those also, that is to clear the board."

"OK, now I get it."

"So, if you are stuck, you turn over another card, and you keep turning over cards until you get one that is contiguous to one of the ones you can see, but on the left is a Joker that looks like a Sphinx, so if you are stuck, you can use this Joker and it allows you to continue. And if you win, you get points, and if you get enough of those...., you can win $1,000."

"So, why did it cost you money?"

"Because you're on a timer, like Beat the Clock. You have to wipe out all the cards in, say four minutes, and if you use the Joker and get lucky, you can win. But if you keep losing, the screen asks you if you want to Level Up."

"And all your BrainSpace friends appear?"

"Right. Now you get it. If you ask one of your friends to join you, you can not only race him in the game, but you get an extra Joker, or, if you don't want to suck someone else in, you can *buy* a Joker for, say, $1.20, two Jokers for $2.00, three for $2.75 and so on. And that's how I got hooked."

"So you spent $240 buying Jokers?" Rudy asked in total surprise.

"That was last month's bill. This month could be worse," Sally-Ann confessed.

"And did you win any money?"

"I got credited $300."

"You mean, you really owed $540?!"

"I feel like such a dope."

"Sal, I'm not going to say anything. You know what you have to do."

"Stop playing?" she asked.

"No, send the bill to your friend Cathy."

"I can't do that."

"Well, it's all her fault. Either that, or level up."

"Thanks," Sal smiled. "I knew you'd understand."

"Good, kiddo, as long as you learned something." Rudy gave Sal a friendly kiss on the cheek and got up to leave.

"Congratulate Chessie for me, will ya?"

"Sure, Sal. And don't worry, mum's the word."

"Thanks."

The weeks seemed to fly by, and Chessie found herself spending more time at home, doing her work by Skype and email.

"I had a dream that you rearranged my room," Rudy said one morning.

"Well, it is a mess," Chessie retorted. "Lucky I didn't move you into the basement."

"Thanks," Rudy said, giving Chess a kiss. "Going in today?"

"No. Mike's been pretty good. I'll go in tomorrow."

Rudy took the train by himself, using the time to continue his dialog with Codebreaker Morant. "Something is up," Codebreaker wrote. The train pulled in. Exiting with the commuting crowd, Rudy grabbed a coffee on the run and made his way to the office.

Bill, head of the business department, was a good ten years Mort's junior, just a few years older than Rudy. With an MBA from Weselyn, Wall Street Bill was handsome and flamboyant, forever showing up in a bright new suit or outlandish flashy tie. Driving a Tesla Roadster which he bought after trading in his Porsche, Bill appeared to be more attached to his car than to his family or girlfriends. Married twice, Bill had been engaged three times since his last marriage. He had a nine-year-old son from the second marriage who he always talked about, but who he never seemed to have the time to see. Bill's pod had an old photo of his son, a copy of a painting of a fox hunt in Great Britain, and of course, a half-dozen pictures of his car.

"Bill," Captain Whitmore called him into the office. The captain, as always, had the elegant air about him as if he came from another era. With his thin moustache, bowtie and pin-striped suit, he was remindful of many of the actors from the 1940's. William Powell was the one that people most often associated him with.

"These are box seats for the Met game. Ty Cobb's in town. If you don't take your son to this game this weekend, I am going to have to let you go."

"Thanks, captain." Bill's eyes welled up. Ty Cobb! Where'd he pull that one from? He ran over and gave the captain a kiss to the great surprise of both of them.

Rudy, Mort and Sally-Ann watched the episode through the glassed enclosure. Although they began to laugh when Bill kissed the captain, their merriment shifted to compassion when Bill came out of the enclosure tear stained.

"The captain had you pegged, Bill," Mort said. "You're more attached to that car of yours than to your kid."

"It's just when I see my wife, my former wife, that is, it reminds me of how I screwed it up, how I blew it big time."

"You have a chance to make amends," Rudy said. "I'll give you two-fifty for the tickets and then you can get a new sound system for your car and take your kid for a ride."

Bill looked up in shock, and then he started to smile. "Thanks, bud. It's nice to know I've got a friend in Rudy Styne."

"Just trying to help."

"I know you are," Bill acknowledged smiling.

Rudy parked his laptop at his pod. Unlike the others, his was adorned only with current articles. When he was at work, that was all he tended to think about. As he did every day, before logging on, he walked into the kitchen to put his box lunch into the refrigerator.

"Hey, what's this?" Rudy came out waving a big yellow sheet, reading from it: "'Notice! As of September 17th, one week hence, all items not properly tagged with these yellow stickers,' he held up a packet of stick-on stamps, 'will be tossed.' Now what is this all about? Who wrote this?"

"Have you seen the inside of that refrigerator?!" Sally-Ann steamed. She was dressed in a full-length peach chiffon pants suit whose top flowed like a rippling stream as she ran up to make her point. Her eyes ablaze, Rudy looked back somewhat in awe of the subtext of the anger that flowed from her.

"Look, I've given everyone one full week's notice. Have you seen the crud in there! That cream cheese jar's been there since last December! Are you going to open it?" she glared.

"No." Rudy said sheepishly.

"No." Bill responded meekly.

"I'm certainly not going to touch it," Captain Whitmore said, raising his hands in an expression of complete concession. "Sally-Ann, you have the full backing of the head honcho. You do your thing!"

"Thank you, cap'n," she said as she marched into the kitchen and returned with a few choice items which she held with two fingers at a great distance from her head. "I bring to your attention a mystery meat sandwich wrapped loosely in wax paper, which if memory serves well, has been in this refrigerator for well over two months, the skeeviest butter dish I have ever seen..."

"Here, here." Bill chipped in.

"A rotting tomato, a half open can of soup, a tin foil ball of something that no-one dare open and some other crap I can't even bring myself to touch until I get special gloves from the Atomic Energy Commission! Mr. Styne has before him the Refrigerator Declaration and a stack of yellow stick-on sheets. I hereby proclaim that anything not tagged by Thursday will be tossed."

"Way to go!" Mort shouted, to cheers and applause which broke out amongst the rest of the reporters.

"Rudy, when you get a chance," the captain said from the doorway of his office.

"Yes, captain," Rudy entered the office.

"How's Chessie doing?"

"She's fine, going to work until the end."

"Good for her. Saw her on *Road Show*. And the wedding plans?"

"Everything's copasetic."

"Rudy, I've given you a big assignment. The Internet is probably the most important advance to come along since, I don't know, the advent of moveable type? It's simply unprecedented."

"What about the steam engine or the television?"

"Let's not split hairs. You get the idea." The captain didn't say it as a question.

"Antibiotics, the airplane."

"Yeah, I know, and contact lenses and the remote. But I'm talking about now, Rudy. Now! Security's the thing. The privacy issues alone are monumental. We have the shadow web where all sorts of criminal activity takes place undetected, and then there's thievery, illegal wire transfers of vast sums of money, the posting of millions of business people's private passwords from LinkedIn on a hacker site, the problem of viruses, worms and Trojan horses, the attack on corporate websites when hacktivists took down Visa and Paypal when they stopped supporting Wikileaks, the ability to even turn on some unsuspecting schmuck's webcam for Christ's sake, and what about national security. You remember *War Games*."

"Of course," Rudy said, quoting the CIA director, "The next Pearl Harbor…."

"…. could be a cyber attack. I know the quote," the captain said finishing Rudy's sentence. "We're in a guerilla cyberwar here, Rudy, so, keep that in mind when you look at this."

Captain Whitmore handed Rudy an article about the "Nerd Brigade," a group of anarchists and cyber-thieves who hang around international airports and major business districts in key cities like London, Paris, New York and Berlin with wireless devices that can pick up information on computer chips embedded into fancy new credit cards, passports, and even cell phones and laptops. Rudy skimmed the article quickly. In one instance, a man's entire bank account was wiped out and his home sold while he was away on an extended business trip traveling through Europe. Interpol tried to follow the wire transfers of the monies stolen, funds in excess of $15 million, but they were not sure precisely in which country the cash was eventually dumped. Guesses ranged from Switzerland to the Cayman Islands to Uruguay. The guy returned to a house that had not only been sold, but all of its contents were gone as well!

"Jesus!" Rudy said.

"You think that's something," the captain said, "look at this one." It was a story about Bill Massie, CEO of Toronto Pharmaceuticals. After taking a short vacation in Fiji, he found when he returned to his office, that he had been locked out of his own computer because his password had been changed. When he finally gained access to his hard drive two days later, he found that his plans for a major takeover of Genklone had been usurped. Kerzcyk Interlukin, one of his key competitors, had instead purchased Genklone, and so a deal worth three quarters of a billion had been dashed. Without this new merger, his $7 billion company now risked filing for Chapter 11. That rumor alone caused the stock to drop in two days from about $8 per share to under 25¢. And the kicker was, the people who shorted the stock may have been the very ones who stole his information in the first place.

"And then there was those cyberattacks by Beijing into Google's G-mail accounts, gossip columnists for Rupert Murdoch's *The World* newspaper hacking into the phones of a thousand or more British politicos and celebrities, cyberattacks on the Pentagon and NATO, most likely by foreign governments, Wikileaks accessing the Secret Internet Protocol Router Network or SIPRNet, used by the government to transmit classified information, the Israeli cyber-dismantling of an Iranian nuclear power plant by seeding Iran's computers with a slug virus, numerous cities shutting down cell-phone use in blocked out areas during times of potential crisis, China Telecom's re-routing of a quarter of the Internet through their own servers and, along with the Russians and North Koreans, setting up Trojan malware on US infrastructure platforms such as on water treatment facilities, chemical plants, pipelines and electrical power grids. And then there's the deep web, thought to dwarf in size the surface web used by a whole host of desperados for illegal trade from arms dealers and Jihadists to drug running and child porn. However, with all that, the captain's favorite was still the blatant hacking of on-line poker games rigged so that those in the loop could see all hands at once and therefore never lose.

"We got security holes up the Wazoo," the captain said, "and on the social front there is this never-ending battle between MugShot, Formspring.me and MyPlace. Not only are the youth dealing with unwanted sexting, mean-spirited unfriending, cyber-bullying and invasion of privacy issues on a scale unprecedented, these sites are also crashing not just because or their rapid growth, but because of predator tactics by advertisers, hackers, scavengers and pedophiles. If you want technical help, just let me know."

"Okay, captain, but I first want to stay on point with my contact with Codebreaker Morant."

"The FBI would give their eye-teeth to get hold of that guy," Whitmore said. "You know, he's on their Ten Most Wanted list."

"That's the whole point, captain."

"Yeah, well maybe I should just pass this through legal." The captain was referring to residual obligations linked to remnants of the Patriot Act.

"What happened to Freedom of the Press?"

"What about aiding and abetting?"

"Are you saying I shouldn't have told *you*!"

"Maybe Rudy. He's not a good guy."

"I'm a reporter, captain. Look at it from CBM's point of view. He's drawing attention to holes in the system, flaws in software programs."

"And that makes it right?! What about that 'Ever yours' email? Damn thing practically took down Norway and Sweden, severely crippled most of the rest of Europe and actually succeeded in shutting down Webskate Wireless right here in New York for 8 very long hours. Losses were calculated into the billions."

"Billions seems a stretch, captain. You're forgetting that Morant attached a suicide payload to his own virus, which demobilized it shortly after launch."

"How long is shortly?"

"Thirty-five, forty minutes."

"And in that time, he infected 7% of all computers on the planet?"

"More like .07%, captain."

"Whatever, Rudy. It still included some banks."

"I think that was the point. He's forced the authorities to re-think the whole on-line banking thing. Codebreaker is telling us something important."

"Come with me," the captain said, "I want to tell this to everyone." Whitmore entered the main area and called the crew to attention. "People," the captain said, waving a flyer, "I have a memorandum from Robert Zozzie warning all employees to shut off their computers each evening. Do not just put them to sleep. I have also been advised to change all passwords. Zozz has recommended the use of random letter codes with passwords changed on a weekly basis."

"Oh, great!" Sally-Ann said. "I'm never going to remember some non-sensical chain of letters."

"And I must warn you," the captain said seriously, "Zozz expressed quite clearly that you are not to put your password on a file on any computer. You keep them in your wallets. Is that understood?"

"Yes, sir," they replied.

"To reiterate, as of today, all old passwords will no longer be valid." The captain handed out new passwords to each person in the office.

"Zxgron62yo! How in hell am I going to remember this?!" Sally-Ann read.

"Hell, you got an easy one," Mort said. "Mine is oq4657nryzb."

"Shush," Bill said. "These walls have ears."

"*Oooohhh!*" Mort responded sarcastically.

"Suppose, say, Mort is out and we need to get into his computer?" Rudy asked.

"I'll keep a list of the passwords in my safe in my office. Any other questions."

"No, sir, Captain Hikgenerptget."

"That will be all, Mort," the captain said.

"What brought this on?" Rudy asked when Whitmore was out of earshot.

"The captain's computer was broken into," Sally said.

"How did he know?"

"Because he keeps a record of his logins. He was not here last Wednesday, and yet there are two logins for his name at that time.

"Captain, may I see you?"

"Yes, Rudy. Come on in."

"Was anything important taken from you?"

"It was more the feeling of being violated. My computer feels unclean. Rudy, I want you to look into this." As the captain talked, his computer farted.

"Can't you get rid of that?" Rudy said stifling laughter.

"I'm ready to chuck the thing out the window. I've had Zozz up here six times on this. He said the virus is imbedded into a login system which triggers my speaker, and he says it has been replicated as many as 15 times throughout the hard drive."

"At least it doesn't smell," Rudy said laughing.

"Well, not yet anyway!"

Rudy emailed Zozz and set up a meeting. Robert Zozzie had been with the company for just three years. Shortly after graduating from RPI, Zozz came down to the city and set up a computer consulting firm, but the captain liked him and offered him a permanent position allowing Zozz to moonlight as well, as long as it didn't interfere with his job at MT.

Zozz's office looked like a hurricane had ripped through it, charts and books and papers scattered all over the floor, several computer screens on and another machine that regulated all the data that came into the main website.

"You see this list, Rudy?" Zozz said. As usual, his hair was tied back into a pair of ponytails, he wore a muscle shirt to show off his array of tattoos, he wore a blue and red tie, which simply hung around his bare neck, and a pair of blue jeans worn at the knees. Zozz was also trying to grow a beard. His face always seemed to have a three-day growth.

"What is it?"

"This," Zozz said, "is a list of attempts by computer hackers to enter our system."

"But it looks like there are hundreds every minute!"

"There are. These assholes use high-speed computers and they simply use a variety of techniques to target all the major media outlets, industrial sites, military computers, the list is endless."

"Well, who's doing it?" Rudy asked.

"Sometimes it's foreign countries like Russia, China, Uzbekistan or North Korea, sometimes it's professional hackers like Wikileaks or Anonymous, and other times it's just kids fucking around."

"Why can't we trace them?"

"We can, and we do, but frankly, the amount of hacking is so massive, that, for the most part, the government or powers that be just do nothing and hope for

"Will our system be safe?"

"Yeah, and Santa's sleigh will be on time this Christmas too. Well, I'll see you later, buddy." Zozz gave Rudy his famous smile, slapped his hand the way a baseball player would after hitting a game-winning homerun and turned back to his array of winking machines.

Rudy thanked Zozz for his time and took the elevator back up to the office. He sat with the group over coffee and then returned to his pod, punched in his password and logged on. As he began to type the lead line to the story he was working on, his computer made a sputtering sound and the screen collapsed into a dot in the center. And then he read the words, "Oh, Shit."

"Hey," Mort called out. "My computer's down."

"So's mine," Sally-Ann said.

"Mine too," Rudy found himself saying, even though something in the back of his brain sent him a different signal. He thought, at first that Zozz was playing a practical joke, but, over the phone, Zozz said he had nothing to do with it.

"It's a viral attack," Bill proclaimed.

"What the hell's going on?" Captain Whitmore exited his office and walked briskly over to the maze of cells where Rudy's, Mort's, Bill's and Sally-Ann's work spaces were located.

"Oh Shit!" he read from each computer. "What's this all about?"

"Bill says it's a virus," Sally-Ann said. "Bill, isn't that right?"

"Yes, I've seen one like this before."

"Where was that?"

"My son's got a computer game which ends with a dot like this and the words 'The End'."

"And that's your proof?" Whitmore asked.

"Yes."

Just as the captain finished, all the screens in the office changed to read, "Only kidding." Then, the words broke apart and morphed back into the original screen that had been in operation before the attack.

"I don't like this at all!" the captain barked. "We've got sensitive info here and what about exclusive breaking news. Get Zozz up here! We've been violated. Rudy, you've got big shoes to fill. And Sally, Mort, get on the phone and find out if any other magazines or newspapers were hit."

"Look at this!" Bill exploded as he rotated a small TV monitor so the group could see.

Chip Reynolds of CNBC News was on. "Oh, expletive has appeared on thousands of computers in corporative offices throughout the world. Although most of the calls have come from New York City, where we are based, through satellite link-ups and email, it appears that similar viral attacks have appeared in England, Italy, Russia, Thailand and Australia.

"We have here Ashley LaPolla from MIT's codebreaker lab to comment."

The scene shifted to an image of a young gal dressed in blue jeans and a colored t-shirt with the name Ashley LaPolla, Ph.D. superimposed below her face. "So, Dr. LaPolla, what do you make of this?"

"We have a very sophisticated viral inoculation. NTroodr, which we believe is the name of the cracker, has uncovered a security hole in the software of Windows 12.17 linked to an e-mail subroutine that in turn is yoked to the main root of Microsoft's DOS."

"Hold on a second professor. For those of us who are not computer savvy, can you put this in layman's terms?"

"Of course."

"Let's start with the term 'cracker'."

"In computer lingo," Ashley began, "a hacker now is generally seen in a positive light. It's a term for a savvy computer programmer. A cracker has malicious intent."

"And, a root system?"

"The core or nerve center of the computer."

"Now, how is it that all computers broke down at the same time?"

"We think he's got a virus linked to the calendar, and it's set up like an Aids virus. What NTroodr realized was that if he could create a virus that could wriggle itself into the very viral guard that was protecting the computer, the software that was purchased to protect the computer would be the safe harbor for the virus to hide in! And, since it's synched to the calendar, once a particular date and time is reached, which NTroodr chose as today, the virus is released, timed to explode simultaneously around the globe.

"I have not had time to diagnose it, but my guess is that once the virus is launched it sends out duplicates of itself which lie dormant throughout random computer and in email accounts, only to be triggered once again at some future point in history."

"So, you think this will happen again?"

"You can bet on it."

"And why would someone like NTroodr do something like this?"

"Egomania. To give his life meaning. The ability to become a God. This outbreak is one of the largest recorded in history. This is why I think it's just a matter of time before NTroodr appears again, and probably tops what he did here."

"Is he malicious?"

"This particular attack appears to be mostly benign but with the ability to control the destiny of men, one never knows."

Rudy went back to his pod and ruminated. He had never heard of NTroodr before and was wondering why this MIT gal was so sure it wasn't CodeBreaker Morant. Something she said resonated with something CodeBreaker himself had once said. He looked over his notes and then Googled this Ashley LaPolla.

THE CHURCH

Chess simply radiated that day, in her wedding dress with that special glow which emanates because of the promise of that new life growing inside her, and making its presence already known.

The word love was inadequate for Rudy, so he made up words to describe his feelings for Chessie Barnsworth, Chessie B, Chess, Cheskacheers, Buddie love, Scrunchkins….

Charles Koswell had flown in from Jakarta where he was covering yet another student uprising. As his tux had not been cleaned, Charles rented one from Penguin Rental. In a rush, he chose based on his jacket size and did not take into account the fit of the suit. The pants were baggy and heavy and chafed his legs, and the shirt, which was starched, never seemed to sit properly on his shoulders. Impossible to tuck in, Charles decided to try to compensate by tightening the cummerbund, but when he did, the shirt simply buckled causing his jacket to stick out.

Charles reached deep into his pockets searching for the rings. "Where the heck are they?" he mumbled as he waited for the rest of the guests to arrive and the ceremony to begin.

Overflowing with relatives, colleagues and friends, all dressed in their finest, a number of them gave a hoot when one very long stretch limo pulled up to the front door and Rudy and the rest of his core family flowed out and made their way up the steep front staircase to the entrance of the regal church. Designed by Christopher Woodcock, the 18th century sailor and architect, the church resembled a schooner with its clapboard spire rising up much like a main mast to a dizzying height of 165 feet.

Rudy nodded to Captain Whitmore who was standing near the curb talking to Charles Koswell, and then he leaned over to give his mother a hand.

"Rudy, is this your lovely bride?" the good captain kidded as he approached to meet Rudy's mother.

"Captain, this is my mother, Gladys Styne. Mom, this is Captain Dean Whitmore."

"Oh, you're the boss. So good to meet you after all this time. Hello Charles," she said.

"Hey Gladys," Charles replied. "It's about time you got your son hitched."

"May I help you up the stairs," the captain said.

"You told me he always wore suspenders," Mrs. Styne said to Rudy, "but you didn't tell me he had such penetrating blue eyes, and that he was rather handsome. Yes, Mr. Whitmore, I'd be more than happy to grab your arm, as it looks like a long way up from here to the front door."

Mrs. Styne placed her hand in the captain's bent arm, and together, they ascended the steep stairway to the entrance of the chapel. While Rudy continued greeting other attendees, he continued his conversation with Koswell.

"Charles, I'm very happy you could come."

"Well, I did have to pull a few strings to get re-stationed in New York for a week before I go back."

"You've been in Jakarta how long now?"

"Four months. I like it there, but you know me. I also like to be where the action is, like Odessa or Mecca. But now that I'm over 50, they see me as old and tend to give the hot spots to the younger crew."

"I enjoyed your op ed piece on the rise of skin heads in Austria," Rudy said as he reached down with a huff and a tug to pull aunt Helen out from her car.

"You don't really expect me to climb those stairs," aunt Helen, easily 250 lbs, declared. She stepped out of the sun and leaned her head way back to eyeball the vast church spire that rose directly above the entrance. "And who is this dashing gentleman?" Aunt Helen reached out to shake the man's hand.

"This is Charles Koswell, a writer for the International Herald Tribune. He's agreed to piggyback you up the stairs," Rudy deadpanned.

"Koswell, huh!~ I wanted to meet your boss. No slight intended Mr. Koswell, but all I've ever heard over the last umpteen years is what a great man Captain Whitmore is, and I was hoping….."

"You mean you don't want the piggyback?" Koswell asked.

"Oh, I do want the piggyback. I just want to meet this Whitmore fellow."

"He's up at the entrance with mom," Rudy said.

"Gladys! Gladys!" Aunt Helen shouted as she drove her massive weight up like a freight engine, step by step, raising her skirt with her hands to keep the bottom of her dress out of the way of her feet. After rising 6 of the 10 steps required, aunt Helen started to puff, and then she teetered as she tried to lift her weight to the next hurdle. Like a shot, Rudy and Koswell caught her by her bottom before she tumbled backwards and pushed her up, with great effort, the last four steps.

Sweating and panting, her hair already disheveled, aunt Helen's eyes wandered rapidly to find a chair or bench to collapse into. "So you're Whitmore," she huffed, now spying a chair. Greeting the captain, she artfully coaxed him to aid her to it. "I hope you realize what a fine journalist you have in Rudy Styne," she said, her eyes boring into the captain's.

"Oh, I wouldn't go that far," Whitmore kidded. "He can write a sentence and turn a phrase, but now that he's getting married, I'll probably have to find him a sedentary job, like copy editor."

"Executive editor," aunt Helen twisted the captain's arm and forced him to sit with her. "That would be nice. Modern Times could use a fresh look, and Rudy's just the kind of person to get you to help that look along…."

A second limo pulled up and all eyes fell on Chessie. She emerged arm and arm with her father and stepmother. Her face was glowing, her outfit laced with golden threads scintillating in the sunlight. Rudy looked down. Their eyes met. The energy between them was so intense that the crowd burst into applause. Chessie turned a shade of red.

The ever dapper Chas Barnsworth leaned over, gave his daughter a fatherly kiss, and took command of the moment. He guided Chessie and his wife, Sylvia, to the entrance of the chapel.

"Now Rudy," he shouted up to the front, "get away from my daughter! You will have plenty of time to see the bride during the ceremony. I want to enjoy the last fifteen minutes as the only man in her life, unencumbered!"

Ignoring his father-in-law to be, Rudy tried to push forward to give his bride a kiss, but playfully, but directly, Mr. Barnsworth interceded. "Now shoo, Rudy. Get away."

Smiling at the banter and catching a wonderful gleam from Chessie's eye, Rudy capitulated. He turned and entered the groom's quarters at the back of the chapel. There he could wait with his mother for the service to begin.

A violinist played a lilting melody until the crowd was finally seated, and then the organ played an opening piece to begin the procession. Leading the way was Chessie's niece, Loie, just four years old. The tiny flower girl was dressed in a light peach-colored lace dress, white bow and a halo of white flowers which were placed around the top of her head. Remindful of a Greek cherub, she held a bouquet of gardenias that wafted a delightful perfume which complimented the little girl's radiant smile. Sylvia Barnsworth kicked her biological daughter, Adeline, Chessie's older stepsister.

"What, mom?" Adeline whispered.

"Your daughter's shoes, Adeline. They're dreadful," Sylvia whispered under her breath.

"Tell me about it. She said the shoes that came with the dress hurt her feet and I guess, she kept her jellies hidden and slipped them on when we weren't looking."

Little Loie looked up at her mother and grandmother and beamed. The heels of her bright neon purple jellies flashed green and yellow lights with each step. Titters rippled through the crowd, but the flower girl's proud grin was infectious. Sylvia's scowl transformed to match her precious granddaughter's smile. Surprising herself, she picked Loie up when she reached the pulpit and planted a big wet one on her cheek.

"Granny," Loie squealed to get away, wiping her face with the back of her hand, she scooted to her place beside her mother.

After the ushers and bridesmaids filed in, Rudy found himself strutting. He winked at his mother, Gladys Styne who was still at the back of the church, and wondered for a fleeting moment, just who she was talking to. And then it came to him. It was an ancient man named Abraham Maxwell, who he remembered as some distant uncle. Vague memories of uncle Abe, as she referred to him, rattled his soul. A fragment of a memory of being taken to the Museum of Natural History by the old man when he was a boy rippled through him. Glassed-in animals, antelopes, the big cats, a Kodiak bear, a foggy memory of a wooly mammoth, gargantuan skeletons of Goliath-sized dinosaurs in a great hall, and a skeleton of a great blue whale drifting off the ceiling, floated through his mind, as he received a start, back to reality, when Charles kicked his foot and he took his place by the pulpit.

ELIAS & DEBORA MAXWELL

1906: Elias looked up at the sign posted above the entranceway of a long red-brick building: Maxwell-Bavarian Machineworks and beamed. His building. Steel supports, a flagstone base and lots and lots of windows half of which overlooked the rushing tributary which ran to the Iller River located there in southern Bavaria. With a labor force of over fifty, Elias prided himself in knowing nearly everyone by name.

As he walked into the factory a sensation overtook him that he had never experienced before. He felt larger, felt his being expand, felt his arms extend through the lathes, the presses and assembly line, felt his essence flow out through the windows through the spray of the cataract flowing through the waterwheel beside the massive generator, felt his shoulders rise to the ceiling and his head explode through the roof where it crested above the burgeoning hamlet.

From this position, Elias could look north towards Munich, east towards Salzburg, west to the Swiss Alps, or to the near south, to Kempten, perhaps the oldest town in the region, where his new automobile dealership had just opened up. In partnership with his wife's uncle, Adolf von Rosensweig, Elias had become an assimilated entrepreneur. He gazed behind him, upstream, past the series of cottages that housed his workers, past the stylish homes where his managers lived, past the long private lane lined with rhododendrons to the hill, his hill where his mansion lay.

Elias Maxwell, son of Rabbi Hillel Maxwell and grandnephew of Judah Baruch Maxwell, most venerated cantor, was a capitalist. To the chagrin of his family, he was also a convert. A Protestant.

"We will have the doctor perform the circumcision," Elias proclaimed as his wife lay sweating in her bed, her newborn son, Abraham, already suckling.

"He will have a bris, and he will be Bar Mitzvahed, like his father before him, and like his father and grandfather before him. You may try to renounce your heritage, Mr. Elias Isaiah Maxwell, but you will not...." Debora broke down in tears.

A sense of pity and disgust swept through Elias. "I want a modern wife, Debora. We are no longer in the shetl. It is time for us to become Bavarians. As you know, Jews cannot own property, they cannot hold political office. They live as outsiders, inferiors!"

"Oh, so now my husband, wants to be mayor."

"I would be a good mayor. But with a Jewish son, impossible."

"And your father. You want the rebbi to convert as well?"

"My son will *not* have a bris. Why must you be so selfish? How can you take this great joy from me?" Elias demanded. "You want your new Abraham to grow up with a yoke on his life, a cloud over his head, a stain on his record, when all we have to do is give up pagan beliefs. It's nearly 1907, for Chrissakes! Why can't you wake up to the new world? Do you think I can run my operations and be successful as... as a Jew?!"

Debora felt her son begin to gasp. Aunt Ella, who was midwife, grabbed swiftly, and brought the boy firmly to her chest. Cupping her hand she swatted his back soundly. He hiccupped and burped. In spite of himself, Elias smiled.

Although her hair was messed, and there was sweat upon her brow, Ella still expressed elegant regalness and air of authority. She turned to face her nephew. "You vant a healthy son?" she said in Yiddish, her stare deflating the businessman as he shrank back twenty years to his life as an eight-year-old tearing through Tante Ella's kitchen, as she prepared Seder dinner. Swiping a pastry to her chagrin as she swatted his backside, he would scoot out the door, his mouth half filled with delicious treat.

"May I hold my son?"

Ella looked at Debora who turned away. Elias wheeled and rumbled down the stairs unable or unwilling to take on the two women, at least for now. There would be another day.

From the porch, he looked downstream beyond the factory to the blur of downtown Kempten seven miles in the distance. He felt he could almost read the bright new sign of his automobile dealership. He knew precisely where it was, across from the town square right in the center of the little metropolis.

He called Gunter, his manservant, on his new intercom, and had him bring the new Royce roadster up to the house and park it by the front door. Donning riding gloves and goggles, he pushed past and stepped into the driver's seat, commanded Gunter to "crank it up" and put the automobile in gear.

"I expect my shoes to be polished by the time I return."

"Yes, sir," Gunter said.

Steering the Royce around the semi-circular driveway, Elias put his arm out of the window the way he had been taught to make a signal, then he made a left turn and sputtered down the dirt lane. It was late spring. The first purple buds of crocus were beginning to peep throughout the lawn, the rhododendrons were also beginning to bud.

A brood of pheasants crossed in front of him, the driver instinctively braked to a slow crawl. Watching the strutting mother followed by a trail of six chicks, Elias felt a sense of pride since he considered them part of *his* estate, when suddenly, out from nowhere, the male swooped, fluttering dangerously close to his head, warning him off, causing him to duck, as the brood disappeared quickly into the brush. The vehicle lurched and rumbled over a moving object. Elias cut the wheel and slammed the auto into a maze of branches.

Picking rhododendron buds from his windshield, the driver shook his head to get his bearings. Removing his goggles, he loosened his collar as he watched the cock reappear to attack the animal he had just run over. A red fox lay smashed in the center of the driveway, it's neck broken, eyes still open, pecked at by the regal ring-necked bird. Elias would later swear that this bird had looked squarely at him in the eye to tell him that he too should protect his flock.

Debora sat up in bed and began to sob. "It's all right," Tante Ella said, handing her back the boy.

"Why is he so stubborn?"

"He vants to be a success. Is that really so hard to understand?"

"But is it worth the price of our heritage?"

"There is nothing new here, Debora," Tante Ella said. "Rabbi Sinschwartz has told us that intermarriage is as high as 40% in Hamburg, over 25% in Berlin."

"What will happen to our essence?"

"There are still many good Jews. We have survived for thousands of years."

"But what can I do, deny my son a bris to placate his pigheaded father?"

"Appeal to a higher authority, my dear."

Alone in the garden, Elias listened to the plaintiff melody of his great uncle's voice swirl out the sitting room and echo down the hill. Because of the fame of this renown cantor, Elias' father, Hillel, the cantor's nephew, was able to gain a post at Ben Zion Temple in Weissenbach, just over the border in Austria. It was the largest synagogue in the region.

Well aware that he was part of the educated aristocracy, Elias knew he had grown up with a silver spoon. But he also knew that it was not his father who "built a machine shop from scratch to turn it into a major industry," Elias mumbled as he paced outside. "Nor did my father erect a complex to house my workers. And he did not negotiate with goyem to obtain a lot in the town square to start an automobile dealership...."

"Are you coming in?" von Rosensweig nudged as he came out to fetch his reluctant business partner. "Or do you want your brother to hold the boy when the rebbi makes the cut."

"My brother! If Simon so much as touches...." Elias spouted. Throwing his cigar down, he joined his wife's uncle and marched inside. Von Rosensweig led him to the crib. There before them stood the whole clan. They numbered over forty. Although his mother was no longer alive, Elias' father appeared vigorous and self-assured. He stood arm and arm with his sister, Tante Ella, beside Debora, their eyes aglow with images of this new and "perfect child." And like a Goliath, also stood the cantor, his great uncle Judah.

"Eli, you been pissing in the woods?" the cantor cajoled, loud enough for the entire forty to hear.

Shrinking beneath the comment, the convert did his best to hide his revulsion as he watched the relatives break into laughter. He gained some comfort to see that his younger brother did not smile with the others, but rather, came forth to pat him reassuringly on the back.

"Congratulations," Simon said.

"Thank you, brother," Elias replied.

The mohel looked Elias in the eye. With a disdained air of resignation, the new father reached for a yalmuke and plunked it on his head.

Debora's eyes sparkled. Were those tears of joy or sorrow? Elias could not tell. A voice inside took over as he recited in Hebrew by rote the appropriate prayer. As he did so, he felt a large hand on his shoulder. Wheeling, he glimpsed clearly the ghost of his dead mother and the ghost of her father as well. "Wake up, schmuck," whispered the dead Grandpapa Izzie.

During this strange interlude, Elias looked over to the living, his father Hillel and granduncle Judah were dovening in his direction. Tante Ella's soothing voice and gentle hand smoothed Baby Abraham's shoulders. The little one lay on his back, in the crib. A smile of contentment.

The mohel took center stage, stating that this tradition would not interfere with young Abe's ability to marry and reproduce when he reached proper age.

"May I say something," Elias found himself saying, the images of his dead relatives still powerfully hovering in his psyche, "that is, before the surgery begins?"

His father nodded assent, which halted the procedure for a moment.

Elias moved his gaze from his father and granduncle to his wife. "I know I have come from a blessed family, and I know I have not been a religious man. But I am a good man, and I respect my father and his uncle, my wife and her wishes. Abraham Maxwell has been born the religion of his mother, and he will be circumcised in a matter of moments in accord with a tradition that is thousands of years old. There is no easy answer for someone of Jewish ancestry in this world. The real world. I only wish the best for my son." He nodded to proceed.

The mohel chanted the sacred prayer as he brought out the cutting instruments. Capping the boy's penis with a little metal hood, he took out a small very sharp blade, held it next to the protected phallus, and sliced off a ring of foreskin.

Baby Abraham pierced the room with his shriek, as the family applauded and the feast began.

"Thank you," Debora said to her husband. She stood in deference by his side, her eyes still welled with tears.

"I know I'm an ass," he whispered as he gave her a kiss. "I'm only trying to survive in an unforgiving world."

"I know," she said. Their lips met. It was the first time they had kissed in nearly two weeks.

"There is a telephone call for you, Mr. Maxwell," Heidi, the maidservant said.

"Did you get the man's name?" Elias asked. He was sitting in the sunroom reading his newspaper. It was a Saturday morning.

"Count von Zeppelin, sir."

Elias flew from his seat, and picked up the phone.

Grabbing his gloves and riding goggles, the master of the house walked briskly to his roadster, pushed Gunter aside to crank the engine himself. Firing it up with a "humph!" he stepped into the driver's seat, put it in gear, barreled down the driveway and raced to his dealership. There, he waited with his partner, von Rosensweig for the great aeronaut to appear.

Elias had sold six automobiles in May, eight in June and now he was going to begin July with a sale to, of all people, Count von Zeppelin.

"This vehicle rides well, sir," von Zeppelin proclaimed, shouting from the passenger side.

Elias saw opportunity and took the great aeronaut on a ride to his industrial plant. Passing the Count's great airship which was docked in a nearby wheat field,

Elias gazed on its gargantuan size and nodded humble approval.

"We also repair and build engines," the entrepreneur offered as he followed the river-road to the factory, Debora's uncle perched precariously in the rumble seat. "My kid brother is a master mechanic in charge of the machinists."

"Perhaps you could provide new engines for my airships?"

"I would be honored," Elias beamed, just as he pulled into the site of Maxwell-Bavarian Machineworks.

"What do you make of Orville and Wilbur Wright?" Simon hit the Count broadside as he emerged from the plant, his face stained with grease, ratchet in hand.

"I take it, you are Simon?" von Zeppelin said.

"I am honored to meet you, sir." Simon clicked his heels and nodded his head. "I let the workers out for a break just to watch your great airship float into our area earlier in the day."

"This is a beautiful part of the country," von Zeppelin said.

"Thank you," Simon replied, whirling to allow, with a gesture, the workers to stop their machines once again so that they could gaze out the windows at this amazing national hero. The Count reached for his captain's hat, gave them a wave and they broke out in smiles and applause.

"The Wright brothers have gone beyond Lilienthal's motorless gliders, that is for certain," von Zeppelin replied, "but for long distance travel and multiple passengers, I don't see how you can better my behemoths."

THE WEDDING

"Charles."

"Rudy," Charles Koswell leaned over and whispered, "I can't find the rings." As he spoke, his shirt buckled and popped out. Koswell stood up quickly to try and tuck it back in, but a number of people in the audience noticed and quietly chuckled. Gladys Styne used the moment to scurry along the side and take her seat in the front.

"I know," Rudy grinned cryptically.

Pain began to overtake Koswell's expression, but something in Rudy's demeanor settled him. "I may have left them on the seat in the cab that brought me," Charles admitted.

Rudy smiled and surreptitiously handed Charles the rings back, which the taxi driver had spotted when Charles exited the vehicle to enter the church. "You did," Rudy said.

"Whew!" Koswell said.

Chas Barnsworth looked over to his daughter and beamed. Chessie was not a little girl anymore. Her fly-bye marriage to Luke had been a total mistake, here and gone in literally a matter of months, and then she almost repeated her mistake with Cornelius Jefferson's kid, Jack. But Jack had been a gadabout, and Chas had sadly given Chessie the name and phone number of Jack's mistress, Taylor Harriman, grand-niece of Wall Street tycoon Roland Harriman. Chessie had had inklings, but had still fallen for "the lug" as she called him.

The polo matches, sailboat races to Block Island and Martha's Vineyard, trips to Puerto Rico and St. Martin where he had condominiums, and dinners with the political elite and corporate heads from the city flashed through her mind. Clutching her father's arm, Chessie stared at a stained glass window and thought back.

She had driven over the Whitestone Bridge to snake her way along the Hutch to Mamaroneck, Taylor's home. It was a small bungalow nestled in a forest that abutted Redview Golf Club. Parked in the driveway was a coral Corvette convertible with a license plate that said 1M-GR8.

So very clever, Chess thought. Two years out of college, she had taken to Jack right from the start. His slick black hair, barrel chest, self-possessed swagger. She was even attracted to his God-awful vanity. She had fallen big time. Resigned, she rang the bell.

"Fore!" Instinctively, Chessie ducked as a golf ball careened off the wall beside her and bounded into the bushes.

Dressed in red checkered pants and a paperboy cap, Rudy Styne sprung from the course and apologized profusely. Their eyes met. Although he looked goofy in the outfit, there was something in his manner. She recognized him from the city, and he recognized her. "Chockful of Nuts, right?" he said as he fished the bushes for the ball.

"Yes," she said as one might say "Ahhh, that's where I know you from. Small world."

"I can't play for beans, but Senator D'Pardo insisted, and it's the only way I could… OK, here it is."

Chess looked up to see the senator standing on the green, golf club propped squarely between his legs as he leaned on it and waited, a triumphant grin…. "Come on, Styne!" he trumpeted.

"I think I'll let him win. It will be good for his ego." Rudy tried to take his eyes from Chessie's. Taylor answered the door and Chess entered.

"May I come in?"

"Make yourself at home," Taylor replied.

"We're engaged," Chessie said as she looked over the lynx who was dressed in spiked high heels and a maroon velvet one-piece cotton jump suit that clung to every fold of her body. "When's the last time you saw Jack?"

Taylor looked her over as well. "Ms. Barnsworth, I've known Jack since we were in high school. I've been married twice and Jack's been engaged maybe four or five times. It's hard to keep count."

Chess had the urge to deck her, but instead, she surveyed the room and looked at the framed photos of Taylor in bikinis, evening gowns, blue jeans and shirt tied under her boobs, while riding a horse, out on Jack's sailboat with two other couples. "When was this taken?" Chessie was referring to a photo of the two of them riding on one horse.

"Last Spring," Taylor said. "But it's not what you think. As you know, we are just friends." As the bitch continued, Chess glanced out the back window to watch Rudy Styne shank a shot that careened off a tree and plop into a pond. She couldn't help but laugh.

Seeing herself out, Chessie sat in her car for a moment to reflect. She decided not to return to the highway, but instead entered the golf club and waited at the 9th tee.

Rudy looked up as he followed his 3-iron shot. The ball bounced long onto the green, rolled to the cup, hovered and dribbled in. He had an eagle, his first ever! Unable to contain herself, Chess burst into applause.

"Senator, can we break for a quick lunch?"

The senator saw the beautiful girl before them. "Sure, kid. Take ten. Nice shot."

"Thanks."

Rudy and Chessie split a Nathan's footlong. It was so natural, but at the same time, they neglected to swap numbers. Fortunately, they ran into each other again in the city, at that Chockful of Nuts. Well, maybe that time, it wasn't such a coincidence…..

"Chess, we're on," her father said, bouncing her mind back to the present.

"I know, dad. I'm very happy."

"I know you are, Chess. Unless you want to give him up for that Jefferson kid."

"Dad!" Chess poked her father in the ribs.

The organist hit *Here Comes the Bride*. People craned their necks. Dressed in an ivory-colored laced wedding dress with her hair adorned with a ring of orchids, Chessie walked down the aisle, her arm locked in the firm grip of her father. She rested her other hand contentedly on her bulbous stomach. The crowd giggled a little, but it was in good humor. Stunning is the only way to describe her regal demeanor with her head erect and antelope stride. Mr. Barnsworth held back a tear as he guided her to the podium and took his seat next to his wife, Sylvia. She gave Chas a quick peck.

The feeling of having 250 people all on your side caring for you, was a feeling which swept over the groom as he nodded to each friend or relative that caught his eye and waited for his bride to take her place beside him.

Pastor Benedictine leaned over and whispered, "Try to keep your glow down to a dull radiance, m'boy."

"I'll do that, father."

Chess thought about how her stepsister generously offered to let out her wedding dress to make room for Chessie's growing stomach. She thought about how much she loved Rudy, how happy she was that her family could be here to celebrate the wedding, how wistful she was that her mother could not attend. She felt she was looking down from heaven. She knew she was.

Chess looked over to her stepmom, happy for her dad. Squeezing her husband's arm, Sylvia smiled in return. Chessie felt the break, and her father let her go. As she took her place beside Rudy on the pulpit and their hands intertwined, Mort, from Rudy's office jumped up. "Father," Mort said seriously, "could I interrupt the proceedings for just a moment?"

"If you must," Pastor Benedictine said. Mort walked over to the wall behind the pulpit, grabbed a chair and stood upon it. Reaching as high as he could, he released a catch which allowed a large banner to unfurl. Dropping to the floor, the picture was that of the classic farmer with pitchfork and wife with tight bun standing next to him, but in place of the pitchfork was a long shining shotgun. The crowd sat stunned as Mort returned to his seat.

"OK," Mort said, stern-faced. "You may continue."

"Thank you, Mr. Dufas," the pastor said, laughter erupting from the audience.

Rudy leaned over and kissed Chessie's belly, and everyone applauded.

"Do you Chessie Barnsworth take this man, Rudolf Styne, to be your lawfully wedded husband, to have and to hold, from this day forth, till death do you part?"

Chessie turned squarely to face her man. Their eyes locked. She looked deep into the hazel of his eyes and he returned the gaze in kind. "I do!" she said, "Definitely."

"And do you, Rudy Styne, take this lady, Chessie Barnsworth, to be your lawfully wedded wife to have and to hold from this day forth till death do you part?"

"I do," Rudy replied.

The pastor was silent for a moment and then continued. "If any person has a reason for these two people not to wed, let him speak now or forever hold his peace."

"He must have a bris!" a voice in a noticeably German accent cracked the silence.

"A what?" the pastor called out.

"A bris, a bris." The voice called out from the rear as heads turned about.

A spry old man with eyes that radiated light, dressed in a shimmering pin-striped brown suit, a wide autumn tie that seemed to hark back to the days before the Great Depression, and a black fedora typical of the ones worn by Wall Street moguls continued. "You don't know what a bris is?" Abe removed his hat and placed it in front of his stomach as he spoke. "It's a snip, just a little snip of the head of the penis taken by the mohel. After a prayer, of course, on the 8th day. You are having a boy? Am I right?"

"If you say so," Chessie responded, Rudy whispering his name to her, "uncle Abe." Chessie completed the sentence to the astonishment of the crowd. "But I am getting married right now. Does that not please you?"

"Do you know of any reason why these two people should not get married?" the pastor repeated.

Mr. Barnsworth and several other attendees arose with mixed emotions, not quite sure what to do with this dark sheep.

"No, father, no," uncle Abe said with a wave of his hand that caused Barnsworth and the others to sit back down. "They are in love. Can't you feel it? I'm just making a point. A bris. That's all. Proceed."

"Are you sure?' the pastor knew how to milk a moment.

"Quite. I'm satisfied," the elderly gentleman concluded.

Uncle Abe wrangled a seat by moving some people over near him and motioned once again for the pastor to continue.

"I now pronounce you man and wife. Rudy, you may kiss the bride."

Dom, dom, didom.... The chapel bell pealed. Rice showered the couple as they exited the church and took their limo to Chessie's great uncle Hoxie's estate where the reception was to be held.

After the couple walked down the aisle and out the door, the guests also retrieved their cars so they too could make their way to Hoxie's horse farm and country place. Situated on twenty-six acres in the heart of Locust Valley just three miles from the church, turning into the property, the entourage snaked its way up the rhododendron-lined entrance way. To the left, a pair of Arabian steeds could be seen snorting and cavorting, but then they stopped still like statues to watch the cars enter the estate.

It was October and the trees were bursting with color. Two bright white circus-sized tents were sprawled out below the mansion between the swimming pool and rose garden. The main tent was where a band was already playing, and the smaller one housed the buffet. Marble statues of Greek gods at the sides of each tent seemed to beckon the guests to explore various other sectors of the substantial estate. Some of the attendees walked to the corral to get a better look at Hoxie's horses or perhaps pet them. Closer to the mansion was the swimming pool. Placed in a natural setting, it's most impressive feature was a statue of Neptune, holding his trident in one hand and the reins to four horses in the other. The statue stood in front of a lush man-made waterfall that tumbled into the inviting kidney-shaped pool.

Hoxie Leviman, the third husband of Chessie's maternal great aunt, now deceased, had made his money in optics, Hoxie binoculars, microscopes and telescopes. Built right there on the Island for over forty years, they were considered by many to be the finest known. Hoxie Optics did over $10 million last year, in magnifying glasses alone.

When Corning went Chapter 11, after the breast implant fiasco, Hoxie Leviman increased his sales force fivefold and saw his market share quadruple. Now, well into his 80's, Hoxie looked like a man just getting ready to move into his second wind.

Once the main tent was filled, with 250 people taking their seats, side flaps were raised to reveal a Cinderella stagecoach led by two white stallions that galloped into view. On the ride to the tent, the newlywed couple reflected on that odd moment with uncle Abe. "My head is spinning," Chessie said. "What was that all about?"

"I don't know," Rudy said. "When are you due?"

"Maybe we'll have a girl," Chessie said as the coach reached the tent.

The horses brayed to a great round of applause, and then out popped the newlyweds. The band played their favorite song, "I Want To Make It With You," which the couple danced to: "*Hey, have you ever tried, really reaching out for the other side? I may be climbing on rainbows, but baby, here goes.*" The couple twirled around the dance floor, that unmistakable gaze zinging between them. "*Life can be short or long, Love can be right or wrong, And if I chose the one I'd like to help me through, I'd like to make it with you.* Then, the number changed, Rudy asked his mother to dance, Chess, her father, and so on, until the floor was filled with couples. Through the grooving, with Rudy back with Chessie, she said, "Look at that."

Rudy peered through dancers to hone in on two old men sitting off to the side in deep conversation. It was uncle Hoxie talking with great intensity to uncle Abe.

"Is he chewing him out?" Rudy asked.

"No. It's something different. I've never seen my uncle like that. I think he's crying. Maybe I should go over."

Rudy watched Hoxie wipe away the tears and reach over with a strong arm to grab Abe's head and bring it to him. It was a kiss on the forehead, Abe lowering his head as if blessed. Something odd was happening. "I think we should let them be," Rudy said.

When the dust settled, before dinner was served, Rudy's mother took the newlyweds aside. "I must apologize for uncle Abe's behavior," she said.

"There is nothing to apologize for," Chessie said.

"I hope you two are not mad at me," uncle Abe approached. Close up, he looked ancient, but sturdy.

Mrs. Styne gave Abe a big smile and planted a kiss on his cheek. "No, uncle, I was just saying that there were other ways for you to make your point!"

"What is your point?" Chessie asked.

"Ladies and gentlemen!" The dapper wedding coordinator interrupted the festivities to make an announcement. "Can we gather around," he continued from center stage, "for the toast. Uncle Hoxie will give the toast."

The lord of the manner jogged up to the microphone. With an estate of incalculable value, old man Hoxie seemed to garner respect simply by his demeanor. "I have known Rudy Styne for a number of years. Ever since that crazy incident with that psychic. Eh, Rudy?"

Rudy smiled and nodded as did many of the crowd who had read Rudy's best selling account of some clandestine remnants of the cold war. *ESPionage* ran six weeks on the New York Tribune's best seller list.

"And during that time, I have seen the love flowing between this fine man and my niece, and it fills me up. I came into this family a number of years after Chessie was born, but I have always felt accepted, even after my beautiful wife Anna passed away. And so I was just bursting with happiness when I found out that Chess and Rudy were going to get married. Since I don't have any children of my own..... Well, I wanted to put this beautiful wedding together."

Hoxie then stopped talking. He was obviously choked up and everyone just waited through the awkward silence. Struggling to speak again, he just lifted his forefinger as if to say, "Give me a minute."

The MC attempted to come up, to return a happy edge to the festivities, because that was what he was paid to do, but Hoxie put a hand up. "No, sir, please sit. Let me continue. Chess, I was overflowing with pride and happiness during the ceremony when this old man, I know I'm old myself, but he's older than me, making this big *magilla* about a bris. 'What the hell is he talking about?' I said to myself, and I saw Chas stand up and a few others, and I myself was ready to move over to stop him."

Hoxie looked over to Abe who was sitting beside Gladys, tears welling up in his eyes. "And then, as he walked out, he said to me, 'Hoxie, is that you?' and I looked and said. 'Abe Maxwell, could it really be you?' and he nodded and I knew. This man who sits with Rudy's mother, Abraham Maxwell, the genius who started with his father a premier airline in Germany more than a decade before the second World War, is the reason I stand before you tonight. I would be long dead if it were not for this man, for we were both prisoners at....." and then Hoxie whispered, "Auschwitz, a horrible horrible place. And it was this man who sits here before you, who helped me escape. So, to you Abraham Maxwell, I thank you.

"I want to wish Chessie and Rudy all the happiness in the world. To see the great love you two share brings joy to my heart. I have asked Pastor Benedictine to say a blessing, and then we shall hear from the best man."

Charles Koswell led the toast. "As best man, it is my responsibility to say a few nice things about Rudy Styne. I know uncle Hoxie is a tough act to follow, but I will do my best."

Koswell then went over to Abe Maxwell and shook his hand. There was a standing ovation. Koswell waited and then put his hands up to quiet the crowd. "But on a more serious note," he looked around to try and milk a laugh, "I would like to begin by saying that we have clear evidence that Rudy Styne is not one of the brightest bulbs on the planet." Charles put his hand to his ear as a prompt.

"Why is that?" the audience asked.

"Because he invited Mort to his wedding!"

"Here, here," blurted the crowd.

"On the other hand, that he could capture the most beautiful girl on Long Island is a counterpoint in his favor."

"Here, here."

"Many of you do not know this, but I first met Rudy at a coin show over twenty years ago. I remember because although there were large crowds, we were almost the only people at the ancient coin exhibit. We were both admiring a very old coin of the beautiful princess Larissa dated from about 300 B.C., and Rudy said to me, 'I hope some day to meet a girl like this.' Do you remember?"

"Yes, I remember," Rudy said.

"Good, because today, a generation later, you can tell yourself you have fulfilled your dream. And, I can tell you from personal experience, Chessie is a rock, someone you can rely on in times of crisis. I have been in life-threatening situations with Rudy and Chessie, and have found them both to be bold in the face of death. With machine guns blaring....."

As Charles spoke, his cummerbund began to unravel. He tried to continue, but his shirt popped out, so his talk was cut short to a mixture of applause, bravos and laughter.

ZEPPELIN

1909: Simon's full clipped beard gave him an edge. Only 16, he could pass for nearly twice that age, and so he had the respect of the many workers at his brother's factory. A natural talent with his hands, Simon could pride himself in being able to fix broken machines that many perceived to be unfixable.

Thus, when Elias learned that von Zeppelin was having a problem with the motors in his airships, he planned a trip with his brother to Lake Constance to look over the problem.

"Gunter, I'm leaving you in charge of the house," Elias told his manservant. Gunter Linzman stood next to Debora at the foyer, his wife Greta, at his side.

"Thank you, sir."

"You're welcome. Now, go out and start that automobile for me."

"And what about me?"

"Gunter knows who the real boss of this house is, my dear."

"Give me a kiss," Debora said. Elias approached and held her. Their lips touched. "How long will you be away?"

"A few days. A week at most. Simon has his heart set on seeing this Wright fellow in Paris. Maybe I can talk him out of it. I'll see."

"Be careful, Elias. I get afraid sometimes when you go."

"Where's Abe?"

"With Gunter, Jr., most likely down by the creek."

"Well, say good-bye for me."

"Of course I will dear. Oh, give me a real kiss, will you!"

Elias motored down their long driveway and found himself looking for his son. He took off his goggles as they tended to mist up this early in the morning.

"Papa! Papa!" Abe shouted as he raced up a hill to catch up to his father. Elias pulled over and Abe vaulted in. "Can't I go to see the Zeppelin, papa?" Gunter Jr., nearly seven years Abe's senior, stood by quietly.

"Maybe next time. Uncle Simon has to fix it first."

"Mama wants you to be careful."

"I will, son, and I want you to do something for me."

"What is that, papa?"

"I want you to be the man of the house while I'm gone. Will you do that?"

"Yes."

"And will you give me a hug?"

"Yes." They embraced and Elias set the boy back down on the ground. "Gunter."

"Yes sir," the 9-year old boy said.

"You'll look out for my son while I'm gone?"

"Yes, sir."

"Good." Elias reached into his pocket and removed two coins, giving one to Abe and the other to Gunter, Jr. They placed the coins in their respective pockets and watched Elias drive away.

Simon looked at the clock: 6:45 a.m. God, he was amazed at how much self-discipline his brother could impart. He dragged his body out of the bed and threw open the window.

"Hey, let's go," Elias shouted up at the window.

"All right," Simon said, "I'll be down in 15 minutes."

Elias paced the front lawn. He couldn't believe Simon wasn't ready. Unlike himself, his brother lived in a modest home provided for him by Elias. Since it was Elias who had started the company, he would receive the lion's share. And because he was the first-born son, he was also entitled to his father's entire estate. Simon was pleased to receive this house as a sign of Elias' generosity, but he was also upset that nearly half his wages went to pay off the mortgage that his brother had given him.

"I don't think we should take the automobile," Simon said. "Friedrichshafen is almost 75 kilometers and there is no assurance that we will be able to refill, or that the roads will be passable. We can get a coach from Kempten and be there by nightfall."

"Nonsense," Elias responded testily. He checked his watch for the fourth time. "The canny von Zeppelin assured me that we could make it by auto and that the refill stations in Isny and Wangen are in working order."

"You know best, big brother." Simon adjusted his goggles and cranked up the motor before jumping into the passenger seat. "We have to go by the machine works so I can get my tools."

"Why didn't you bring them here?" Elias railed into him. "You knew we'd be going and we're already late."

Simon stewed in silence. Sometimes he absolutely hated his brother. He was never good enough. Elias would only point out his shortcomings. Wasn't it he who had designed a new crankshaft for the Lauffen engines, and hadn't he caught the design flaw in the brakes of the Rumplers before his brother sold no more than two defective cars?

Not only had he saved the company, and Rumpler, great embarrassment and a possible lawsuit, Lauffen also paid a pretty penny for the use of the engine patents. And all his brother had given him was an extra month's salary.

"When you own your own machine shop, and pay your own patent attorneys, you can make your own profits." Elias had instructed, "but until then..."

"Ya, ya, ya," Simon mumbled.

"What was that?"

"Oh nothing." Simon ran into the machine works and emerged with a large trunk of his special tools. He placed them carefully on the back seat. "Did you bring Abe's autograph book?"

"What are you talking about?"

"Abe. He wants von Zeppelin's autograph."

"I'm sure we can pick up a sheet of paper when we get there, or maybe even get him a photograph."

"Signed?"

"Yes, signed. Anything else?"

"No. I think we are all set."

The Bavarian hills were in bloom, the farmers having begun their planting of wheat, corn, barley, alfalfa and potatoes.

"Look out," Simon shouted as he instinctively ducked. Up from the trees descended a *whoosh* as Gustav Lilienthal, in one of his new gliders, sailed overhead.

Elias watched in disgust, but Simon beamed.

"He wants me to work with him, so we can enter in the upcoming competition." Simon watched, his eyes ablaze as Gustav managed a wave. Then Lilienthal banked and sailed down a hill towards von Rosensweig's castle.

'I thought his brother dying would have been warning enough," Elias harrumphed.

"But Otto Lilienthal is a great German hero," Simon responded, "and the fact that Gustav wants me to work on the concept of a tail design, I think, it is a great opportunity."

"I suppose you still want to go to Paris, after we go to the lake."

"Elias, of course. Wilbur Wright! My God! He's got a motor in his glider and he's shipped it all the way from the United States. Even Wright credits Otto Lilienthal as being the first to achieve heavier than air flight. The key he said,... wait, I brought his article." Simon turned to the back jump seat and began to rifle through his tool chest, as Elias brought the Royce to a swift halt.

"Look, Simon. That will have to wait. I can't risk hitting a bump in the road and losing my best mechanic."

"Here it is," Simon began to read.

His enthusiasm was so infectious that Elias found himself easing his countenance. "All right, all right, we will go to Paris, if you fix von Zeppelin's motor."

"Maybe he'll fly us there."

"Simon, I wish I had the ability to dream like you."

The two brothers passed the time by discussing their opposing views on the role of religion in modern Germany as the car sputtered over the hills. At the first refill station at Isny they stopped for breakfast and a cup of coffee.

Elias complained to the waitress at the slow service. "This town is no more than a fart in the road. If it didn't have that filling station, I don't think it would have even known it rated a name. Waitress, let's go!" he shouted.

"Ellie," Simon ignored Elias' ever-present edginess, and used an old nickname to try and change the mood, "When I saw Gustav glide overhead, my mind just reels with the possibilities. I foresee a day when aeroplanes will deliver the mail and be used to transport passengers."

"I'm all for supporting your dreams, and I'll even support your request to enter flight school in Munich as soon as you have trained a few adequate replacements. But I don't understand how you can compare a device that is little more than a small toy with the great airships of von Zeppelin. You know as well as I he has the capability of transporting 20 or more passengers to every corner of Europe, North Africa and western Asia. There's even talk that von Zeppelin may attempt the Atlantic."

"I agree, but it is not a matter of one or the other. Certainly in military encounters, von Zeppelin's giant airships would remain as sitting targets, whereas a flying heavier-than-air propeller-driven craft would be more elusive and maybe nearly impossible to shoot down."

"Why all this talk about war?"

"It's the Kaiser. He's upset particularly about all the internal conflicts in the Balkans. I don't think the Serbs will ever get along with the Turks."

"So, what does that have to do with us?" Elias suddenly became more aware of the road and a look of concern entered his face. "Simon, you have the map. Which way do we go? Look at that crazy sign."

"We follow the Argen. That's the way the coach goes. What were we talking about?"

"The Balkans."

"Oh, yes, Ellie. I'm surprised you don't see it. If civil strife breaks out again there, Austria and Hungary may be called in on one side and Russia on the other, and then we would have a real battle on our hands.

"What would Germany do?"

"Well, it could depend on Turkey or the French or the Brits for that matter. I think we turn at this post right here."

"But the river goes left."

"I know, but the sign for the city we just passed said right."

"Thanks, kid. I'm so busy trying to steer this monkey, I must have missed it." They took the right fork which took them to a hill. Sputtering over the rise, the duo looked down to the majesty of Lake Constance with the regal metropolis of Friedrichshafen to the west.

"There, there, do you see it?" Simon said excitedly.

"Oh my God," Elias breathed. Off in the distance they could see what looked like a giant whale floating beside a mammoth-sized barn. "It's simply gargantuan."

"It sure is, big brother," Simon said. "You could fit nearly a dozen homes inside it."

"That many?" Elias gasped.

"End to end, Elias, end to end."

Elias accelerated. The auto careened over a mogul and they found themselves air bound for a second.

"*Whoa!*" Simon shouted and Elias braked instinctively. They decided on a more leisurely pace and drove that way to the hangar.

Dressed in full military attire, with a robust complexion and well-manicured beard, Count von Zeppelin came out to greet them. He was an older gentleman, well into his 70's but carrying this advanced age very well.

"The problem is in the second engine," the Count said pointing up above the passenger gondola to the intricate machinery that was housed to turn the propeller.

"And how am I to get up there?" Simon said.

"On that, I'm sure Helmut will send down the lift."

"What about my tools?"

"Just put them on the lift."

Simon tilted his head back to gaze upon the great craft.

"It's so silent," he sighed.

"Well, that's the problem, isn't it?" the Count responded. "The left engine's been purring all week like a contented cat, but three days ago, it sounded like an explosion and now it won't turn over at all."

"Why don't you just replace it with another?" Elias asked.

"Excellent question." The Count guided the loading lift down and helped Simon step aboard. "We've got three other ships in production, few spare parts and no spare engines." The Count shouted the last few words to Simon who had already arisen nearly 40 feet straight up, and directed the balance of the conversation to Elias. "My engineer said your Simon is the best. Naturally if we have to change engines we have to change engines, but I want to exhaust all possibilities first."

Simon looked down and watched the two men diminish in size accordingly as he rose into the passenger compartment, accepting Helmut's hand to make a safe transition.

"It's over here," Helmut said, leading Simon down a long plank that ran the length of the ship. "We will have to let out some hydrogen for safety's sake, but the more gas we let out, the less stable the ship will be."

"Everything in life seems to be a trade-off."

"You can say that again, sir," Helmut said.

The craft floated silently. Though docked, they were still above the tree line, so Simon took a quick opportunity to peruse the landscape. He gazed across the great lake towards the Swiss Alps. France lay just beyond. If only he could cut the tether and float gently up, he'd be in Paris in no time.

Elias grimaced as he looked up at his brother wasting time as he often did, daydreaming.

"No doubt he is thinking about flying," he said apologetically.

"I understand completely! Herr Maxwell," the Count replied. "I too am a dreamer." They watched the ship begin to quiver as Helmut released the gas from the chamber closest to the broken motor.

"I'm sure he will be able to fix your problem." Elias straightened his collar. "My brother just takes a little time to get started."

"Yes! I'm sure." With that, the Count waved his hand as if to say "leave them be until they are done," and departed.

As Elias watched Simon stare off into space, an anger arose in him, he could hardly contain. His face turned red as his brain began to explode.

Although forty feet above him, Simon did not have to be a telepathist to realize he was about to be reprimanded. He spun to make his way back to the distressed engine, but as he turned, he stepped on a screwdriver someone had dropped by mistake, and his foot kicked out from underneath him. Flailing his arms like a frigate bird about to take flight, he tried to regain his balance but could not and he fell back in a series of small steps that took him to the edge of the gondola. With his body disproportionately positioned to distribute his weight to his upper torso, he flipped backwards over the railing and caught his left foot on one of the riggings. Now he was dangling head first out of the great ship. Catching the accident in progress, the Count, although himself and elderly man, raced up the scaffolding to the ladder that led to the dirigible and scampered up nearly four flights of stairs and over to the gondola, arriving just as Helmut did. The two of them struggled to grab Simon's foot and stabilize him so that he could reach up to the rail and pull himself back on board.

Chugging from the climb and seeing his entire life flash before him, Elias arrived just as Simon righted himself back on board.

"My brother, my brother," Elias stammered. Instinctively, he ran over and gave Simon a hug and a kiss, his eyes streaming tears. "My only brother. Simon, Simon, oh my Simon."

"I'm alright elder one," Simon replied. "I was only testing the strength of the Count's rigging." He grabbed the cable that had saved his life and gave it a hearty tug.

Simon gave the Count and Helmut a broad grin. "All right Herr Helmut, take me to your infirm engine."

Elias slumped to the floor, overpowered by a rill of tears. His jaw began to quiver and a cry was released from deep within.

Simon placed his arms around Helmut and Count von Zeppelin and led them along the catwalk away from his brother. "He gets like that every time I fall off one of these things."

Through the hysteria of his woe, Elias could not help but begin to laugh. Exhausted, he managed a look to say that he loved his reckless brother in part because of his very ability to twist a potential tragedy into a witty put down of his elder brother.

"Elias, when you are ready why don't you come to the boat house and we will set sail and leave these two gentlemen to their work."

"I'll be right along, Count," Elias managed, emotionally drained, unable to fully understand the depths of the feeling that had come over him.

Von Zeppelin led Elias to a boatyard at the edge of the lake, its dock peppered with sailboats and small rowboats. "Come aboard. It seems to me, young man, you could use a break!"

Elias had to laugh to be called a young man. But from the elderly Count's point of view, Elias realized, he was. Gingerly, he found a spot to grab a hand rail, and stepped aboard. "How big is she?"

"Forty foot. I have a larger ship, but that requires a crew. Have you sailed before?" As the Count spoke, he began to untie the various ropes that held the ship in place.

"This is my first time."

"Can you swim?"

"That I can," Elias replied. "I spent my later youth near the River Iller which runs through Kempten. Every summer we'd go to a lodge on one of its tributaries and that's where I learned to swim."

"You need to get back to that tributary, my good friend. You are tight as a drum. I tell you this, Herr Maxwell, you will have to ease up if you want to ever make it through the next decade or two." The Count threw Elias a line.

"How often do you get out?"

"As often as I can." The Count untied the last rigging, pushed off and leaped gingerly aboard. "Quick, give me that rope and duck!" The boom swung around and the sail caught wind. "I only wish the motor on my airship could run as well as the motor in the new automobile you sold me," the Count mused.

"I have great confidence in my brother, sir. And while we are complimenting each other, I would like to take this moment to congratulate you on the rigid body construction on your new airships. What a superb advance."

"It's changed the aerodynamics dramatically. But this motor problem has really rattled my cage. I've had my mechanics replace just about every part we could, but still the engine won't turn over."

"If we fix it, and I believe Simon will," Elias challenged, "can we not supply you with the next round of engines for your new craft?"

"If your brother fixes this engine, I think I'll just hire him right out from underneath you." the Count cajoled. "Duck!" he commanded, and the boom swung around again as he tacked and followed the wind towards the outskirts of the nearby city. Gulls flew by and glinting silvery fish leaped completely out of the sea.

"Even the fish can fly here," Elias pondered aloud. The Count nodded in agreement. "But I have to warn you about stealing my brother. I fear he is not interested in airships as much as gliders. In fact, he wants me to allow him to leave for Paris where Wilbur Wright will be showing off his new motored glider as soon as we are done here."

"It's a clever toy, I'll grant those American brothers that, but totally unsuited for carrying multiple passengers or for traversing great distances. He's going to dive!" the Count shouted out. Elias watched an osprey hit the water full throttle and surface with a large fish in it's talons. The Count discussed the details of sailing with Elias and allowed him to steer the vessel back to their home base.

Simon was waiting with Helmut, both men with large grins. "Do you know that the wing of Wright's plane operates in the same way as that sail?" Simon said, pointing.

"So, if I turn these sails horizontally, my boat will fly too?" the Count replied.

"In theory yes, if the speed were great enough and the length of the sail increased to offset its significant tonnage."

"But my great airships are not theory, my good man."

"I know, and I think they shall always have their place. But for speed and maneuverability, I believe the aeroplane is the wave of the future."

"Maybe it's figs and potatoes," the Count mused. "Are you sure the engine is back in working order?

"Yes," Simon said matter-of-factly. Helmut nodded in agreement.

"Then stay the night and I'll fly you to Geneva where you can catch a train to Paris and see that crazy American."

Count von Zeppelin's signature resembles his invention!

WRIGHT IN PARIS

"If we get separated," Simon shouted, "I'll meet you at the tower."

Simon turned and pushed forward through the crowd, Elias looked up at Eiffel's great edifice. He had wired Debora that they'd extended their stay so they could go to Paris to meet Wilbur Wright. He let Simon go off so he could take his own time to walk towards the tower, his mind still racing with the majestic thought that he had just been in the clouds, that he, Elias Maxwell, son of a Jewish rabbi, had flown in a Zeppelin with Count von Zeppelin himself. They had been higher than the birds, above the tree line, above the masses. Something shifted in his self-concept. He often felt part of the privileged class, but that flight put his self-concept into a whole new category.

The crowds had numbered in the tens of thousands just to get a glimpse of von Zeppelin's magnificent airship. Newspaper reporters, watching the Count sign autographs and pose for photographs, placed the story of his jaunt above that of Wright's European arrival. Elias thought that he too might have been captured in a newspaper picture. He'd have to try and get a copy.

Elias thought back to the last time he had been at this site. It was the World's Fair which he had attended with his uncle when the Eiffel Tower was first built. 1889. *My God,* he thought, *19 years ago,* and now another sizeable throng to witness Wilbur Wright demonstrate his new aeroplane. The crowd was almost as large as the one that had greeted von Zeppelin when they had landed by Lake Geneva. Young boys, bearded men in suits and gentle ladies all running to greet them, to greet *him* just because he had been aboard, flying above the Alps, looking at homes beneath the clouds as if they were small toys, watching the moving dots which he knew to be carriages travel down a road, the thrill of being up there, as if he were a god. And now with a contract with the Count, he was moving into a whole new industry.

Whoosh! Elias ducked as Wright's box-shaped aircraft appeared as if by magic from behind a blind of hedges, startling the crowd, and then motored along the midway before it landed off in the distance.

True, the flight had taken only seventy-three seconds, and even that seemed an eternity, but how could one compare such a rickety single-piloted toy to a giant airship that could carry a large party of men a distance of hundreds, or, if the Count wanted, thousands of miles. Wright's invention was a fad, much like the unicycle craze that had taken over much of Western Europe during the first years of the century. Elias wanted Simon to be happy. He could afford him this whim. He knew Simon wanted to feel free, so why not indulge him? For Simon had earned it, fixing unfixable motors, redesigning a series of cables to secure von Zeppelin's gondola in a more sturdy fashion, imparting that air of confidence to convince von Zeppelin that Maxwell-Bavarian Machineworks could produce better engines than the Count was presently using.

Von Zeppelin, had been cautious, fearful that Elias may have been more talk than substance. But then Simon described his plans on how he could build even more efficient motors, and he answered every question thrown at him, hiding nothing, knowing full well that what he said could be used by the airship manufacturer to create his own motors without MB Machineworks. But Simon also knew that the Count was a man of honor, and so they had secured a contract with von Zeppelin for six full-scale airship motors, and that was just to start.

If the army were to begin to construct a fleet, as rumor suggested, then there was little doubt that this production would be spearheaded by whoever von Zeppelin recommended, and right now it was clearly he and his brother.

Wright's plane looked like a long cage made out of grocery boxes, with square wings, nothing like the elegant gliding apparatus that resembled the wings of a giant dragonfly that Lilienthal had designed. And where Lilienthal took off from a standing position and dangled his feet beneath, Wilbur Wright lay flat, his head peering ahead of the wings, all on top of a machine that had replaced the graceful curves of Lilienthal's device with hard edges.

Nevertheless, no matter how fragile and unnatural the propellered box looked, there was no denying, it flew, and that's what mattered. Elias thought he could see his brother tearing at breakneck speed towards the landing area as his mind drifted back once again to his own flight on the great airship, the quiet sensation of floating with the clouds, of being a cloud.

"He's going to come to our plant," Simon told his brother later as they boated down the Seine and exited by the Church of Notre Dame.

Elias looked up at the myriad gargoyles that leered out from the medieval edifice's many tented roofs. "Who?"

"Wilbur Wright of course! I told him we could produce aeroplanes for him in Bavaria if he so chooses. He was concerned, of course, about patent infringement, complaining about an American named Curtiss, who was stealing his ideas and trying to place the priority for motored flight onto Lilienthal, which wasn't so. I took the liberty, Elias, of telling him we would be happy to pay royalties."

"You're very generous with my capital, Simon."

"He earned it, Ellie. Don't you see, this is just the beginning? I want to build these aeroplanes more than anything."

"More than the motors for von Zeppelin?"

"Yes, even more that that."

After dinner, the brothers parted, Simon opting for a midnight stroll along the Champs Élysées, Elias choosing Madam Homage's evening of earthly delights.

"If Debora sees these, she'll absolutely kill me," Elias told his brother when he returned to their room the following morning. On the bed lay a dozen postcards of flavorful nude women posing.

"I don't know how you can do this, Ellie. You're a happily married man."

"That's exactly the point, Simon. When you get married, you will understand."

"I will never understand. You are my brother, and I love you. But you have sinned before the eyes of God."

"And that's the one I sinned with!" Elias guffawed, as he pointed to a plump young lady examining her naked body before a full-length mirror.

"Her?"

Elias grinned broadly. "Hey, boychick," he said, reverting to a Yiddish accent. He clumped his brother playfully on the side of the head. "We're on our own."

"What are you talking about?" Simon remarked, rubbing the side of the head where he was slammed.

"God, he ain't here. When are you going to realize that God is a human creation to keep the masses in tow?"

"You built a factory, you signed a deal with von Zeppelin, you slept with a harlot, so now you are smarter than God?"

"I would prefer a mistress like von Rosensweig has, but that is too messy, and I know Debora would never approve."

"You mean von Rosensweig's wife knows?!"

"Of course she knows. You can't keep something like that a secret forever, unless you have separate businesses."

"You mean like another factory in Paris?"

"Paris is too far. I'd settle for Munich or Salzburg."

"But don't you love Debora?"

"Of course I love Debora, but I'm talking about a man's needs. Here, you better hold these for me."

Elias handed Simon the postcards, and Simon found himself looking through them with an odd mixture of revulsion and lustful curiosity. "I can't keep these," he replied, trying hard to hand them back.

"Look, just until we get home and Debora unpacks my things. I took you to Paris to see this Wright fellow, didn't I?"

"You were just as interested as I in Mr. Wright's aeroplane."

"Simon, really. How can you compare that frail flying box-cart to von Zeppelin's majestic floating airships which encompass the size of a dozen houses? Let's not get side-tracked on the fad-toy of the day."

"It's not a whim," Simon retorted, throwing his brother's cards upon the floor. There, among the cards was a photo of von Zeppelin signed "To Abe Maxwell." The two brothers exchanged glances. "I'm going to build an aeroplane. Already Lilienthal's brother is advancing the design of his glider to take into account the success of the Wright brothers, and there will be a competition in Harhollenzeim next Spring. Every aeronaut in Europe will be there trying to figure out how to combine these two inventions into one elegant design. And I want to be in on it."

"And who is going to pay for this venture?"

"The best design will be awarded a prize of forty thousand francs."

"You will build von Zeppelin's motors. If the Kaiser asks, you will build motors for his army as well, and you will take these cards back home for me. And if you do all that, we can then discuss the creation of this other aeronautic whim."

Elias stood firm.

Simon considered his options. He couldn't proceed without the use of the plant. He bent down, gathered the cards and tucked them into his luggage. "I'll pick up and hide your dirty secrets," Simon spat back, handing the von Zeppelin photo to Elias as he continued. "And I'll build von Zeppelin's motors. Mother of God, Elias. I want to build those motors. What I'm talking about has nothing do with airship motors. I'm talking about a glider to enter into that competition. Now that his brother's dead, Lilienthal's aching for another partner. I know he knows he can never replace his brother, but that's what fuel's my fire. And once I build that glider, then maybe I can figure out how to put in Wright's designs which would add a motor and propeller. Why, and I ask you this in all seriousness, why do you want to rob me of this one thing that will give me such satisfaction? I don't understand."

"Because it's stupid. This Wilbur Wright thing is a game for a child. Even if he gets it to fly for a few miles, do you really think he's ever going to get his flying box to carry more than one or two people? Von Zeppelin's got a cruise ship that floats on air, that lets you sleep soundly in your own bunk bed and eat dinner up there. It's safe, it's quiet, and it can land practically anywhere. Wright needs hundreds of feet to land. One bump in the road and he is dead meat. And as I understand it, the wind has to be right as well. We are not boys anymore, little brother. We are men. And men build airships."

"There is something dead in you Elias, and that is why you turn to Madam Homage and her den of iniquity."

"Iniquity! You sound like a religious nut. You're living in the clouds, like the Wright brothers. You want to build a glider and make a fool of yourself, who am I to stop you."

Elias was about to slam the door to go to his room, when he realized that he had only booked the one room. So he walked back to Simon and slapped him across the face. Immobile, Simon absorbed the hit.

HONEYMOON

"One hundred, ninety-nine, ninety-eight, ninety-seven, ninety-six, ninety-five.... One hundred, ninety-nine, ninety-eight, ninety-seven, ninety-six...."

Chess slept quietly, out like a light, a smile of utter contentment on her lips, her hands folded placidly on her fertile womb. Rudy on the other hand readjusted, got up, took a piss, rolled over, counted backwards, prayed for sleep.

The alarm annoyed him. It seemed that just as he finally got to sleep, it went off. He pressed it for ten more minutes and finally fell deeply into oblivion.

"Rudy, let's go. The plane leaves in two hours."

"Christ." Rudy bounded out of bed and into the shower. "I don't mind the going. I just hate the leaving."

"Cut the philosophy, big boy. We're out of here in fifteen."

"Yes, ma'am." He scrubbed himself vigorously with the wet face cloth. "Where are the bags?"

"They're in the car."

"You put them in the car and you're six months pregnant! Don't do that."

"Come on, I'm healthy as a horse."

Rudy pulled their new yellow Bug out of the driveway and drove like a madman to the highway."

"Which way you going?"

"L.I.E."

"Forget that," she said. "Take Lakeville and just cut across the Island. We can get to JFK that way."

Rudy took her advice as they bypassed the Distressway. 6:15 am and it still didn't matter. Chessie had been right. The L.I.E. was bumper to bumper. There was no way they would have made the plane if they had taken the highway. *Where do all these people come from*? Rudy thought.

"Hey, get out of my way!" Rudy shouted. "Did you see that asshole?"

"Rudy, take it easy. We'll get there," Chessie said as calmly as she could.

"Do you have the tickets?" Rudy scooted around a turning vehicle and ran a light. A lady at the cross street flipped him the bird.

"Did you see what she did!" he said indignantly.

"Well, my dear, you deserved it." Chessie said. "You're driving like you are out of your mind."

"But suppose we miss the flight!" he snapped.

"What of it, kiddo. We're on our honeymoon."

"But we...."

"But we what?"

"Well...."

"If we miss the plane, which we won't, we'll just catch the next flight. We're not on deadline, so relax."

"Yeah, you're right. We can catch the next one." Rudy hit the accelerator, jumped a double yellow line to weave around two cars to get to a clear straightaway. He took the Southern State, just two exits, yet it took nearly thirty-five minutes. Traffic was at a dead halt, two miles outside Kennedy. He scooted onto a shoulder and drove the breakdown lane able to save a few more minutes by gaining the airport exit early.

"You're impossible."

"Yeah, but you love me."

"Who said?" she said.

"You did, last night. If I recall."

"I must have been drugged," Chessie cajoled.

"Uh huh," Rudy said. "That's not how I remember it."

"Hmmmm."

They checked their bags at the outdoor counter with twenty minutes to spare.

"I told you we'd make it," Chessie said.

"Lucky I passed that Mercedes on Southern State," Rudy said. "Did you see the way he was moping?"

"I wouldn't call 70 miles per hour moping, Rudy."

"Well everyone does 75, 80 there. You know that. Oh, my God, I think that's him!"

A tall slim gentleman in a pin-striped suit brushed by them. The man placed his keys and Rolex into a basket, put them through the X-ray machine along with his briefcase and shoes, and walked through the metal detector.

"Quite the dapper man," Rudy commented as he waited for his carry-on to pass through the conveyor belt.

"Very funny," Chessie said.

"What do you mean?"

"What do I mean, the guy looks like your twin brother."

"You mean that?" Rudy had to admit, that although the man looked considerably older than he, there was a certain *je ne sais quoi* that was awfully familiar.

The man looked back with that 6th sense that people seem to have when they know they are being watched. Rudy did not avert the gaze. Their eyes locked. And for the briefest moment, the two felt as though they had entered each other's soul and found that they were one and the same.

As one, both men touched their face as if they were checking a blemish in the mirror.

The inspector handed the man back his watch and keys, causing the two to break the magnetic connection they had made. The man then turned suddenly and disappeared down one of the corridors.

"Boy that was eerie," Chessie said.

"What was?" Rudy had not returned to their plane of reality yet. A burly man behind them pushed over to grab his luggage. Mechanically, Rudy grabbed his own carry-on and also Chessie's and together they sat down to put their shoes back on. Then they walked down the hallway.

"Which gate?"

"Sixteen, Rudy. Weren't you paying attention when we checked in?"

"Sixteen, yeah, right," he said, his mind still transfixed.

"You cannot beat first class," Chessie said.

They took their seats and soon, the plane ascended. Hot towels for their faces, a full three-course breakfast, cheese omelet, fresh fruit plate, bagels warmed to correct temperature, coffee and real pastries.

"I think I'll have an after breakfast aperitif," Rudy said.

"You're kidding, it's 7 in the morning."

"Couleur and cream," he told the flight attendant. Chessie enmeshed herself in the new *Good Housekeeping*. Rudy never understood how she could stay with the same magazine for what seemed like weeks. As she read, he drifted off, make-up sleep from the night before. Somewhere between being awake and dreaming, he entered a portal into his distant past. He felt as if he were a child again, only the images were not familiar, a scantily clad lady with long legs reclining at a window seat, she seemed European, Old World ways, and yet, the dream felt vaguely correct.

"Die spärlich bekleideten fraueleine festsetzen...."

Rudy drifted father. His fingers pressed tired eyelids as his brain sloshed in this sea of cerebro fluid. Backwards his mind fell, backwards, before Chessie, before Modern Times, before college, before high school and grade school, kindergarten, before, before, before.... A strange man with a rough beard who smelled of musk, tossed him in the air as an image of himself slumbered below him in his crib.

"Rudy, do you want lunch or what?"

"What? what?" Rudy mumbled, still emerging from the dream.

"Lunch?" Chessie repeated.

"Yeah, sure," Rudy said.

"You know, I have to say, I feel funny having a honeymoon and all, being..."

"Pregnant?"

"Yes," Chessie said as she wriggled her bottom to readjust.

"Would you like any juice or cocktail?" The stewardess came by to hand the couple two pillows and a pair of dark blue flannel blankets.

"We're on our honeymoon," Rudy offered.

"That's nice." The stewardess raised her eyebrows to acknowledge Chessie's bulging midriff.

"Love child," Chessie reassured her. "Do we really have to do this brisk thing. I mean, if it's a boy?"

"Bris. There's no k. I don't know. I mean, I barely even know this uncle Abe. I don't think he's even my real uncle. My mother seemed so peculiar about it. She insists he's a close relative, and then there was that unbelievable moment with your uncle. Did you know he was a Holocaust survivor?"

"I'm ashamed to say I didn't. You know, Rudy, uncle Hoxie also mentioned that Abe owned an airline in southern Germany."

"You mean Bavaria," Rudy got pedantic.

"Well, we are going to Verona and Milan. I looked on a map. Southern Germany, I mean, Bavaria, is only about five hours north by car. We could go see that Walt Disney castle."

"Neuschwanstein?"

"How the heck did you know that?" Chessie was amazed.

"Because I was thinking the same thing. Googled it last night. We could skip Milan and scout around up there. What do you say?"

"Sounds like fun," Chessie said.

"I did locate an airline near there," Rudy said, "MB Airways according to *Wikipedia* started in Kempten, by a Gunter Linzman," Rudy read off his computer. "That's got to be near where this uncle Abe's place was."

Rudy looked out the window. They were already high above the clouds. The hum of the engine, an easy bank and the plane readjusted to some slight deviation in direction, shafts of light, peeking over the cloud cover. Then, daybreak, sunlight blasting through the window. Chessie leaned over to give Rudy a kiss. Her lips seemed to melt onto his, her touch was tender. His loins stirred.

"Do you see that guy over there reading the paper?"

"Who, him," Rudy asked.

"Yes. Who does he look like?"

"I don't know, but if you tell me who it is, I'll probably agree."

"Roman Polansky. And Jill Eikenberry is sitting next to him."

"Jill Eikenberry. Where'd you pull that one out from?"

"*LA Law.*"

"I know. *LA Law*, but that's gotta be, I don't know, six or eight lifetimes ago."

"I just saw her on some cable movie channel about a lady who retires to live in the jungle."

"Oh, and what about the guy behind you."

Chessie sneaked a peak and burst out laughing. "My god, it's Burt Lahr," she whispered.

"It is, isn't it? And that's Margaret Thatcher sitting next to him."

"Unbelievable. Should I try to get her autograph?"

Suddenly the lady spoke to call over the flight attendant and out popped this aristocratic British accent. Rudy and Chessie did their best to stifle their laughs, easing themselves back into their respective niches. Rudy was reading a book on the people who funded Hitler. Chess was immersed in *Good Housekeeping*.

"I know it's light reading," she said reading his mind, "but I like it. It has everything, recipes, short stories, interesting other tidbits, so stop giving me that look."

"Did you know that Henry Ford was one of Hitler's greatest supporters?" Rudy reviewed the relevant chapter with her.

"Hated the Jews big time," Chessie said. "I think he funded the Nazis through some duchess or baroness."

"How did you know that?" Rudy inquired just as he read a passage about that in his book.

"*Good Housekeeping.*" Chessie smiled as Rudy surveyed the scene once again and Chessie's face cracked a smile.

"You just read that over my shoulder, didn't you?"

"Well, you're so slow, Rudy. I finished that page five minutes ago."

The plane landed in Milan. Rudy and Chess were to stay three nights and then drive straight to Venice, loop back to Verona and return to the states from Milan. "Look," Rudy said, "we can skip Milan, go right to Verona and take the car up into Austria and then to southern Bavaria. I'll see if we can get a room in Neuschwanstein. We can see the castle and drive through Kempten and Ravensberg and see if we can find anything to corroborate what uncle Hoxie told us about Maxwell Airlines."

"But what about Venice?" Chessie said.

"Well, we've got ten days. I think we can do that, too. Let's say we drive straight to Venice, spend a couple of nights and swing back through Verona. You can see, it's a straight run up through Austria."

"Oh, yeah. I see it. We could lunch in Innsbruck, and then go right to Neuschwanstein. We can do this Rudy. I'll get cracking." Chessie took over the computer. Using Expedia, she was able to book a room at the Hotel Caveletto off St. Marks Square for three nights in Venice, two nights in Verona at the Cleopatra and four nights at the Mueller House at the base of Neuschwanstein Castle in Bavaria.

Rudy had had visa problems in Italy from a previous trip, but with help from the state department, the bugs had been worked out. They sailed through customs, got a car at Avis and drove it to the Avis station on the outskirts of the ancient mushrooming island nation, Venice. A water taxi took them down the Grand Canal, under the Bridge Rialto and on toward the hotel. Traffic was moderate on the waterway, *vaperattos* and motor boats zipped by, as gondolas moved along in more leisurely fashion. The Caveletto, which was two lancs off St. Mark's Square, was just a short hop and one bridge from Harry's Bar.

Chessie had been to Venice before when she worked as a staff photographer for *High Life Travel,* but Rudy had never been there. He was amazed at the majesty and history of the place, the organized and colorful chaos of the Grand Canal, the age of the buildings, the amount of tourists and the number of pretty gals in short skirts that dotted every landing.

"Hey," Chessie said. "Get your eyes back into your head, kind sir!" Chessie read from the guide book which told them that many of the buildings were constructed as far back as the 12th century.

It is just amazing," Rudy said. They watched the throngs walk along the water's edge and found themselves particularly amused by the tourist groups, most seeming to come from China. The groups were easily seen as blocks of floating baseball caps all of one bright color, such as orange, blue or red.

Their water taxi turned off the main canal and led them through a back channel past a stable of gondolas right to the very steps of the hotel with water sloshing over the bottom landing. They checked in and unpacked. Rudy wanted immediately to take a gondola ride, but Chessie said he had to see St. Mark's Square, and so they did. Their hotel had a sense of privacy, slightly off the main loop. However, once they rounded a corner, Rudy became overwhelmed with the drama of the grand square and the Bell Tower which rose over 30 stories. They found a spot and just sat.

Many of the people were focused on the pigeons, hundreds bobbing and hobnobbing for handfuls of corn that the braver tourists held courageously in their hands for the classic St. Marks photo, a Disneyland take on Hitchcock's *The Birds*. Macho men and young girls surrounded by scores of their feathered friends, not only pecking for corn, but perching on them and mating on the square as well, males with their iridescent shimmering green necks puffed out three times their normal size, undulating their throats, dovening to their respective mates, females tittering amongst themselves, tolerating, but also flattered by the interest. A young cock approached a slim gal bravely courting her with a sooth cooing until a bigger brute suddenly appeared and off like a scaredy-cat the young cock flap-flopped.

Chessie was rooted on a large white pigeon who seemed to be virtual king of the square, but Rudy found himself instead, focused on the swallows, their silent bat-like flutter shifting into speedy dives and banks, circling with misdirection and sudden swoops, in rhythmic syncopated figure-eights, moving to the left or right to avoid an obstacle or snatch a tasty flying morsel. Like fighter-planes on overdrive, they followed one another in twos or threes, coalescing in squadrons, chirping as they zipped past, reversing directions, peeling off on different routes, with all of this action off-set by serenely gliding seagulls floating high above along invisible currents.

The line to go up Bell Tower looked to take about an hour, but that's what Rudy wanted to do, so they waited. As they stood there, Rudy had a dramatic feeling of déjà vu. "We should go to Murano," he said.

"I thought you'd never ask." Chessie gave a sigh of relief. "Waiting on this line is just too crazy. We can catch a *vaperatto* and be there in no time."

They left the line, walked past St. Mark's church and the Doge's Palace and stood at the water's edge waiting for the 42 water taxi.

"I know everyone says this," Rudy said, "but I feel like I have been here before, or that my ancestors have been here."

"Well, I really have been here before, kiddo, and I can state with authority, there is no grander place. I've never been to Murano, though and can't wait."

The water bus soon arrived. Along with a small crowd, they hopped on board. The trip was quick, the long side of a half hour, and there they were in the island village of Murano, the *vaperatto* letting them off right by the glass works of Alphonse Alphonso, with a sign that said, "Established 1680."

"Wow," Chessie said, "they've been here forever."

A wizened old man, sitting in the sunlight called them over with a crooked finger. Chessie waved nicely to the man as she whispered to Rudy, "Come on. I want to see the town."

Rudy waved in kind and they walked by to head into the heart of the village, which really was a series of side shops that lined both sides of the canal.

As they passed the man, he reached out and tugged Rudy's jacket. "You come back!" the man said in passable English. "I will wait." The man lifted a finger to tap the side of his nose, as if he knew something.

"Sure," Rudy said, and on the duo went, meandering through the streets, stopping into different shops to look at chandeliers and pendants and gold-tipped goblets, urns and vases and an angel which Chessie wanted to get for the top of her next Christmas tree.

After about an hour, they found themselves directly across the canal from Alphonse Alphonso's glassworks. Out of all the places they saw, none compared with that very first shop for size and range of objects for sale. "Do you know who that old man is?" Rudy asked the friendly lady who sold *mille fiori* ashtrays and statues all made out of colored glass.

"You mean him!" She pointed to the antiquarian across the canal who still sat in the sun.

"Yes, him."

"That's Pepé Alphonso. He could be 100 years old. His father was Alphonse, himself, one of the greatest glass blowers from the late 1800's, early 1900's."

"Was he wearing a Jewish star?" Chessie inquired.

"Probably. There has always been a strong Jewish community here in Venice. The Alphonso's are one of the oldest families in the region of Jewish origin. There's a small temple around the corner. You should see it."

Rudy felt the urge to return to speak to this ancient signor, but Chessie said, "Let's go."

"Where?" Rudy said.

"To the temple. If we are to give our son a bris, we might as well learn a little about these people!" she smiled.

They turned the corner, and there, tucked in an alcove was a miniature synagogue. The door was open and they entered. The windows, of course, were stained glass, the temple felt ancient. It was made of stone but it did not feel damp and that was probably because there was a stove off to the side that radiated an even heat. Behind glassed-in windows were old photographs.

One series of a wedding caught Chessie's eye. "I know this is crazy Rudy," Chessie began, "but this man here, the photo is dated 1912, is named Maxwell, and he is remindful of your uncle Abe. Rudy peered at the photo and read, "Iris and Simon Maxwell."

"It's a common name," Rudy said. But the man did look familiar. There was no denying it.

"Look at the way he's standing," Chessie said, "the way he cocks his head, just like your uncle Abe."

"You got a point." Rudy agreed with the perception.

It would have taken them a while to circle back so they opted for a *vaperatto* which instead hopped them quickly across the narrow canal to their initial landing spot. Pepé was still there, waiting. "Come here," he motioned again with his crooked finger. "You are a Maxwell, are you not?" he said.

"No," Rudy said. "I do have an uncle by that name."

"Abe?" the man said.

"Rudy felt he had been hit by a jolt of lightning. "Yes," he said. "How would you know?"

"I was at Simon Maxwell's wedding back before the Great War," Pepé said. "I was a small boy, with a terrible crush on Iris, Simon's wife…. ahh, she was…" he paused to kiss his knuckles and throw out his fingers, *"primo!"*

"So who is Abe?"

"Simon's nephew. Elias Maxwell's son. Maxwell Airlines. We are cousins of Iris. Come. Help me up."

Rudy reached down and helped the old man to his feet. He hobbled with some difficulty but then began to pick up a bit of momentum. Pepé took them into the glassworks. Inside was a demonstration by one of his grandsons blowing glass. They stayed long enough to watch the grandson create a horse rearing on its hind legs. "That's for them," Pepé told Antony. "Dip it." They watched Antony dip the hoofs and tail in a vat of molten gold.

"While it cools, come!" Pepé repeated. He led the couple into a back room. "That one." He pointed to one of a number of photo albums on a shelf. Rudy took it down and the wizened nonagenarian opened it. With wrinkled hands, he pointed out photographs of the wedding. "That was me!" The old sepia-toned photo showed an adolescent steering a motor boat with Iris and Simon Maxwell dressed in their wedding outfits. The next photo was a close-up of the couple. "Here," he commanded. "You take it."

"No, I couldn't," Rudy said.

"I won't take no!" the old man said.

"Rudy, we could scan it and mail it back," Chessie said.

"All right," Rudy said. "Thank you." He tucked the photo into an inside jacket pocket.

The old man insisted on walking back with them. "Iris was so happy that day. It was the greatest day of my life," Pepé revealed. And then he broke down into tears, collapsing into his chair which was situated in the setting sun, by the *vaperatto* stand.

Antony came out, and handed the glass statue of the horse to Chessie. "You can't leave without this," he said. "Oh grandpapa," he said. "Not again. This happens every time."

"What do you mean," Rudy said.

"Did he tell you the wedding of Simon and Iris was the happiest day of his life?"

"Yes."

"What about your own marriage and the birth of your children?" Antony was scolding his grandfather.

"Yes, yes," Pepé said. "I am an old fool. Can you forgive an old fool, my grandson?"

"Of course, grandpapa." Antony reached over to Chessie to take the horse back. Wrapping it in newspaper, he placed it in a box lined with bubble wrap and handed it back.

"Thank you," she said.

"Come," Pepé said to Chessie as he walked them to the *vaperetto*. "Give an old man a kiss."

Chessie leaned forward and the old man whispered into her ear. "No matter what they told you, Abe Maxwell is this man's grandfather. He is no uncle. Go, go!"

Rudy shook the old man's hand and shook Antony's as well.

"Show Abe!" Pepé said, pointing to the photo. "You show him, Simon and Iris Maxwell. Good-bye. And tell him, it's from Pepé! "

Rudy had difficulty sleeping that night. Upon returning to their hotel, they had gotten directions from the concierge to Al Conte Pescoar, an Italian restaurant several bridges away with outdoor dining. Having no trouble finding the place, they had enjoyed a tasty dinner right on the canal. The way the seating was, they ended up sitting with a couple from Cuba who talked about the pain their countrymen endured for many years, and the difficulty they had in being prevented from visiting their relatives who lived so close to their isolated island. The wine kept flowing, and when it was time to leave, they parted reluctantly.

Strolling through the dark alleyways, they missed the key byway and found themselves totally lost, going over a bridge they knew to be wrong, thinking they could recover, when, in fact, they could not. Rudy felt a panic overtake him, as they retraced their steps, and that startled him. The anxiety attack coming on so suddenly, with the realization that this friendly city of canals could turn on a dime into an imponderable maze. What really surprised him was how truly narrow the correct alleyway was that led to the bridge that took them back to the Caveletto. How was it that he had not noticed that feature when they walked so easily to the restaurant when going in the other direction? That is what troubled him the most, his lapse of observational abilities. In fact, he had argued with Chessie, but she insisted that this very slim byway was the way to go, and garl darnit, she had been right. So when they finally settled into bed, he found himself wrestling in his sleep and he had a nightmare. In the dream he found himself in a long line of workers and tramps, walking slowly around a cold city block to get to some essential function. From an alleyway came a man in a cape who he thought of as his brother, who simply cut ahead of everyone, way in front, leaving him behind. And yet, he was the only one outraged, everyone else simply accepting placidly the interloper's brazen move. He awoke in a sweat.

Chessie was fast asleep. It was 5 a.m. and the sun was just making its presence known. He got dressed, exited the hotel and walked the silent streets keenly aware that this was a very ancient place. So many bridges and ghosts and narrow alleyways, winding passages, silent moored gondolas, a sleeping town with its teeming past, intoxicating present and burgeoning future. Rudy thought about all the storefronts, their trip to Murano, Pepé and the glassworks. He passed mask and puppet shops, one that had religious icons, two simulated rare bookstores, a window front with enameled jewelry, several upscale clothing stores, a music studio. The city was awakening. Young hip ladies in high fashion attire, pin-prick nose studs, long straight hair, tight skirts, high heels, extended strides, some text-messaging as they swiftly walked to open up their respective places, men in pea-green overalls with wheelbarrows delivering the morning goods, gondoliers taking the tarps off and polishing their boats, getting them ready for the day. Rudy saw Venice as a place of apprenticeship, so many young workers' entrance into the high life. One gal smiled at him, made his day.

Chessie was up when he got back. She had already showered and was out on the balcony sketching a rooftop scene. After breakfast, they walked past Harry's

Bar to a photography shop. There, they got the picture of Simon and Iris scanned and emailed to Rudy's computer. After obtaining correct postage, they took the original and mailed it back to Pepé.

That task completed, the newlyweds took a leisurely gondolier ride down the main canal. The waterway was alive with activity, so many boats, so many people just enjoying themselves. Chessie leaned into her man. He put his arm around her and held her tight.

Over the next few days, Rudy found himself staring at the picture in his computer. If Abe was his grandfather and not his uncle, as Pepé had told Chessie, then this man, Simon, would be his great grand uncle – Abe's father's brother. So, who was Abe's father?

Rudy punched Maxwell Airways into Google. There was really nothing on it. He tried MB Airways and again it came up that it was started by Gunter Linzman right before WWII. According to one article, BMW, which stood for Bavarian Motor Works had a monopoly on the name Bavarian Motor, so Linzman reversed the letters, and thus, MB, was born, an acronym that really stood for Motored Bavarian Machineworks and later Airways. Rudy knew a little about the Treaty of Versailles, which restricted Germany after WWI to creating only non-powered aircraft, in other words, gliders. Linzman's company was one of the first, along with others like Junkers, Udet and Messerschmidt, to build motored aircraft, once the ban was lifted. Rudy also read that the letters MB denoted precision in flying instruments and also motors. However, one article, which was translated from the German, traced the letters MB to altimeters and motors that went as far back as 1915.

After Venice, Rudy and Chessie picked up a car again and spent several nights in Verona. They toured a few medieval churches, the street and home where Juliet of the play Romeo and Juliet supposedly had lived. They watched a play in the coliseum, a grand ancient amphitheater which competed with Rome's for its majesty and awe-inspiring size.

The following morning they took Route 45 north through Austria, arriving in time for lunch in the ski town of Innsbruck, the mountains towering over them in the background. It had been a four-hour drive, and just two hours later they were in Neuschwanstein. Considering how many wars had been fought between and within such countries as Italy, Austria and Germany, Rudy was amazed how close everything was. Driving from Italy to Germany was not much different than driving from his mother's house on Long Island to Chessie's friend Al's place in Vermont. And yet, during that short run of just six hours, they went through three countries, two highly different languages, and three or more highly different localized cultures.

Coming out of the mountains, they drove along a farm belt for many miles, until, all of a sudden, tucked into a large hill in the distance, they could see two distinct castles. The bottom one, built by Ludwig's father, was yellow and more traditional looking, with squared off parapets, and a circular feel to it, but the top one was what it was all about, mad King Ludwig's Disney-like blue castle.

Driving into town, Rudy and Chessie had to laugh to themselves, because, much like Venice, they saw more sets of tour groups from China, each gaggle dressed en mass with the same flaming red, yellow or green baseball hats. Then they rounded a corner and found themselves driving by a group of about thirty Muslims, all on their knees, praying to Mecca, bowing on their prayer rugs in unison. They turned another corner, and there was Mueller House, a regal looking hotel sandwiched between the two castles. It really was like a fairy land.

The lady of the manner was cordial, and hip. She spoke English with almost no accent. She asked the couple if they would like their clothes washed, and the couple gratefully agreed. This hotel would be their base for the next four nights. From there, they would tour the castles, and also take day trips to Kempten and Ravensburg, which they read were two of the oldest towns in the region.

Rudy grabbed the map, and out they went, arriving in Kempten less than an hour later. "This is where MB Airways was supposed to have started. All operations, according to the articles, have been moved to the outskirts of Berlin, with another smaller division near Munich," Rudy read. "Maxwell Airlines, according to Pepé, also began in these parts. I think we should just start at Kempten and see what's what."

"Okay, Rudy. This is fun. I feel like we are on a real adventure. Hey, look!" Chessie said. "Turn right over there."

Rudy followed her directions. They saw an old brick building with the words "MB Motoren Werkes" painted on a sign that arched over the entranceway. They drove in. Rising above the empty row houses and abandoned factory were two giant smoke stacks. Painted on one, in very faded but discernible letters was the word "Maxwell."

"Wow!" Rudy said. "This is heavy."

Rudy started to get out of the car to snap a few photographs, when suddenly a man holding what looked like a long iron rod, came running out from a side house, screaming, *"Privateigentu! Privateigentu! Steigen Sie das grundstuck!"*

"Sorry," Rudy said, raising a hand to stop and put the man at ease. *"No spreckensie German."*

"Private land! You are trespassing!" The man spoke in an ominous tone.

"Let's get out of here!" Chessie said.

Rudy dove back into the car and off they drove. "That was weird!"

They passed a row of sizeable rhododendrons and then high on a bluff an old boarded up mansion that overlooked the land. Everything was run down. The house looked cold and empty, and it felt very sad.

"What do you make of that?" he said.

"You mean the name Maxwell on the tower?"

"Yes. Is it Motor Bavarian Airways as *Wikepedia* says, or is it Maxwell-Bavarian Airways, as all this suggests?"

"Either way," Chessie said, "it's clear from what you showed me, that the Linzman family has been running that company for over 60 years."

"That's not what Pepé said," Rudy reflected.

"I know, but he's remembering back fifty or seventy-five years," Chessie said. "Come on. I found a great restaurant in Ravensburg that runs along a river. You want to have lunch there?"

Chessie's eyes were gleaming. How could he resist? This Maxwell stuff was interesting, but it really was a side line. They were on their honeymoon. When they returned to their hotel at the end of the day they found that their clothes had not only been cleaned, but everything had been pressed and folded as well, including their underwear. "What a luxury!" Rudy said.

"Yeah, well don't get any ideas!" Chessie shot back.

"Are you trying to say you are no Mrs. Mueller?"

"Can't put one over on you!" Chessie continued to pull his chain.

The couple spent the rest of the next few days as tourists, taking in the area, eating at local restaurants, purchasing tchochkas that caught their fancy, even spending down time at the hotel to simply sit in the sun and read. Believe it or not, Chessie was still working on her *Good Housekeeping* magazine. Rudy was reading a Michael Connelly novel about a lawyer who got trapped defending a man he thought was innocent of murder, only to find out that he had gotten it dead wrong.

The grounds were neatly kept. Rudy was trying to relax, really trying, but one of the gardeners kept eying him. The man would work the rose bushes, rake a little, disappear and then reappear. It seemed as if he kept finding things to do, so as to return to their orb.

"What?' Rudy finally said.

"Excuse me," the gardener said in passable English. "But are you Mr. Linzman's son?"

"Linzman, what are you talking about?" Rudy said. Chessie put down her magazine and looked at the man who returned the gaze and then stared back at Rudy.

"MB Airways," the man said. "I heard you talking."

"I know Gunter Linzman is MB Airways. That's easily found on Google," Rudy said.

"No, no," the man said. "Rolf Linzman, the son. You are not Rolf's son?"

"My name is Styne," Rudy said. "I just have one of those faces."

"No, you are his twin," the gardener said. "I know what I am talking about. Wait, you sit there," the man said. "I be right back."

"Chess, this is so odd," Rudy said.

"I know," Chessie replied, "but everybody has a look-alike, you know that. Look at Tom Brady and Matt Damon or Tina Faye and Sarah Palin."

"How about Dave and Kevin Kline?" Rudy offered.

"Come on, I'm serious."

"Okay, Jerry Orbach and Martin Landau."

"Michael Jackson and Diana Ross."

"I thought you were serious," Rudy said.

"I am Rudy." Chessie stifled a laugh. "I got one. Joan Rivers and Jennifer Grey."

"All right, enough!" Rudy said. "You know, we should get packing. We're leaving tomorrow morning."

"This is the best honeymoon I've ever had, Rudy."

"I just hope it's mine." He patted her stomach.

"Rudy!" Chessie gave him a playful slap.

The gardener never returned and so the duo went back to their room, packed for the next day and rested up to be ready for the evening. "Let's eat here."

"No, that guy creeped me out," Chessie said. "I found this Greek restaurant, about a mile from here. They have entertainment. It'll be fun."

"Whatever you say. Should we get reservations?"

"Might as well," Chess said. "I'll call the desk."

Dinner was at eight. They dressed for their last major meal before their return to Milan. They had booked a hotel right at the airport, so this would really be their last relaxing night. Directions were easy, and they arrived at Zorba's at ten of.

The walls were filled with photos of celebrities, mostly Anthony Quinn and photographs depicting the movie *Zorba the Greek*. Rudy could see that one of them was in color. On closer inspection, he found it was an oil painting, and when he looked even closer, he was surprised to see that it was signed by Quinn himself. And there were Quinn signatures on other photos as well, spanning decades. One in particular caught his eye. Quinn looked to be about 68 years old and he was shaking hands with, there's no other way to say it, Rudy's double. "Who is that?" Rudy asked the maitre de, a three-piece jazz band playing softly in the background.

"Anthony Quinn, of course," the man said.

"No, the guy he's with."

The maitre de looked at Rudy and looked at the photo. "Are you teasing me? It looks like you, but that was twenty years ago. Dimitri, look at this." The maitre de called over an older man who was wearing a red Fez. He seemed to be the owner.

"That, Rolf Linzman, and you are his spit image. You must be his son, no?" He spoke in a thick Greek accent.

"No, he's not that much older than me. So, what was he doing here?" Rudy asked.

"MB Airways. They used to have big manufacturing plant in Kempten. But that was closed down, I don't know, it was just ages ago."

"Would it be possible to obtain a copy of this photo?" Rudy said. "I don't need it today. You could scan it some day when you get a chance and email it to me?"

"Sure, boy," Dimitri said. "Karl, get his computer address. Two glasses of wine on me!"

"Thank you," Chessie said.

"No problem," Dimitri said. "But you only get one sip. You know, the bambino!"

"Hah!" Chessie said.

Dimitri took over ordering. Starting with hors d'oeuvres, the dishes included sausage wrapped in grape leaves, fried eggplant, small potato pancakes, a big Greek salad with olives and feta cheese, and the main course, savory lamb souvlaki, stewed whole tomatoes and carrots, turnips and green beans seeped in a honey sauce. Dimitri sat with them through much of the meal, telling them his life story and then returned later to join them for dessert.

The flight back home was restful. Rudy reflected on the last leg. Mrs. Mueller either knew nothing about Rolf Linzman, or would tell them nothing. He suspected the latter. Having had such an exciting trip, the downtime sitting in first class was a welcome respite. Rudy soaked in his novel, and Chessie, having finished her *Good Housekeeping,* began reading a book on Greek cuisine.

THE 4TH REICH

A commuter on the subways for so many years, Rudy felt like he was traveling on a luxury liner when he boarded the Long Island Railroad for work each day. He found his usual spot, kidded a bit with the bridge clique and worked on some ideas before the train pulled into the city. Detraining, he snaked his way through Grand Central, going, as he always did, through the underground passageway that surfaced through the Roosevelt Hotel at 46th Street, just two avenues away from Modern Times.

"So how was Bavaria?" Sally-Ann asked.

"Oh, Jeeze, I forgot your bumper sticker."

"Thanks a lot. I asked you to get me one simple thing," Sally-Ann huffed. Rudy reached into his satchel and removed the present. It was a small replica of Mad Ludwig's Neuschwanstein castle. "Here you go." He placed the powder-blue fairyland icon on her desk.

"You remembered! Rudy, You remembered!" Sally-Ann bounced up. Unable to control herself, she gave him a brisk hug and placed a wet kiss on his cheek. Turning red, as Mort and Bill looked on, she sat back down and resumed her typing as if nothing had occurred.

"Rudy, can I see you?" Captain Whitmore stood at the entrance of his office, his thumbs characteristically welded to his ever-present plaid dark green suspenders. Whitmore's pencil thin moustache and bushy grey eye-brows lent an air of accomplishment to his disciplined demeanor.

"Yes, captain."

"Take a seat."

Rudy found a comfortable chair and let his eyes wander to the one-way window that overlooked the street. There, he watched the parade of humanity pass along 5th Avenue. The captain spun around in his turret chair. He was studying the crowd through a pair of binoculars. "Here, look at this guy!" The captain pointed to a man reading a newspaper as he walked and handed Rudy the bonocs.

"I can practically read the headlines," Rudy said. "Looks like *The New York Post*."

"That was my guess," the captain said. "Look, kid, I know you just got back from your honeymoon, and Chessie's pregnant. But what I want to know is, can you travel? I mean, I can probably keep you predominantly New York based once the baby arrives, but...."

"Sure, captain. No problem. Just no more trips to Bhutan. At least for now. What's up?"

"We want to do a piece on the new Deutschland. I'm thinking of a title: The 4th Reich. Daimler-Chrysler, Spinnwebe Republic, Sieberlink, Bertelsmann Publishing House. What do you think?"

"You forgot Deutsche Boerse."

"Did I?" the captain said reflecting on Germany's new presence on Wall Street. "Maybe you should just lead with Deutsche's take-over of the New York Stock Exchange."

"I like it," Rudy agreed. "You want me to go back to Germany?"

"Yes. I've got something set up with Heinz Gruuban at Spinnwebe...."

"Gruuban, I can't believe it. I'm definitely in. If he gets Webnet."

"Exactly. He'll be bigger than Bing."

"Wasn't he a Nazi?" Rudy ruminated.

"No, that was his father, Gustav. Everyone knows that photo with him talking to Waldheim in their SS uniforms. But we are past all that."

"Are we?" Rudy said. "Isn't that the whole point?"

"I don't know, son. Follow your instincts. But if you dig any dirt about a guy that big, we gotta be certain."

"You know, if he gets Webnet, he'd have a virtual monopoly on wireless Internet, cell phone and picture phone service throughout Europe. That search engine and broadband platform Webnet is developing...."

"Like YouTube?"

"Yeah, I think they're calling it U-View. I read one article that said it would be slicker than Hulu."

"I doubt that. But see what you can find out."

"When's the meeting?"

"Next Wednesday. I want you to take Kimberly."

"Chess's not going to go for this."

"Talk to her. She's the best photographer we have, and we're going to need someone to make those stiffs lighten up."

"We've got to set down some rules here, Rudy. We just got back from there."

"It's a coincidence. What am I gonna do?"

"All right, maybe I can buy that, but traveling with a harpie is quite another thing."

"Come on, Chess. I work with her every day."

"Yeah, and if she had her way, she'd work with you every night."

"Are you jealous?"

"Damn straight, I'm jealous. You're not going. If she goes, this is non-negotiable."

Rudy gazed into her bright green eyes. And got lost. Chessie reached out her hand. There lips touched, tongues darted.

Dressed to the nines, with spiked heels, a skirt that showed mostly thigh and form fitting sweater, Kimberly Attison entered the aircraft. "Business class, not too shabby." Since she was bilingual, and had lived in Germany for nine years, her father was German, she would act as the guide.

"I'm amazed that the captain sprung for it," Rudy said. "He usually makes me go tourist."

"The captain's also booked us at the Charles. He wants us to be, how did he say it," Kimberly cleared her throat to do her Captain Whitmore imitation, "'You've gotta be top drawer.' He's got us a two-room suite with fax machine and Internet service."

Rudy and Kimberly were on the red-eye. Unable to sleep, Rudy opened up his laptop and logged onto GoGo, the airline's provider of Internet service. In the midst of one of his searches, Rudy became alarmed when a box appeared. *"ATTENTION!* Savior Security Center has detected malware on your computer!!" Not happy, Rudy looked over at Kim. She was fast asleep. He'd have to deal with this on his own. He read the rest of the warning. "Impact of Vulnerability. Remote Code Execution. Virus Infection: Unexpected Shutdowns."

"Just great!" Rudy mumbled to himself. If he didn't do anything about this, his whole trip could be screwed up. Knowing he had most of his computer backed up on a separate drive at home, Rudy opted to take the plunge. Worst case scenario, he could use Kim's laptop or even buy another. He went to Savior's website, paid his $29.95 through Paypal and let the game begin.

A stewardess walked by. He flagged her over and ordered a whisky and ginger ale. Returning his eyes to the screen he watched as a chat box appeared requesting that Rudy shut off all peripherals and allow one Anis Ramone to take control of his desktop. This was frightening to think that some unknown entity who he hoped was essentially honest, and not some scam hacker, would commandeer his computer, and while he was in flight, to boot. A few questions were asked, and then the technician asked for full permission to take control. Rudy at first declined and here's how the rest of the session went:

1:09 AM: You have denied full permission to Technician. A support representative will be with you shortly.

1:09: **Anis Ramone**. Hello, my name is Anis Ramone. I am a LiveAdmin Corporate certified computer expert. We will be performing remote administration of your system. Could you please provide your email address so I can identify your service package?

Customer: Rstyne@ Moderntimes.net What happens next?

1:10: **AR**: Thank you for your order. We will run a comprehensive analysis on your computer and remove all spyware malware and virus infections. We will optimize your Mac's speed and performance. During this procedure your personal files and data will not be deleted, accessed or copied. Your presence is required in first couple of minutes of this session. If you own a laptop, make sure that it is plugged in and charging.

1:11. **AR**: First we will reboot your system. Please save your work and quit all open applications, except LogMein. You will be automatically reconnected once your Mac boots up. Please confirm if we can proceed with reboot process.

1:11: **Rstyne**: Should I quit?

1:12: **AR**: Yes, please.

1:13: **Rstyne**: Should I quit Entourage, Word, Safari, textedit, finder, which ones?

1:13: **AR**. All, please except this chat window.

1: 13: **Rstyne**: Including the web-browser and Savior? Or do I leave these two. I can't quit finder.

1:14: **AR**: Quit Safari but please leave Savior. Thank you.

Rudy wondered how Savior could access his computer if he logged off the Internet. Obviously they could. This information alone was gold for his article and well worth the $29.95. As he was thinking, Rudy decided to copy down their exchange. He'd show Captain Whitmore when the article was nearly complete, and they could then decide what they could use. But during the process of scribbling down their dialogue – he couldn't save it -- another screen came up superimposed over their dialogue. Rudy looked at his choices. He could press the Permissions button, which would begin the scan, he could Deny the request and just get out of the entire process or he could push a Red Panic Button which was clearly there to stop the entire process at any time. He pushed Deny.

The second screen disappeared and Rudy continued copying down the dialogue which was still there underneath.

1:15: **AR:** You've denied me full access.

Damn right! Rudy thought.

1:15: **Rstyne**: Sorry, I pushed the wrong button. [Rudy lied.]
1:15: **AR:** No problem.
1:15: **Rstyne**: Where are you located -- just for curiosity?
1:15: **AR:** Our staff is located worldwide. Our technicians are available 24/7 from USA, England, India, Paraguay, Bulgaria, Romania, Serbia and Turkey.

Rudy noticed that she either avoided a direct answer to the question, reframed it or simply misunderstood. The answer certainly intrigued him. Why the Balkan states and some obscure location in South America and not some major outlet in European countries like Germany, Italy or France? Or Brazil for that matter? He also noticed that neither China nor Russia was on the list.

1:16: **AR.** Shall we proceed with the reboot process?
1:16: **Rstyne**: Yes, but I'm also interested to know where you personally are located, what state/country?? Thanks.
1:17: **AR:** Bulgaria. You're welcome.
1:17: **Rstyne**: Now what will happen?

Rudy continued to furiously write down the continuing dialogue, before he clicked the permissions button.

1:18. **AR:** We will proceed with the reboot process. After that, we will create a new username that will be used for this maintenance task. Finally we'll start the scan.

Rudy gave permission to allow Rescue to take over his computer and reboot under their own password. He then read the response that sent a chill through his bones:

1:21. **AR:** You have granted full permission to AR. To revoke, click the Red X on the toolbar. AR is rebooting your computer.... Connecting.
1:22: **AR:** Now we will briefly take control of your desktop, when prompted for, please enter your admin password. Please note that we do not see or store your current password. We will create new admin user which will be deleted after successful maintenance task. Please inform us when we can proceed.

"OK," Rudy typed.

1:24. **AR:** Thank you. Remote control started by Anis Ramone. We will now commence installation of our software. During this procedure we will have control of your desktop, keyboard and mouse. Please note that repair service might take up to 210 minutes."

Holy shit! Rudy said to himself. *That's almost 4 hours! His computer could be clicking till five in the morning. I hope I did the right thing,* he mumbled to himself.

1:39. **AR:** At this point, your presence is not required, but feel free to monitor our progress. Please refrain from using keyboard and mouse during this period.

Feeling a bit like the astronaut Dave in *2001: A Space Odyssey* capitulating to the computer HAL, for the next few hours, Rudy watched in amazement, dazing on and off as a virtual arm from 7,000 miles away reached out to take over *his* laptop and scan *his* entire computer. The reporter looked on in awe as three multi-colored rectangles suddenly appeared in rapid fashion: a black window in the top right corner with bright green writing, a blue window in the center at the top with white writing, another black window but this time with bright orange writing in the bottom right corner, the dialogue box with AR still on the left top corner and, like an oscilloscope, a series of streaming graphs in yellow and blue at the bottom of the screen.

Rudy stared at the RED BUTTON in the chat box which apparently gave him the ability at any time to take back his computer, as he continued to monitor all the action, which, for the most part, was situated in the top right black window with green lettering. File after file came screaming down as the program scanned and scanned for a full two hours. Finally, AR came back on the chat box.

3:19: **AR**. Your computer repair service – virus/spyware * malware removal has been completed. Service report including video feed will be sent to your email. Thank you again for your purchase of Savior Security and have a nice day!
3:20 AM. Remote control by Anis Ramone stopped. Session has ended.

Rudy checked his email. There he found a link to the website that not only had a video accounting of the entire scan, but also the following full report:

Malware: Threats disinfected: 4. Issues resolved: 4.
Repaired system permissions.
Removed old log and temporary files.
Cleaning out old system announcements.
Removed stale files from /var/rwho.
Removed scratch fax files.
Rotated fax log files.
Rebuilt whatis database.
Done login accounting.

"What is whatis?" Rudy mumbled to himself while nodding into sleep mode. Three hours later he received a friendly elbow from Kim. The plane was landing. Munich time was 6:20 AM. He had a few moments to scramble to the bathroom before the Please Be Seated Sign appeared. The plane touched down.

Deplaning, Kimberly seemed transformed, and when they entered the terminal, she just took over.

"Styne," Kimberly directed, "get the bags and I'll get the car." Speaking fluent German, Kimberly got the directions to the rental place and also found the best spot to pick Rudy up. "I'll meet you downstairs by the yellow and blue bus stop. It should be right across the street from the exit."

"Do you think it's best we split up? Suppose one of our bags are held up?"

"Look, if we run into trouble, then we'll meet at the baggage claim." Kimberly rocked an imaginary cell phone. "That's a worst case. See you in twenty. We Germans are pretty efficient."

"Well, I'll give you pretty," Rudy smiled.

"I'll take that as a compliment." Kimberly turned a few heads as she strutted down the walkway and disappeared into the crowd.

Twenty minutes later on the pick-up island, Kimberly pulled up. Driving a white Honda, her car looked like every other rental that zoomed by. "Rudy," she called out, after he got in, "you are not going to believe this." She was breathing heavily. "I got to the stop early and told you to get into the car. This guy, I swear, he was your double, even the same clothes, but as I looked, he was older, gives me a glare like I'm cross-eyed. 'Do I know you?' he says in German. I was flabbergasted. Before I got a chance to mumble I was sorry, he had hailed a cab and was off."

"What are you talking about?"

"Your, dead-ringer, and don't mean just your spitting image, I mean your frigging clone, right down to that adorable dimple in your chin! Everyone has a doppelgänger, Rudy, everyone knows that. But this one was the real magilla!"

"You're nuts."

"I am, am I?" With that, Kimberly pulled out her cell phone and showed Rudy an image she recorded. It was a profile, almost from the back, of a man getting into a cab. Shot through the rear window and blurred, Rudy couldn't tell if it looked like him or not. But something about the guy's body language, the way he hunched his shoulders as he bent to get into the car.... something about it rang true. It was another experience of déjà vu. There was a nuance to the picture that was unmistakable even if Rudy couldn't see the face that well. He thought back to that previous incident at JFK with Chessie.

"Have you ever seen your dead-ringer?"

"All the time," Kimberly said. "Don't all dumb blondes look alike?"

"But you are not even blonde."

"Well, I used to be!"

Kimberly certainly knew her way around Munich. Like a shot, she got them to the hotel where they unpacked, grabbed breakfast and then headed over to Spinnwebe Republic. The company was set along the River Isar which ran near the university, through the heart of the city.

The river seemed more like a creek than a major byway to Rudy, but Kim straightened him out on that score. Rather than entering Spinnwebe by the main road, she chose a path through the park that took the duo past an area of rapids where the locals donned wetsuits and surfed the rough water.

"Wow." Rudy stared at the unexpected site, and used his cell phone to take a picture.

"Enough!" Kim tugged him by the shirtsleeve. Yanking the reluctant tourist from the magical spot, she led them through a charming park past the university to the entranceway of the burgeoning hi-tech conglomerate that was fast becoming one of the jewels of the region.

Encompassing five buildings constructed in a style compatible with the local Bavarian architecture, even though the buildings were modern, they looked like they had been there for centuries. The lawns were green, the flowers in bloom, the place felt distinctly like a campus.

A male receptionist greeted them at the main hall, gave them badges, and walked them to a structure that resembled a church with tall spires and stained glass windows. "The boss' place," the receptionist said. "You're expected." They entered.

The structure had an impressive atrium with an expansive open staircase that wrapped around to a second floor landing where most of the offices were, and a window two stories high that looked out to the river. Streams of sunlight poured onto the floor. Rudy waited for Kim to take photos of the setting, but then, like a shot, she ran up the staircase to take a long view. He opted for the elevator. He stepped in and pressed 2.

Kimberly took several shots from half way up of the view of the river. She tried to take a decent shot of the atrium, but, with the glare, she thought it better to shoot from the second floor overlook. With her back to Gruuban's office and leaning over the railing, she snapped a bird's eye view of a large bronze statue of a spider in a spider web which was positioned near a tropical garden and indoor waterfall. Trapped was a bronze statue of a scantily clad maiden remindful of the White Rock girl, arms and legs flailing as if she had just fallen into the web, her breasts sensual, her nipples erect.

Rudy barely looked up when the elevator doors opened, and when they did, as he exited, he found himself colliding with an elderly gentleman with a distinct air of success about him.

"Sorry," Rudy said, grabbing the man quickly as he almost caused the fellow to tumble.

"You should look were you are going, young man," the older man said curtly in German.

"Excuse me?" Rudy said in a way to convey that he did not speak German. Their eyes locked. "*No spreken sie German.*"

"You are Rudy Styne!" The man spoke in a shocked voice in English with a German accent.

"*Yavol!*" Rudy said, trying to deflect an uncomfortable moment. Kimberly walked over just as Herr Gruuban came out of his office.

"Ms. Attison, Mr. Styne!" Heinz Gruuban approached. He looked to be a man in his mid-40's. Wearing no tie, with his shirt open several buttons, and hair from his chest exposed, Gruuban's pants were precisely pleated and perfectly fit. Rudy also noticed alligator shoes, and sleeves rolled up to reveal a large diamond pinky ring on his left hand, and the obligatory Rolex on his wrist. He was smiling, but he had an odd strained expression. "I see you've met Mr. Linzman. I was just telling him about our meeting. The 4th Reich. A little bold, but kind of catchy."

Rudy was flustered. "Linzman?" he managed.

"MB Airways," Kim whispered to get him back on track.

"We were just in Kempten." Rudy said.

Gunter Linzman stood for a long moment. There was an uncomfortable silence, and a subtle sense of disconnect between Linzman and Gruuban. Mr. Linzman finally said reflectively. "We shut that plant in the 70's. Most of our operations are closer to Berlin."

"Lufthansa absorbed them," Gruuban explained, "after the war."

"But we always kept out identity." Linzman defended himself. "We were the premier airline, we didn't cater to the masses, and when the time was right, we bought back our stock."

"And Lufthansa never complained," Gruuban explained. "Everyone made money, didn't they Guntie!"

Linzman spoke in a quiet tone. "Yes," he said slowly, "Everyone was happy." Linzman looked again at Rudy for yet another pregnant pause. "So, you're Rudy Styne?" he found himself repeating.

"None other."

"Would you mind?" Kimberly motioned with her camera.

Linzman looked at his watch and then reached out to shake Rudy's hand. "You are the reporter from the United States." He either was ignoring Kimberly or he didn't really process what she had said.

"Guntie," Gruuban spoke in an obligatory tone of congeniality, "you are welcome to stay."

"No, I can't. We've had our little chat."

"A photograph, gentleman!" Kimberly said in a tone to brighten the moment. The two men looked at each other expressionless. *"Fur das amerikanische Publikum!"* Kimberly said more loudly, in perfect German, a big grin on her radiant face.

"Ah, fur das amerikanische!" Herr Gruuban repeated.

Linzman made a gesture of acquiescence. He stepped back and stood next to Heinz Gruuban. In mechanical fashion, they put their arms around each other and pasted on smiles. Kim snapped the photo. "Another," she said and then clicked off several more.

The older man returned to Rudy and grabbed his hand once again. "Would you have dinner with me tonight? You and of course your lovely friend."

"Hey, Guntie," Heinz said. "What about me?" Gruuban was much younger than Linzman, and it was clear, at least to Rudy, that the use of the 'Guntie' nickname did not sit well with the older gentleman. They conversed in German. Kimberly translating in a whisper as they talked. "Mr. Linzman is telling him that he'll have the entire day with us. He just wants us for the evening."

"We'd have to be nuts not to do dinner, right?" Rudy whispered back as he stared at the older man trying to put all the pieces of the puzzle together.

"He's CEO of one of the most prestigious airlines in Europe, Rudy. It's just what you are looking for."

"I'll pick you up at your hotel?" Linzman said after finishing his conversation with Gruuban. "Say, seven?"

"Seven it is," Rudy said.

Linzman walked into the elevator, but not before placing his hand on Rudy's shoulder. It was a comforting gesture. Rudy was not sure what this was all about, but he knew he would find out soon enough.

"Thank you," Rudy found himself saying. Gunter Linzman simply looked back at him with an expression of compassion as the elevator doors closed.

Heinz Gruuban welcomed Rudy and Kim into his sumptuous enclave. There was mahogany all around. The view of the river and the city was inspiring. The tall Palladian windows were augmented by a broad stained glass trim which ran the perimeter of the ceiling. A continuation of the church motif that graced the exterior, the colored glass allowed a panoply of colored ambient light to filter in.

"When did you start Spinnwebe?" Rudy began. Gruuban was a genteel host and spoke freely about his attempts to acquire Webnet which would clearly make his company the largest web provider in Europe with a search engine that had already gained two more market shares from the giant Google.

"It's not just email, apps, web and search, you know," Gruuban explained. "Webnet, of course, has U-View a digital broadband video platform that, believe it or not, dwarfs the combined abilities of YouTube, NetFlix and Hulu. Although Apple still leads the world in smartphones, we're creating a new ecosystem that's simpler, faster and more efficient. Already, we have deals with Nokia to produce our own smart videophones, MyPlace to integrate our social networks, Scope for digitalizing motion pictures and for web video-uplinking, and we have a pending partnership with Turner-TimeWarner for broadcast rights for their film and TV archives. And we also have pending deals for the syndicated libraries of every major Western network."

And so it went for the next three hours. Rudy's mind was blown. The new capabilities for creating a multimedia device three times the size of a Backberry, but smaller than the typical laptop would combine computer, television, camera, videophone and traveling library all in one device. "You could call it a souped up iPad or Surface tablet," Gruuban said, dismissing the Kindle as completely obsolete. The world was changing so rapidly. Kimberly had assured Rudy that he had asked the right questions, and he got it all on tape, but his mind was elsewhere. There was something about Mr. Linzman's grip on his shoulder that overshadowed this fantastic meeting with the CEO of a company that was ready to combine technology equivalent to the best of Apple and Microsoft with that of Verizon and the TV networks.

"Mr. Gruuban," Rudy was listening to the playback as Kimberly drove.

"Come on, let's take a break," Kim interrupted. "I'll take you to one of my favorite places, Hofbräuhaus, on the Platzl.

The famous pub was easily the grandest beer hall Rudy had ever been to. Feeling as if he had stepped into a scene from *Sound of Music*, men playing accordions, trombones, hand-held glockenspiels and a big base drum, marched through the aisles dressed in lederhosen, complete with high socks, well-pressed shorts with colorful plaid suspenders and mountain hats with feathers in them.

Intertwined with the performance, waitresses pranced by dressed exactly like St. Pauli Beer girls. Theirs was an exuberant buxom blonde in a low-cut white blouse, with black midriff waistband, very short red skirt, bright white stockings that stopped tantalizingly two inches below the hemline with garter belts that disappeared into the netherland, and black heels laced up to above her ankle.

"Vat vould you like," she said through the cacophony.

Rudy smiled as Kim ordered two beers.

"Is that all?" the gal flashed some cleavage and batted her eyelashes.

"She's really pushing it," Rudy commented.

"Just turn the recorder back on," Kim replied in as serious a tone as she could muster. They grabbed their beers and found a more private corner so they could continue to listen to the tape.

"Heinz," Gruuban said on the tape.

"He wanted me to call him Heinz," Rudy spoke.

"I know, shush," Kim said. "Turn up the volume. You're taking notes aren't you?"

"Of course." Rudy pointed to his noggin as the tape continued.

"Heinz," Rudy asked on the tape, "if you gain the kind of control you are really seeking, that is, the creation of an Internet media giant on a scale that would rival the cell phone companies, MugShot, YouTube and the TV networks combined, what safety precautions would you be taking against a cyber attack?"

"Redundancy, back up, cyber-eye and parallel circuitry," Gruuban said.

"Cyber-eye and parallel circuitry?" Rudy asked.

"Take the terrorists that use the web. We now have the capability with Internet GPS to locate almost instantaneously any cyber attack with pin-point accuracy, and I'm talking within a six-foot radius on any spot on the globe."

"Russia too?"

"Naturally. As you know a lot of cracking comes from disgruntled factions of the old Soviet Union. We think that Digital Sky might be behind it." Gruuban was referring to Digital Sky Technologies, the Russian counterpart to American Satellite, that now had a major share of Facebook. "We pass this information to the proper channels. We've already had several key arrests. And I can tell you, you do not want to be arrested for fucking with the Internet particularly if you live in Russia, Iran or China."

"Are you talking death penalty?"

"You will clean up the language, no?"

"Of course, Mr. Gruuban."

"Heinz."

"Heinz. And you are saying this is foolproof?"

"Nothing is foolproof. But we are close. You see that building over there?" Gruuban pointed to one of the buildings on the far side of his campus.

"Yes."

As they listened, the St. Pauli girl, carrying two more overflowing beerstynes, somehow found their new location and plunked them down. Foam splashed on the table which gave the excuse the waitress needed to lean over and display her ample cleavage, as she mopped up the overflow. She had a star tattooed near her nipple on her right breast. Trying to ignore the sexual tension of the moment, Rudy and Kim clinked glasses and they went another round.

The tape continued, "The entire building is set up for R and D for technical, hardware and software advances and security. And please, Ms. Attison."

"Yes."

"No photos there. Okay?"

"Of course," she said. Kim nodded to Rudy and they continued listening.

"And this parallel circuitry?"

"We have relationships with several satellite companies to set up alternative wireless paths for banks, government agencies, VIP's and so on. These are wholly different frequencies which are incompatible with public airwaves and thus incompatible with the hardware sold on the open market. Our parallel network operates on a firewall protected entirely separate system, that is, an alternative Internet highway on a totally different orbital platform with password encrypted access, all of this set to go, if indeed we were attacked, along mainstream lines."

"How can you possibly maintain security?!" Rudy inquired.

"Very easily," Gruuban said, a slight sense of satisfaction to his voice. "Every machine sold has a serial number. And all equipment comes with a standard tracking device. Through a GPS IP address tracking system, every signal sent or received on our VIP network can therefore be pinpointed. We will also be setting up a second tier for non-VIPs who are willing to pay for extra protection. And this is all separate from our mainstream operation."

"You mean, if other machines come on or spy on this separate line, you would know?"

"Now you got it."

"And that is why you were meeting with Mr. Linzmann?"

"It's no secret he wants to compete with LandSat. That's part of the reason. We are also just friends." Gruuban was talking about MB's entrée into the field of satellite production, launch and maintenance.

Rudy handed the checkout girl a credit card, and they stayed a few moments longer to watch a Bavarian dance performed on stage. On the ride back to the hotel, Rudy checked his email as Kim rattled the cage.

"They were arguing when I got up there," she said.

"About what?"

"I'm not sure. I distinctly heard Heinz mention Rolf Linzman, which seemed like a relative of Gunter's."

And then his phone went off. Kimberly looked over at Rudy's expression. "What's wrong?" she said.

"That was a nurse. It's my mother. She's had food poisoning and her liver seems to be shutting down. She's at a hospital out on Long Island, and they are already thinking about a liver transplant. They want to make sure she didn't also suffer a heart attack."

"My God," Kim said. "What do you want to do?"

"I've got to get home as soon as possible. Who knows, she may need part of my liver. I'm just going to grab my luggage and take the next available plane."

"What about Linzman?"

"Do you have his number?"

"No. He was just going to meet us at the hotel."

"You meet with him and apologize for me. I'm sure he'll understand."

RABBI

Rabbi Sinschwartz looked out at his congregation and sighed silently to himself. True, the synagogue had a solid core membership that numbered over sixty-five families, but many of the members were, well, they were just plain old.

"Rifka," he said to his wife during holiday brunch, nodding hello to Simon Maxwell, the only remaining member of that family who still attended services.

"Yes my love."

"Look about you. What do you see?"

"I see the largest Jewish Congregation in all of Lower Saxony.

"But where are the children?"

Rifka rattled off the names of twenty or more, but she knew where this was headed. Only last week two more families had dropped out because of assimilation. That had made eleven families gone this year, and nearly a third of the congregation gone in the last four years.

Jobs and opportunities were scarce because it was predominantly an agricultural region. True enough, there were a few manufacturing plants such as Maxwell-Bavarian Machineworks. But much of the real labor in the region was low skilled. "Trained monkeys," the rabbi had commented one Sunday afternoon to Rifka's dismay. But she understood some of the animosity to the statement. Elias Maxwell was a convert. Yet another prominent Jew who had turned. And Jews tended to be merchants or traders, or they sought high skilled careers like lawyers and doctors and accountants. This meant that people were leaving town to go to the cities where there were well-endowed universities and more opportunity. Out of the 130 fully paid members, nearly half were over the age of 50.

"It doesn't take a genius to do the math, my dear," Rabbi Sinschwartz said again as he watched old Phillip Brownell shuffle across the floor to pile another helping of baked fish, pickled herring and bagels onto his plate. With bent head, squashed down nose, green complexion and a bottom lip that stuck out like a dinner plate, the old man wheezed as he walked such that every step looked like it could be his last. Simon was always amazed that Brownell was still on the planet. And the funny thing was, Brownell looked that way, with literally one foot in the grave, for as long as Simon could remember.

"I've heard the Maxwell boy can read," Mrs. Bromberg came over to the rabbi's table with her youngest daughter, Angelica, who was nearing 20. With a pinched face, twisted lips and a tendency to wear her dresses hiked too high on her hips, everything about Angelica was off kilter. Rifka could read her husband's thoughts: The odds of Mrs. Bromberg getting her daughter married off were getting slimmer with each passing month.

"If he can read," Angelica spoke with a shrill voice that tended to make the hair on the rabbi's arms stand up, "then he should learn Hebrew."

The rude girl had hushed the table, for she dared to say the obvious; the best and brightest young Jewish boys were not only not getting Bar Mitzvahed, worse, they were becoming Christians! And why? Because their fathers were agreeing to trade their heritage for a few more German marks.

"Elias wants to become part of the *Volk*," Angelica's mother agreed, her words stinging the air like salt going into a wound.

"Debora will want him Bar Mitzvahed," Rifka tried, attempting to stave off a wash of depression which threatened once again to overtake her husband.

"How do you know he can read?" the rabbi inquired. "He's only three."

"I saw them in Kempten's meat market the other day. He was reading to his mother a newspaper article about an upcoming aeroplane race."

"In Champagne?"

"Yes, Rabbi," Angelica said. "Simon, oh Simon," she shouted too loudly as was her custom, creating an awkward scene by drawing attention to herself.

Simon was still talking to Mr. Brownell. He helped hold the old man's plate, as Brownell heaped another pile of food on top, and then hobbled back to his table so that he could snort more down.

"He's handsome, isn't he?" Mrs. Bromberg said to the rabbi's wife. "He and my Angelica once danced together at the Brierwitz bar mitzvah."

"Mother! That was seven years ago. We were thirteen! Am I never going to hear the end of it?"

"Seven years? Was it that long? Simon! Simon!" Mrs. Bromberg called him over by motioning with her fingers before he had completed his aid to Mr. Brownell.

Simon wanted to steal out a doorway or engage Klinemann or Eisler, or anyone else in conversation, but he had to be friendly. He ambled over.

"Yes, Mrs. Bromberg. Angelica, Rifka, rabbi."

"Angelica here tells me that your nephew can read."

"It is true rabbi. He can also multiply three and even four digit numbers in his head."

"You don't say," the rabbi responded cautiously. "Does his grandfather know about this?"

We write him frequently, but after the stroke. I am sorry. I hope and pray my father will survive. But he is very feeble, too ill to travel. That is why we are planning a trip before the end of the month."

"He will see Elias too?"

"That is for Hillel and God to decide."

"I see," said the rabbi. But that doesn't excuse Debora. Why is it I never see her at services? You know she is welcome."

"She feels odd. She doesn't want to cause more strife."

"You mean, she figures she can wait a few years before she deals with the Bar Mitzvah problem?"

"Yes, rabbi. Abe's only three and he's bright enough. What am I saying! He seems to be on the level of genius, and she figures he has at least three if not five years before she broaches the subject...."

"Of religious training?"

"Yes, rabbi. She is hoping that Elias will come back or at least give his tacit approval after he is more established..."

"With the *goyim!* It's a *shonda!*" Angelica spoke again so loudly that the janitor, Mr. Ottoman, who was not Jewish, turned to look at her.

"Angelica, that is not a term we like to use," the rabbi cautioned, nodding a reassuring smile in Mr. Ottoman's direction.

"I'm sorry. I never say the right thing, do I? I suppose mother here is going to ask you, Simon, why you have not asked me to dance with you since the last time."

"We danced?" Simon really hadn't remembered. But he also knew immediately that he simply should have kept his mouth shut.

Tears cascaded down Angelica's eyes before she had a chance to hide her face, so she turned quickly. "It's all your fault, mother!" Knockneed, she ran from the room.

"I've tried to get her to grow up, but here she is, still an untouched maiden at nearly 20, and she continues to make an ass of herself."

"Evi," Rifka said as kindly as she could, "sometimes I don't think you understand her."

Simon felt trapped yet again by Mrs. Bromberg. He had never danced with the bushel-puss, as she was known to his friends. Holding hands during a hoorah was not dancing. And now he remembered that she had spun with him and licked his face, that day, seven years ago. He thought she had been drunk that afternoon, they all could sneak wine at the Bar Mitzvahs in those days, and it was one of those, oh one of those nutty moments. He was half-drunk himself. Should he straighten things out? "Why not call on Debora," Simon said to the rabbi as he watched Mrs. Bromberg's daughter run from the building. "I know that she is proud to be a Jew. It's my brother that's the problem."

The rabbi thanked Simon who excused himself so that he could light out after the embarrassed Bromberg girl. He found her down at the big oak tree by the stream.

"I hate her. I hate her. I hate her," Angelica found herself unable to contain her rage as she tore at her own dress and ripped out a clump of hair. "I want to lick you now. What can I say? Will you let me lick your hand, Simon?"

Grabbing the girl with both hands to prevent further destruction of her clothes, Simon decided to come clean. He would tell her the truth. "Angelica, listen to me. You cannot say such things, particularly to someone you know does not love you."

"But I pine and ache for you."

"No you don't. Forgive me for saying this. But you are frustrated."

"How can you say such a thing to me!" Angelica reached out to slap him.

"You misunderstand me," he said grabbing her hand in a vice-like grip. "You are loud and draw attention to yourself."

Angelica reached over with her mouth and began to lick his fingers. "And you are not?"

Flushed, Simon let go of her grip, and they walked farther into the woods.

"Rabbi Sinschwartz came by the house," Debora said. "He wants our Abraham to attend schule."

Elias, who was driving, turned to look at her.

"It was Mrs. Bromberg's idea," Debora added. Elias had decided to make the drive to Austria without Gunter so there would be more room in the vehicle for the long journey.

"Mrs. Bromberg. That's Angelica's mother, isn't it?"

"I think it is, yes," Debora said.

Elias gave Simon a knowing stare through the rear view mirror. He was sitting in the back seat with Abraham. Elias looked long enough to cause Simon's face to redden.

"Of course. It's hard enough for those who stay Jewish," Elias said as the automobile sputtered on. "But being a Polish Jew. *Oi vey!*"

"Elias!" Debora exclaimed. "You're speaking Yiddish!"

"Vat can I say," he continued in an exaggerated Jewish accent. "Sometimes it just slips out. Christ forgive me!"

"Is that a joke, papa?" Abe was leaning forward with his elbows on the front seat.

"Yes, it's a joke," Debora said, rustling Abe's hair.

"Just don't tell *my* papa!" Elias said, "or he'll never see me."

Simon put Abe on his lap and joined the conversation. "Ellie, the best you can hope for is that he still sees me!"

"So that you can announce your engagement!" Elias said innocently.

"You're engaged?" Debora said. "Who's the lucky girl?"

"Who's the lucky guy?" Elias smirked.

"Ellie's just busting me. There's no girl in my life. He just wants me married so he can dig his talons even deeper into my loins." Simon turned to Abe. "And then he thinks I can help get him into the good graces with your grandpapa."

"Grandpapa loves me," Abe suggested.

"You're our in," Elias said, winking at Simon again through the rear view.

"Grandpapa loves all of us," Debora said. "Even the *goyim* behind the wheel!"

Elias started to give his wife an awful stare, but she glared back. Then suddenly, the two of them burst into laughter.

"So, now I'm *goyim?*" Elias declared.

"Papa, you're Jewish *goyim*, somewhat like a French German or a Serbian Croat." Abe was proud of his analogy.

"Or a sour Kraut," Simon jabbed. They waited for Abe to get the joke, and then again the group burst out in sounds of merriment.

The Daimler chugged up the great mountain and careened over the other side, and then up over another rise to an overlook where they stopped to enjoy the view. "Weissenbach," Simon proclaimed, pointing out the location on the map for Abe.

"Can we take a photograph, papa?"

"Yes we can son. Simon, will you set it up? We'll put the little *tatellah* in the front."

"So, he is your darling boy," Debora said, tears in her eyes.

"Of course he is my *leibling*," Elias said, staying in Yiddish.

It was as if, for a moment, a great burden had been lifted for the master of the house. Now that his family was in Austria, Elias did not have to pretend to be something he, underneath it all, truly never felt comfortable being. "Here, let's use this." Huffing, he pulled out a suitcase from the trunk to create a seat. Taking center stage, he sat upon this square thrown, placed Abe on his knee and positioned Debora to stand behind. She placed a hand on his shoulder. With the mountains and hamlet in the background, Simon held the camera steady and shot the picture.

"You must change plates," Debora insisted.

"It went very well," Elias said.

"Can't you just do as I ask?"

"Well dear, aren't you the bossy one."

"Oh be quiet, oh great one, and stand over there beside your brother. And so, Elias and Simon stood side by side.

Although Elias had nine years on his brother, for the briefest of moments they were each transported back two decades. Instinctively, they put their arms around each other. Elias cocked one hip, and put on his self-assured swagger which only made Simon grin more broadly. Click, the photo was taken. It was an instant classic and they all knew it.

Tossing the suitcase and camera back into the trunk, the Maxwell clan tumbled back into the car, and rumbled down the hill into Weissenbach.

"What are you doing?" Debora said, as Elias took a right turn and headed up an unpaved lane. "Grandpapa lives by the synagogue on the other side of town."

"He's taking us to visit grand uncle Judah Baruch," Abe said.

"How did you know that?" Simon asked.

"Papa told me, didn't you papa?"

"I never said a word, but I did think it."

The graveyard had headstones dating from the 1500's. Many of the older ones were faded and difficult to read. "There's the big oak tree," Simon shouted.

They made a left and a right and wound their way to the Maxwell plot. Four generations of gravestones going back to the 1700's. They passed a grave which said "Henny Jountow."

"That's uncle Henny," Elias recalled. "He fought with grandpa Judah for an aisle plot. *You die first, you get the aisle*," Elias repeated in grand uncle's voice the famous family story. Down three spots, they saw the grave, Judah Baruch Maxwell, 1838-1910: Husband, Father, Cantor. He was dead less than a year.

"Is this Hebrew, papa?"

"Yes my son, it is." Elias knew that Abe was well aware that it was Hebrew.

"It's very pretty. What does it say?"

"The Lord is One," Debora said.

"One universe. It's all nonsense," Elias prattled. "Of course there is only one universe."

"One God, Abe," Simon said. "Judah is trying to tell you even in death, there is only one God."

"Don't fill him with poppycock, Simon. Some men feel the need out of a weakness to look to a God, to create one as a way of escaping their own responsibilities."

Out of the blue, a small green falcon lighted on grand uncle Judah's grave. It cocked its head and looked Elias in the eye. The group were stunned by the delicate, yet powerful majesty of the rare bird.

"Are all these dead people with God, mama?" Abe said after the bird flew off. Abe watched his father and uncle continue their endless philosophical bicker and then he began to cry. "Mama, mama. Why does papa always disagree with uncle Simon?"

"Oh stop your crying," Elias chastised. He turned and stormed back to the car.

Debora reached down to grab a few stones to place on granduncle Judah's and uncle Henny's graves. "We do this to remember them," Debora said. Abe reached down and placed a stone on each grave.

They drove in reflective silence through the bustling town, past a bank, a jewelry store, quilt shop and general store, and two interesting clothing shops Debora had planned to go into, then on past the synagogue where their father had been the rabbi for over thirty years, past a blacksmith's shop where the boys had each first learned how to shoe horses and ride them, past Betsy Villardy's house, Elias' first love, and then through the gated entranceway which led to the home the Maxwell boys had grown up in.

It was a three-story edifice with large columns holding up the front porch, six steps to reach it, and inside, a sizeable foyer giving way to an impressive mahogany staircase set back towards the rear. A large kitchen and dining room were off to the left and a sitting room/library converted into a bedroom was to the right. Now, Hillel would not have to walk the stairs to get to bed.

Aunt Ella came out to greet them, ushering them into the dining room. "He's very ill. The doctor said he suffered a series of strokes just two nights ago."

"How long?" Elias put it bluntly.

"The doctor says he'll be lucky to survive another 30 days."

"My God," Debora gasped. "Will he see Abe?"

"He will see you and Abe and Simon."

"And Elias?"

"I'm sorry, Debora. He was firm."

"What did he say?" Elias inquired.

"He said the day you converted was the day you died."

"But I saw him just three years ago, well after my conversion."

"Your father only agreed to see you because he was traveling with uncle Judah for Abe's bris and because of the family. I think he was hoping that once your son was born, perhaps you'd wake up. But, obviously.... Debora, why don't you and Simon take the boy in. I'll stay here with Ellie."

"Do you want to see grandpapa?"

"Yes, momma. Very much."

"He said he could never forgive himself for, how did he put it, 'giving you the time of day'," Tante Ella said after Debora and Abe were out of earshot. "You're dead to him, Ellie, I'm sorry."

"He's overdramatic, too Jewish," Elias shot back.

Abe looked at the big house. He recognized it from the photos of his father and uncle as two boys standing at the front porch in their children's outfits. The building smelled of stale air and unpleasant medicines. Abe held his nose, but Simon reached down gently and pulled the boy's hand away as they entered Hillel's room.

"You must be a man when you see grandpapa."

"Your face looks funny, grandpapa," Abe blurted out.

The visitors looked about. Formerly the rabbi's living and reading room, most of the library was still intact, with rows of leather-bound and other weighty books still upright on shelves against the back wall. Here was the place where many of the religious leaders of Austria and Hungary had spent endless hours discussing the fate of their people and the role that the ancient biblical texts should play in modern Jewish life. The couches had been removed and replaced with a bed, which was straightened rather than made. Stacks of medicine bottles stood along a window shelf.

With a regal presence, Hillel sat back in his large well-worn brown leather sitting chair. Yet, he was shocking to look at, because his face sagged miserably on the left side, and his left arm hung limply by his thigh.

"Come here my boy," grandpapa rasped, his voice somehow still forceful. "Let me see my grandson." The old man reached out with his good arm and swept the boy off the floor and onto his knee. Debora reached over and gave grandpapa a kiss. Simon approached cautiously.

Elias had always been Hillel's favorite son. This had never been a secret. And even now, perhaps a month from death, he still placed Elias first even though he had the first born son excluded from the room.

"Let me see you, Simon." With little Abe fixed securely on his knee, Hillel reached over to give his second son a handshake.

Simon moved fast, but not fast enough. Hillel grabbed the fingers before Simon could imbed his thumb against that of his father's. Hillel crushed his son's knuckles with an iron grip.

Wincing, Simon spoke. "You look tired, papa."

"You have a kiss for me?"

"Of course, papa."

"I've been told that this nephew of yours can multiply three-figure numbers in his head."

"It is true, grandpapa," little Abe chimed in.

"Good. Simon," Hillel said, releasing his grip and smiling sadistically. Simon kneaded his injured fingers with his other hand as his father continued. "Get me that paper over there." He motioned with his limp arm which flopped in the direction of his desk.

Simon walked over and grabbed a sheet of calculations and brought it back. "And my glasses."

"Yes, papa."

"Holding the paper so that the boy could not see, he said, "Are you ready?""

"No, grandpapa," the three-year-old startling the old man with such brazen assurance.

"Why not?"

"I must be standing if I am to calculate."

"All right, all right. You can jump down."

Debora was not going to take a chance. She rushed forward to help the boy to the floor.

"You ready now?"

Abe inspected the tough old rabbi. He hadn't shaved in two days. His expression was contorted from facial paralysis, and his robe seemed to reek of pungent medicinal smells. But at the same time, there was something vibrant about his grandfather; this great rabbi he had heard so much about, that he had spoken to on the telephone and which he had heard had attended his circumcision. "Can we start with an easy one, rabbi?"

Abe's use of the word in place of grandpapa and the nature of the request took Hillel by surprise. He gave Debora a look which said it all. He knew now that he did not need to test this boy, but they had come this far. "How much is 3 times 27?

"81."

"32 times 54?"

"One thousand seven hundred and twenty eight," As Abe spoke, he paced the floor like a small man on a mission."

"675 times 4,240?"

Abe walked to his grandfather's desk and sat at the table, as Hillel furiously wrote these numbers on his pad. Rolling his eyes, Abe spoke. "Two, eight, six, two, oh, oh, oh," he said emphatically, peering into the eyes of his grandfather.

"May I have this?" Abe had picked up a small magnifying glass.

"Of course, Abe, of course. But I want you to do something for me."

"What is that, grandpapa?"

"I want you to describe this entire room to me."

Abe began his description from the seated position, but then stood and circled the room. He described the many books in the bookcase, the Oriental rug, the leather chair and hospital bed. One had to be imported as Hillel had wanted one with an adjustable height. He described the window and drapes, the gas lamps on the walls, the contents of the bookshelves, the names of the medicines that lay on the shelf beneath the window, the small wastepaper basket, the various carved icons which were placed on a small coffee table, and so on. When he had finished, Hillel spoke again. "I want you to do me another favor, Abe."

"And what is that, grandpapa?" Abe stood before his grandfather with legs spread apart, his arms folded in front of his chest.

"I want you to describe me and remember this day for the rest of your life."

"I could only do such a thing if papa were in the room with me." Abe spoke firmly with no pause in his response.

Hillel looked down at the small boy. They traded expressions. The look of joy and sense of pride he had for his grandson vanished. "Leave!" Hillel commanded, sweeping his arm dismissively across the lot of them.

Simon interrupted. "Debora, take Abe with you to the car and wait for me." He spoke with such fortitude that it took everyone by surprise. She hushed the little boy away.

When they had left, Simon turned to face his father. "Papa, you have been a rabbi for over half a century, and yet, here you are, a month from your maker, and you have learned nothing!"

"You will not speak to me like that!"

"All I ever wanted from you was an ounce, one tiny ounce of the love you showered onto Elias. Instead, you crush my hand like I'm eight years old so that it still hurts."

"You always were a little *fagalah*."

"So that is what this is about. You are so unsure of your manhood, even now you have to dominate and sour your relationship with your only grandson."

"His father is dead to me."

"His father, your son, is waiting outside for one sign. And maybe if you gave him that sign, he would not have become so cynical about his,... rather, your precious religion. Can you really be so cruel? You who have been taught to be a religious leader."

"Elias is dead to me. How could he, how could any Jew abandon their Judaism?"

"Charity begins at home," Simon said.

Hillel reached to the arm rest, placed his almost dead hand on one rest and used his good arm for the other and struggled to get up. Tante Ella appeared from the hall and rushed to his side.

"Simon, give me a hand."

The dutiful son walked over and helped his father to his feet.

"Take me to the window. Open it."

Simon struggled with the lock and tried to raise it up but couldn't. Having propped his body against the wall, the old man reached down to the window with his good arm and pushed it open with a mighty shove.

Elias, with his wife and son beside him, looked up as Hillel looked down. Their eyes locked.

"*Brecht zich a ring, tsefalt di gantseh kait*," Hillel shouted down. Stumbling for a moment, he moved back towards his seat, Tante Ella helping him. "Send him up," he said collapsing into the chair.

Simon motioned with his arm. But Elias stood fast.

"It's all right, papa," Abe said stepping away from the car, the little boy pulling his father towards the house. "Grandpapa wants us to come up."

"One link snaps and the whole chain falls apart," Elias repeated his father's utterance in a low voice. "Honey, I don't know what to do."

"You have no choice. You will never forgive yourself if you stay down here. He's willing to see you. It was your son who made this happen."

"What did you say?"

"I told him I would remember this day always if grandpapa saw you, papa." Elias grabbed his son's hand and entered the house with Debora holding the boy's other hand. Taking a deep breath, he entered his father's room.

Hillel looked into his son's eyes. Elias returned the gaze in kind, a forced smile shared between the two of them.

"Debora, bring the boy here." The old man looked down at the boy. "Abraham, you are, at three years old, a wise man. Promise me one thing."

"What is that, grandpapa?"

"That you will grow up to be a good Jew."

"I promise."

"Not just promise. You must swear an oath!"

Abraham took in a breath, looked at his father, who stood there noncommittally, and spoke. "I swear an oath!"

"Do you hear that Ellie? Do you hear that!" Hillel proclaimed. "Say it once more and then give me a kiss."

"I will be a good Jew, grandpapa."

"And you will remember this day always."

"I will remember always."

Hillel scooped the boy up once again in his good arm and gave him a long kiss as he hugged him close.

Little Abe felt he could sense the very presence and vibrations of his ancestors going back centuries, so strong was the force that his grandfather emanated. "God is inside us, my grandson," Hillel whispered. "Inside us all, including your papa."

"God, here? Where, grandpapa?"

"All around. Isn't that so, Ella?"

"Of course, rabbi. God is everywhere."

"Now, take them down and send Simon up to stand beside his brother."

Tante Ella led Debora and Abe back to the car and Simon came in.

"Mit in hintn zitst men nit oif tsuei ferd."

"Father, I can and I do. In fact, I ride four horses with this behind." Raising a finger for each "horse," Elias spelled out: "Maxwell Bavarian Machineworks. One." He held up his first finger. "Automobile dealership." He held up two fingers. "Simon's airplane factory and motors and parts for dirigibles. Three. And my family who I drove 200 kilometers to see you, is four. Four horses and," Elias held up his thumb, "if I become Mayor, five horses. Five, papa. Five horses with one behind."

"You are smart for a businessman, Ellie, but your red apple still has its worm. I look at you and I see a proud and successful exterior. But on the inside, you are bankrupt. I say again, you can't sit on two horses with one behind. You think you can run your little empire without God?"

"How many times must I go over this with you. Jews cannot own land in greater Germany. They cannot hold office. They live on the periphery of society. So what do you suggest? That I change the world? That I tell the Kaiser to change the laws restricting these people?"

"These! You call them 'these' ?! I may be old and decrepit, but you are the dead one."

"Oh, what do you know of the outside world? Jews are second class citizens. I don't deserve that fate. I am smart. I know how to run businesses, so why should I not succeed?"

"So now Rothchild and Petchek are second class! And what about Jacob Schiff? From across the seas, from Wall Street, no less, this great Jew, the JP Morgan of the Jews, lends the Kaiser, Wilhelm himself, lends *him* money to build his defenses. And Schiff supports Japan, mind you, a whole country, against those anti-Semites in Russia. The atheists, I spit on them! Is that the work of second class citizens?"

"Those are the megawealthy, papa, the exceptions. And Rothchild and Schiff are not living in Germany. Even Petchek has his main steel mills and mining facilities in Prague. Yes, it is true, they have their presence in Munich and Berlin, but they are international. I am German and proud to be German."

"That is my point, my son. Simon. Tell him."

"Tell me what?"

"Papa thinks we should move."

"Move, are you mad? My whole life, over 15 years of building up my business, is back there in southern Bavaria. That is my home. And where do you expect me to move? To here, which is a little better than Germany. Anti-Semitism is rampant in Austria as well."

"The Danes welcome the Jews, and they have many of the best manufacturing plants in all of Europe. Or go to Belgium, or Budapest, or London. There is an ugliness, a deep ugliness in the Kaiser and his anti Jewish rhetoric. It can come to no good, Elias."

"You just don't understand. I am not like you," Elias countered, a haughtiness entering his argument.

"How can you so lightly dismiss 3,000 years of tradition? We are a blessed people. I want you to pray with me. Stay for Shabbis. God will forgive you if only you ask him back into your heart. You are dying Ellie. You can no more renounce your Judiasm than I can renounce my son."

"But you have renounced me. I have not seen you for three long painful years, since Abraham's circumcision, and then you only really allowed me to come, to see him."

"Twist it any way you want. It was your doing, but God is watching Elias. You trade your soul for a pot of kopeks. But are you any happier? NO! You are miserable. A miserable small man. I grieve for you." Something switched in Hillel's brain. "Now be off," he said dismissing Elias with the flick of his wrist. "Simon, you stay."

"But papa," Elias reached out.

"I told your aunt I would try. It was against my better nature, but you are dead to me. I will never lay my eyes on you again."

Dramatically, Hillel shielded his eyes with the back of his hand. Elias dropped his head and walked out.

"I can't be in the middle of this, papa. He is my brother and my business partner."

"Business partner, my *tuchis*," Hillel said disdainfully. "From what I understand, you have, now let me calculate, yes." Hillel paused to stare at the ceiling. "Carry the three and divide by seven. Zero percent of his business. Am I right?"

"Yes, but..."

"But, but, but. I know it is a bad thing to split an estate, and tradition demanded it go to the eldest son. But a company with one's own brother! And he treats you like an employee. Wake up, Simon. It was always implied that he would share the wealth with his blood brother. Not to split up land, but material assets is a whole other thing. You are his slave, the brilliant idiot."

"That is not so. He's opened up an aeroplane manufacturing plant with me as partner."

"You have this in writing?"

"No, but...."

"No, but what? That's your brother. My eldest son turns his back on God, and worse, turns his back on blood. He is nothing but a greedy *swinehundt*. You get a contract in writing giving you a piece of this new plant. Do you hear me, Simon?" Hillel paused for a response.

"Yes, papa."

"In writing. Any man who denies God will sacrifice his brother. Some of the worst anti-Semites are Jews. You mark my words. Now give me a kiss and return with a signed document so I can see with my own eyes that this old man can be wrong. You do that, and I'll stop saying Kaddish for my other son."

Hillel lumbered over to the window. Struggling with his good arm, he raised it even higher and shouted to the car, his words bellowing out the driveway and down the street. *"Yisgadal, va yisga dash, mei rabon,"* the prayer for the dead.

Down at the car, Elias put his hands on his ears to block out the verse that every Jew, even those that had converted, knew by heart. And so, the Yisgadal continued to ring in his ears until he donned a yarmulke himself and verbalized the prayer two months later at Hillel's funeral.

BLOOD RELATIVE

The North Shore Hospital out on Long Island seemed more like a hotel, at least from the outside. The landscaping was immaculate, the plantings bright, colorful and cheerful. Gladys Styne's room was on the second floor in a wing that overlooked a garden of multi-colored dahlias.

"Mom."

It took Rudy's mother a moment to focus. With IV's and painkillers pouring into her, she was disoriented, "loopy" was how Chessie would later describe it, and not totally certain as to just where she was. "Rudy, is that you?"

"Yes, mom."

"Do you want to have tea?" she rasped.

"Mom, we're in the hospital. We can't have tea."

"I know that dear," she said. "Now come here and give your mother a kiss."

Rudy approached and gave her a hug and kiss on the cheek. The color of her cheeks were a sallow yellow.

"You're filling out nicely," Mrs. Styne said to her new daughter-in-law. Chess approached and followed suit. "I'm so happy for the two of you."

"How you doing?" Chess asked.

"The doctors aren't sure yet. We're in a wait and see, *Ouch!* mode," Gladys Styne grimaced in pain. "But they say the worst is over. They think I had a reaction to some clams I ate in Freeport."

"You know, my DNA was not compatible?" Rudy said.

"DNA?" Mrs. Styne's eyes were watering and she still seemed not totally there.

"Well, how can that be, mom?"

"What are you talking about?" Gladys turned to look out the window.

"Genetics, mom. It doesn't make any sense." Rudy considered the moment, and then just blurted it out, "Am I yours or not?"

"What kind of question is that!" she turned back to face him squarely. "Of course you are mine. I remember it as if it were yesterday. You were a breach baby."

"I know, and I was coming out arm and foot first...." Rudy began, before his mother continued.

"Don't be rude to your mother, Rudy. They cut me stem to stern just to turn you around. But once I saw you, believe me, you are mine." Rudy's mother looked over with soulful loving eyes.

Rudy didn't know how to respond. "Then what's going on?"

Gladys Styne hesitated.

"Is this man really Rudy's uncle?" Chess asked, showing Gladys a picture of Abe Maxwell from the wedding.

"He didn't tell you?"

"He called Chessie's child-to-be his great grandson."

"It's a boy?"

"No, mom," Chessie said to her mother-in-law. "I mean, we don't know yet. So who is he?"

"You went to Germany, I hear. Let's have tea. Tell me about the trip. I remember when I went with your father to Paris, but that was so long ago, before you were born."

"Mom, you're changing the subject. How old is that guy anyway?" Rudy inquired. Rudy didn't really know his father as he had died before Rudy was born. To Rudy, he never really thought of himself as having a father. All he really had was a few old photos of a man he didn't know and had never met. Gladys was leading him on a tangent, and he wanted answers.

"Abe?" she said.

"Yes, Abe?"

"He could be 96. He's at least 93 as I calculate. *Ouch!*" she cried out again, obviously still in pain.

"93, my God! And he's not my uncle, is he?"

"No."

"But he's related?"

"Yes."

"Then how could Chessie's child be his great grandchild? Is he my father's father?"

"It's more complicated than that, Rudy," Mrs. Styne said with sudden clarity. "You are my child. I gave birth to you. That's all there is to it."

"So, what's this about our genetic codes?" Rudy said again. "We don't match."

"So they don't match. I'm not an expert in genetics. Look at aunt Helen's eyes. They're blue. No one else in the family has blue eyes."

"If Abe is Jewish, how is he related to me?" Rudy asked.

"Why is that important?"

"I don't know. This man I hardly know showing up now, out of the blue. And his interest in a German airline. All I want to know is what's going on?"

"Rudy, I'm not really myself right now. They said I almost died yesterday. It's up to Abe to tell you these things. He made a promise to tell you at the bris. It's only a few weeks away. You've already waited this long...."

Rudy could see it was fruitless to continue. For now. Whatever it was, she had held this secret for 38 years. "Okay, mom." He gave her a kiss.

"That's a good boy. Chess, give me a kiss. You'll come while Rudy is away? We'll have tea?"

"Of course, mom. We'll have tea."

Chessie had stopped working, with her so close to giving birth, and Rudy's mother still in the hospital. "I just think it is better if I stay home now," she said to Rudy.

"You really quitting?"

"Well, Jake is letting me take an extended leave. It's kind of the law now anyway, but I think he's being generous. It's better this way. I'm sure the auction house can survive without me. And I can still do a bit at home by working on line."

"Whatever you say," Rudy said. "It just means I'm going to have to commute by myself. You think she'll be all right?"

"Your mom?"

"No, the first lady."

"Well, you don't have to jump on me."

"I'm sorry, Chess. She just really got to me, all that talk about tea."

"I think it was the pain killers, Rudy. My father got like that when he had bypass surgery. He kept ranting about how all Chinamen, as he called them, were stealing American jobs. It lasted about a week. I'm not sure your mom completely knew where she was."

"Maybe, but there is something else weird going on, and I wonder why she just doesn't tell me."

Rudy was distraught, rolling it all around in his mind. *What did she mean, she gave birth to me? How could that be if our DNA is not compatible?* Rudy hopped in a cab. He had a meeting downtown with the notorious Wall Street mega-upstart T-Dan Mulrooney who was in a bidding war against Heinz Gruuban for Webnet. Owner of U-View, the do-it-yourself multimedia broadband giant that was dwarfing in capacity the present technology of any competitor, Gruuban had led Rudy to believe he had it locked up, but then T-Dan came along, and suddenly U-View was a very hot commodity with the stock of its parent company, Webnet, literally quintupling over night. As usual, Rudy was running late. As he passed 23 Wall Street, he caught sight of a picket line. It seemed to be a protest against the German airline, MB Airways and its CEO. Rudy searched his mind. How could he forget the guy's name? He just saw him. "Lunzman? Lugman?" he said aloud.

"Linzman, "Gunter Linzman, CEO of MB," said the cabby.

"How do you know so much?"

"I own stock in Rockwell," the cabbie said. "If that schmuck takes it over, the Germans will be in control of everything, so they might as well control the defense department while they're at it, right?"

"Right," Rudy said.

As the cab scooted by the stock exchange, Rudy perused the picket line. It was filled with a scattering of mostly old men, Holocaust survivors, he guessed. This was a new thing, Jewish groups going after the large German concerns that were making inroads into US companies. One of the men was holding a placard up with a picture of Linzman crossed out with a big Nazi sign, another held a sign that said M=Maxwell. It took Rudy a minute to process it all, and by that time, the cab was several blocks away. He looked back through the rear window. One of the men looked like uncle Abe! He'd have to put his foot down with his mother. Who the hell was this guy? Rudy did not want to wait another two months for the kid to be born and this bris thing to take place to find out. He wanted answers now.

T-DAN

Not yet 30, there wasn't a humble bone in T-Dan's body. An arrogant narcissist with a spike beneath the center of his lower lip, a lavender silk shirt open to the navel and a pirate's earring the size of the Hope Diamond, T-Dan was flanked by two young gals with dark Phoenician eye make-up, tight ponytails, viper-red lipstick, spiked heals and the shortest matching black-leather skirts imaginable. Aside from the ample cleavage the girl on the left had as compared to the one on the right, the only other difference between them were their sashes. The one on T-Dan's right wore a yellow sash, and the one to his left, a sash of psychedelic orange. The chemistry between Rudy and T-Dan was non-existent. The interview did not go well. Rudy was reminded of Leona Helmsley. "Only the little people pay taxes," she had said. It wasn't totally clear what Mulrooney was really up to.

The ultimate cybergeek, T-Dan had been a math prodigy in high school, an MIT dropout and software genius having made his first billion ripping off a fellow student's project by getting a patent on a program that linked search queries and buying habits to IP and email addresses. The court battle was vicious, but T-Dan took no prisoners. Before the age of 24, with feature articles in *Wired, Rolling Stone* and *Forbes*, he was already one of the ten richest men in America. Voracious, with a temperament to make Donald Trump look like a wuss, T-Dan now wanted to change the Internet from a free access intelligence highway to one for pay. "Would you like a bitch for a quickie?" he said, nodding to either one of the gals at his side, when Rudy entered the penthouse suite.

"Thanks, but I already had lunch," Rudy said. "I hear you are in a bidding war with Heinz Gruuban for Webnet."

"Bidding war. You gotta be kidding. That guy's small potatoes. I've got access to one hundred times the capital he's got."

The plan, as Rudy came to find out, was for T-Dan to boost his revenue stream to several billion dollars a week. The idea was to start with micro-payments for every uplink or download any person on the net made, "Say ten or fifteen cents. Anybody can afford that." But his real plan was to obtain the credit cards of the masses and then double the fees every nine months. T-Dan's ultimate goal involved the transformation of U-View which was owned by Webnet, into a multimedia broadband platform that would compete with cable and radio, and also dwarf comparable, but less advanced capabilities in comparison to U-View's main competitors, YouTube, Netflix and Hulu. But, to do all this, T-Dan would have to obtain controlling interest in Webnet, a stock Gruuban already had a major stake in that was now already selling at over $500/share. Mulrooney would require an enormous amount of capital to overtake Spinwebbe's position. So, where would he get the funds? OPM, other people's money, where else?

"All we do," T-Dan said, "is issue more stock of Diamond Head." This was the on-line cyberonic awesome wicked virtual reality game company that made its mark by interfacing with BrainSpace, the social networking Internet site connected to the laptop and cell phone of literally every high school and college kid in the nation. By giving out cash payments to the top 100 highest game scorers every month, Diamond Head had created a frenzy, quickly overtaking and essentially replacing other games like Farmville. Everyone knew some geek who had earned a thousand dollars within the last thirty days. Using a combination of subliminal cuing and a simple reward system, T-Dan had tapped into the pleasure centers of the brains of the youth, and then spread it to the adult world through BrainSpace, his social network that was fast replacing every major competitor. By muscling out the investment banker who had backed the two software junkies who had started Diamond Head, T-Dan had gained control of a company just six weeks before its IPO. That deal alone bagged him a cool $400 million when the company hit the market at $5 a share, and jumped to $85 within three hours on opening day. And his revenue stream, through the gaming division was netting him tens of millions of dollars a week.

"If the government can print more money, so can I? Heh?" T-Dan glared at Rudy.

"How do such obnoxious people become so successful?" Rudy asked rhetorically when he returned to the office.

"You should have worn a low-cut blouse," Mort suggested.

"Very funny. Is that how you got that interview with Michael Jordan?"

"God, how old is he?" Kim said. "He must be in his 60's by now."

"Hey Rudy," Bill called out, "Comere! You gotta see this!" Bill motioned broadly with his arm. Rudy walked over.

Sally-Ann was looking at a photo of Gunter Linzman, that Kimberly had taken in Munich. "Rudy," she said, "this guy looks like he could be your father."

"What are you talking about?"

"His looks. He looks like you."

"What are you nuts? The guy's an ex-Nazi," Rudy said dismissively.

"You're kidding?"

"No, I'm not. A cabbie told me."

"Then it's gotta be true." Bill put a serious expression on his face and nodded appropriately.

"I googled him," Rudy said. "I should have gotten the cabbie's name as a source. This Linzman guy goes all the way back to the war. What do you think MB was doing at the time! They were making war planes for Hitler."

"Mort," Sally-Ann called out, ignoring Rudy. "Whadaya think?"

"No doubt about it," Mort said, looking at the picture Sally-Ann had emailed to him. "Spitting image!"

"Bite me, Mort," Rudy said.

"Let me see that photo again," Bill butted back in. He looked Rudy over from head to toe. "Hello, poppa!"

"Rudy," Mort stuck his two-cents in, "stand next to the computer so we can get a better look."

Grimacing, Rudy picked up his iPhone and stormed out of the office.

IRIS

Several years had passed. Roberé von Rosensweig, one of the most handsome *bons vivants* in southern Bavaria, decided to get married, again. Embarrassed for the philanderer, Simon balked about attending the wedding.

"Let me make this as clear as I can, young brother. You will attend this wedding or you will be out of a job and out on the street," Elias exploded.

"You would really sack me over this?" Simon said in wonderment.

"Do you know what kind of position you would put me in to make excuses? He's my partner's brother, for God's sake, and Debora's uncle. You will not bring shame on me."

"Half-brother, which makes him a half-uncle."

"So, he's a half-uncle. You're going."

"Elias, I have taken about as much as I can from you. I think we both know I could go to Fokker or Junkers, and in an instance gain employment."

"You wouldn't dare."

"I'll tell you what," Simon said, detecting the fear that had overtaken Elias' tone of voice. "You will give me a 10% share of the business, in writing, and double my salary as of tomorrow, and I will attend yet another von Rosensweig travesty of marriage vows."

"I'll give you 5% share and increase your salary 20%."

Simon was shocked that Elias had given in so easily. "I am honored that you take my statement at its word."

"You are my brother," Elias managed, averting Simon's eyes, shocked by his own generosity. It was true he had moments of guilt for having taken advantage of the bloodline. He would have had to have paid a non-relative as much as three times for the work he got out of Simon, but he couldn't be too generous. He had his own expenses. Simon knew nothing of high finance, and it was he, not Simon, who had taken the risk.

"I will agree under the condition that Maxwell-Bavarian Machineworks create an official aeroplane division and that I receive 25% of all net revenues from such a division."

"And will you pay 25% of the start-up costs?"

Simon caught his brother's gaze and hesitated only momentarily before he opened a closet and reached for his suitcase.

Debora and little Abe sat in their roadster at the base of Simon's home, en route to Roberé von Rosensweig's castle. They waited for Elias to emerge with his brother. As Simon had noted, Roberé was the half-brother of Adolf, Elias' financial partner in the machine works. Much younger than Adolf, Roberé was a gadabout who Debora barely knew. Her only real memory of him was his jet black hair, disarming smile and piercing blue eyes. Her father was dead, and Adolf von Rosensweig had been a good uncle, almost a replacement father who Debora had seen weekly and sometimes daily for as far back as she could remember. But Roberé was someone she hardly knew. Her grandfather had remarried, and Roberé was part of a different family. Reaching in front of the driver, Debora squeezed the horn three loud times. Startled, Abe started to cry. "We are always twenty minutes late," she shouted up to the window where her husband and brother-in-law could be seen. "Come on, let's go!" she screamed.

"Simon, you can't do this. You can't just leave me," Elias said, hearing the faint entreaty from his pain-in-the-ass wife.

"You'll do fine without me. You can train Gunter or his son. They'd be only too willing to learn, and look at all the money you will save. I should have listened to father all along. 'You are exploiting your own brother.' That's what he told me, but I didn't listen!" Throwing a few essentials into a bag, he continued, "I'll send for the rest as soon as I get a place. Fokker's got a plant in Denmark, and I think I'll probably go there." Turning towards the door, without even a backwards glance, Simon rumbled down the stairs.

"You're not going to the wedding?!"

"What for? He's the brother of *your* partner, not mine."

"All right, all right," Elias shouted, but Simon kept going.

"An aeroplane division. 25%. All right. What more do you want?"

Simon reached the front porch and caught Debora's eye. She was holding young Abe trying to soothe him as the horn and the long wait had made him cranky.

Simon dropped the bag by the door and looked back up the stairs at his brother who stood forlornly at its apex. He suddenly looked older.

Elias knew he felt older. With the Kaiser stepping up production of von Zeppelin's airships, Maxwell-Bavarian had more work than they knew what to do with. There would be important people at this wedding. But the fact of the matter was, without Simon's mechanical genius, the entire operation could fold. With so much dependent on one man, Elias realized that Simon would have to begin training additional master mechanics.

"Gunter," Elias said as they returned to the roadster, "I have suggested to Simon that we branch out into aeroplane manufacturing."

"I'm pleased for you, sir," the driver said.

"I think my husband just offered you a new position," Debora said.

"I'm happy where I am, ma'am. Perhaps when Gunter Jr. is old enough, he can take such a position."

Debora stared off and rubbed her chin pensively.

Elias looked over at her. If she was so smart, did she also know about his Parisian peccadillo? One glance in her eye confirmed his worst fears. "You're babying the child," Elias scolded. "Let him sit up here with me like the little man he needs to become."

Nearly six, Abe preferred to sit between his mother and uncle Simon, whom he loved dearly. "Thanks papa," he said seeking the best tact. He scrambled over the seat and crawled beside his father, turned around and actually winked at his mother and Simon.

Elias reached out with a stiff arm and placed it tentatively around his son's shoulder.

Set atop a foothill with the Austrian Alps behind, Roberé von Rosensweig's castle loomed. Dating from the 14ᵗʰ century, the Niederkraudt castle had a rich history beginning with Count Albertine, who constructed the first third of the edifice in 1385, to his grandson, Prince Niederkraudt, who tripled its size in 1465. In 1643, a great battle from the 30 Years War was fought there. The descendents of the Niederkraudts were thus able to hold out until reinforcements came from Kempten. But by the mid-1800's, the fortunes of the Niederkraudts were in decline and the castle was sold to a cousin of Elizabeth Hapsburg, wife of Franz Joseph. But this cousin had come on hard times, and von Rosensweig's father was able to purchase the castle and its grounds for a modest sum. Since his eldest son Adolf already owned a large estate, and his second son, Debora's father, was no longer alive, the father left the castle to Roberé, who supported the place by becoming a gentleman farmer, leasing out it's 200 acres for a share of the profits.

Gunter pulled into the driveway. Spanking new cars and horse and buggies were parked in different fields separated by a large barn and servant's quarters. The Maxwell family stepped from their automobile and Gunter drove off to park it. There was the sense that the outdoor festivities were winding down, which meant they were late. Elias shot Simon an angry stare.

Von Rosensweig appeared a bit tipsy, that was Simon's sense of it. Already past 40, by spring of next year, Roberé would have a new wife who was barely 17, Rebecca von Eppenstein. This engagement party alone was the cost of a yearly salary for an upper echelon executive.

"Purchased her for 20,000 pfennig," a corpulent young soldier snickered.

"Hold your tongue, son," Elias cautioned. Turning on Debora, he commanded, "Go off now to the chapel, and take Abe with you. I'll meet you shortly."

There were so many lovely people milling about on the great expanse of lawn. Debora looked about. Near the band were the von Stauffenbergs with their twin ten-year old sons Alexander and Berthold and a third child, another boy, little Claus. Debora didn't really know them, but she knew of them and nodded hello. What she wanted was to go over and meet the bride's family. She had known the von Eppensteins from synagogue, when she was a child and had spent many giddy moments with Rachel, the older sister of the bride. She only had so much love to give, and she knew that if she ever turned it off, it might never turn on again. Therefore, she reached over to Elias, kissed him tenderly on the cheek, avoided his stiffness and whispered. "Dear, I want to love you, but if you cut off my spirit, I will be reborn with another mind."

He looked at her questioningly.

"If it is all right with you," she spoke in normal fashion, so others could hear, "I would like to say hello to the von Eppensteins, who are old friends. And then we can meet up at the chapel."

Elias saw his whole life flash before him. His partner, Adolf, Debora's uncle, half-brother of the groom, began to approach. Was he ruler of his own house or was he just another castrato like so many of the Jewish men that he knew? "Sounds good," he managed. Abe in hand, she walked off.

"Now, who the hell are you?" He wheeled and confronted the cadet who seemed to be waiting. The young man whose face still contained baby fat, had added to his uniform a bright yellow silk scarf which flowed from his neck like a feathered wing. He stood there fondling a large pinky ring made out of a shiny red stone, perhaps pink sapphire, or more likely, a pale garnet, as he replied.

"Hermann Göring, Herr Maxwell," he said clicking his heels and bowing slightly, "Dr. Herman von Eppenstein's godson."

Elias knew the doctor. He was the bride's uncle, respected in both the Jewish and gentile communities, and wealthy enough to own two castles, one in Austria near Salzburg and another near Nuremburg. Von Eppenstein waltzed over, his arm draped around a blonde German lady.

"Elias, I see you have met my godson, Hermann, here," von Eppenstein said, putting his arm around Göring's shoulders. "He has joined the air force, learning to be a pilot. I believe he is taking flight lessons with your brother."

"Come on," Simon grabbed Göring's arm and led him away. Göring pushed Simon away briefly as he reached over to give his mother a kiss, wet lips on lips.

"I'll see you later, Hermie," Göring's mother Fanny said as Elias, somewhat stunned, put two and two together.

"Hermie?" Simon teased, when the two youths were out of earshot.

"Hermann," Göring corrected, a sense of indignation to his voice. "The same first name as my mother's latest tart."

"I thought von Eppenstein was your godfather?"

"He was only a family friend when I was a baby, but now," Hermann raised his eyebrows, "I'm his protégé. He likes to take me hunting, and who doesn't like to do that. Why don't you join us next Saturday?"

"On the Sabbath?"

"Sunday," Göring corrected. "I'll just ask God-daddy to change the date. You know how to get there?"

"Of course," Simon said.

Everyone knew von Eppenstein's castle in the Alps at Mauterndorf. Hermann and Simon watched from afar Debora and little Abe conferring with the bride's sister, Rachel, and the two proud parents. The father of the bride, Sigismund von Eppenstein, nodded recognition to Hermann, who he obviously knew. As Debora bent his ear, Sigismund smiled also to Simon. Certainly, Simon deduced, Debora was explaining just who he was, her brother-in-law, MB Machine Works' chief mechanic.

"You've got guts," Simon said, turning his attention to his podgy friend, trying to decide if Göring's affectation with the scarf was just a feminine attribute or a perversity.

"You mean this?" Hermann replied as he gently stroked it.

"Yes, and your 20,000 pfennig comment."

"I've known Rachel and Rebecca since we were children." Göring kissed the scarf and let it fly again in the wind.

"How, so?"

"They're my godfather's nieces. That was their father Sigismund, talking to your brother's wife. He imports raw goods, fruits and vegetables from Persia, and also coal for the Kaiser." Moving away from the crowd in a conspiratorial manner, Göring placed a hand to his mouth so he could whisper. "It has always been my belief that my gracious god-uncle, if there is such a word," he added as an aside, Simon grinned, "had introduced his two lovely girls into the secret of their femininity."

"You don't mean!" Simon began, truly shocked, finding himself looking back at Sigismund von Eppenstein with a different eye.

"No, not intercourse," Göring said, "digital stimulation of their, well, I like to call it, since there are two of them, their cliterati. It would be the plural, you know."

"Orgasms?"

"Of course." Göring postured with a knowing wink. "As their father, he assumed the duty of bringing each girl to that pleasure when they reached early puberty. Rachel practically told me as much years ago."

"And she's all right?"

"I'm sure Roberé's made a deal with the father for the younger one. I always knew her as Little Beckah!" Göring said, ignoring Simon's question.

"What kind of deal?"

"For von Eppenstein's grandkids, Little Beckah's kiddies to be."

"I'm not following."

"Roberé's a no-account gentleman farmer, nowhere near as successful as his half-brother, Adolf, nor as successful as your brother, for that matter."

"This doesn't look too measily to me." Simon gestured to the vast expanse of lawns, the medieval castle, riding stables, path to the river.

"True, but he got it as an inheritance. He may be land-wealthy, but cash-wise, he's piss poor, and so with a move like this, Roberé gets to keep his castle, and continue the charade of his so-called upper breeding. And with all this pomp, he gets to marry a von Eppenstein, not your everyday Jew. It's a wink between two older men as they barter the life of this babe in the woods."

"What's that supposed to mean?"

"This grand palace of Niederkraudt." Hermann spread his hands as if they were wings. "The great von Eppensteins get to place a daughter here in her own castle, and she's a quarter century younger than Roberé. You've taken math, haven't you?"

Simon nodded as it all began to dawn on him.

"On top of that, Roberé's got his own daughter from a previous liaison to marry off."

"Liaison?"

"I won't stand on ceremony, you can call it marriage. In his case, same thing. But he doesn't have the funds to cover a wedding. The father of the bride and all that. He needs capital."

Von Eppenstein footed this?" Simon looked over the array of foods, tents on the lawn, the five-piece orchestra, open bar, small legion of waiters and waitresses."

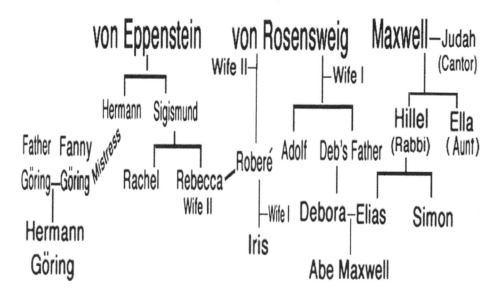

"Of course, Roberé didn't spend a dime. But, von Eppenstein will need a lot more than slight of hand to give his daughters proper fare. I practically grew up with them. They were always at my god-daddy's place, to them, uncle Eppie. I give this marriage three years, max. I bet you anything."

"Marrying her so he can divorce her later for money? You're kidding?"

"I am?" Göring continued the gossip. As they dickered, and Göring could really get under his skin, Simon noticed a lithe young lady eying a dish of hors d'oeuvres. "Hermann, we shall have to continue this another time." Göring saw the gal himself and quickly understood. "See you next Sunday," Göring said. "And don't forget, I'm still in for those flying lessons."

"You've only mentioned them fourteen times."

"If you were an elephant, I'd only have to tell you once!" Göring gave Simon a rousing slap on the back which encouraged him to go in the direction he was heading.

Simon waved his hand in a friendly parting gesture and approached the cuisine table.

"It's a tough decision, isn't it?"

"Yes," the young lady agreed. "The lox looks so inviting, but so does that chicken wing, and I simply can't imagine trying both."

Simon took the chicken wing, slabbed on a piece of lox and put the whole thing in his mouth. "You mean like this?"

She tossed her head back and laughed.

"What's your name," he garbled as he reached deftly to remove the bones.

"Iris, and you?" she said still smiling at his prank.

Simon put up a hand to pause so he could finish chewing. She waited, never losing her effervescent smile. "Simon," he chewed... "Maxwell."

"And you're related to the bride or the groom?"

"Neither, but if I had to choose, and between you and me, I'd rather not, I'm linked to Roberé through his brother, who is my brother's partner and uncle of my sister-in-law."

"Now wait a minute," Iris bantered. "Let me get this straight. Your brother is married to Roberé's niece?"

"Now I'm going to have to think about that." Simon pondered. He feigned reaching for more lox and chicken wings, but settled for a grape. "Partially, my dear. To be technically correct, half-niece. And you?"

"I too am linked to Roberé. He is the half-brother to the father of your sister-in-law who is my late half-uncle."

"Which makes you?...."

Iris waited for it all to sink in.

"Your second cous..., your, your father!"

She nodded yes with Simon stepping back to contemplate.

"It's very simple, really. Nineteen years ago, daddy married mommie, and fourteen years ago daddy fell in love with my babysitter. But her two children are too young to come to this event on their own, or too unofficial. They never did marry, you know."

"Oh my," Simon stood off and watched as Roberé, at the far end of the lawn, nuzzled his bride-to-be and she giddily reciprocated.

"So, this would be his second official wife?" Simon asked.

"You got it," Iris said. "And an unofficial one with two progeny on the side."

"Ohhh," Simon now fully understood. "I see."

"Would you like to take a walk?"

Iris glanced at her father and returned her eyes to Simon. As if they had known each other since childhood, she grabbed his hand and they scooted away.

It had been a dry season, the moat nearly empty. Tightrope walking a series of rocks, the duo forded the petering stream and followed a trail through a field to a tended wooded area where the path continued to the river.

"Do you live with your father?"

"Of course not. I hardly know him. It's true he charms me when he comes over to join me for a horse ride or take me out in his new automobile." Iris paused and stood back to get another look at Simon. "That's where I know you from!" she continued. "Your brother owns MB Factories, doesn't he? And you work at the shop."

"How do you know?"

"Because daddy had a breakdown. It was about a year ago, and we were near your brother's factory. 'I think this is where they make the parts,' daddy said, and he returned with you."

"I remember. You were sitting in the front in a yellow dress."

"It was coral."

"Of course, coral. I remember."

"You don't remember at all."

"Did I open the hood, jiggle a few wires and pretend that I was going to charge your father a hefty sum?"

"Yes," she conceded.

"Maybe I didn't notice your dress, but I did notice you."

Iris found herself blushing. They reached a rise in the woods where a large stone outcropping allowed an unobstructed view of the tributary. "This is my favorite place." She steered Simon out onto the rock. "It leads to the Enns. Some day, if you want, we could take a boat ride."

"I would love that." Simon reached over to Iris' shoulders and brought her forward. Their lips touched and lingered. Simon had never felt such a flood of deep emotion. He looked into her eyes and she returned the gaze with equal fervor. Her face began to flush, and then she grabbed him hard and hugged with all her might. They fell to the ground and kissed again. "Shouldn't we get back?"

"Do you think we'll really be missed?" She shocked him with her response.

Debora touched Rachel on her arm. "Răch," she said to the bride's sister.

"Debora, I'm so happy to see you. And who is this?"

Little Abe looked up at the pretty lady from behind Debora's skirts, obviously taken by her beauty. He knew she was going to lean down and give him a kiss, and he knew he wouldn't mind.

"Isn't he the most precious little man!" Rachel declared. "How is it that we let so much time elapse between visits?"

"Does your sister know what she is getting into? There was a debate whether to come at all, but Elias insisted. He couldn't insult his partner, and I knew it would be a chance to see you."

"Rebecca knows what she's doing. At least she knows he's been married before, and that he even has a daughter older than she is! Where is Iris?" Rachel looked about. "Isn't that your brother-in-law?"

As Debora turned, Abe wrestled his hand free and galloped off to jump into Simon's arms. "You have a pretty girlfriend, uncle Sye-Sye."

"Simon," Debora said, "this is Rebecca's sister, my good friend, Rachel."

"Hello."

"I see you've already met my... what will you be to me?" Rachel said to Iris.

"I think I would be your step-niece."

"I'm very confused," Rachel said, trying to work it out.

"Well, I'm not," Simon interjected. "This is already turning out to be one of the happiest occasions I have ever attended."

"You feel hot," Abe pushed at Simon's face, and so he put the boy down, his complexion turning ever more shades of deep red.

"And what's your name?" Iris asked.

"Abraham," the boy replied. "I'm going to fly in a glider just like my uncle Simon some day."

THE LODGE

"So, you really think the aeroplane will replace the Zeppelin for passenger travel?" Hermann Göring picked up his shotgun and fired at the rising pheasant, missing.

"I never said that, Hermann. It's simply a faster way to transport mail, or for wealthy individuals to traverse great distances. I was averaging nearly 120 kilometers per hour during the prelims for the Munich to Cairo to Munich race."

"You've registered?"

"Of course."

"That's over eight months away. I'm impressed," Göring admitted.

Simon followed the next pheasant quickly, his buckshot easily taking down the grand bird. One of von Eppenstein's bird dogs lit out after it.

"You're two ahead of me!" Hermann barked, finding it difficult to hide the feelings of jealousy that swept over him. "Next time I'll be in that race."

"God willing," Simon said automatically. "But first you must learn the glider."

"I'm not sure God has much to do with it. It's more a matter of whether my god-daddy will spring for the ship. And here he comes."

"You boys all set?" von Eppenstein was flanked by his second of three bird dogs, one still with a pheasant in its jaws.

"Yes, sir," they both replied.

"You each got a kill?" They each nodded yes.

"Then that is our quota for the day," von Eppenstein placed a hand on hip, bringing his rifle back from the sky. "Lugar, take these to Billingham," von Eppenstein told his second.

"Billingham?"

"The chef, stupid!" Göring practically shouted, slapping Simon heartily on the back.

"Nice shooting, young man," von Eppenstein said. "See Billingham before you leave and he'll have your birds plucked and ready for the roaster."

"Why thank you," Simon replied.

The three men were all dressed in high boots, jodhpurs and bright shooting parkas. Hermann moved with authority, a slight swagger to his gate. He led Simon to a hill that dropped off quickly to provide an overlook for miles and miles of farmland, and off in the distance, von Eppenstein's castle. "We could launch here," he suggested.

"I think you've found a perfect spot, Hermann."

The lodge, which was a good ten kilometers from the castle, was rustic but well-kept. Made out of hewn logs, it had two great support beams spanning a cathedral ceiling. On the far wall, a bear's head was centrally mounted, flanked slightly below by the heads of two antlered bucks. The west wall was mostly window. It overlooked the land and a sizeable lake which shimmered in the wind reflecting thousands of sparkles from the afternoon sun. Hermann's mother sashayed in. A tall exotic slightly plump blonde lady, Fanny Göring was dressed in a tight-fitting off-white pants suit made of silk, low cut in the front, exposing a lace slip, as it clung to every sensual curve of her supple body. Demanding attention from every eye in the room, she said hello to Simon, and then planted a succulent kiss on her son's lips that left Simon with a queasy stomach.

"Talk is you are going to marry von Rosensweig's daughter," she said to Simon. She let go of Hermann's hand and wrapped her arms possessively around von Eppenstein who had just entered the room. He reached over as she gave him a cheek. He planted a lascivious kiss wetly.

"I admit it, Madam Göring, I am smitten by Iris, but we have only just met."

"Take my advice," Madam said as she directed the servants to begin the meal, "propose as soon as you can. Life is short."

"My God, Emma. What's the rush?" von Eppenstein cajoled.

"Oh, you are right, dear. I think you should wait, like we have, Simon, for at least eight years."

"We've only been dating six years," von Eppenstein said.

"And soon it will be eight, Ritter."

"Mother, he is Jewish," Hermann startled everyone.

"And what does that have to do with anything?"

Hermann countered, "How is it Godfather that you are Jewish and you own land?"

"You forget, my dear boy, I am of nobility and immune to local statutes."

"Yes, you, Petchek, Rothchild, Warburg and Rosensweig. And what about *your* brother?" Göring turned to Simon.

"Ultimately, he sees religion as a mass delusion, but for practicality's sake he converted years ago. He is no longer Jewish. He's a Protestant just like you."

"Yet, his father's a rebbe," Göring teased mocking poorly a Yiddish accent.

"I don't think the Kaiser minds at all, now that we are supplying him with motors for his automobiles and tanks," Simon remarked, coming to the defense of his family, realizing at once that he should not have let such personal information slip. Nothing had been signed and sealed yet.

"What are you saying?" Hermann asked.

"MB Machineworks produces engines for von Zeppelin," von Eppenstein remarked.

"So?" Madam Göring was trying to follow the conversation.

"There's talk of war," Hermann said matter-of-factly.

"The Kaiser's building a sizeable army and increasing Zeppelin's fleet. Isn't that so?" von Eppenstein turned to Simon.

"I want to manufacture aeroplanes, not just build one here or there for racing," Simon changed the subject. "Would you be willing to invest in production facilities?"

"You mean a fleet?" Hermann jumped in. "Aeroplanes. I do love them, momma. Godfather, what do you think?"

"Why do you think Hermann invited you here?" von Eppenstein boldly suggested. "Surely, not to go hunting."

Göring shot a mean look over to his godfather who brushed the look aside. Simon was not pleased with the undertone. "I will talk with my brother about offering you a prospectus."

"We will look it over," von Eppenstein said. "Come. I think dinner is ready."

Simon ran back and forth from one corridor to the next. Two of the machine presses were down and the one in working order was emitting an ominous screeching sound.

"Can't you fix that?" Elias shouted, embarrassing his brother in front of two workers and the pressman.

"We've got two machines down, and we're asking too much from this one. Look Elias, you can not expect me to oversee these men, fix broken machines *and* operate two of the presses as well. I think it is time to modernize and take on Hoffmann's shop before someone else purchases it."

"I am not throwing my money out the window on fancy new and unproven machinery just so that you can expand us into aeroplane design. It is folly."

Simon stopped the one working press and took Elias to the side. "Von Eppenstein is willing to fund me if you do not," he said quietly out of earshot of the workers. "I'm training Gunter's son as you asked, but of course, he's just a teenager and it will be years before we can seriously consider him. I think you need to start hiring some top engineers from the universities."

"You think we are made of money?"

"Let me be blunt, big brother. In your own tight-fisted way, you have been generous with me, but my passion is aeroplanes. So, either you fund this expansion, or I go out on my own. The choice is yours."

"You are awfully high and mighty for a seventeen-year-old."

"I've had a good teacher."

Elias sat stiffly, not hiding his sense of impatience and boredom as Simon listened transfixed to abstract mathematician David Hilbert argue with a young Albert Einstein and Max Born about a problem associated wind turbulence and drag. They were sitting in a lecture hall at Göttingen University with a dozen or so professors and scholars who were listening raptly to Theodore von Karmen's presentation. Von Karmen, a short Jewish man, was an expert in aerodynamics. Simon had contacted him and von Karmen had invited them to Göttingen to see the facilities with their own eyes. For a college town, it was too cosmopolitan, Elias thought. Too many austere buildings, not enough trees. He realized how fortunate he was to have a place with space and greenery.

Von Karmen approached and whispered, "Please forgive me. We'll be just a few more moments."

"Albert," von Karmen said, "you are going to have to account for the random action of wind shears and calculate in laminar flow." Von Karmen scribbled a series of calculations on the board as Einstein and Hilbert jotted these calculations into their respective notebooks.

"Albert, you want to join us?"

"No," Einstein said. "You've given me much to chew on. I think I'll just stay here with Professor Hilbert and hash out this last sequence."

"If you need me…"

"Yeah, yeah, Mr. Expert, we know where to find you," Einstein said.

"I'll give them the weekend and see how they do," von Karmen said with an air of total confidence. "Come on," he gestured for Simon and Elias to follow him by nodding to a path which led to the other side of campus.

With von Karmen in the lead, Simon took his brother to Professor Prandtl's wind tunnel where von Karmen had fastened an aeroplane. Simon guessed it was a stripped down Bleriot. It was a large hangar, over 100 feet in length, somewhat narrow, but easily able to house two planes end to end. Theodore handed earmuffs to each man and then motioned to an assistant who turned on a huge fan at the end of the tunnel. Suddenly a terrific draft was directed toward the front of the plane. Von Karmen pulled a lever which released a steady stream of smoke and then he walked over to cameras positioned at different areas and shot several photographs so that he could chart the movement of the draft around each wing. Beaming, Simon looked over at Elias, who returned the gaze with a begrudging nod.

AEROPLANES

The developments in flight technology advanced at breathtaking speed. Where the first Wright Brothers flight was measured in fractions of minutes, just six years later flight time was measured in hours. This had been a watershed time for aeroplane development, and Simon had argued, cajoled and eventually pleaded for Elias to invest, "to be part of the game." Louis Bleriot had just captured the attention of the world by being the first to fly the English Channel. Nearly 50,000 people cheered him on. Simon too was enthralled and speculated about entering the Reims Air Meet to be held in France. He told Elias that he could work with Lilienthal, whose gliders he had already flown in, who was now attempting to place a motor and propeller on board. But Simon's plans were colored with a heavy dose of wishful thinking.

"The Cairo race is already one too many," Elias sliced.

"Papa," Abe chimed, "there will be Voisins, Bleriots, Wrights, a Morane, two Antoinettes and even a Curtiss. I've read that Bleriot will have the fastest planes there."

"How do you know so much?"

"It's in *The Bavarian Ledger*, papa!" Abe tore from the room and returned with a scrapbook.

"Where did you get this?"

"I've had it for two months. Great uncle Adolf gave it to me."

Simon knocked on the front door, as a prelude to simply opening it, as was his custom.

"Hello, Abe."

"Uncle Simon!" Abe's eyes lit up, for Simon had given him a small color photo of a Henri Farman plane.

"It's an advertisement for cigars," Simon pointed out.

"Cigars, hmmm," Elias pondered. "Simon, this will divert funds away from vital concerns."

"Elias, look at the leaps and bounds already achieved in six short years. We're in on the ground floor. I've already built the motor and forged the propeller. And we have one of Prandtl's best students at Göttingen."

"The man I met?"

"Yes, Theodore von Karmen. He has agreed to help us on wing design. If we were to enter this race and come out ahead...."

"You could be killed. And then what would I do?"

"You're being too dramatic."

"Simon, you know as well as I, we can both rattle off the names of a dozen people that we knew personally who have died or been severely injured from crashing aircraft."

"I have them here, papa." Abe opened his scrap book to the back page to his list of injuries and obituaries.

"Ernst Mayhau!"

"You hadn't heard?"

"When? Simon. I saw him only last May?"

"It was a freak accident."

"Freak! What happened?"

"Some say it was a gust of wind, but I think he made a mistake when he tried to avoid a flock of birds."

"It says here that he fell out of the plane."

"It flipped over. Cally Hall saw the whole thing."

"And the plane righted itself and landed safely!" Abe added to the total astonishment of his father.

"My God, Simon. I don't want you flying."

"That was a fluke. I realize there is some danger. But isn't that our challenge, to make the plane safe for flight?"

Elias ruminated for a long time that night. He paced the bedroom and the halls, then he donned his hat and coat and strolled the grounds. The moon was full. Little Abe ran to the window and looked down at the long shadow of his papa disappear down the lane.

Strangely, Abe found it comforting, the full moon casting a greenish glow into his room. His eyelids became heavy and he wrapped himself back into his bed to fall back asleep.

Not Debora. She could not sleep with her husband missing from the bed, and he, of course, as she knew, realized this, so he turned back.

"I'm sorry, Debora. I'm frightened for Simon. How can I keep him from building this plane? He's working with top aerodynamic engineers, he's doing it on lunch breaks and on his own time. He has his heart set on entering this race."

"Stall him," Debora said. "In the end, you must let him. But have him set up a reasonable timeline, maybe several years, so that he can assure you that he'll have a dependable product."

"You make good sense, my dear."

"Thank you."

"In spite of my harsh exterior, I'm concerned for his welfare. Obviously he's going to test this plane, and if he gets hur.... I can't run this factory without him."

"Then why don't you treat him as a partner instead of an employee?"

"What has that got to do with what we are talking about!" Elias stormed. "You're always hocking me about how unfair I am, when meanwhile, he has his own house...."

"Which you own...."

"No matter. He does not bring in the revenues. He had nothing to do with raising the capital."

"You have no choice," Debora repeated. "If you deny him this, no doubt, he'll do it anyway. At least he will have your blessing and maybe then you can have some say as to how he will proceed."

"Why can't he stay on the ground? We can get any whippersnapper to be a pilot."

"He is a whippersnapper, Elias. Don't you see? He wants to be part of the game. He wants to fly. Can't you understand it's all the rage. Look at little Abe, like the Thomas boys and Schumann's kid, he's enamored with stories of the newest flight record broken, length of time in the air, speed, altitude."

"I can't believe he's only six."

"Dr. Havenmacher says he's a prodigy."

"So, I suppose you want me to build a plane for him, too?"

"Very funny, dear." Debora leaned over to give her husband a kiss.

After talking it over with his partner Adolf von Rosensweig, Elias put money down to purchase an 80-acre farm that abutted his land and commandeered the barn there to allow Simon to create his own airways division of Maxwell-Bavarian Machineworks.

Having studied the designs of the Wright brothers and Curtiss' aeroplanes from America, the work of the Brits and the other Europeans, Simon correctly realized that the most advanced flying craft were now being built just a few hundred kilometers away in France.

"I think the Bleriot's are the best," he told Elias.

"But Abe tells me that Curtiss has the combined speed and distance record."

"That may be so for today," Simon replied, "but I'm willing to bet that the glory days of Orville and Wilbur and his American followers will be eclipsed by Bleriot or maybe one of the Germans in just the next few months."

"What do you have to do to win?"

"You mean besides risking my life?"

"No! Simon. I don't want any risks. I do not want to build a flying coffin. If you are really going to start this aeronautics division, I want you around to reap in some of the gravy."

"Give him Tuesday mornings and most Thursdays," von Rosensweig interrupted.

"And what about our profits?" Elias demanded of his not so silent partner.

"Elias, we're already at near full capacity with automobile production and filling part requirements for von Zeppelin. Expanding in aeroplane design and manufacturing is the next logical step."

"If anything, we should be making dirigibles," Elias countered.

"It's true, brother, that dirigibles are best for passenger service over long distances. There is already talk about commuter flights to England and North Africa, but for speed there's no comparison. Bleriot just logged over 140 miles per hour!"

"For air mail delivery?"

"Yes. But think also about the advantages in border defense and reconnaissance. If we could rig a camera to a floor window we could log troop movements in Western Russia and Turkey.

"And battleship positions." Von Rosensweig's mind suddenly came alive.

"But Adolf, I am also afraid to become overextended. Motors for automobiles and airships, additional parts for the German air fleet. Won't we run the risk of diluting our resources?"

"Maybe, but you have to admit that our greatest resource is standing right here. And if Simon's passion is in aeroplanes, we have to placate him or deal with a very disgruntled worker."

"Simon, we can allow you a day or a day-and-a-half per week," Elias replied.

"And evenings?"

"You can do anything you want on your own time."

"You'll let me build my racing plane?"

"Why don't you just purchase a — which one did you say?"

"A Bleriot."

"Yes, Simon. Get the Bleriot. You said it was the best," Adolf agreed. "This way you could spend more of your time maintaining it and getting some flying time in."

"You two just don't understand." Simon paced. "You think I'm a mechanic? After all of I've done, redesigned half the motors in the shop, made changes on the pulley system for the blimp that even the Count thanked me for."

"We're willing to get you a plane. What else could you want?" Elias demanded.

"To build it from the ground up. Every nut and bolt. Work in a wind tunnel. Make it aerodynamically sound."

"And you think you can construct such a plane for this year's race?" Elias asked skeptically.

"I have already blueprints, and mock-ups for the motor, propeller and fuselage. The key will be wing design and the tail."

"I thought a tail is unnecessary."

"Elias, did you ever see a bird without a tail? Let's not tamper with God's greatest ideas."

"But Fokker has made it clear, he does not need a tail."

"Fokker will change his tune when we beat him at Champagne!"

DICKIE

Chess was knitting a miniature sweater, having already finished a pair of mittens and a small toque. Her stomach was bulging buoyantly beneath swelling breasts.

"How do you know it will be a boy?" Rudy had picked up the mittens and eyed them.

"I don't."

"Well, this is blue, isn't it?"

"It's teal, Rudy. Boy or girl, as long as it's healthy."

"Why don't we just do the test?"

"I don't want to know. I can't explain it. This little being growing inside me. I'm trying to tap into its energy beyond whether it's a male or female."

"Teal, schmiel. That's blue, Chess. You think it's a boy."

"Come here." She reached for his hand and placed it on her stomach.

He felt the firmness of the taut compartment.

"Close your eyes," she whispered. Rudy did. He sat down with her and tried to commune with this new life-form growing inside her. She placed her hand on his and they sat like that for what seemed like a timeless hour.

"Teal, huh?" he finally said. "What color you doing the pants."

"You tell me."

"Avocado."

"You sure you want to go alone?"

"I'd like to take you, Chess, but, and you tell me if I'm wrong. You'd just as soon stay here and relax."

"I know, Frisco sounds exciting," she said. "But, yes, I'm happy staying here. Been that," she added.

"I should be back by the weekend," he said.

"You really think you saw uncle Abe picketing Linzman?"

"Yes, and if I had the time, I'd try to see him now. I've got to know who he really is, who I really am. But I've got a great lead on NTroodr and I'm not going to get sidetracked. There's a Pulitzer in this if I pull it off. Why don't you feel mom out."

"I'll try, Rudy, but I don't want to make uncle Abe the reason I go visit her."

"Yeah, you're right. Worst comes to worst, we should find out the truth when the bambino arrives."

Rudy didn't mind flying. In fact, he liked it. What he didn't like was schedules. All this hurry up and wait. They wanted you at the airport two hours early for an international or coast to coast flight, and then, half the time, the flight was delayed. You had to be there hours early, then they could, and often did, leave any damn time they wanted.

Rudy had packed light. He had stuffed it all in a carry-on. Speed and ease of movement was his style. He placed the bag on the conveyor belt, took off his shoes and walked through the metal detector.

Beep!

"Take your belt off," said the lady. She was a skinny broad with long straggly black hair, a dark complexion and odd accent. He guessed Pakistani, but Indonesian would not have surprised him. He smiled at the irony of his inability to tell between such a large potential difference.

"What are you laughing at, sir." She spoke with a distinct British accent.

"I'm not."

"You looked at me and smiled. Empty your pockets."

"I already did."

"Guard!" The lady called out with such a loud voice that people as far away as the fast food stands turned to see.

Rudy pulled out his pockets and lifted both hands in a move to try and alleviate the tension. He started to walk through the metal detector once again, but two burly security policemen collared and dragged him to a changing room.

"Excuse me, Jed," Rudy read the name plate, "but that gal's out of her mind and clearly abusing her power. I'm a well known reporter for Modern Times. I travel practically weekly."

"So, why are you giving her a hard time?"

"That's the point. I didn't. She's got a bug up her you know what."

"She said you refused to empty your pockets."

"They were empty. When the metal detector went off, it must have been my belt. She wouldn't let me walk through after I removed it."

The other guard shot Jed a look, and it became pretty clear that this was not the first time this employee had caused a ruckus.

"We will have to pat you down," the other guard said.

"Be my guest." Rudy lifted his arms in a passive manner. "I'm all for security and even for your guys patting me down. My point is, she's fucking nuts and you and I both know it. Can't you get her reported?" Rudy couldn't believe he had cursed to these men. Why was he always so angry?

"That's not our job, sir," Jed continued to expertly pat Rudy down, moving both hands between Rudy's legs, up and down his thighs, around his buttocks, midriff, up under his arms.

"I'm a reporter and a patriot. But if the security staff is plain wacko, given to power trips, when guys like you know about it, then something's seriously wrong. This'll make a good story, Jed."

"Turn around," Jed said frowning. Expertly, he slid his fingers into every one of Rudy's pockets.

"I'm saying *she's* the security threat," Rudy said. "Don't you get my point? You need someone with real eyes, not some weirdo."

"You did something to tickle her feather," the other guard said.

"I smiled and she took it as an insult."

"Don't give us that crap. Your belt should have been off from the start. You know the drill. You said so yourself. You told us, you travel every week. Now, get back in line. Your bag will be at the end of the counter."

"Thank you."

"You're welcome."

Rudy looked at the clock. He had lost a good twenty minutes. He had about seven minutes left. He hated to be rushed as he liked to peruse the newsstand before boarding, to pick out a paperback to read, or grab a magazine or two. Now he was pressed for time. He tried to choose ones he didn't normally read, *The New Yorker, Harpers*, maybe *Vanity Fair*. It was just his way to make the trip a little more interesting. Sure he had his laptop. But that was all his stuff. This was a chance to pick up the work of some of his colleagues, his competitors. He saw the words "MB Airlines" on the cover of one and grabbed it. He didn't even know what magazine it was and then he rushed to the boarding area.

The flight to San Francisco had a stop in Chicago, and there was a maintenance problem on the receiving end. They could route through Phoenix or wait it out. Either way, the flight was delayed. The stewardess put 20 minutes on the board. Rudy guessed it would easily be twice that. He was tempted to go back to the newsstand and grab one of his more traditional choices, but a bird in the hand....

He opened up the magazine. It was the German publication *Deutchland*, written in English for an American audience. The lead story was about a coup de tête in Qawatar, a small island nation in the Red Sea off the coast of Ethiopia. Just forty miles from the Gulf of Aden and formerly a protectorate of Saudi Arabia, Qawatar, often confused with the wealthy and well-known peninsular nation of Dalwat Qatar, had won its independence from Yemen during one of the Arab Israeli conflicts in the mid-1960's. A fishing village island ruled by different warlords for centuries, Qawatar had remained out of the public eye until oil was discovered in the early 1980's. After a fierce, but brief civil war, Sheik Motahanni had seized control.

Over the next 20 years, the Sheik upgraded his fishing fleet, built hotels and resorts and began negotiating with Harvard University with plans to transform the local college into a world-class center of learning. But now, there was a coup and the Sheik was believed to be in hiding.

According to sources in Yemen, after the coup, the salaries of the entire Qawatari army had been doubled with General Rachman Mohammed bin Anwar installing himself as replacement kingpin. Astoundingly, negotiations with Harvard continued and a new public works desalinization project was announced to build an irrigation system to create farmland where there was now dry desert. "With 20% of all revenues from oil placed in a public treasury to fund housing, farming equipment, schooling and training for all Qawatari citizens, we plan to become a totally self-sufficient nation," bin Anwar said. According to the article, the construction of the desalinization plant was being undertaken by a German concern, Linzman Enterprises, a division of MB Airways.

The article then went on to discuss the history of MB Airways, which was described as an elite division of Lufthansa for a half century before breaking off from its parent company when the Berlin Wall came down in the late 1980's. Since that time, MB has acquired Maiden Airlines, the feisty British concern, as well as several smaller French, Italian and Finnish airlines and two wind farms in Norway and the Netherlands. It was rumored that MB was now negotiating with Rockwell & Marlen Airbus for a possible take-over and that it was also moving into the satellite industry with a broadband capability that would dwarf in capacity and speed all existing mass media, cell phone and Internet providers.

"What is the success to MB Airways? many people are asking. The answer seems to be twofold, the impeccable service on their flights and their ability to keep fuel costs down -- all due to the brilliant maneuvering of Rolf Linzman, son of the company's founder and president, Gunter Linzman."

Chessie decided that if Rudy was going to Frisco, she'd take her own little adventure. There was an ad for a flea market out on the Island. And it was near Wading River, which happened to be where she used to summer with her family, on Long Island Sound. When her mother was alive. That sounded good. She'd give it a go. Taking the car out, Chess decided on the leisurely route, along Route 25A. Following her GPS, she turned off the road right before the hamlet and came to a town square where about fifty tables were set up.

Chess felt a sense of excitement as she parked and made her way through the throng, eying chotchkas, thumbing through clothing racks, sizing up several paintings. A small brass statue of a boy holding a bouquet of balloons caught her eye.

"Why don't you buy it?" a young man said, looking her over in a way she found oddly discomforting. The item had a price tag of ten dollars, but was advertised at 50% off. She peeled off a five and took the piece.

"Thanks," she said to the lady behind the counter, and moved away. But the young man trailed after, so she weaved through a few more stalls, snaked her way to the car and drove off. Instead of driving back to the house, she decided to continue on, drive through Wading River and search out her former summer home. There was the dirt road, and she took it.

The house, really a summer cottage, was not set up for winter. The place looked abandoned. It had been over ten years. Chess thought back to how, as a little girl, her mom, when she was alive, would lift her in the water, how she'd run after the minnows in the shallows and try to catch some in a cup, and how her father and uncle used to take a tire and swim out together on it to that rock, way out, perhaps 100 yards from shore. The house sat on a high cliff along with several others, a good sixty feet above the shore. She tried the door but it was locked. Walking to the back edge of the property, Chessie looked off in the distance towards Connecticut, searching the horizon for that rock.

Taking the long staircase down to the beach, two full flights, she reached the rocky/sandy shore. Taking her sneakers off, she began to walk the shallows, finding herself looking for minnows. Thinking back. The young man who she had seen at the flea market, appeared as if from nowhere, and began walking beside her. Unlike Chessie, he was not barefoot, but stomped in the waters plopping in his shoes.

"Hello, Chessie," he said. "It's been a long time."

Chessie tried to put a place and time to the face. How did he know her name? she thought. He seemed sweet, but....

"I'm not sure if I know you," she said.

"Remember camp? You were a counselor."

Chessie got a pensive far away look in her eyes, but nothing registered.

"We used to be in love. At least I was in love with you," the young man said, startling, yet also flattering her.

Chessie moved away, but he followed. Barefoot, sneakers in hand, she ran up the long staircase and tried to get to her car. Breathing heavily, she began to realize that maybe this was a dream.

Lying in the bed, she felt the man's presence and she could hear his breathing. He was sitting on the bed right beside her! She could feel his body heat by her thighs. Afraid to open her eyes, she felt frozen, not sure what to do. Maybe if she just kept her eyes closed, she thought, he'd disappear. She waited and waited, but he was still there, hovering. She wanted to scream, to kick him off the bed. Frozen, she continued lying there, and then slowly, she opened one eye and looked about. No one was in the room. She was alone. It would have been easy to simply write this off as a dream, but there on the bed was that small brass statue of the boy with the balloons she had purchased. She found herself missing Rudy all the more, but knew it would be several more days until he returned.

Rudy had expected to arrive in Frisco early evening, but with all the delays, he got there after midnight. He notified the desk clerk to wake him at 7. After breakfast and waiting till 10 a.m., he gave Chessie a call to let her know he had arrived and then called his contact. "Dickie, I'm here."

"You downloaded Savior, schmuck, I can't believe it."

It was just like Dickie to not even say hello. "You hacked my computer?!" Rudy was aghast.

"Hey, old buddy, I'm just looking out for you. You know how to get here, don't you?"

"Did I open myself up?"

"Nah!" Dickie said. "It's a scam, particularly for the Macs, but they're probably legit. The problem is, now they have your credit card number and your password."

"What should I do?" Rudy thought back to the plane ride over to Germany and how through the paranoia of losing access to his laptop, he allowed a nerd from Bulgaria to clean up his computer."

"I wiped them and changed your password, you're cool," Dickie said. "Just call up your credit card company and get a replacement."

"You what!?"

"What," Dickie said, more as an accusation than a question.

"All right, what is it?"

"Boscoe, what did you think it would be."

"Very funny, Dickie. Did you really change my password?"

"Nah, I didn't do anything. But I did remove their ghost watcher, younno, a covert Trojan. I don't think you have anything to worry about. So, get your ass over here."

Rudy loved the Bay area, the energy of Berkeley, all the bridges, the streetcars and incredibly steep hills of San Francisco, the skyline and water views, the sense of the land itself being alive. He crossed Golden Gate and headed into Marin County where Dickie was holed up. Dickie, who had always been overweight and a bit of a schlub, with his trademark disheveled hair and dirty fingernails, was an old fraternity brother from college. One of the fortunate few, he had been in on the ground floor when Google started up, had cashed out half his stock when it had peaked a few years back, and made another fortune selling his data mining program Blitz to Microsoft which was now incorporated into Bing, their innovative answer to the giant Google. Rudy figured Dickie to be worth an easy thirty million, but he still lived like a pauper, in the same house in Sausalito, the one he had been in for twenty years. At least it had a view of the bay.

From the outside, the place looked deserted, like one of those houses whose door a kid would never knock on, on Halloween. In bad need of a paint job, this was all, according to Dickie, to keep with his low profile. And inside, it was not much better, ratty furniture, old dusty posters on the wall of various rock bands, a broken lava lamp, a half-eaten pizza on the kitchen counter from, Rudy hoped, the night before, currencies from a dozen different countries wrapped separately in their own plastic bags, two-dozen mouses of all different colors and sizes scattered all over the tables and on the floors, and five banks of computers lining the so-called living room which was really Dickie's office.

"Can't do it, old buddy. It's illegal."

"Come on. If I'm right, we will have caught the biggest cracker in the country."

"Listen, Rudy, I'm all for catching crackers, but Codebreaker's now a good guy. That shit was done ten years ago and everything done since has been for one reason only, to alert the system. Why do you think it's Ashley LaPolla? She's got the primo job at MIT, she's on the cable stations all the time. Did you see her the other night on Charlie Rose?"

"Yeah, I did."

"Did you check out her rack!"

"Come on Dickie," Rudy said in an exasperated voice.

"Can't a guy shit yah? I didn't mean to put you down. Was it something she said on the air?"

"Yes," Rudy said, "Exactly. That's what set me onto her. Actually, I admit, I had an inkling before that, and her TV spot just confirmed it. She never even considered the Oh Shit hack as being done by CodeBreaker Morant. Why not? Because she knew *she* didn't do it! I had never even heard of NTroodr until she mentioned him, and that was right from the git-go, as soon as that prank broke."

"You got it all wrong, knucklehead. She just recognizes style. That's what she does for a living," Dickie explained. "Something about the hack told her it wasn't Morant's sig. I can buy that. It's the same conclusion I came to," the geek's geek explained.

"I googled her, Dickie. Turns out she wrote a paper in college on the movie *Breaker Morant*, and look at this." Rudy took out a photo of Ashley wearing a Bryan Brown T-shirt. "That was *his* film."

"Yeah, that and a dime…." Dickie began.

"So, if I'm wrong, I'm wrong."

"It's a helluva a risk, old buddy."

"You told me to come out here, so I'm here."

"I miss my friends. I thought I could give you some advice."

"Oh, come on," Rudy said. "Let's do this! You had no problem hacking me."

"Apples and aardvarks," Dickie said. "You don't know shit from Shinola. She knows everything."

"More of a challenge," Rudy taunted.

Dickie paced the room. He looked back at his college pal and looked at his machines. "Give me her IP number."

Rudy handed it over. He had paid the son of a friend of Chessie's, who worked at LaPolla's lab, to get her computer address.

As Dickie looked it over, Rudy asked, "Won't she know?"

"How stupid do you think I am? And don't answer that!" Dickie said with a harrumph.

"Whadaya mean?"

As Rudy spoke, Dickie opened up a draw and took out what looked like a police radar gun and aimed it out the window at the boats in the harbor.

"What is that?" Rudy eyed the device closely.

Dickie stood up, marched around the room, put the back of his hand against his face like he was Zorro and proclaimed, "Cloak of invisibility, man."

"Looks like a can of Pringle's potato chips," Rudy said, ignoring Dickie's attempt at drama.

"That's exactly what it is," Dickie said, dropping the act. "It's a Pringle cantenna, picks up ambient wi-fi. Here, look at this." Dickie pointed to his computer and out popped a list of nearly a dozen open wi-fi lines.

"What is that?"

"That, my man, is a directory of every unprotected wi-fi network within about a 500 yard radius."

"Unprotected?" Rudy was taking notes.

"Yeah, non-password protected. "You didn't think I was going to search from my line, did you?"

"Holy shit, Dickie. Is this legal?"

"Legal schmeagle. The beauty of it is that the guy in the $6.3 million 75-foot yacht out there won't even know I'm using his Internet service, unless, of course, they trace it back to him." Dickie turned and glared. "And even if they do locate his IP, I'll run the search through the under-web, so no matter what happens, he'll stay in the clear and they'll never know it's me." With that, Dickie logged onto the Internet via the yacht's account and went to Dr. Lapolla's server. "They've logged, of course, every search she ever made."

"You mean, you're gonna break into her server?"

"Duh! How else did you think I was going to do it?"

"I thought you'd hack her computer," Rudy said.

"Boy, you really are dumb!" Dickie sliced.

"Didn't you listen to a word I said?" Dickie gave Rudy another one of his fuck you Prussian stares. And then his expression changed back to a more friendly demeanor. "Look, Rudy, servers get hacked thousands of times per hour."

Dickie spoke matter of factly. But Rudy was flabbergasted. "Well, you went into mine."

"You're a fucking amateur. She's probably got six layers of firewall, and even if I get in, she'll definitely know. This way, there's no way she *can* know. Because I won't be touching her computer at all."

"Unless, of course, she hacks her own server," Rudy suggested.

"You gotta point. But she'd also have to separate me out from the rest of the hackers that hit servers every moment of every day."

"You mean like the NSA?"

"Who are you Eric Snowden?" Dickie shot back as he continue to work the computer figuring out a way to complete entrée. "Hah!," Dickie exclaimed, "we're golden, piss brain, golden. Take my word for it." Sometimes Dickie could speak with such disdain in his voice that he could make Rudy feel like he was an inch tall.

"And that would be crazy, right?" Rudy asked, trying to ignore Dickie's bullshit side.

"Exactly. Not gonna happen."

"Well, what about the server?" Rudy continued taking notes.

You're kidding me."

"Yeah, I'm kidding you. Listen, meathead, just go visit a server sometime yourself, and check it out. They're running against automatic searches that can occur at a rate of billions per second, hackers looking for inroads, and occasionally they get lucky. How else do you think they got into NATO, the White House and the computers at the Pentagon?"

"Billions of times per second?!" the reporter needed verification

"Well, millions, anyway."

"You're telling me servers get hacked every second!?"

"Jesus, Rudy, yes. Every fucking second, every fucking minute, millions of hacks per second, billions per minute, zillions of hacks per day. Like I said, these are automatic searches, it's not like some schmuck pressing buttons. These are fucking automated worms digging day and night for inroads," Dickie softened.

"Undetected?"

"Technically, not undetected, hard to trace. We're talking about the deep web old buddie, so, it's not whether or not I'm detected, it's whether or not I can be identified."

"So, maybe you use TOR or Freegate?" Rudy was referring to two well-known software programs that could bury a hacker's identity.

"Jesus, Rudy. I thought you knew all this shit. No, I'm not gonna use TOR or Freegate. The NSA's all over those! I'm using Calhoon."

"Calhoon? What's that?"

"It's a derivative of Haystack, a nifty that masquerades and encrypts the log-on so the server doesn't even know he's being searched, and even if he finds out, he can't track the source because the source is interwoven with innocuous traffic and hidden by 10,000 intermediaries, compounded by most of this shit happening in the undernet. Half the intermediaries I'll be using are themselves undetected by the major search engines. The way I've got it rigged, even a sniff will send the tracker to a video game site."

"Wild Goose?" Rudy guessed, referring to a maze video game that was the new rage.

"You know me too well, Rudie Toot Dudie."

The chums exchanged Cheshire grins and clanged fists and then Dickie sat at his computer and logged on. Dickie had worked at Google since it all began. He was a software genius, and it was true, he had stolen some of their search secrets, but he had also done a lot of the work to help make Google Google. So they never did catch his back door. The whole thing took a fraction of a second to uplink and download and about twenty-five seconds to print out. "You never got this from me." He handed Rudy a stack of about fifty pages. "You want it stapled?"

"Only if you run me off another set."

Dickie raised his eyebrows and then he laughed, pressed a button, and out spit another set. "Come on, I know a good seafood place."

The restaurant, Salla's Fish Grill, was just three blocks away. They walked. Right on the dock, it had an entrance in the shape of a shark's mouth. They took a window table. As Dickie studied the menu, Rudy stared out at the magnificent view, across the bay, of the city.

"Hey babe," Dickie shouted to the waitress who was rushing by with a big tray of hot food.

"I'll be with you in a second," she said scooting past them.

"That's one helluva of a long second," Dickie poked when she finally returned.

The waitress was standing there, pencil in hand ready to take their order. "Would you like another minute to decide?" she ignored his comment.

"Would that be an actual sixty-second minute or a give or take minute?" Dickie stared her down with one of those looks that conveys to the receiving person that he or she is a worthless piece of shit.

"Probably the latter, but either way, I'll be right back." She rushed off, trying to deflect an awkward moment.

"What do you want? It's on me, old buddy," Dickie said.

"I think I'll go for the stuffed sole, Rudy said.

"Excellent choice. Waitress! Waitress!" Dickie shouted and curled a finger to get the girl back sooner.

"What'll you have?" she said.

"My man'll have filet of sole. How's the crab legs? Are they fresh?"

"Fresh frozen. We fly them in from Alaska every other day."

"Fresh or frozen?" Dickie asked petulantly. "Can't be both."

"Frozen," the waitress said.

"They any good?" Dickie said.

"Of course they are."

"Okay, I'll get the crab. Bring an extra cup of butter when you bring the crab."

"Sure. Anything to drink?"

"Two beers," Rudy interrupted. "Thank you."

"You're welcome," she disappeared.

"What was that all about?" Rudy asked.

"What?" Dickie said. "Hey, remember that girl from college with the nose ring and the red hair?" Dickie moved the conversation to the good old days.

The duo then relived some of the old frat stories, how they got five broads drunk and got them to shed their clothes and go into the hot tub which Dickie still had in the back of his house. "Do you remember the tits on Angie. God they were beautiful."

"Is that all you ever think about?"

"What else is there?" Dickie opened up his wallet and pulled out an old crinkled photo of Angie topless. Rudy stared at it trying to keep a straight face. Dickie looked him in the eye, a sly smirk on his lips and that was it. They both just cracked up.

When the bill came, Dickie asked Rudy to cover the tip. They left the restaurant and walked back to Dickie's place.

"Why don't you stay over? You want a hit?" Dickie lit a joint as they walked. Rudy nodded no. "We can have breakfast at the dock. You can still catch the plane. Come on, have a hit." Dickie tried to hand it off, but Rudy wouldn't take it.

"You do your thing, kiddo. I'm just gonna pass," Rudy said. "It's unbelievable, you still smoking that shit!" Rudy did not say this in a deprecating way, but rather with some sense of awe.

"It's medicinal," Dickie said, holding his breath, cracking up with the stupidity of the joke. "It's some really good shit."

"I can tell," Rudy said. He hadn't touched grass in ages, and he certainly wasn't going to start now. "I know you don't care about the money," Rudy said, "but you've got so much now. Thirty, forty mil, am I right?"

"Give or take."

"So, why not set up some type of foundation or scholarship fund?"

"You still want to save the world, don't you?"

"Yeah, I do. And if I had your resources, I think I could."

"I don't know, maybe you're right," Dickie said. "You wigged I had you cover the tip?"

"No," Rudy lied. "My whole trip's covered. I probably should have picked it up myself."

"Yeah, as long as it was covered. You probably should have."

"I think you should save your money for a rainy day," Rudy said. "You never know when you might need ten twenty mil." He spoke sarcastically.

Dickie looked reflective. "It's all just sitting there. I live on a shoestring. It's like it's not really mine."

"I don't think you ever grew up," Rudy said.

"Sounds like you're having a kid," Dickie replied.

"Nail on the head, my friend."

Dickie had missed the wedding, so Rudy filled him in and told him about Chessie's pregnancy. Rudy had to admit, although Dickie was one pain in the ass, heck, he had always been one big pain, it was great to sleep at his friend's pad, a real throw-back. And like the old days, after the sun went down, they sat in the hot tub and reminisced till two, three in the morning. Breakfast was awesome, on the water, near all the yachts, with that fantastic view of Frisco. "I can see why you stayed," Rudy said. "But you should find yourself a girl."

"I'm afraid she'll want me for my money."

"I'm not telling you to get married. But find someone, Dickie. The clock doesn't stop."

"Yeah, I know, I know," Dickie said. "Knock'm dead, bro."

En route to the airport, Rudy tracked down one more lead, reporter Joanie Rush, who had lost her job at the *San Francisco Chronicle* after uncovering a major telephone hacking scandal that had rocked Hollywood. *The Chronicle* had claimed that her lay-off had been the result of normal cutbacks which had plagued the industry ever since the Internet almost put them out of business. But Joanie wasn't buying it.

"My investigations were leading me to Joshua Dilly," Joanie said, "and that's when I lost my job."

"But Dilly doesn't even own *The Chronicle*," Rudy countered. They were sitting on a park bench that overlooked the Golden Gate Bridge.

"That's the point, Rudy. Don't you get it?"

"No, I don't. I guess I'm dense."

"If Dilly owned the paper, then I would definitely have a case," Joanie said, "but he is a close friend of Mrs. Worst. Do I have to spell it out anymore than that?"

Joanie was referring to the head of the Worst family fortune that controlled *The Chronicle* along with one of the local leading TV networks. She also owned several professional sports teams.

"Everyone knows Dilly has hacked the cell phones of just about every major star in Hollywood. He's as bad as the Brits, and I was this close to uncovering the proof when my world just came tumbling down.... I'm not kidding, Rudy. I actually found a dead parrot with a rose in its mouth floating in my toilet. Do you know what that does to your psyche?"

Rudy looked Joanie over. Still beautiful and pushing fifty, Rudy could definitely detect a residual sense of fear in her eyes, additional wrinkles in her face and her once natural blonde hair now much more speckled with grey.

"Joanie, maybe you just need a rest."

"You can say that again, Rudy. I've always tried to fight the good fight. But I was naïve. It never occurred to me that my own newspaper would actually deep-six such a major story and deep-six me. That's what's so insidious about it. The very safeguard we have against abuse of power has now become the source of such abuse! Make that your story."

"What are you going to do?" Rudy commiserated.

"I can set up a blog. I can move back to New York, which I really don't want to do, and hope I can get a gig maybe with *The Times*, I could try cable, or *60 Minutes*, or I could just forget it, go to Europe for awhile and regroup."

"Joanie, I admit I like the last idea. I understand what you're going through," Rudy continued, "but I just want to be clear...."

Joanie cut him off. "Do you, Rudy? Do you, really?"

"Well, all I can say is I do have a sense of it, and I know what it means to be shut out of a story."

"Yeah, I remember that whole superpsychic, Soviet cybernetic parapsycho scene."

"Exactly, Joanie, but we did get it out there."

"Yeah, through *The National Tattler*. Hah! In a million years...."

"I know, you'd never go that route, but published is published," Rudy countered.

Switching gears, Joanie stood up to point out a tall ship that was coming up the bay. "You just don't get views like this in the Big Apple," Joanie said.

"Yeah, and the earthquakes don't compare either," Rudy quipped.

Joanie watched the crew of Coast Guard sailors stand in formation spread out along the yardarms, a giant American flag waving atop the tallest mast. Many onlookers along the shoreline spontaneously stood and saluted. "I see sights like this and I feel, for a moment, patriotic." She turned back to face him. "So, are you going to help me, or not?"

"Now, wait a second," Rudy said. "Don't pull that on me, Rush." Rudy used her last name. "I told you up front, I was looking for that cracker who's threatening to take down the Internet, and you said you had a lead."

"Oh, fuck you! Rudy Styne. You're just like all the others." She reached out and literally gave him a shove on the shoulder, and then she turned and stormed off.

Rudy sat there taken for a loop. Not quite sure what to do, he reached for his cell phone, and watched Joanie answer hers. "If you come to New York, I'll speak to Whitmore. How's that?" Rudy said.

Joanie turned to see that it was really he who had called her. She slowly walked back. "I'm sorry, kiddo," she said. "I know it was a dirty trick."

"So, you really don't have anything on this cracker?"

She nodded no. The sky roared above them. They both looked up to see a very large airplane soar overhead.

"I heard the weather in Tuscany is good right about now." He smiled.

"Maybe you're right," she said. "Take a little time?"

"Yes," he said. "A little time. You deserve it. It will do you good."

Joanie stared at him for a minute considering. Then she nodded, reached over, gave him a brief hug. "Maybe you're right," she whispered, and then she turned and walked away.

Rudy got back into his rental and made his way to the airport. He waited until he was seated on the plane before opening up Dickie's package. It was, without a doubt, a search of every Google entry the MIT professor had made for the last four months. Dickie had coded his program to reduce redundancy. In other words, if Ashley LaPolla searched a topic once or one hundred times, it only appeared on the sheet once, but with a number next to it to identify how many times she had searched that site. It ran 50 pages, two columns, double sided. Everything was there. She googled scores of articles on cracking and famous hackers, computer speed, GPU's (graphic processing units), MIPs (millions of instructions per second) and broadband, the Cray computer, history of the Internet, Skype, onion sites, Larry Gates, Steve Jobs, and other founding fathers, robots, the singularity AI, the DIA, SIRI, SIPRNet, DARPA, Shadow Web, Deep Peep, DropBox & Digital Sky, Julian Assange, Eric Snowdon, Jacob Appelbaum, Anonymous, paywall and the Kaminsky attack, Wikileaks, Echelon, iCloud, Whit Diffie, Sabu, Al Gore, Justin Frankel, Austin Heap, satellite relay systems, ambient social networking, streaming video, Wi-Fi, Napster, Gnutella, key escrow, Wget, Nullsoft, BitTorrent, Base64, web-TV and LimeWire, TOR, Blockfinder, firewalls, Freegate, Haystack, Skipjack, Undernet, Evil Genius, encryption, identity theft and PGP (pretty good privacy), spyware, Trojan horses, data mining, phishing, and browsers, poisoned servers, crossword codes, nanobots, UNIX, Bitcoins, Bing, the Silk Road, Red Hat, Phrack, Fancast, Netflix, Nexus, Apple, Hulu, Microsoft, Surface tablet, Gogo and Google, glitches, frozen computers, back doors, repurposing, relay systems, dumpster diving, server migrations, repatterning, countermeasures, carnivores and skeleton keys, spoofing, swatting, cyber-rooms, sniffing, sexting, spiral tracking, Pandora and Quora, Beluga, Yobongo, Group.me and twittering, B-ugly, Bouncing dot, ByteMe and Bitbandit, firewalls, poking, pinging, Palantir Technologies, passwords, qubits, viruses, worms, Catphish and cloning, Chinese symbols, hotels in Europe, sex toys, spanking, spiked high heels, hermaphrodites, bustiers, G-strings, thongs and tongue kissing, Playgirl, clothing sites, Territory Ahead, Bryan Brown photos, Breaker Morant, Topkapi, I-Robot, War Games, El Topo, Elvis Presley, Social Network, Norah Jones, U2, IP, spam filter, search engine, military sites, think tanks, banks, insurance companies, foreign governments, virtual space, cloud computing, E-Tablet, Qawatar, major networks, Turner Classic, Disney, CEO's, David Bowie and Charlie Rose.

From the rhythm of the list, it seemed that she started by linking NTroodr to the people at Google, Bing, Webnet, Yahoo and Microsoft, and then she went to Bulgarian, Russian and North Korean sites, some in Australia, but she kept coming back to T-Dan Mulrooney, Spinnwebe and Heinz Gruuban, HuffingtonPost, Ello, Modern Times, Mother Jones, Jon Stewart, Wolf Blitzer, Rudy Styne, Captain Whitmore, MB Airways and both Gunter and Rolf Linzman.

Rudy felt certain that Ashley was closing in on who NTroodr was and also that she probably suspected that he himself was on her trail. There was no getting around it. He had to approach her, but how to do it without bringing attention to Dickie? Would she know that she'd been compromised? His heart was racing. She was CodeBreaker Morant, he was sure of it. Was she searching for NTroodr because he was her competition or was she out to catch him? Rudy had to interview her and see if he could somehow trap her. The power that Dickie had at his fingertips, his ability to invade literally the lives of virtually anybody, it blew him away. Could a person truly hide his or her IP address and search anonymously? Maybe he could ask her that.

VENICE

It was early spring, 1912. Simon had thought about it hard and long. Should he borrow one of the new automobiles, Elias would probably allow him. But then, there was the expense of gasoline, the ruts, the distance required to travel and the problem of the location of the petrol stations. And on top of that, he'd be beholden to his brother and he wanted to do this on his own.

The thought of Roberé walking his daughter Iris down an isle with his child/bride giggling on the side, the hypocrisy of inviting dozens of cousins and business acquaintances of his brother, and the problem of having Iris' divorced parents on the receiving line was just too much.

Simon banked his propellered glider, caught an air current, and felt the rush of wind across his face. As he looked down over the patchwork of trees, farm houses and fields of green, he searched for the hill where Roberé's castle lay.

Trying a maneuver he had learned at Göttingen, he swooped down to pick up speed and directed the craft to follow the circling buzzards where he suspected another thermal lay. Yes, he caught it and spiraled ever higher.

Iris had paid the farmhand dearly for the use of the estate's best horse and carriage, and for his silence. She stood at the rise and paced. They had chosen this field because Simon had said that it would be the easiest to land. Further, there was a barn there where they could store the plane.

Scanning the skies in anticipation, Iris strained as if to peer through the very mountain tops. She watched two egrets fly by and then a great heron. But was that a heron? It looked too big. Her heart pounded and a sense of joy swept through her on a level she never could have imagined.

Yes, it was Him! Her heart beat so rapidly she felt almost as if she herself could flutter up to meet him. Waving a large orange, yellow and purple scarf she had purchased on a trip to Milan, she pranced back and forth like a filly testing her young legs.

Simon saw the signal. He considered the wind and potential landing sites. He had walked the area at the time of Roberé's wedding, so he knew the best strip to land, but there was a cross·current and he didn't think he could make the drop clearly. He tilted the wing-lifts and soared so close to his beloved that she hit the ground startled. Missing the barn by less than two meters, he banked sharply, leveled and forged a path. This had been his back-up strip. The wings sliced through the overgrowth like a scythe cutting a swath through a wheat field. The glider touched ground and halted.

Taking off his goggles, Simon began to unstrap himself, but Iris was too fast. She leaped instead into the cockpit, and draped her pulsating body over her brave champion.

"Wait, wait," he tried to say as she showered him with kisses. Yielding, he simply turned his head towards her and reached out with his loose hand to hold her head and run his fingers through her hair. Her mouth was soft and sweet, her eyes clear, her expression pure.

"And you thought you were in heaven five minutes ago!" she said helping him from the craft

"Are you sure Mr. Schwigmann will find the plane?"

"Don't worry, I told old Schwiggy how important it was. He'll be here before dinner time with his two sons. I know Christopher is aching to see your craft."

"And they'll tow it into the barn?"

"No. They'll come all the way up here and plop it on a cow patty! Don't worry."

They walked, hand in hand, along the path left by the landing. Both felt at ease, a natural energy flowing between them. Iris could not believe how right everything felt, how comforting Simon's grip was, how much she loved the smell of his skin. They stopped at a pond that was as still as a mirror. Simon looked at his reflection.

"What are you doing?"

"I'm trying to lift one eyebrow." Simon wrinkled his forehead, blinked with one eye and raised the eyebrow of the other. "Now, you try it."

"No," Iris said.

"Why not?"

"It might give me a headache. I know you think it's a sign of intelligence, but I don't think so. It's just a place for old men to put their monocles."

This tickled Simon in a way that made the two of them burst into laughter. Simon turned to face her and looked deep into her eyes.

"What?"

"Shush," he whispered, continuing to gaze at the multi-colors and flecks of gold imbedded in the spokes of the green part of her irises. It was a magical mandala pattern that glinted and seemed to rotate into a whirlpool portal to the very essence of her being. "There's a world in there."

"Your world," she replied.

"Will you marry me?"

"I will Simon Maxwell. I will."

"Will you have and hold me till death do us part?"

"Simon, you're too serious. Not if you fly recklessly. I'll tell you that." She reached up and kissed him first quickly and then deeply. "I want to have your babies," she whispered.

"Right now?"

"No, goofy," she said, her face flushed crimson.

"Tonight?"

"Maybe."

They stepped into the carriage. Iris took the driver's seat, Simon letting her – not because he didn't want to drive the buggy, but because if she wanted to drive, he wanted her to have what she wanted.

"What did you tell Elias?"

"The truth."

"That we plan to elope?"

"Yes."

"What did he say?"

"At first he got angry."

"That you were leaving the factory for two weeks?"

"No. He got over that quick enough. But he was hurt."

As they spoke, the buggy made its way south, through the foothills of Bavaria and on into the Alps of Austria.

"From Innsbruck, we can catch a train to Milan and change for Verona, then on to Venice."

"I can't believe it." Iris' eyes sparkled and her long sandy brown hair fluttered in the wind.

"You look like you've taken enough clothes for a sojourn to the new world," Simon said, referring to the large trunk which lay in the back of the buggy.

"My mother insisted I take her wedding dress."

"She didn't oppose?"

"She was all for it. She liked the daring aspect. Said she'd tell my father tonight. She would phone him."

"So, he still doesn't know?"

"One way or another, he knows. I told his stupid wife she wouldn't need to be bothering about me much longer."

"Was she jealous of you?"

"Relieved, I would say. So you never told me."

"What?"

"About Elias."

"Oh, him. His eyes filled with tears. I'm not sure I have ever seen him in such a state. 'I'm hurt that you wouldn't want me,' he said. 'What are you talking about?' I asked, concerned that he would insist I stay at the plant."

"So, what's the problem?" Iris looked off at a heard of cattle and then a number of women riding horses over a steeplechase.

"Best man. He wanted I should ask him to be best man. Can you believe it! All that time he's taken the lion's share from our endowment, he creates a factory that I have to run, pays me less than he pays the new foreman that he just hired for our turbine division, and he's hurt because I won't ask him to be best man!"

It had been a long ride, but the horses were strong. Off in the distance, nestled at the base of the great chain of the mighty Alps, they could see the hearty town of Innsbruck, it's freshly painted frescoes and clean city streets, dwarfed by the sheer rise of the mountain tops. From their vantage point of the massive panorama, it looked almost as if it were a toy village, its pristine buildings sparkling in the crisp clean air.

"What did you tell him?"

"That he was my best man, that he was my only beloved brother and he would always be my best man."

Iris let out a broad grin, snapped the reigns and brought the horses up the main street, her mind swiftly taken by all the pretty shops. A young lady and her boyfriend in bright colors pedaled past them on a bicycle built for two. Eying a block that contained three out-door restaurants, a store for Paris fashions, another of linens and one of eye-popping pastry, she pulled the carriage to a halt.

"And how did he take it?" Her eyes darted between each establishment while they conversed.

"He burst into tears and gave me a kiss. He also gave me a check equivalent to nearly half a year's salary!"

"Why Simon," she turned to face him, "he may love you almost as much as I do!"

She looked a bit weary from the long journey, but in some odd and mesmerizing way, it made her appear all the more alluring. Simon found himself embracing and kissing his fiancé with such passion that people stopped in the street and applauded.

Embarrassed, he quickly tied up the horses and guided Iris into a local hotel.

"We've missed the train by nearly an hour, and the next one will not be here till tomorrow morning." He hesitated for the briefest of seconds. "We shall get two rooms and then let us change for dinner."

"Oh, Simon," Iris said, a slight pleading lilt to her voice. "That clothing shop closes in 45 minutes." She motioned through the window to the Parisian establishment next to where the horses were. "You get the rooms and meet me at the bakery in half an hour."

Before he could respond, Iris was out the door scurrying across the street. He watched as she dabbed her face with powder from her purse and straightened her hair, fixing her appearance in the reflection of another shop. And then she slowed her gait, cocked her head and stepped assuredly into Madam Fleury's Fashion Center.

Iris had trouble falling asleep. They had no chaperone and would be married within 24 hours. What would be the harm if she stole into Simon's room to snuggle beside him?

Simon heard the latch open and felt her presence as she tip-toed in. "I can't sleep," she whispered, bending down to kiss his forehead.

Simon looked up to see her eyes sparkle and her hair glisten in the moonlight. He breathed in the smell of her perfume and felt the softness of her shoulders, the smoothness of her cheeks as she suddenly felt his heart increase its pace threefold. Rolling out of bed and wrapping a robe around the two of them, Simon led Iris back to her room. "We've waited this long," he said.

Iris stood before him at her door. She knew he was right, but every cell in her body ached to be near him. Her face flushed deep red, her body broke out in a sweat and she swooned, Simon catching her before she struck the floor.

Deftly he swept her into his arms and carried her to her bed, kicking the door shut behind him.

"Stay at least a little while," she pleaded.

He felt her hands go clammy, her nightgown had become pasted to her body. "I'll be alright in a few minutes," she assured him. And so he sat beside her and comforted her as he waited.

"Just a few more minutes," she said. "I feel safe, so right to be beside you. I will make you a good wife."

"I know you will, and I will make you a good husband." He watched her eyes shut and found himself staring at her perfect face, her clean complexion, slight smile and look of contentment. He felt his lids grow heavy.

The sun pouring through the room pierced his reverie. Simon awoke curled up beside his fiancé. She was still asleep and groaned as he stole out of the room and into his own.

The train ride to Verona was speedy and majestic, particularly at the beginning as they barreled through the great Alpine passes. From Verona, they changed rails for Venice arriving at the regal city-state while the sun was still high in the sky. Simon stood in awe at the effervescent waterway. Catching a *vaperetto*, it would take them by water through the heart of the city and then out to Murano, the well-known glass manufacturing town where Iris' uncle lived. Thirty-five minutes from the heart of Venice, the couple would be married at a chapel on that quaint isle.

"It's really a series of small islands, beyond reach from the edge of Venice," Iris told Simon. Their ceremony was scheduled for nightfall, so Iris suggested they take a leisurely tour before they left for uncle Alphonse's place.

Awed by the majesty of the Grand Canal, Simon stared in wonder at the lush villas and palazzos that lay along its banks, the numerous gondolas and steam-driven boats which motored back and forth.

Iris had been to Venice several times with her parents when they were married and with her mother after her divorce. She watched with delight Simon's look of fascination. She pointed out the dates of construction of many of the buildings. "There, that is Palazzo Balbi where Napolean watched a regatta in his honor in 1807. Oh, and that's the Gritti Palace." Simon nodded. "We stayed there with mother and father in 1902 when the Campanile collapsed."

"What is the Campamile?"

"'n' not 'm,' Campanile, the tower at Piazza St. Marco, by the Basilica."

"You mean, besides the Doge's Palace?"

"Yes, of course. Oh Simon, isn't it wonderful! That's where Galileo demonstrated his telescope and showed the Doge Leonardo the moons of Jupiter."

"Whatever are you talking about?"

"Simon, don't you know anything! Have you never looked through a telescope at the heavens?"

"I am only a humble machinist, Iris."

"And pilot."

"And pilot, my love."

"Oh, you're so much more than that. Some day I will show you the moons of Jupiter, and if we are really lucky, the rings of Saturn as well."

"You have seen those with your own eyes?" Simon could not believe it.

"There! Look, there!" Iris jumped so high she startled some of the other passengers. They have rebuilt the Campanile! We must get off!"

"But your uncle. They are all waiting for us, no?"

"It won't take long. So we will catch another waterbus. They come twice every hour."

"It is true," the boatman said. "If you want, I can deliver your bags when we get to Alphonse's."

"You know my uncle!"

"Naturally," the boatman said. "He told every one of us captains to look out for his delightful niece and her Bavarian fiancé."

Simon looked at the man who, to his surprise, responded in Yiddish. "You worry more than a Jewish mother with three ugly daughters!"

Simon tried to tip the captain, but he would not take it. "Do not worry. Your bags will be safe. If you stay two hours, you will probably get me on my next go around." And then in a loud voice, the captain called out, "Piazza St. Marco." Most of the crowd stepped off the boat.

Iris thanked the captain and followed suit. She ran past the palace and up to the red-brick tower. "It's over 100 meters high," she said. "Are you ready for the climb?"

Without waiting for a response, Iris tore up the stairs. Huffing at the top, Simon caught up to her. He put his arm around her and squeezed. She nuzzled in as together they looked over the vast complex of canals and bridges. Simon's eyes were drawn to a line of gondolas making their way through the main waterway like a fleet of wooden swans. "Wow!" he whispered.

"Wow indeed. Do you see those islands there." She turned him the other way and pointed to several islands just a few kilometers away.

"Yes."

"That is Lido Beach, and further out, you see it?"

"Yes."

"That is Murano. Come, we still have time to see the Basilica and maybe some of the palace."

"Wait. Give me a few more minutes. This city is like a magical fantasy. All the great buildings, the waterways, all the activity. I want to remember this moment forever."

"So, it was worth the climb?"

"Look, a violinist in the square, and all the pigeons."

"We can go down and listen, but if we hurry, we will still have time to see the Basilica, or if you wish, the palace."

"It's funny how you can feel the presence of God in the synagogues of the gentiles," he said entering the Basilica which was just several paces from the tower. Awestruck by the size and intricate beauty of the Grand Chapel, Simon took in its mosaic ceiling and carvings, the stained glass windows, magnificent statues and great domes.

"I know. Do you think underneath we really pray to the same God?"

"I think there can be only one."

"Then what about Jesus?" she said. They stared up at one of the many paintings of Madonna and child.

"As far as I know, he was a rabbi, and a son of God, as am I."

"But so many gentiles hate us."

"Yes, and there are many Jews who hate to be Jews."

"That can't be so."

"Well, what about my own brother. He has converted, you know. With his own father a rabbi, and his uncle, the greatest cantor in all of northern Austria."

"Come," she said. "Let us gain a glimpse of the Doge's Palace as well."

"I've had my fill of buildings right now. Let us sit in the square and listen to that violinist and feed the pigeons. Maybe we could eat those open-faced tomato and cheese sandwiches I see so many people trying."

"That is pizza."

"Is it Kosher?" Simon said

"Do you care?"

"It is not me who cares, but my Kosher stomach. Every time I mix meat and dairy or dairy and pickled food it goes into conniptions."

"I think if we stay with cheese and tomato and bread, you should be alright."

They sat by the violinist and munched. Iris looked at the far end of the piazza, a wistful look to her eye. The violinist approached to play a lilting melody, it's sound echoing and fading quietly throughout the great square.

"What?" Simon said. He found himself staring at the fulsome handlebar moustache that graced the musician.

"Oh, there are so many shops to see and streets to show you...."

"Shush," Simon commanded.

"But, but..."

"Shush." Simon reached over and gave his beloved a soft but firm kiss, and then he left his finger on her lips to seal them. "Shush," he whispered. "Just listen." The violinist continued to play, giving the couple a nod and a wink.

Iris struggled with herself. She had so many thoughts, so many things to show him. She did not want to miss the Doge's Palace and all those glamorous shops. But at the same time, she began to appreciate a certain sereneness that her beloved exuded.

A flock of pigeons flapped by, banked around the square, hooked back right towards them and coasted to a stop. Iris watched a large cocky male enlarge his throat three or four times its normal size. The neck reflected an iridescent green as he cooed and then imposed his bold chest onto an unwilling female. He gained a position to mount her, but she flew off leaving him standing there clearly dumbfounded. Simon caught most of this and smiled at Iris. They watched an old man in a tan striped suit, cane in hand, head bent, traverse the square. He had suffered a minor stroke and walked with a certain deadness to his right side.

Two girls holding hands in bright colored skirts raced past. Coming from the other way, an elderly lady with the smallest dog Iris had ever seen on a leash, tottered by.

Two musicians joined the violinist, one playing an accordion and the other a flute. Iris watched Simon listen to the mixture of sounds and also the voices of other travelers, and then she heard the wings of pigeons. It dawned on her that she had never really considered – that was the word, considered – the sound of wings beating with the orchestra, for it was an orchestra, although a very small one, the echoes of each of the instruments separately and together, bouncing off the buildings of the great piazza. She began to study Simon's face as he continued to stare serenely at this new and breathtaking environment, and as she did so, it seemed, at least to her, the world began to move more slowly. The people seemed as if they were crossing the square at a turtle's pace, or at separate turtle paces, in rhythms different than the one she was so used to.

As she watched and listened, she also began to connect the day to the night. She had been drawn to Simon right from the start, the way he worked so patiently on her father's broken car, where she was champing at the bit, wanting to go, go, go, and yet she also recognized her own patient deliberation during those nights when she took out her stepfather's telescope and watched the heavens. Sometimes she would be out in the night for hours and a servant would have to be fetched to drag her back in. Why was it, she realized, that she never lived her days the way she lived those nights? It was clearly one of the reasons she had been attracted to this man, a fellow who marched to his own rhythm, not caught up in the mindless chatter of the social world she was so enmeshed in. That is why she had decided to elope with him.

They did not have to stay in the hypnotic grasp of the social climbers, the shallow existence she felt whenever she was near to her father's sycophants. But she also recognized a seething ambition in Simon as well. He wanted to expand his brother's operation from automobiles to, my God, aeroplanes, to a new exciting but dangerous world where people die, but also a place of almost magical wonder, to be able to defy gravity and soar with the birds! He had done this, this man who could sit so serenely when they were in the most exuberant city in all of Europe.

She marveled as he looked over to her and spoke with no words. He wanted even more silence from her, even more, even more, even more.

She would obey.

"So that's where we are staying," he finally said, looking at a map of Venice that was printed on a placemat. She could see his mind reeling. "How far is Murano?"

"Once we get on the waterbus, we will be there in no time."

"And they are expecting us?"

"Simon, don't worry. Everything is set."

On the one hand, Simon did not like the idea that he had left all these big decisions to someone other than himself, a female no less, but another side of him completely trusted Iris, and that part of him reveled in the fact that he could actually find a mate, a partner, as she had called it, with whom he could rely, even depend on.

Their *vaperetto* passed a large sailing vessel which reminded Simon of a pirate ship, and then the craft moved out into open water and over to another group of islands really were not very far away.

Motoring into a large channel, the *vaperetto* pulled up to what looked almost like a railway station. "Murano," the driver called. Along with the throng, Simon and Iris disembarked.

"This is where they make Venetian glass," Iris said. "My uncle comes from a family that has lived in Murano for centuries. He will meet us and take us to the rabbi."

Uncle Alphonse stepped from a doorway just two storefronts down from the dock and stood silently. He watched as his niece and fiancé disembarked. "Iris," he waved.

Simon watched as she ran to him, moving in a flowing manner. He swept her off her feet and twirled her around before giving her a kiss as he held her before him.

"You've grown up so much," he said turning. "And this must be Simon." The men shook hands. "Follow me," Alphonse said.

"What about our bags?"

"Don't worry, my good man. They arrived a couple of hours ago safe and sound." He pointed to a brick wall bathed in late afternoon sunlight where their bags sat in plain sight. Simon gazed above several colorful potted plants to the sign that was hung there: Alphonse Alfonzo's Glassworks.

"Your place?"

"My place. But there is no crime in Murano. This is a small village and everyone knows each other. There is also a thriving Jewish community. We Jews have been traders and merchants here for centuries. Venice is the hub of Europe, and we are one of its suburbs. At one time, before all was combined to create the single state of Italy, Venice was the most powerful nation on the planet."

As he talked, Alphonse led them quickly down a series of ally-ways, over several bridges, and then along a narrow lane that ran along a canal which led to a small temple.

Simon was introduced to the Alfonzo clan, a Jewish merchant family who could trace their roots back 300 years, just in Venice alone. Iris' mother was a first cousin and each of the family members asked about her.

The chapel was austere, but it also had fantastic stained glass windows, multi-colored Hebrew letters, Jewish stars, images of old men at the wailing wall, a burning bush, and Moses on Mt. Sinai holding the Ten Commandments. Simon found himself transfixed by the weighty portrait. He took his place at the pulpit.

"My grandfather designed that one," Alphonse's son Pepé said. A youth of only 12, he had been designated best man.

"I've never seen such magnificent work," Simon said.

"We're all artisans here," said Pepé. "Grandpa remains the master."

"Master?"

"Glassblower and artisan, and he trains my father and his brothers and cousins, and he also trains me. Tomorrow I will show you."

The rabbi gave them a look to indicate that the service was about to begin. Two other uncles and two cousins held the chuppah, or canopy. The cantor began his ancient chant and then uncle Alphonse led the bride up to the alter.

Simon had fallen for Iris the very first time he had gazed upon her, that time her father's car broke down, and he felt a reawakening and a new level of palpitation when he met her again at her father's wedding extravaganza. But now, a new feeling came over him, one he knew he would never experience again with any other lady. The overwhelming feeling of love that overtook him caused him almost to stagger as it swept throughout every pour of his body.

Smiling and self-assured, Iris looked over at him. Surreptitiously, she raised and lowered her eyebrows and smiled. He found his eyes rooted on the folds of her delicate eyelids. He couldn't explain his fascination. He felt emotions well up and suddenly he collapsed in tears.

Iris understood. And through what could only be called a regal presence to her countenance, everyone waited patiently. Taking out a handkerchief, the rabbi handed it to Simon who blew loudly. *Honk!* A few people including the groom burst into laughter, Iris reached over and brushed a tear from Simon's face and then the rabbi began the marriage ceremony.

After a rousing night of dining and dancing, the couple decided to take a midnight stroll. The romance of Murano was contagious. They meandered down lanes and over bridges and simply lost track of time.

"These islands are so compact, I feel we will be seen as fools if we cannot find our way back to the inn."

"To consummate our marriage." Iris said matter-of-factly, mischievously.

"Yes."

Just then, a gondola appeared. It was Pepé. "Come, young lovers. I'll take you home."

Simon could not stop his heart from pounding, the two of them as Adam and Eve, under the sheets. He found himself lying alongside Iris, one leg draped over her thigh, his head on her chest, her nipples erect, her breasts just millimeters from his lips. Gently, she guided his head to them and he kissed each one, lingering, as his entire body quivered. She held him to her as tight as she could until his breathing slowed and he felt more at ease.

"I've never..." he began.

"Nor, have I," Iris said. "Just kiss me and see where we go."

Simon moved up to be on top of her and he pressed his body as close as he could. Her lips were soft and sensual, so much so, that he was in awe not only of her great beauty and receptivity, but of God's very act of creation. He felt blessed. They were nose to nose, Simon simply lost in her gaze.

"Where'd you get it?" Iris asked.

"What?" he asked.

"That iron poker between us. Did you steal it from grandpa?"

"I don't know where it came from," he perked, "but I know where it should go."

Iris guided the tip and brought him in. He entered a world that brought forth a vision of whirlpools and spinning colors, mostly of sparkles and purples. Their movements were never hurried as they melded through the long sweet night. Neither could quite believe the level of joy that they shared as one.

The sun burst through the window the following day, lighting up the entire room with a series of brilliant streams of yellow light. Iris lay on her back, her bare breasts exposed unashamedly. Simon kissed each one and moved to her lips. Her smile was so broad and delightful that he felt it competed with the very light from the sun.

"You get the closest shaves," he teased as he rubbed his cheek next to hers.

"Well, I wish I could say the same for you." She bantered in return, as she reached up with a gentle hand and stroked his morning stubble.

Pepé was waiting for them at breakfast. Impatient to show off the glassworks, they deliberately ate more slowly just to test him.

"If you take any longer eating," Pepé countered, staring at a pocket watch, "the master may be finished for the day."

"But it's only 10 a.m.," Iris offered.

"He begins at 4:30."

"In that case," Simon gulped the last of his coffee, grabbed Iris' arm and nudged her and Pepé outside.

"It will be faster by boat." The boy took them to a small motorized craft which got them to the glassworks in what seemed like two minutes.

Grandpa Alfonzo nodded for them to sit. The all-stone room was a mixture of coolness, almost dampness and also incredible warmth because the kilns were open and blasting heat. The master was twirling in the fire a large globule of glass which lay at the end of a long dark pipe easily two meters in length. He removed it from the heat and then began to blow and work it with a tool that seemed to be a combination of pliers and cutting instrument. Before their eyes, an elephant emerged. First came the ears and four legs and then he pulled the tusks and long sinewy trunk. The appendages were pulled so that it reared on its hind legs. The self-standing piece continued to be stretched and molded as the master continued to manifest numerous details, ridged patterns on the trunk, the folds under the eyes, the brush at the end of the tail with accents for the hoofs and tusks which were dipped in gold. The beast seemed to come alive, its proportions and expression nothing short of perfect.

"It's a wedding gift," Grandpa Alfonzo said, "which we will wrap and ship to your house so you won't have to worry about breaking it."

As Iris reached towards the object, grandpa shouted. "Don't touch. It's still quite hot!" Embarrassed, she retreated.

"Don't worry," Pepé chimed, "his blow-torch is worse than his bite!"

Everyone, including even grandpa burst into laughter. "Come," grandpa said, leading the couple from the building into a sunny courtyard where a grand lunch was prepared in the couple's honor. Three violinists serenaded with grandpa taking the first dance with the new bride. They stayed the night, but disembarked at first light.

"You must return and see us again," Pepé said. He led Iris and Simon to the *vaperetto* which took the couple back to Venice proper.

"This is for you," Iris handed Debora a silk shawl she had purchased in St. Marco's Square.

As was the style and custom of their ilk, the wives of Maxwell men were expected to dress in conservative attire, mostly drab browns, grays and blues. Debora had an eye for flair through her father and his brother, but like so many other ethnic women of her day, she feared standing out. "We walk in shadows," Elias' mother had told Debora early on, when the new bride had come in one day in a bright yellow dress and matching bonnet. She kept the outfit but never wore it again.

Dazzled by the myriad of colors that rippled through the fabric, Debora's eyes glistened. "Thank you," she repeated. "Thank you." Almost in a tender manner, she began to fold the scarf back up to pack it away, Elias silently nodding to her movements.

"Oh you simply must try it on," Iris said, ripping it from Debora's grasp and giving it a firm snap. "This is more than a scarf, Debora." Iris spun as she unfurled the piece.

"I had no idea it was so large."

"You can wear it as a shawl." Gently, Iris draped Debora's shoulders with the multi-colored fabric. It was a view of the canals during a flower parade.

"I never realized Venice was so splendid," Debora found herself saying. She caught a glimpse of herself in a mirror and then walked over boldly to get a better view. A something arose in her as she stared.

"You look like a gypsy," Elias' comment cut like a lawnmower through a bed of violets.

"Momma, why are you crying?" Abraham looked up at his mother, his head cocked in wonder and sympathy.

"Your papa wants me to be grim and proper."

"Elias," Simon said, "if you can not appreciate how lovely Debora looks in this new scarf, you should consider seeing that new psychologist gaining all that press in Vienna.

"Sigmund Freud," Abraham announced, turning sheepish when he saw his father's expression.

"I was being kind," Elias replied. "I could have said she looked like a..." he mouthed the word silently positioning his body so that Abraham hadn't a clue.

"And this is for you," Iris said, handing Elias a cigar-tip snipper. "Let's hope you don't reach for this at the wrong time," she deadpanned.

The silence lasted about 14 seconds before Debora got the joke and began to laugh. Simon too burst out in hysterics, and then young Abe began to cackle. "Papa, now you can clip momma's toenails," he managed, tears flowing down his eyes. Debora broke out into a big grin as Elias tried to keep up the façade. Debora draped Abe in the shawl and he wiggle-walked about the room, mimicking the geese that so often frequented the lawn.

As the little Maxwell circled the room, a thought began to dawn on him. "Hey," he said, "where's my gift?"

"We weren't able to find anything for you," Simon replied.

Disappointed, Abe was not quite sure if he believed his uncle. Simon was always bringing him something, a tchochka, a little toy, a strange shell or colored stone, but something.

"What's that?" Iris asked, pointing out the window as an aid for misdirection. Simon used the second to bring out a marionette of a boldly colored orange and black tiger. He hung it on the back of a chair right behind the boy.

"I don't see anything," Abe replied. "Where?"

Moving her eyes as if she were following a scurrying animal, Iris led her gaze back into the room and over to the chair right behind Abe.

"Oh," he said, initially startled. "A tiger."

"Yes," Iris said, and it's still alive."

"Is not."

"Is too."

"Is not."

"Is too," Iris declared. Grabbing the cross-piece handle, she made the puppet move. Using a bit of ventriloquism, the puppet, whose name was Jaguaro, spoke to Abe, and then Iris had it "walk" along the hallway. Having practiced for a few days for just this event, Iris held her audience spellbound as she caused the big cat to stalk, and leap, and lift a paw and turn back to eye her new nephew.

Amazed, Abe ran over to play with Iris and the puppet, and she showed him how to manipulate the strings. Debora left the room to tuck her scarf away and prepare tea with the housekeeper, Greta, leaving Elias to talk shop with his brother.

ROLF

Rolf Linzman knew his father was acting strange and he had an inkling why. He wasn't blind. He had seen that boy, yes, he was a man, but Rolf thought of him as a boy, in the airport, twice. And yes, he looked just like him! He had never gotten along with Marlina. She had never accepted him and he had begun to put two and two together.

He looked nothing like his blonde blue-eyed mother, Marlina Krupp Linzman, daughter of Otto Krupp, progeny of the great Krupp Cannon & Artillery dynasty, the largest producer of armaments in greater Germany. He never took to her, and she never took to him. They didn't think like each other and he never once got the feeling that he was loved by her, even all the way back to childhood, the cold buxom ice-goddess, walking around in her skimpy underwear, asking him to help her fasten her bra or clip her toenails, he hated her.

When she touched him, and it was only when there were other people around, a shiver went through him, as her family looked at him askance, trying to figure how a Krupp, married to a well-built fair-skinned blue-eyed Aryan like Gunter Linzman III, heir to MB Airways, could give birth to a Middle-eastern mite.

And when he had accidentally slammed her with the cricket bat, and she swore at him and called him a "dirty Jew," sure, he was only eight years old when it happened, still, he knew now, forty-something years later, that he had done it on purpose. Right on the side of the head! He had hit the ball, the couch, the pillows and her. *Thwack!* Marlina, for he could not call her "mom," had cared more for her cousins than she did for him. Pretending, always pretending that she cared, when he knew the truth, she wished him dead.

But he would deny her that wish, and live. He would use the Linzman name, although he never felt like a Linzman, and the Krupp connection, and play the game and prosper. And the more successful he became, the more he flaunted it in her face. Even as a tot, he would stay with her dutifully before her bath, when she wanted company, when she would sit at the window seat in just a towel and apply that God-awful smelling depilatory to her legs, pretending he couldn't see her crotch as she then asked him to wipe the white shit off, that piercing acrid smell that bit into his rhinencephelon, the wads of tissues coated with slimy leg hairs. How he hated it as he gritted his teeth, and brought her her skeevy stockings, helped her clip them onto the bottom of her girdle because she had a date with his poppa, her Guntie. He would do it all, put the silly clothes on she wanted him to wear with the matching plaid top and bottom shorts-set, comb his hair with that thick glop so he could form it into a dumb pompadour to make him look taller, and wear those stupid clip-on bow-ties and the suspenders that held up his socks, and uncle Petar's moth-eaten woolen underwear that itched, and smile and bow and shake the hands of all of her relatives who despised him. If she could play the game, so could he.

But Rolf was also haunted by who he really was. He would look in the mirror for endless moments comparing his features with that of his mother's father and try to find some point of comparison, try to figure out why he was an only child, and on top of that, one with the nose and complexion of a Semite, when every female Krupp other than his mother dropped blonde, blue-eyed babies like pfennings pouring from a Monaco slot machine. Families with three, four, five and more. All his Aryan kin. Talk about a black sheep! If he hadn't dared his first cousin Amy, to lick his private part when he was twelve and she was ten, he may very well have gone off the deep end. Because now he had a hold on the Krupp clan with "their" secret, "their" special way to enjoy his titillation at every family gathering whenever he and Amy could sneak away.

Through the years, they would become more bold in their pursuit of the illicit, touching each other under the table during dinner, bringing her to climax in sight of everyone, probing every orifice with their tongues during sleepovers, and when they were older, screwing as often as they pleased.

"I'm pregnant," Amy had told Rolf the very day he turned eighteen.

"Is it mine?" He would do to her what the family had done to him.

"How could you even ask?"

"How do I know?" he said, lying through his teeth.

"You fucking Jew bastard!" she had said, slamming him like a freight train full throttle.

Rolf thought back to that slap, the red imprint of her hand on his face that turned yellow and then purple, that knocked him to the ground, that kept him out of sight for weeks, that sense of total shame. And the kick that followed, that hit him squarely in the left nut, that sent a stabbing stinging pain that rippled through his scrotum and tore at the bottom of his gut, that stunted his manhood for months, nay, years and years on end. A permanent injury. She stopped his orgasms for what seemed like forever. And even later, years later, it still hurt, whenever he came. Was she ever even pregnant? He thought back. She had to have been. How could he lie to himself about such a thing? Self-deception, the story of his life. A doctor must have dealt with it. He never saw her that way again. Of course they would be in the same room at family functions and funerals. But he kept his distance. She was married soon after to an overweight lout, a Krupp manager, no less, that treated her like Queen Tit. And so he winced whenever Amy was simply in sight. That stabbing pain in his testicle reawakened. And she knew it, daggers in her eyes when she gazed his way, that look of utter contempt. The Aryan had crippled the Jew once again.

And it was then that he began to form the idea that he was a Jew, but how could he be? His father, Guntie, for that is what his friends called his old man, who, in fact, he did resemble, was always solicitous, even gentle with him. Putting up with a son's obnoxious ways. How he would use such foul language in mixed company or discuss masturbation in front of his aunts when they visited, how he would get drunk and get into car accidents and treat his dates like dirt, and to really rattle the cage, defend Stalin whenever they visited grandpa Krupp. "How did you ever tell Hitler from Charlie Chaplin?" he would ask the old bugger. Why would his father even care? Unless he really was his? But how could he be? Rolf had seen the birth pictures. Marlina *had* given birth to him. How many times did he have to hear the stories of how he was a breach baby, how they had to open her stem to stern to turn him around and bring him out. She would tell him that story it seemed every other month as she asked for company when she sat after her shower, still wrapped in that towel in her window seat to paint her toenails. "Dear, would you do the cotton?" And ever the perfect son, he would place the little soft white balls between each toe as she applied the nail polish with her tongue out and her pinky extended. He hated that medicinal odor of the polish. "All right, all right, you can leave," she would suddenly say. "Go, go, go." And out he would run as he heard one of her great farts that howled through the hallways, and her verbal explosion of "Oops," or "Ahhh."

He would run out of the house, out past the barn, and out through the woods, to his special place that overlooked the Iller River, by that odd gravestone that said "Simon Maxwell, loving brother, 1892-1918." A gravestone all by itself, situated by the massive oak tree, high on the rise, the one that could be seen from the river for miles. The tree where hawks the size of bowling pins rested. That's where he would sit and gain comfort. Just 26 when the Maxwell had died. He would stare at the tombstone and reflect as he looked at the image of the bi-plane that was etched above Simon Maxwell's name. He must have been a flyer, Rolf thought. But then, when he was fifteen, they moved away from Kempten, never to return, to Berlin, a city split in half by Germany's enemies. "At least we're on the good side," his father, Guntie, would say.

If it wasn't for his papa, Rolf didn't even want to think about how horrible his upbringing would have been. Because as rotten as he was, and he was rotten, spoiled and mean, his father was always there, protecting him. But why? He knew his father's love was genuine, but he resented it, and he couldn't help it. Mad at the world, he took it out on the one person that had ever shown him kindness, his father. But there was a reason. Rolf knew that his old man had a secret, this great CEO of MB Airways, Gunter Linzman III was hiding something. He guessed, a secret love, and it was this, this hidden thing that might tell him who he really was.

And now, with his virtual doppelgänger showing up in airports, at Gruuban's office, this Rudy Styne, New York City reporter, he was the key. Rolf knew it, but he also feared making contact. For he was now in a dangerous game, very dangerous, organizing a coup in Qawatar; what was he thinking? Competing with airlines like Delta and American who, themselves were purchasing oil refineries to keep their fuel costs down, that's what. But still, people had died, regimes had changed.

Nevertheless, Rolf now experienced the feeling of raw power, that it was *his* actions that altered history, that gave him a charge better than any roll in the hay. To control the lives of others, and make them all pay.

He was sure his father was deeply upset with him. Papa suspected. But didn't know for sure and that gave him a certain cushion. Yet, Rolf also knew deep down, that he had let his papa down -- big time. And now, his father was acting distant. A wall was growing between them that affected him more deeply than he ever would have suspected.

If he could succeed with Gruuban to take over Webnet and U-View and talk his father into completing Phoebus, their satellite production and launch company, they would then have email, phone and search capabilities that would be virtually omnipresent, a real rival to Microsoft, T-Mobile and Google combined. Then it would be worth it. He would gain back his father's respect and even get his mother to kiss his ass.

The problem was NTroodr, this entity, whoever he was, who knew his every move, who infiltrated his cell phone conversations and emails, who left his fucking little hints on purpose. And this meant that NTroodr also knew of his role in the Qawatari coup, and the cracker wanted Rolf to know he knew. People had been killed because of his actions. And what would really happen if papa found out?

"I just had a meeting with Heinz Gruuban, Rolf, and I'm not happy about it," Gunter Linzman said to his son.

"So I heard," Rolf replied. He was sitting in his father's Berlin office with his feet on the coffee table slouching back into the sofa. "I also heard you met my doppelgänger." Rolf stared fiercely into his father's eyes. He respected his father, but he was also constantly in competition with him, trying to increase on his own the market share of their company and pushing the envelope as far as it could go.

"Gruuban told me that it was you that was behind the coup, Rolf. That's not what you told me. I thought you were negotiating with the Sheik when this whole thing blew up, and now I find out you were the cause of it."

"So, what if I was?" Rolf said icily. "You know as well as I, we can't rely on the market to dictate fuel prices. But now, with our hands tied to the new powerbase at Qawatar, we should have total assurance that we can keep our costs down. And, if Gruuban secures Webnet, we will have a competitive advantage impossible to usurp."

"People were killed. Does that not matter to you?"

"As I understand it, papa, you and your grandfather were supplying Adolf Hitler with fighter planes during the war. The ultimate Nazi, am I right? Tell me there is no blood on your hands?"

Guntie looked at his son as a lifetime of thoughts tore through his mind. How could it be that the war had occurred so long ago, and yet it always seemed as if it were yesterday? And why was it that this Rudy Styne looked like Rolf? And then there was Abe Maxwell showing up after all those years. He had to be at least 95, Guntie calculated. He had thought Maxwell had been dead for fifty years! He needed to gain back the offensive.

"You raped your cousin Amy when you were 18, didn't you?"

"Is that what you have thought all these years?"

"I had to shield you. Everyone knew."

"We were lovers, papa. We fucked more times than Bayer has aspirin tablets. Raped! I used to finger her while we all sat around the Christmas table and sang winter carols. Hah! Why do you think we always sat together? Raped! Give me a break. You are really pitiful, old man."

"That's not what she said." Gunter tried not to let his son get to him.

"What can you expect from a Krupp? How many thousands of slaves did they kill? And anyway, what does that have to do with anything?"

"Your passions, you cannot control them."

"You're listening to a pack of lies from a bunch of mass murderers, upper crust ones, I'll grant you, but butchers nonetheless, who you know are liars, and you lecture me about controlling passion? How about truth, where does that fit in?"

"What the hell are you talking about, son?"

"Rudy Styne, Who is he? Is he yours, or not! How many children do you have?"

Guntie looked at Rolf. Now pushing 50, although intellectually brilliant, his son still had the emotional make-up of a three-year-old. Guntie didn't know what to do. He himself was not really sure who Styne was. Surely, he had to be an offspring, but how could that be? He was at least a full decade younger than Rolf, and he had been faithful to Marlina ever since her pregnancy. The old man held the answers. Gunter suspected the truth, but he had yet to spend time with Rudy Styne. And, even if he knew the truth, how could he trust Rolf, when he had raped his own cousin and now staged a coup in a small island nation? And yet, Guntie did not really know how to lie.

"Son," Gunter began, "there are things you do not yet know. Of course I have been aware of the trouble you have had with your identity for as far back as I can remember. But you are my son, and that is the truth."

"And what about momma? Am I her son, or not?"

"It's complicated, my boy. Momma gave birth to you. You know that, and she loves you in her own way."

"By letting me cut her toenails?"

"It has been hard on all of us, Rolf. But here, in this office, we don't talk toenails. We talk business, and we need to focus on some giant steps you want to take. I let you absorb a half–dozen of the smaller European airlines, I let you talk me into starting a satellite division. I met with Gruuban to discuss the Internet, and

I agreed that we would benefit if we were to partner with him once he lands Webnet and U-View. But I want the truth about Qawatar."

"What about Rockwell?"

"That has nothing to do with Qawatar! You have to understand, that's a merger I've been working on for 20 years. It would give us a central position in the American market, so we could get back to my passion, supersonic jet planes and the possibility of intercontinental commuter space flights."

"Yeah, yeah," Rolf interrupted coldly. "Berlin to LA in forty-five minutes. Even if it were feasible, papa, you think the American public is going to let a German concern control their space industry?"

"Rockwell is a public company, Rolf. We get enough stock, it's ours. Underneath, the American people understand that it was Germany who gave them their advanced propulsion systems in the first place. History says it was the Americans who got to the moon first, but we know better. It was German ingenuity, German know-how and German technology. I am simply positioning myself to reclaim our birthright. That is the dream that has haunted me ever since our crushing defeat at WWII."

"But you hated the Nazis. You told me that many times."

"I'm not talking about Nazis. I'm talking about Germany's sacred destiny. Have you never comprehended how much your father loves our scientists, Hendrik Lorentz, Max Planck, Otto Warburg, our flying aces, Max Immelman, Ernst Udet, Baron von Richthofen, Melitta von Stauffenberg, Willy Messerschmidt and interplanetary visionaries like Werner von Braun. It was our technology behind America's great rise in the 1950's. There would have been no space race without German brainpower!"

Rolf had seen his father angry before, but this was something different, a certain intensity that his father had never really revealed before. He decided to stir the pot. "Then how is it that you married a Krupp? That family was one of the first backers of Adolf Hitler. They've hated every political and social cause you have ever cared for. Even I know you feel guilty about the Jewish thing. So why a Krupp?"

"Your great grandfather played a role. He believed in Hitler, and because of that, you and I are here today. Though humble in his beginnings, he ended up wining and dining Otto Krupp and I fell in love with his daughter. It was as simple as that. I was blind to the rest."

"And I'm her son? You really want me to believe this?"

"You have to give me time, Rolf. You've been spoiled from the day you were born. You've been an ungrateful and immature brat for most of your life. And you've got a deadness about you. I've given you some freedom at MB, and now I find you've used your influence and the power of my name to overturn a government. Have you really lost your mind? We are talking about people's lives here. We could be brought before The Hague."

"I hadn't thought of that," Rolf admitted.

"Well, now you have. We need to iron out a lot of things before I open myself up to the likes of you."

Guntie knew, the second it left his mouth, that he had said it wrong. He wanted the moment back, to change the wording, just a momentary slip, but it was too late. Rolf was out the door before he could say, "I'm sorry, let's talk this out." and now what was he going to do?

The big issue for Guntie was MB's exposure in the Qawatar imbroglio. What was Rolf thinking? Guntie would have to make a few calls, but he also thought he might have to hide certain financial transactions and create, if he had to, an alibi for his son, and maybe even one for himself, too.

AERIAL RACE

Simon traveled weekends to Göttingen to test various aerodynamic designs in von Karmen's wind tunnel. He met with Junkers who agreed to fund research on his curved wing if MB Airways would agree to share any discoveries that might be patentable.

"Hugo Junkers is a man of his word, Elias," Simon told his brother now six weeks into the project. Uncle Adolf was also present. "No single individual is going to own a monopoly in this field, and if we create an alliance now with Junkers, we will have an in with a man who is likely to become the largest aeroplane manufacturer in Europe."

"What about Fokker?"

"The Kaiser talks of marrying them, but Fokker is Dutch by birth, so the Kaiser doesn't have much leverage. His best option is simply to keep him interested."

"Junkers is also not German."

"I know, Ellie, but either way, we would be best to go in with him, rather than Fokker who is much more unpredictable. Also, Junkers has deep pockets, and if we should succeed, we may also end up supplying patented parts to Fokker...."

"And the French, if we are lucky."

"I like the bi-planes," von Rosensweig offered.

"They're sturdy, that's for sure, uncle Adolf. But the more wings, the greater the drag. Von Karmen agrees that the monoplane streamlined is best to take advantage of minimizing boundary layer drag."

"You're losing me, Simon," Elias said. "Do what you want. But you must promise that you will not sacrifice safety for speed."

"I've got to keep the plane light if I want to win."

"You are missing the point, Simon," von Rosensweig took over. "We are letting you enter this race, but Elias and I have talked seriously about this. It is much more important that our plane finish the race. Stability and trustworthiness must be the key. Let the daredevils go for the speed record."

"But, uncle Adolf, why else..." Simon protested.

"Simon, I will close your shop tonight. This is non-negotiable. Men may die three months from now." Elias paused. "Let me be blunt. "Winning the race is not, I repeat, not our primary goal."

"Elias, I don't understand. What is the point if I cannot try to win?"

"The point is to see all of these other planes in action. The point is to participate, shore up our alliance with Junkers, or Sopwith in Britain, or Nieuport in France if you can. Think about it. The winner will have his little day in the sun, but what about tomorrow? He will have to top that speed and so on. Our goal is to gain a contract with the Kaiser to build, say four to six aeroplanes that will be reliable to deliver the mail. Speed must take a back seat to dependability."

"Simon," uncle Adolf added his piece, "Listen to your brother. Our goal is not to win, but to finish with a plane that will be viewed as sturdy. If Farnam or leBlanc...."

"Or that daredevil Garros..."

"Yes, Garros, want to go for speed or altitude, let them. You are to play this cautiously," Adolf continued. "Finishing is winning. That is to be our motto."

"I just don't understand him," Elias said at the dinner table. "I've given him everything he has asked for, and all I want is for him to be cautious."

"He's headstrong," Debora said. "Do you like the brisket? It's a family recipe from Mrs. Dieter."

"The meat market, momma?"

"The grocery store and meat market, my little one."

"It's got tomatoes in it, doesn't it?" Elias guessed.

"It's always got tomatoes in it," Debora said. "The secret ingredient, that's what I'm asking about."

"It's a fruit," Abe said, tongue to the top of his lip. "Apple juice."

"Right!" Debora said.

"How is it that you don't go to the Kosher deli?" Elias asked.

"Oh, I do, sometimes. I'm not a fanatic, Elias, I just like Dieter's. There always seems to be something new and interesting there."

"Delicious," Elias said, a rare twinkle in his eye.

"What are you so happy about?"

"Papa just sold Mrs. Dieter's husband a Daimler luxury automobile. Right papa?"

"He'll buy one every year. Momma, pass the gravy, would you."

"Yes, dear," Debora said to her husband.

Wrench in hand, Simon looked up as Iris approached. He was making final adjustments to the gas line. "What are you wearing those for?"

"Simon, you told me headgear and goggles are necessary, and I'm certainly not going to go up without a flight jacket or without my Harriet Quimby flight boots!"

"Your Harriet Quimby flight boots! Iris, I simply can't let you go up."

"Simon, this is not a matter for discussion."

"But it is dangerous up there. You could get hurt."

"Even killed, Simon?"

"Of course. It's out of the question."

"Because why?"

"Because you could die."

"I'm not sure I'm following you. Why should that be a consideration?"

"You want to die?"

"That's a risk I'm willing to take."

"I forbid it."

"On what grounds?"

"Because you are my wife. Because I love you. Because I could never forgive myself if anything ever happened to you."

"Maybe I'm dense, Simon. But I've still yet to understand your point. You're worried that something may happen to me so I cannot fly?"

"Yes, exactly."

"I'm willing to take the risk. I have already told you this."

"But what would I do without you?"

"Ah hah!" Iris' eyes sparkled as she approached the plane and placed one foot up onto a tire. "So, it is really not my death that you are so concerned with so much as that you would be lost without me. Do I have it right?"

"Iris. You're putting words into my mouth. This is still a very dangerous sport. Three aviators were killed at the Paris to London meet just last year, and six more were badly injured."

"And out of the 43 planes that entered the race, only 14 made it to the finish line."

"Yes. That is right. How do you know this?"

"Because I know everything about how dangerous this is. Can't you see what I'm trying to say?"

Iris walked directly up to her husband and faced him squarely eye to eye. "I'm going up with you. And if you tell me it's too dangerous once more or that maybe I will be killed, I will forbid you from ever flying again."

"You will forbid me! Have you lost your senses?"

"Are you so obtuse, Simon? Is that what it is, or are you so selfish that you cannot see that you simply have no choice? If you want to pursue this, this...." Iris searched for a word, "outrageous and foolhardy adventure, a path that adds years to my life every day, every moment you take flight, then you must simply understand that I am being tortured. Can I stop you from being an airman? Can I?"

"No."

"Then we must do this together. You want to enter this year's Aeronautique Internationale, am I right?"

"Of course. You have known all along this is my goal."

"Munich to Rome to Athens to Cairo and back again through Istanbul."

"Well, yes."

"And how many planes are being entered?"

"I don't know, maybe 65."

"And how many will complete this race?"

"How can I know that?"

"Well, you told me just last year 25% of the flyers were injured or killed and nearly 75% of the planes entered either crashed or were unable to complete the route."

"That was last year, dear. We have made tremendous progress in a year. My guess is that...." Suddenly, Simon stopped.

"Go on," Iris goaded. "Go on. You've made progress. So out of the 65 planes, will you say half will finish?"

"That's still a bit optimistic."

"How many?"

"Perhaps thirty-five, forty percent."

"And how many will crash and die, Simon. How many? Five? Three? Two? Will it be one out of every twenty flyers that will die?"

"Hopefully there will be no fatalities."

"Hopefully?"

"Yes, hopefully."

"I'm going up with you on this test run."

"Iris, we have already had this discussion. I forbid it."

Simon stepped into the cockpit as Gunter spun the propeller. His fourteen-year-old son, Gunter Jr. stood by and watched. Iris gave the boy a thumb's up sign and a big grin, and the boy grinned back. "Are you strapped in?" Simon asked and Iris turned back and shouted "Yes."

"Then we're off."

The plane sputtered down the runway until the propeller began to build up momentum and the vehicle picked up speed. Iris felt as if she were in a racing car, when suddenly there was an enormous burst of power and, *Whoosh!* up it rose.

Iris shouted, nearly shrieked for joy. There they were, above Elias' big factory, above the worker cottages that lined the road, above the Iller tributary as it flowed past the Maxwell estate, and on to the river, which they followed past the town of Kempten, and then Simon hooked back towards Fussen. Flying low, following rolling fields dotted with vast patches of farmland, Iris saw in the distance a series of mountains jutting up with two castles prominently positioned on the first major hill.

"Mad King Ludwig?" she shouted back to Simon.

He nodded yes and steered the craft over the lower castle, Hohenschwangau, which was yellow in color and squared off, and then he banked up the mountain, following the spiral staircase-like road, to the eye-popping fairytale palace in blue at Neuschwanstein. Designed for Ludwig in the late 1800's to capture the flavor of a medieval palace fit to house the Holy Grail, with its numerous parapets, draw-bridges and spires, Neuschwanstein was set high, perfectly visible from Pöllat River Gorge which it overlooked, as well as the great plain that Simon had followed to get there. Iris reached over to Simon's shoulder, leaned her head on her extended arm and wept.

"Time to go home," Simon shouted back.

All Iris could do was simply nod in agreement, her eyes filled with a thankfulness that filled her husband's heart.

SIMON'S ASSISTANT

"Cecil Sneedmore. Yes, I know of the Sneedmore engine," Elias said as he stood by his desk awkwardly wondering why Simon had brought a foreigner to the plant.

"And the Sneedmore circular biplane," Cecil said proudly.

"Yes, of course. Well, very nice to have met you," Elias tried to turn his attention back to some papers on his desk.

"He flew it all the way from East Church," Simon said.

"England?!" Elias looked up. He saw a swarthy man prematurely balding, with tufts of hair sprouting above his ears and an enormous set of sideburns that melded into a big handlebar moustache. Formally, they shook hands. "Here? You flew it across the Channel and all the way through France and Switzerland?" Elias was astounded.

"It was slow going, but yes. It took me two weeks."

"Two weeks! You'd have been better taking a train," Elias humphed. But he was intrigued. "And it is here, in Kempten?"

"Yes. Your brother has asked to go up for a ride."

"Across the English Channel you say?"

"Yes."

"Well, I don't understand. If you could fly the channel, how could it take you two weeks?"

"Repairs, mainly. Also weather conditions. I lost nearly three days on the Swiss border."

"How did you manage the Alps?" Simon asked.

"I didn't, of course. I flew the valleys. Wind shears took me down on two occasions, and I had to wait for supplies from East Church." Cecil looked out the windows to the west as if he were trying to see England. He wore a heavy brown leather flight jacket, high boots and trousers that flared out at the thighs. Hanging off his shoulders was his leather headgear and goggles, and he also had a pair of flight gloves which were hooked to a belt loop. A lanky fellow, mostly elbows and knees, Cecil had sunken cheeks and a round snout that resembled the nose of a clown, as it sprouted from between his great moustache.

"And you came here for what purpose?"

"I've hired him, Elias. I talked to you two months ago about this."

"Now Simon, we are always talking about hiring mechanics, but that's a far cry from inviting a man from half way around the globe...."

"He's only from England. Why don't you look at the craft before you make us both sorry," Simon tried. "Come on, Ellie. Show Mr. Sneedmore your new MB roadster."

"I'm very impressed with your factory, Mr. Maxwell," Sneedmore said. "It's so tidy, and the workers, they all look so efficient."

"Looks can be deceiving, Mr. Sneedmore. Come then. We'll ride to Simon's hangar and take a look at your whirligig."

A manservant brought the car around. Elias took the driver's seat and Simon fooled his brother by sitting in the back with his guest. Elias realized he'd been made the fool to look the part of the chauffeur, but he didn't mind, and in fact felt safer with his brother to look out for him while a stranger sat behind in the back seat. He had never heard of the Sneedmore motor, let alone the Sneedmore Whirligig, but he was not about to let this foreigner know this.

As the vehicle approached the hangar, Elias got sight of the monstrosity Sneedmore had designed to fly across Europe in. The aeroplane, if you could call it that, had its motor situated behind the pilot. The front wheels were angled out, and there was also a set of back wheels so the contraption did look sturdy when on the ground. What perturbed Elias were the so-called wings. The vehicle looked more like a squashed bagel than an aeroplane. "And you flew all the way across Europe to meet me in this?"

With a perfect scaled down model of a Nieuport painted blue, held high in one hand, little Abe stood on the kitchen chair to pontificate. Moving the model in a flying motion, he took Elias by surprise, interrupting his father's daily ritual of studying through his monocle the morning paper as he ate breakfast. "Count von Zeppelin," Abe began, "was born in Baden in 1838 and served as a liaison between the King of Württemburg and the Union Army during the American Civil War. It was at that time that the Count first went aloft in military observation balloons. Nearly forty years later he constructed his own. Zeppelin's greatest contribution was twofold. One," he held up one finger, "to implement a design of rigid construction, and two, to create separate chambers to hold the hydrogen."

"How do you know all of this?" Elias asked.

"I read it in this book Tante Ella brought me," Abe replied.

"You have a brain, child," Tante Ella said knowingly. "Elias, you remember your cousin Wilson?"

"Little Willie. Yes, I remember. He used to throw matzoh balls at me during Passover."

"Do you remember that he also memorized the entire Torah?"

"Yes, I remember," Elias said.

"Word for word," Debora and Abe jumped in having heard the story a dozen or more times.

"You can all make fun, but he had the gift like this little one." She reached down and gave Abe a gentle kiss which affected him in an odd way. He looked into her eyes. There was a delicate regal beauty to the thin crinkles of translucent skin that created her eyelids and laugh lines. Abe felt he could see right through this thin covering to see his great aunt's very lifeblood pulsing inside her cranium.

"And where is cousin Willy now great aunt?"

"He works in a patent office," she replied, her eyes wistful.

"What is a patent office?"

"It's a place where people register their inventions."

"You mean like uncle Simon's valve cover for your automobile engines, papa?"

"Yes," Elias replied. "So Tante Ella's favorite cousin Willy spends half his life memorizing the ideas of others. Forty-one years old, with the brain capable of enormous feats of memory and he's never once come up with a thought of his own."

"He logs other people's thoughts, that is true Elias. But he has been very valuable to that office."

"And what do they pay that great genius? A clerk's salary, that's what! It is a tragic waste. You listen to me my little brainchild."

"Yes, papa."

"I want you to give me a new thought every week."

"What is that?" Abe stood there dumbfounded. As smart as he was, his young mind simply could not yet grasp the abstract idea.

"Something new," Elias barked, "not someone else's thoughts. Not thousand-year-old facts about someone else's life, like the Count, which is very interesting, I do agree, but still, that is someone else's thoughts. Someone else's life. I don't want you to end up like your cousin Willy, memorizing endless reams of minutia, being little more than a glorified replacement for a filing cabinet."

"*Whaaaaaa!*" Abe began to wail, the tears streaming from his eyes like great rivers.

"Now you've scared him!" Tante Ella chastised.

"I only wanted him to do something," her nephew paused and then continued the sentence, "original."

"*Whaaaaaa!*"

Flying from the kitchen came Debora. "I leave you alone with Abe and Tante Ella for two minutes and you've gotten the boy to tears. Are you proud of yourself?" She glared at Elias.

"*WHAaaaahhh!!!*" Abe now began to scream and wail so loudly that he managed to scare himself, and so the crying continued to escalate. Debora swept the boy into her arms and began to cradle him against her body as he kicked and screamed and tried to push his mother away.

"You never learn!" Debora lit into her husband as she continued to cradle the child and stormed from the room.

"What did I do?" Elias lifted both hands.

"He's barely past the age of six," aunt Ella said, "and you are treating him like he's a man." Ella moved into the sunlight to nestle herself into her favorite sofa. Curling her knees up and slipping off her shoes, she tucked her feet under the far pillow.

"Well then, how am I supposed to treat him?"

"Hug him. Play with him. And don't worry that he'll turn into cousin Willy."

"But I'm concerned. What a total waste," Elias spat. "Wilson's father thought he was going to raise the next Spinoza. Willy this and Willy that. It was all he ever talked about, and all I remember is what a little monster he was."

"And why was that?"

"Because they catered to his every whim. They thought he was their ticket to glory and riches. I don't want that for Abe."

"What do you want for him?" Aunt Ella spoke with great sincerity.

"To come up with his own thoughts. If I wanted a parrot, I could have gone to Trieste and brought one back."

"You saw parrots in Venice?"

"I said Trieste. But yes, there was an animal store there. They had little parrots too, the size of sparrows and more beautiful fish than you could ever imagine. Debora had to practically drag me out of there."

"Well, I can tell you this Ellie, you keep chastising and scaring the boy, that's just what you're going to end up with."

"I don't know what you mean." Elias asked, truly stunned.

"All he wants is a little attention. Some love and attention. You want him to have original ideas, then you come up with some of your own and show him." Aunt Ella sat back and gave Elias one or her stares.

"That's Simon's forte," Elias shot back. "I build businesses and make money. My little brother is the idea man."

"Where is Simon?" Ella asked.

"He's working like crazy with that English fellow Sneedman."

"More," Debora corrected, having returned. Abe had gone up to his room to play with yet another aeroplane model he was building.

"Sneedmore, whatever. He and Simon want to enter an aeroplane in the next race."

"Isn't it awfully dangerous?"

"Auntie, that's exactly what I told them. Four aeronauts died in the last race. That's four brothers or sons."

"Or fathers," Debora said.

"And for what?" Elias asked rhetorically. "The airship is so much more safe and reliable."

"Simon says that the future is in aeroplanes," Debora reflected.

"I admit he is sometimes right, and Sneedmore corroborated..."

"Man," aunt Ella wryly poked.

"Sneedmore? You're joking with me?"

"That's not allowed?" Tante Ella cracked with a smile.

"Whatever," Elias said, "the British fellow with that nose that glows in the dark, with those god-awful sideburns and moustache. He said that Great Britain is building hundreds of planes. We have to keep up."

"What does the Kaiser think?" Ella asked.

"The Kaiser is still fully behind von Zeppelin. But his brother is interested in aeroplanes now that Krupp has built anti-Zeppelin cannons."

"No!" Debora reacted viscerally.

"There's no stopping the Krupps when it comes to killing machines. But that's good for us, because it's much more difficult to hit a plane, so government funding remains a possibility."

"But, Elias, if they fund you, won't you lose your autonomy?" aunt Ella asked.

"It's a problem. You're not as dumb as you look, auntie."

"Coming from you, I'll take that as a compliment," Ella said matter-of-factly.

*   *   *

"We could fly the plane there," Simon was bent over a table in the conference room studying a map.

"That's out of the question," Elias replied. "You said the wings fold back. That means we can ship by rail."

"But that still leaves us nine kilometers from the starting gate." Simon took out a pointer, walked over to the map and showed his brother the race: Munich to Rome to Athens to Cairo to Istanbul and back to Munich, with stopovers where necessary, such as on Crete or Tobruk on the down leg and Cypress or Belgrade on the back leg.

"How many aeroplanes are in this race?"

"Fifty-seven, old man," Sneedmore interjected in English. "Eight have dropped out."

Elias preferred to speak German to Sneedmore, but the Brit persisted in English. Where Elias saw this as an attempt to imply some sense of dominance, Simon saw it as an opportunity to practice speaking another language. A chance to express bitterness, versus a moment of opportunity -- that was the difference between Elias and Simon.

"Obviously, we will assemble at the railway station and fly to the starting gate," Sneedmore interposed.

It was the air about him that seemed to imply that he, Sneedmore, a mere mechanic and designer, was the owner of the craft. That is what irked Elias.

"Let's see that log once again."

"Oh, that can wait," Simon changed the subject a little too rapidly and Elias, ever diligent, picked up on it. "I will see it now."

"Elias, we've changed the plane's name to the Maxwell-Sneedmore monoplane."

"Why a monoplane and not a bi-plane?" Elias jabbed.

"To reduce wind resistance," Simon said.

"Bleriot's got the one to beat, and it's a monoplane," Sneedmore again spoke in English.

"Is Sopwith in a monoplane, too?" Elias asked.

"No, he's apparently married to the bi-plane, Elias."

"I'm Mr. Maxwell to you, Sneedmore. Now, let me understand this again. How much capital have you invested in this Maxwell-Sneedmore monoplane?"

"Capital? Why, you're paying me, old man!"

"Well, when you come up with 1400 pounds," Elias began in perfect English, reached over with a pen to vigorously scratch Sneedmore's name out from the new logo, and then reverted back to German, "then you can get your name on one of our aeroplanes." Elias gazed back to Simon with a look of disbelief and then shifted to one of those stares that bore holes through people.

"And what if we win?"

"You get a 5% share, Sneedmore. which I won't deduct from the expenses involved to ship the plane, lodge the two of you and fund the re-fueling booths on the two continents this race is going through."

"But," Sneedmore began.

"I'll tell you what, Sneedmore. You win this race and I'll up your stake to 7.5% of the winnings on the next race, and then you'll have the funds to purchase nearly 25% of the next plane you race in. That's of course if you don't spend it." Elias managed a wink at Simon on his exit.

"He's such a bore," Sneedmore said weakly.

"Oh, and another thing," Elias popped his head back into the hangar. "Sopwith's on a monoplane. I spoke with him and Horace Short just this morning," switching to English, "on the Arco-Slaby wireless."

"You went to the wireless station!" Simon exclaimed, "and didn't take me?!"

"You were flying with Sneedmore." Elias reached into his coat pocket and flipped a rolled up newspaper onto the table:

Professor Slaby Speaks by Wireless
To Aeroplane Designers In England

"Slaby thinks we can get a radio phone on board the craft," Elias spoke English in a proper British accent. "I've invited him down after the race. Tah, tah." Elias disappeared again and Sneedmore, to Simon's great relief, laughed.

"Your brother's quite the card, isn't he!"

"I've always thought of him as the King of Diamonds."

"And how does he see you, Simon?"

"Oh, as a Jack, probably."

"Of Diamonds?"

"Heaven forbid. It's usually Spades, as I'm always the one who's doing the heavy lifting!"

"Then, why do you stand for it?"

"I have a roof over my head. I pay the bills. But most importantly, through him I have, I mean, we have the funds to build this Maxwell-Sneedmore monoplane!"

"You mean you will put my name back on?"

"Not on your life!"

"Hah!"

Abe looked out the large set of windows and watched the landscape roll by. He held his model Maxwell-Bavarian I monoplane against the pane. One could still see part of the word "Sneedmore" painted over in yellow on the fuselage. The wings were yellow as well, with green stripes, and the cockpit was painted green. Although his first trip aboard a train, Abe couldn't help but fantasize that he was really flying, and that it was he that was soloing his uncle's monoplane, not his uncle Simon. He sat deeply into the big leather sofa of their first class compartment and nuzzled against aunt Ella with his momma on his other side, sitting across from his poppa.

"Where are the boys?"

"They're back with the plane, Debora."

"They're each afraid to let it out of their sight," Tante Ella added.

"Can I go back there, papa?"

"I'm sorry, son. It's too dangerous and there's no heat. You'll see the plane when it comes off the train."

"But I can stay warm by hiding in Sniggerly Sneedmore's sizeable sideburns."

"Shush, Abe," Elias cautioned.

Abe searched for another topic. "What's an armadillo, momma?"

"Why, I'm not sure. Elias, do you know?"

"I think it's a small animal like a rat."

"Why would Mr. Whitworth call his plane a rat, papa?"

"It's not a rat, dear." Tante Ella joined in. "It's much larger, about the size of a raccoon, and it's completely encased in an armor coating. I saw a number of them when I went to the United States in '93."

"That's right, you were at the Chicago World's Fair. I'd forgotten," Debora said. "That's when Stigey was alive."

Ella turned to her grandnephew. "Oh, my little Abraham, I'm sorry you never met my husband."

"But I did, great aunt. Last night I saw him in my dream." Like a ferret, Abe darted for Ella's handbag and pulled out a small photo album she always kept with her. "This was him, in that same hat!" He pointed to a congenial gentleman with a gleam in his eye, who wore a weathered fedora cocked back and to the side like an American cowpoke.

"Yes, that's right," Tante Ella said.

"His eyes sparkled in my dream, just like this picture, auntie."

A subtle but desperate urgency took over Ella's face. She tried to speak nonchalantly. "Did he talk to you?"

"Yes, he did great aunt."

"And what did he say?"

"He said that when you cut the carrots into my soup, you will cut them the size of...."

"Kopeks!" Ella finished his sentence.

"Yes, Kopeks."

Following the story, Debora nodded to Elias who frowned in return.

Tante Ella looked once again at Abe. "How did he look?"

"He looked happy. He was smiling, and let me touch his grey silver hair. It was thin, not rough and wet like papa's."

Aunt Ella turned to hide her tears.

"Are you hurt, great aunt?"

"No dear," she managed before she totally broke down.

"Oh, what absolute rubbish," Elias said. "He had a dream and you act like Christ Almighty came down from the heavens."

"Elias, you know nothing," Tante Ella poked back. "The plane is called an armadillo because Mr. Whitworth has used a great deal of metal to protect its hull."

"You mean like the armadillo protects itself?"

"Yes, my god-child. There were four of them at the zoo in New York."

"How was the great fair?"

"Oh Abe. That was so long ago. They recreated Venice, and it was the first time I had ever seen electric lighting."

The door to the compartment slid open, and Iris entered, her face flushed in red. "Did I miss anything?" Iris' eyes were glistening from the tear-stains caused by the cold.

"How are the boys?" Debora asked.

"Not as cold as I was! I thought I could stick it out with them, but after the hot cocoa was gone and I had to, as Sneedmore said, use the loo..."

"He's such a turkey, isn't he!"

"Debora, he's worse than that." Iris took a seat next to Abe, as Debora moved across to sit next to Elias. Unconsciously, Iris grabbed Abe's hand as a way to warm her own. She rubbed his fingers vigorously and continued, "All he talks about is the 4,000 quid he hopes to win in the race, 'to show Evil Elias.' That's what he calls you, Elias. I know he's joshing, but still. It's you who are funding this venture, and Simon and I are very grateful."

"I hadn't heard that one!" Elias responded. "I hope we do win, as he'll just have to give the money right back to purchase a share in Simon's enterprise. Hah!"

"And when does Simon get his share?" Tante Ella popped in.

"In time, dear aunt. Let's see how they do first. Unless they are also willing to also share in the losses. Are you Iris?"

"I'm not a businessman, Elias. I trust your judgement as my loving brother-in-law."

"That would make you my father's wife's great aunt's through marriage nephew's sister-in-law," Abe calculated.

"Or wife," Iris said.

At this, Abe broke up into hysterical laugher and like laughter of this kind, it was infectious. First Debora broke and then Tante Ella began to chuckle, then Iris joined in. But when Tante Ella moved into a cackle, and Abe began to point at her, even Elias could not contain himself any longer. "Oh, my side, my side is aching," Debora managed. Abe saw his opening and moved over to his mother and poked that side. She tried to retaliate as he giggled, but he had the edge. "Stop, stop. I'm going to pee my panties. Stop. Stop," she shrieked and then jumped up and flew out of the compartment. They all tried to restore a measure of decorum upon her return, but once Abe said, "Sniggering Sneedmore," they all broke up again.

As Simon and Sneedmore worked with four handymen to unload the plane and unfold the wings back into position, Elias called over a carriage and took the ladies and Abe to the hotel.

Unpacking the luggage, Abe was able to retrieve his scrapbook where he had pasted in newspaper and magazine photographs of many of the planes and pilots involved and also pertinent statistics.

"Papa, this is Mr. T.O.M. Sopwith, and here is Vikers and Bleriot. That's Orville Wright, oh and there's Horace Short."

"Do you have a picture of the Baron?"

Elias was referring to Baron leForest, who was sponsoring the race. Elias had not yet met the man so was interested to see how the Baron looked. "Who's he with?"

"That's Patrick Alexander, papa."

"He's older than I thought. You know, Abe," his father said, "he's the first man to jump out of a balloon using a parachute."

"He's not the first, papa."

"Well, he's one of the first to do it and not crack his skull…. Where's our plane?"

"Right here, papa." Abe turned to the back of the scrap book where he displayed nearly ten photographs of what Abe had listed as the Maxwell-Sneedmore monoplane. Elias was going to correct him and then, remembering Tante Ella's injunction, thought the better of it.

"When can we go to the aeroport, papa? I want to get signatures of all the designers."

"What about the pilots?"

"Both, papa. Many are both anyway."

"Bright and early tomorrow morning. But come, we should go back to the train station and check on uncle Simon."

"And sniggering Sneedmore?"

"Shush! Now, we've had our fun, but you mustn't ever say that again, Abraham. You don't want to hurt Mr. Sneedmore's feelings."

"Only if he doesn't snigger at me papa."

"Enough. Come on. Anyone else?"

"I'm coming," Iris shouted as Ella and Debora waived the invitation off. They would rest and take in a shop or two near the hotel.

AERODROME

The sun was just cracking the horizon when the Maxwell roadster took the family out to the aeroport. Even Elias looked on in awe as his brother's plane soared overhead on its way to the starting gate. The race wasn't for another two days, but this part, for Elias, was more important – making contacts, finding out who the competition was, seeing who he could do business with.

The Short brothers had a wing design that even Sneedmore was envious of. If Simon thought it was the best design, Elias would rather do a deal. MB had a light motor and a patented valve cover, they had an in with Daimler, and a patent pending on a tail rudder. A swap could be the best way to go. And the beauty of it from Elias' point of view, was that Short was British. This would give MB a design edge outside of Germany.

Simon and Sneedmore looked down below and waived frantically. For the fun of it, Simon banked and simulated an easy spiral fall as he circled the automobile and sailed the plane towards the landing field. "Holy smokes," he shouted to his teammate.

Barely able to hear him, Sneedmore nevertheless gave Simon the thumb's up sign, for there below were more aeroplanes than each had ever seen before, and so many different designs.

Although the majority were monoplanes, there were also nearly a dozen bi-planes, three or four tri-planes two with flappable wings, five with propellers situated behind the pilots, Gordon Bell's whacky circular flying machine, the Armstrong-Whitworth Armadillo, which looked too bulky to the immediate eye to give the impression that it could ever get off the ground, two planes that looked like bicycles with wings, one whirligig, nothing like Sneedmore's, that had to have been put out there as a joke, and one behemoth with a stack of 8 wings that looked like someone had taken a fuselage and welded to it a giant set of Venetian blinds.

Soon after Simon taxied his craft to his numbered docking gate, Elias motored his automobile into the aeroport. Abe marveled at the thousands of spectators. Although officials had roped an area where the planes were situated and there was a large imposing *Verboten* sign, Elias handed an official an entrée document and thus was able to take his family on a tour of the facilities.

Much like a lord, little Abraham marched out, dressed in his brand new light brown pin-striped three-piece suit and yellow bowtie. Totally absorbed in the moment, he wandered to a small crowd that stood around a tall man who somewhat resembled a walrus, with his big round shoulders and very large moustache.

"Where's Abe?" Debora said.

"I though he was with you," Elias shot back.

"I'm sorry," Iris said, taking some of the blame. "I also thought he was with you."

Becoming frantic, Debora started to run in three directions at once, shouting into the large crowd, "Abe! Abe!"

Elias gripped her arm. "Hush, Debora. You're making a scene. He's a bright little lad, and we will find him. He's probably standing like a statue entranced by one of the planes near by."

Debora looked over at Iris, a pleading look in her eye. "I'll start with the closer docking stations," Iris said. "You should stay here, Debora. This is where he knows we are."

"Momma! Momma!" Debora looked up. Bobbing above the sea of heads, little Abe seemed to float towards them. As he came closer, it became apparent that he was sitting on the shoulders of a tall man with moustache so large that it seemed to part the people as he approached.

"Mr. Maxwell?" he said to Elias, lifting the boy down and extending a hand.

"Yes, Elias Maxwell. My brother is Simon Maxwell, who has entered the race in our new Maxwell monoplane."

"It's Henry Taroon, momma. The British pilot. He gave me his autograph and let me sit in his cockpit."

Debora pulled the man to her, and kissed him on the cheek. "Thank you. Thank you," she said.

"I should try and find more young lost lads if this is how I'll be treated," Taroon said. And then he turned. "And you must be Iris?"

"How did you know?" Iris was taken by the man's handshake. His grip was all encompassing, warm and secure.

"This little wizard," he said, patting Abe on the head. "Tell your husband, I'm hoping he places or shows. Now all I have to find is Tante Ella and I'll be a full-fledged member of the Maxwell clan."

"I'm right here. And as long as you are giving the ladies a kiss...." Taroon leaned over, gave her a peck, stole a quick kiss from Iris who blushed, and then he saluted to all and bid adieu.

"Momma, what did he mean, places or shows?"

"I don't know. Elias?"

"In a horse race, it means coming in second or third."

"Oh, I get it," Abe said, and then he laughed.

"Now, stay close," Debora warned.

"I will, momma." Yet Abe just turned without looking back and began his trek to the next hangar. Elias was about to reprimand him, but Tante Ella stopped him by reaching out with her hand. Then she simply trotted to catch up to Abe and called the others to follow. Debora and Iris moved quickly, and then Elias capitulated.

"There's Roland Garros," little Abe proclaimed. "He was the first to fly the Mediterranean." Abe couldn't stop himself and ran over to get Garros' autograph.

"Here you go, my little one," Garros said, giving Abe a photo of himself which he had on hand. With a flourish, he simply signed his last name boldly along the bottom.

Abe proceeded by rote to describe to his father and mother, his auntie Iris and his Great Tante Ella the names of the pilot and designer of each plane, various vital statistics such as its estimated average speed, range, maneuverability, and any incidental adaptations that were unique.

Although most of the information was readily available in the brochure and accompanying literature, it was still an impressive achievement, and so a small crowd began to follow them around as well. Some even asked young Abe questions.

"What do you think of Leon Morane's monoplane?" one fellow asked.

"You mean the one he designed with Raymond Saulnier?"

"Yes," the man said, masking the fact that he didn't know Morane had formed this partnership.

"It's an obvious copy of a Bleriot, but in my estimation, the M-S I could be an improvement, particularly for reaching high altitudes," Abe said.

"Why has Bleriot clipped the wings of his new monoplane?" a mechanic for the Voisin monoplane being flown by Octave Gembellino inquired, knowing full well the answer.

Abe hadn't noticed the clipped wings and now he did. His mind reeled through the hundreds of pages he had read of statistics and information about the mechanisms for lift, flight and speed, but then replied, "I'm not sure why he would do that, sir. The reduction of the surface area of the wing will serve to decrease wind resistance, but this will also hamper the maneuverability of the plane during heavy wind conditions and ultimately make it unfit for flight."

"Balderdash," Gustav Hamel, the pilot of the plane said, having overheard the exchange.

"You're Mr. Hamel, are you not?" Abe looked up at the mustachioed man, whose goggles stood atop his head like a frog's eyes staring out to each side.

"Yes, young man, and I will admit that Mr. Bleriot cautioned me along the very same line, but our test flight increased our speed by over 7% and the decrease in control was negligible."

"May I have your autograph?"

"Of course." Hamel marched to Abe, reached down to grab his pad and pen and dashed off his signature.

"I would like Mr. Bleriot's as well."

"I'll send him over as soon as I see him, little man."

Abe thanked the pilot, turned and began to describe the next craft in line continuing to carry the small entourage with him on his tour.

"You should have seen it. Hamel came this close to knocking Bleriot's block off," Simon spoke between forkfuls as the family sat at the dinner table and talked about the day. "Abe, you were on the money! Hamel was so cocksure he had the fastest plane. Well, maybe he did, but once that gust hit him during the trial run, well, he was lucky to survive. He should have been thankful, only a broken collar bone. But that didn't stop him. Can you imagine, Bleriot's maybe the best designer out there, but his ego got the better of him. Yet, I have this gnawing suspicion that it was really Hamel who talked him into it. The plane looked like a cork bobbing in the sea. He was lucky he crashed into an unplowed wheat field, because it broke his fall, and just missed Farman's monoplane which had just taken off for its own test run!"

"Where's your partner," Iris inquired.

"With the English, where else? And who do you think he's having dinner with?"

"Sopwith?"

"You got it on the button, Elias. T period O period M period Sopwith. Thomas Octave Murdoch Sopwith had scratched the Bleriot monoplane he was supposed to fly in, the one you heard about on the wireless."

"Yes."

"And now he's flying his new design, a bi-plane called the Sopwith Camel. Sneedmore had spoke of him with such contempt, and that was just on the train ride here. Now he's kissing his *tuchis!*"

"Jealousy, Simon. He's a good enough assistant designer. But when a man is that jealous...."

"What?"

"He's insecure with his abilities," Tante Ella jumped in. "Isn't that what you are trying to say Elias?"

"Exactly."

"So, Abe," Debora changed the subject, "whose got the fastest plane and what chances does your uncle have to win this prize?"

"I only want Simon to finish," Elias interrupted. "Abe, we will listen to your predictions in a minute, but I want this to be perfectly clear. You saw what happened to Bleriot and Hamel. We're in this thing...."

"For the long run," Simon finished his sentence. "I know, but £20,000 pounds can go a long way."

"It's a diversion, Simon. You have to think three, five years down the road." Turning to his son, Elias continued, "Abe, how many planes will even make it to the finish line?"

"The races are averaging 23%, papa. Twelve, maybe fourteen."

"And how many will die?" Iris found herself asking.

"Four will die and nine will suffer injury of varying severity."

"How do you know such things?" Iris had a pleading look in her eye. She turned away and found herself fleeing the room. Simon took off after her.

"Abe, my little man," Tante Ella interjected. "You are *never* so presumptuous as to predict death, particularly that harshly."

"But auntie, that's what the numbers...."

"I don't care what the numbers are. You are not God. It is your position and our position as a family to hope for the best."

"But the numbers."

"You hold your tongue, and show some humility before our Lord when it comes to predicting death. Do you hear me?"

"Yes, auntie."

"All right," Elias said, "now that that is over with. Abe, is there anything else you can tell us?"

"Sopwith has the best shot on the first leg because he's got the best mechanic."

"Who's that?"

"Fred Sigrist, papa. They've already formed a new aviation company together, and, as uncle Sye-Sye said, modified Bleriot's monoplane into a biplane which is all for the better, but it's probably too new to make the whole journey."

"What about Count Hellenstein?"

"He's certainly another to look to, but my guess is that a light sturdy biplane has the best chance."

"That leaves Curtiss on a pirated Wright and Hotchkiss on a Avro." Elias looked pensive.

"And Sopwith," Tante Ella chimed in.

"Abe's ruled him out."

"Are you really that sure, Abe," Elias asked. "Let me put it another way. Which are the best biplanes out there?"

"My money is with Hotchkiss," Abe proclaimed.

"And what money is that?" his mother interjected.

"Momma, it's just a figure of speech!"

Abe's advanced use of the language was a never-ending avenue for surprise, and the adults laughed at the statement, taking the young boy aback before he realized that they were not laughing at him.

Elias continued the conversation. "Well, Abe, that means you are ruling out Graham-White in his Nieuport."

"That's a monoplane, papa."

"Oh. What about uncle Simon?" Debora found herself asking.

"Sniggerly Sneedmore insisted on a French rudder, and they are known to crack in salt air."

"Where'd you find that out?" Elias was astounded.

"It's the alloy of metal that Duvieux chose. It's sturdy and hard, but Horace Short sent it to a metallurgist, and he confirmed that saltwater will change its surface structure."

"How do you know this?"

"I overheard Mr. Short telling Sniggerly."

"You can't call him that, Abe. We already decided. So, I guess that means, I'll have to see Short myself."

"Don't you believe me, papa?"

"Of course I do Abe. But Short may have a solution."

"A small electric current in the rudder will prevent the corrosion from taking place."

Elias, Debora and Tante Ella looked down at this wonder child in total awe. After a long pause, Elias asked, "And how do you suggest we place such a current into the rudder?"

"Connect it to a battery," Abe concluded.

"And how long will that last?"

"Uncle Simon will need to charge it at each stop. I think if the rudder holds, he could finish the race."

Simon gave Iris a long kiss and then walked off to his plane.

"What did he say?" Debora watched in exhilaration the line of aeroplanes for the race. Simon climbed in, turned back and waved at them.

"That he'd be careful." Iris kept her eyes forward, fighting back the tears as she watched Sneedmore approach the propeller to get the MB-1 started.

Abe stood transfixed, one hand in that of his mother's and the other cradled by Iris. The wind picked up. Tante Ella sat in bright sunlight against one of the out buildings as Elias paced in front of them. Moving towards his plane, he was only allowed to approach the starting area. Then he backed off and returned to stand near his family. Abe had counted a small patch of people, estimated its size in relation to the entire crowd and calculated the number of attendees at twenty-three thousand. During a lull in the action, Abe found himself taking out his favorite photo, that of Henry Taroon standing next to his aeroplane with his flight goggles and his enormous mustache. The photo was inscribed "To my Little Partner, Abe." Abe smiled every time he looked at it.

Off in the distance, behind the starting point, Count von Zeppelin hovered in one of his enormous airships. On board were Baron leForest, the main sponsor of the race, Dame Edna, first cousin of the King of Greece, and Kaiser Wilhelm and his brother Henry. The race would start when Dame Edna threw out a bright yellow and orange scarf.

The wind picked up again and von Zeppelin found his craft drifting further and further from view. Along the runway in sets of three could be seen virtually every major pilot from Europe and America and most major designers.

With nearly 60 planes in the race, the Maxwell monoplane was in the 7th tier next to a Voisin monoplane and an Avro tri-plane. The start was staggered allowing fully 15 minutes between each set of three. The entire start would take nearly nine hours.

With mishaps and crashes the actual start took two days. Three planes, including another clipped Bleriot, crashed on take off, and one, a Blackburn monoplane, piloted by a female, M. Denise Oulet, caught fire twenty minutes out, lost altitude and smacked into a tree. Oulet broke her neck, thereby becoming the fourth female pilot to die in the last two years.

A total of 16 planes scratched before the first leg to Rome.

Debora looked over each of the planes and turned to her husband. "My favorite, other than yours my dear," Debora began is…"

"Let me guess," Abe butted in.

"All right."

"The Rumpler-Taube monoplane."

"How did you know!" Debora said in astonishment.

"Because it looks like a large bird with fluted wings and a broad tail," Abe said.

"And how will it do?" Iris asked.

"It needs a beak to cut the wind," Abe said, and then he farted.

"Abraham!" Debora responded in astonishment.

"I couldn't help myself, momma."

"Well say excuse me."

"Only if you promise, momma, not to stand under the Taube when it flies overhead."

"Abraham, that's enough."

By the time the planes had reached Athens, four more had dropped out including the Rumpler-Taube whose tail was ripped, by, of all things, a kite that a boy in Albania was flying, and the race was over for another 15 pilots by the time the lead plane landed in Cairo. Three pilots were killed on the first leg, one was lost in the Mediterranean, and three pilots suffered serious injury from other crashes. One, Colonel Fogley from East Church, had three cracked ribs, a broken nose and a shattered pelvis. Key-Sandal broke both legs and lost an eye, and the last casualty, the flamboyant Dane Eduard Raven, was in a coma and not expected to live. That left twelve planes for the final two legs.

Heeding his son's advice, Elias dispatched a replacement rudder to Belgrade. True, Simon would have to get that far in the old one, but that might make the difference. He sent Sneedmore, who, to his amazement, agreed to go.

"You may not believe this," Sneedmore spoke in German, "but I want Simon to win as much as you."

"And why is that?"

Reverting back to English. "For the sheer sport of it. Certainly the monetary prize is an incentive, but if we win, we make history."

Simon looked back at the shaky rudder and shuddered. He saw an Antonette go down ten miles out of Naples and had heard about the deaths of Fogley and the girl and Dane Raven. But everyone knew the risks. He was catching up to a biplane. It had to be Hotchkiss in the Avro, as Simon had passed Curtiss before Naples. Based on Sneedmore's information, Simon figured there must be at least two Nieuports beyond Hotchkiss and maybe a Farman.

Coordinating officials in five countries sent out two airships two weeks ahead of time to place markers as guides all the way to Cairo. Simon feared going down like the Raven, but he was determined to get to the next leg as long as his rudder held. The extra weight of one of Elias' car batteries caused difficulties in taking off, but not so much in landing. He also experienced a number of shocks when he touched certain metal parts along the floor of the plane. But the wings were sturdy. The Maxwell motor kept purring and the rudder had not crusted as much as he had anticipated. Simon had never seen the pyramids before and was looking forward to circling them and then landing outside of Cairo where there would be a layover. Times would be calculated and calibrated so that the remaining pilots could dine together.

The triangular monuments appeared smaller to Simon than he had expected. He had forgotten about the Sphynx however, and risked himself a bit to swoop down to get a better look. He couldn't believe how close they were to the burgeoning metropolis. Off in the distance, not far from the shoreline, he could see a biplane landing. When he himself arrived at their weigh-station, he was oddly gratified to see seven planes in front of him. Sopwith in his Camel bi-plane was in the lead. He had an eight-hour edge over Billingsley, who in an Avro, was in second. Simon was nearly fifteen hours off the lead, but his brother's words had given him comfort. Thus, he was more at ease than the in-betweeners who cajoled and bickered as to why their plane was at the back of the pack. Sopwith suggested a memorial service for the lost pilots. Simon and most of the others attended. He stood next to Count Hellenstein, who was a fellow Bavarian Simon had once met at Lilienthal's glider production facilities.

After dinner, and unable to sleep, Simon found himself back at his plane, using a torchlight to go over the rudder. He could see that it would probably get him back across the Mediterranean, but he feared it would never get him to Munich.

"It's a message for you, sir," the man from the hotel had come out to the hangar in the dead of night.

"It must be important for you to come out so late," Simon said.

"I'm on duty all night. Everyone is dead to the wind, except for the two of you."

"Tom, how nice to see you."

Sopwith approached the plane and gave it a long look. "I like what you did with the lifters."

"Thank you."

"And that neat design of the folded wing. But I think inevitably, you will sacrifice stability when you collapse wings for transport. You should have flown the plane to Munich from your plant."

"I didn't want to risk an extra flight, particularly with this new hinge design. Sneedmore's got it just right. He calculated the angle of bend here, and welded these pieces for extra grip along the base. But, I'm still concerned about the rudder."

"It looks all right," Sopwith said, but he took out a wrench anyway and rapped the rudder soundly. "Whose idea was the electric current?"

"Your own metallurgist. It was in one of his old papers."

"Come on, Simon. There's more to that story. Who figured this out?"

"My nephew read it and saw the solution."

"I *knew* you had some brains behind this operation. Send him to East Church and I'll hire him on the spot!"

"He's just six years old."

"The little chap who asked for my autograph? Hah! Well, send him anyway. Apparently, it doesn't make much difference." Sopwith stopped in mid-thought. "My God, Simon. Will you look at that."

Simon turned and watched the moon on the horizon rising right over the pyramids.

"I'll be right back," Sopwith said.

Simon watched the eerie scene and tried to envision what type of advanced culture the Egyptians must have had to have erected so many great monuments.

Wearing protective goggles and a light blow torch, Sopwith returned and began to weld a crack in the rudder that, because of its position under a bolt, had been overlooked by Simon."

"You know this is against the rules."

"I won't tell if you don't tell. It's important for every aeroplane to be safe. I look to a day when aeroplane travel will be as common as a trip by train, when aeroplanes even replace the Zeppelin."

And you see such a day?"

"Not in the immediate future. But for speed and ultimate triumph over meteorological whims, the aeroplane is the wave of the future."

"We are one of the few firms that supply parts for both types of craft," Simon said.

"I know. And I know your brother is very proud of you. He told me to look out for you. You've got a new rudder waiting in Belgrade, so you should be all right. Just get there safely."

"I know you are way out in the lead on this, but who do you think really has the best design?"

"You mean aside from me?"

"Of course."

"Well, that's tough. I think the monoplane offers the greatest chance for ultimate speed, but frankly, I think for handling and stability, you've got to go with the bi-plane."

"What about the tri-plane?"

"They would have advantages in trick maneuvers, for loops and spirals and in severely windy territory. Overall, the biplane is more cost effective."

The two pilots drove back to the hotel with the clerk in a new Royce, and each, more tired than the other, stumbled themselves into their respective beds.

Sopwith overslept, so his lead time was cut by nearly two hours, but he was still the man to beat. He had probably calculated that the extra sleep time would pay additional benefits, keep him more alert than his competitors. So he didn't begrudge the decision, and thus took off for Belgrade at 9:23 a.m.

Simon had learned many secrets about reading the wind. At dinner the night before, Henry Taroon, who was flying a Baby Bristol monoplane, began to articulate something that Lilienthal was the first to discuss. Namely that there were pockets of air that spiraled upwards. Many pilots since Lilienthal had experienced such updrafts. Simon himself had used such upsurges years earlier when he was involved primarily with gliders. As Lilienthal had first noted, and Taroon had speculated, this might be a natural mechanism that could be harnessed for raising altitude of motored planes as well. If the upsurge was read correctly. Certainly hawks and seagulls used such spirals, but how would one know where they were located?

"I think upthrusts can be just as dangerous as downthrusts," Rugman, the only tri-plane pilot, said. Count Hellenstein agreed.

"What about speed?" Simon asked Rugman. "Your tri-plane is nearly twice the weight of a Bleriot monoplane."

"Well, there's the trade-off. We know the general consensus is to avoid all wind shifts. But when they come, I've got the stability, whereas a Bleriot flutters like a butterfly in the wind.

"Yours is a Junkers, isn't it?" Simon asked.

"Yes," Rugman said. "Professor Junkers knows what he's doing. What happens when we add passengers and make long distance travel a regular occurrence? Surely, one wants the greatest stability."

"But you're running last in the race," Captain Cornish entered the conversation. Cornish was in a Nieuport monoplane and running third.

"That may be true," Rugman responded. "But as Sopwith informed us, you nearly ditched in the sea when a quick squall rumbled up the bay."

"It wasn't the squall, but what was about it," Cornish revealed. "Odd down-thrusts. That's what took out Strepski. But that's where skill enters into it, and instinct. I picked up speed on the slide and pulled out of the mess just forty feet above the water."

"You're lucky a dolphin didn't jump aboard!"

Everyone laughed at Count Hellenstein's joke, and then dinner broke up.

"I want to thank you for finding my little nephew Abe, that first day," Simon said to Taroon as they left the dinner room.

"Oh, it was nothing," Taroon said. "I enjoyed meeting your family."

"And they, you," Simon said. "Good luck tomorrow."

"You too, brother," Taroon said, the appellation somehow sounding right, coming from this large warm man.

Each pilot would start a staggered release time based upon certain arcane rules that seemed to change at each stop. Each pilot would also keep their time handicaps for the next leg. Times were recalibrated by combining time in the air and certain allowances for ground maintenance. Sopwith was supposed to leave first, but now he wouldn't, yet he would still have nearly a six-hour lead over the first plane out, and several more hours over all the other planes that left ahead of him as well.

For stability, Simon was beginning to agree with Sopwith that a bi-plane would be best. But this race was for speed. He felt, as did most of the others, that these races were important for the spirit of competition, the publicity and for attracting new investors. Simon was of a mind to add his support for Horace Short's idea to break the races down according to design, that is, a race for monoplanes, one for bi-planes and one for tri-planes. He had a feeling that this might be if not the last, one of the last of what Sneedmore called "The Hodge-Podge Races."

Simon was flying in tandem with Cornish as they crossed the Mediterranean and flew the Isle of Rhodes together. Having left shortly before dawn, the water was so still, it looked like a person could simply walk across it. A low fog hovered, the only movement being a lone fishing boat which left a clear trail that stretched all the way to the harbor.

As they approached Rhodes, both Cornish and Simon could see Sopwith coming from behind. Off to the west, dark storm clouds threatened. As the sun rose, the mist disappeared, the wind picked up and the sea now became choppy. A sudden cloudburst, which cut off the sun, came down in a torrent. Portending the deluge that was to follow, it drenched an area no larger than several acres as it tore across the sea in rapid fashion. Now was the moment of truth. Should Simon try and outrun the storm, wait it out on the ground as he suspected Taroon, Count Hellenstein or Rugman might do, or try and outrun it. Cornish pointed out the more ominous threat to the west and motioned he was going down, but Sopwith looked like he was turning right into it.

That is when it occurred to Simon. If indeed the storm were moving rapidly, if he headed towards it by circling back slowly, he might just get by with allowing the darkness to pass in front of him. This could allow him a straight shot to Istanbul without another stop, and the cost would only be ten or fifteen kilometers. But that would only be if the storm were self-contained, and not a monster. He decided to follow Sopwith's lead and banked circling left, while Cornish bid adieu and dropped altitude as he sought a place to land on Rhodes.

Bolts of lighting jagged down in glowing rapidity as Simon continued to bank in retreat. The lightning was what he feared more than the rain, and a bolt no more than 300 meters away, sent a terror through him he had never experienced before. He decided to land instead and began to look for a place as Sopwith came roaring overhead, tilting his wings by banking left-right-left as he surged around towards the tail end of the slickering downpour.

From experience, Simon preferred to take the plane down on a grazing field or a large road which could most often be found by main towns. Those were usually the hardest surfaces, but there was more of a risk to hit a tree or a horse and carriage or automobile. As if by magic, a black cloud materialized overhead, lightning struck and the plane was socked by an electric charge. A ***KABOOM!*** almost threw him from the cockpit. More than one pilot had died being thrown from a plane. Safety belts were still seen as a chicken's way out. But Elias had insisted on a rope to secure Simon in, and now he was glad he had listened. The rope had gotten wet and tended to cut into his thigh, and he had taken it off for the leg from Rome to Crete. But, he had to admit it, Elias was usually right, and that was also what made him so exasperating. Elias could speak with such conviction and be right, and yet speak with the same authority and be flat-out wrong. Occasionally, Elias would admit a mistake, but for the most part, he covered it over. But when it came to mechanics and giving Simon freedom, Elias took the back seat. It made up for his tight-fisted inclination. Simon decided he would insist on a signed contract and 30% of the airline, or he would walk.

Iris had talked of moving to England, as she had relatives there and Simon felt, with this new connection to Sopwith and Sneedmore, that he could set himself up there and work with the best designers in the world if Elias balked yet again.

He knew that Junkers was a man to watch. His metallic monoplane was still in the running and then there was that youngster Fokker, although he hadn't entered a plane in the race. As his mind reeled, Simon realized that he hadn't thought about Iris at all, except as how it pertained to his interests. She was so afraid for him. He had always thought of Iris as strong, but now he realized she was really strong-willed which was different than strong. He reckoned she had courage, but it was of a different sort as in standing up to her father. The one thing she had said that stuck with him was to "place the shoe on the other foot."

It took him nearly 36 hours of flying to realize what she meant. How would he feel if she were risking her life and how would he be feeling if she died and left him alone? He was taking her for granted. His near mishap of being thrown from the plane made it all the more clear. Life was sacred and Elias was right. It made much more sense to finish the race than to risk one's life trying to win it. His plane touched down on a deserted field. He watched with mixed feelings of envy, empathy and trepidation as Sopwith caught the tail end of one storm and pushed forward on the gamble he could beat the next one that was popping over a local mountain range.

The first plane back to Munich was a surprise, the Reissner-Junkers monoplane flown by one of Maxwell's Bavarian neighbors, Count Hellenstein. As the race had started and ended in Germany, the press and awaiting crowds were in a frenzy. Sopwith came in next on his biplane Camel, followed by two monoplanes, Hamel in a Bleriot and Hotchkiss in a Bristol and then Taroon in a Maurice-Farman biplane.

Simon was able to limp into Belgrade, and Sneedmore, to his pleasant surprise, was ready with the new rudder. Nine planes had made it to Munich, and his would be the tenth, if he could just get off the ground.

Abe had kept track. Humbled by his miscalculation of the stunning success of the Reissner-Junkers monoplane, he, nevertheless, was ecstatic. Even though there were nearly 30,000 people at the gate, Abe was in the inside track. He had autographs of two of the three pilots who had died, and was able to obtain a complete set of all who finished. It was waiting the full extra day to see if Simon would come in that caused the young boy to get cranky. Perhaps it was because he had reacted to the great tension that had erupted between Iris and Elias. She had come so far as to have socked Elias in the arm, when he said that Simon had been foolhardy to have entered the race in the first place. Secretly, he was hoping that Simon would finish in the top three, and chided himself for telling Simon to be so cautious. He felt embarrassed when at the end of the day, there was still no word from his brother. Rather than be concerned with Simon's health, and that was the reason Iris had socked him, Elias seemed to her to be more concerned about the image of his company. To finish a day later was, and this was the word that set her off, "tawdry."

A propeller had cracked just 70 kilometers outside of Munich, and Simon had lost nearly 18 hours securing another which he had to pay dearly for. He had seen a small airfield and touched down with still enough time to replace the part and finish on the day that most of the other planes had come in on. But he had hit a roadblock when an ignoramus calling himself a mechanic refused to sell him the propeller without being paid in advance.

Iris had stared at the horizon so long and felt her hopes soar and wane with the arrival of each new plane that she had become what Abe called "a nervous Ninny" by the time Simon finally arrived.

"That's him," little Abe said with authority when a slight dot which looked like a soaring bird, peered into view.

One exchange of glances with the tyke convinced Iris, and she ran headlong out onto the runway. Her heart pounded in her chest as a feeling overtook her like no other she had ever experienced before, pride, wonderment, anger, even some jealousy, but mostly love and yes, joy, pure joy.

Simon saw his lovely mate running and jumping to greet him. His eyes strained down to read her expression as she gazed upwards to greet his. He watched the wind, circled for his approach and set the Maxwell down.

Taxiing to the hangars, he found himself greeted not only by Iris and his family, but also by most of the other pilots all who had stayed to cheer their comrades on.

"Come join us for a drink," Sopwith had said. Simon thanked him heartily, but declined.

"Well, I don't mean by yourself. Take your lovely wife and get Elias to bring his little devil. I want to get the statistics on who had the fastest leg."

"And who survived?" Iris asked.

"Yes. And who survived."

"Cornish had the fastest leg at 117.3 kilometers per hour in his Nieuport," Abe offered at the table as beers were passed around to the adults and a sarsaparilla was given to him.

Sopwith leaned over to the boy and clinked glasses. "And who had the fastest bi-plane?"

"You did, Mr. Sopwith, sir. You knew that."

"Yes, but I want to know why."

"The combination of your lighter horsepower engine and reduction of drag."

"Caused by?"

"I'm not sure, sir. It could be the curved wing, but more likely, it's a combination of factors that created greater overall streamlining."

"I felt considerable drag on that last leg," Simon chimed in.

"The rudder?" Elias guessed.

"I couldn't have finished the race without it and Sneedmore was a heaven sent. But yes, the added weight of the battery and choice of metal. I'm not sure just what it was."

"Go back to the wind tunnel" Sopwith suggested. "I hear tell Junkers practically lives at Göttingen."

"Will you now be producing bi-planes exclusively?" asked Simon.

"It's true, the monoplane won this race," Sopwith said, but I agree with your little one. For overall safety and stability, the biplane is best. Speed is for daredevils."

DRAGONFLY

Part of the ritual of their lives was the reading of the Sunday newspaper on a formal couch Debora had talked Elias into putting into the sunroom. Located at the southeast corner of the dwelling, natural sunlight would filter through the windows and flood a porch that wrapped itself around to the front. It had been a warm day in May, and Greta, Gunter's wife and head maid, had surreptitiously left the outside sunroom door open and then coaxed Abe, who seemed all along to be part of the scheme, to wiggle-walk the half-dozen goslings that had recently been hatched, up the front porch, through the house, through the sunroom and back out. So engrossed was Elias in a newspaper article involving Germany's attempt to bully France into giving them Morocco, that he missed the event entirely. And when Elias looked up, he couldn't understand why Debora, Abe and even Greta were giggling. After burying his head back into the paper, Greta coaxed Abe to repeat the procedure. However, in this instance, she also closed the door that led back out to the porch.

Once the goslings were inside, Debora innocently asked for the very section of the paper Elias was so locked into. When he looked up, there was his son, grinning and waddling with a string of young geese behind him.

"My God," Abe," Elias remarked. "Did you hatch them as well?"

"No sir, but I do take care of them because their mother was cooked by Farmer Munster." Abe paused, and then added, "I took pity on them."

The depth of Abe's answer seemed to startle Elias more than the prank. And so it came that Abe was allowed to tend to these geese and together, the family watched the birds grow through the summer.

It was this spark that was ignited in Elias through Abe's actions that warmed the heart of Debora and helped her overlook so much of Elias' shortcomings, not the least of which was his all too serious manner. They had a string of three idyllic weeks in late June and early July when Elias would get Debora and Abe up at dawn. Gunter, it seemed, was always up ahead of them. He would wipe down the rowboat and position the cushions just so. Abe would wiggle-walk the goslings into the pond. Elias, now in the boat with Debora, would lift Abe above the water just as he reached the shoreline, and then, like Jesus, allow the boy to walk on the water as the goslings followed. Debora would take over the oars and row them out to the middle of the pond.

"Give me those," Elias would command pointing to the oars. Now he would take the boat to the far end and into a tributary which led to the Iller. No matter how fast he rowed, the goslings would keep up, always in the same pecking order, seven of them straight in a line.

Each time, it seemed, they would venture farther, and so on a few occasions, Debora would pack a picnic and the family would spend an entire day on their outing, the geese growing stronger and bolder each time they went out.

An avowed atheist, none-the-less, Elias began to gain a feeling which he could only attribute to "spirituality" that would overtake him when they would depart the pond and snake their way through the tributary, his son's family of goslings dutifully following.

Abe's gleam became infectious. Elias would sing Bavarian ballads and even Yiddish songs as they sat in their boat among the reeds, watching the turtles, egrets and herons, spying a hawk or kingfisher, locating a family of sea otters, and once, even spotting a wild boar, as they bobbed and ate their picnic sandwiches.

Simon and Iris had come for dinner ostensibly to help celebrate Abe's 7ᵗʰ birthday. Debora had invited uncle Adolf and his half-brother, Iris' father Roberé and his young wife Rebecca. Roberé was telling Elias an off-color joke about the Archeduke's wife Josephine and a manservant who used to give her a shave, when Abe came in from the kitchen. He was holding a dragonfly in a jar, which he had caught when it almost drowned in a puddle in one of the ruts in the driveway.

"Momma, momma, look a fly-fly, a fly-fly."

"That's very nice, dear."

"Get that horrible creature away from the dinner table," Elias commanded looking at the drenched bug clinging to a twig.

Tears welled up in Abe's eyes. He wanted to keep it.

"It's alive," Simon said.

"Who cares if it's alive?" Elias shot back.

"Your son cares," Iris found herself saying.

"I do care, sir," Abe said.

"It's a stupid insect, and it will be dead within the hour. Get it out of my sight."

"Elias, you call this insect stupid, but it can do something we humans are only beginning to learn about." Simon opened the lid of the jar and eyed the glistening insect carefully. "I believe if we leave it alone, it's wings will dry and it will thereupon get up and fly."

"It's half dead. Stop such nonsense. It's stupid."

"On the contrary," Simon said. "I believe it is a sign of great intelligence, that this small animal has figured out how to counteract gravity."

"That's all poppycock. It's a blind process," Elias jumped. "Over millions of years, the insects adapt this way and that, some mutate, others die out, and this particular one gained wings. Intelligence has nothing to do with it."

"How can you say that?" Debora found herself saying. "It's a sign from God."

"You see what I have to put up with! What could God possibly have to do with a dragonfly?"

"Maybe God likes the rainbows that you see in the wings," Rebecca offered.

"It's so sad you don't see it," Simon replied. "All of science is based on the premise that God exists."

"You sound like an idiot, Simon. There is no God. It's a human invention to make simpletons like you feel better about yourself...."

"And get us over the fear of dying?" Roberé jumped in.

"I don't understand your point?"

"Man fears death," uncle Adolf entered the conversation. "So he invents a god to placate his fears. God will protect us for eternity."

"Exactly, as long as we are in agreement that he's an invention," Elias said with satisfaction.

"It's moving, dada," Abe exclaimed, calling his father with an appellation he abhorred.

"What did you say!" the father shouted.

"The dragonfly has moved, sir."

"And it will fly again," Simon reassured his nephew. "And Abe, as nice as your father is, he is not right about everything. God does exist, and this dragonfly proves it."

"Balderdash. You are filling the mind of my son up with nonsense. There is no God. It is all a human creation."

"And did a human invent a dragonfly as well?" Tante Ella added quietly.

"Of course not," Elias huffed.

"And you think a dragonfly's flight is merely the work of chance?"

"Exactly, I'm amazed at how primitive your thinking really is. Someone has got to be at the top of the food chain, and it happens to be humans. It's as simple as that."

"But brother, if we want to design an aeroplane to fly more efficiently, aren't we going to try and copy the design of the birds and insects such as this one?"

As his father and uncle continued to speak, Abraham watched intently the dragonfly continue to pump its wings with air and watched its long streamlined body begin to quiver. Debora, keyed to her son, also began to watch, as did the younger von Rosensweig and his wife, Rebecca. In silent communication, they continued a conspiracy of expectation as Simon and Elias battled out the age-old question with uncle Adolf sitting back observing in quiet self-amusement.

"I'm trying to say, Elias," Simon began, "that in some sense, the dragonfly is more intelligent than we are."

"That's just plain asinine."

"They have been around for tens of millions of years," Adolf found himself commenting.

"So, you're on *his* side!"

"Elias, it's not a matter of sides. I simply see his point."

"What is his point?"

"That there is something in the universe more intelligent than we," Debora found herself chiming in.

"God. Is that what this is about? You all believe in God?"

"I do," Simon responded as Debora silently nodded.

"And you?"

"I see their point. That's all I'm saying," uncle Adolf hedged.

"It's all chemicals and nature, pure chance and combinations."

"All great scientists believed in a designer," Simon said, "a watchmaker."

"Well, you can't prove it to me!" Elias took a haughty pose. "There has been more killing, more wars, more ignorance and more fear perpetuated in the name of God. Look at the problem in the Slavic nations. The Croats who are Roman Catholics hate the Serbs who are Greek Orthodox even though both are Christians. And in Russia...."

"The pogroms," uncle Adolf nodded in agreement.

"Exactly. The Jews are hated and forced into squalid ghettos and slaughtered in Russia because they believe in one god and I guess, to some extent, the Russian aristocracy believes in another. And then there are the Spaniards and the Crusaders, and before that, the Romans ...."

"Mesada," Debora added.

"Yes," Elias agreed, believing she was finally coming to her senses. Putting on his monocle, Elias looked each person over, and concluded, "It's paganism."

"What do you mean?" Iris asked. Rebecca nodded to agree in wondering what the point was. It was the first time Iris had connected with her, well, her step-mother.

"Oh, it usually reduces down to my God is better than your God. My God loves me. If I believe in Christ, I will be saved and if I don't...."

"You don't," uncle Adolf poked.

"Paganism," Elias continued, "God worship, it's all the same. You don't need God to survive in this world and in fact, you are better off..."

"To eliminate religion altogether? Is that what you're saying?" Debora asked.

"Of course. It's a liability, a handicap which simply keeps me from my market, reduces my profitability. What good is religion to me?"

"I can only tell you," Simon jumped back in, "that if I design a better aeroplane, a more efficient wing, it will be because I respect the wisdom of nature and will try to emulate her, try to unlock her mysteries."

"Nature is nature. It has nothing to do with God. You don't see the animals praying to God, do you?"

"I don't know what animals think, but I do know that I am in awe of the very process. Think about Orville and Wilbur Wright's minds. Where did their minds come from?"

"Simon, how many times do I have to go over this? It's evolution, one animal blindly evolving into another. Random mutation and survival of the fittest. I thought you understood Darwin. That is science. Your view is mystic mumbo gumbo."

"Then what about this house?"

"What do you mean, this house?"

"This house, how was it built?"

"Simon, now you are being stupid. We met an architect. He drew up the plans, we hired a builder and he had his idiot carpenters bang some nails and bango, a house. Not brain science."

"It did take planning," Roberé interjected.

"Of course it took planning!" Rebecca entered the fray. "That's why humans live in houses and deer hide out in the woods."

"Simon's trying to say that the universe also took planning. Isn't that right, uncle Sye-Sye?"

"Yes, little one. There had to be a designer. You cannot get a dragonfly to fly by chance any more than you could build this house by chance."

"You are creating a false relationship, Simon," Elias said, his voice ever more adamant. "One is human thought and the other is a blind process of adaptation and random change over many millennium. My son brings in a half-dead dining needle and you give him some clap about it resurrecting itself, like Lazarus being raised from the dead. You get my son's hopes up...."

"What's a dining needle, sir?" Abe asked, breaking the tension of the moment.

"It's another name for dragonfly," Elias said, trying to offer a small means of tenderness.

"Well, the dining needle is dining on your plate, dada!" Abe beamed, for in fact, the insect had tested its wings and had landed on the cooked carrots which sat on his father's plate. Transfixed, Abe began to look at the odd creature in a sense, as if it were for the very first time. He noted that it had a green iridescent head and a body that was a vibrant light violet. There were two sets of translucent wings that looked somewhat like mesh stockings that Abe had once seen on, what his father called "a floozy." The large bulging eyes resembled those of a fly, and its head seemed to operate in a dimension completely separate from the torso as it swiveled around like a captain's chair. Turning its head completely around and cocking it, the dragonfly seemed to stare directly at Abe's papa as if to size him up. Iris shared a glance with Rebecca as they squelched their giggles.

Something in Elias erupted. His hand reached up to smash the insect, but at the same moment he caught a look of bafflement in his son's eyes, disappointment in Debora's, slyness in von Rosensweig's and self-satisfaction in Simon's. Elias' hand reached to the side of his head, and he vigorously scratched his brain. It was a nervous habit which was a part of him, and so it could be used to mask his original intent.

"I get too serious with the arguing with my smarty-pants brother, your uncle, Abe. Come, let's release this bug. With that, he grabbed the plate and brought it to a window which he forced open.

Roberé got up with his wife and placed an affectionate arm around his daughter, and they walked to the window. Iris felt a warmth from her father she had not thought possible. She looked up at him and smiled. He reached down and kissed her forehead. "It's nice to see you."

"You too daddy, and you, Rebecca."

Rebecca smiled back.

The dragonfly circled the room and then alighted on Abe's forearm. He held himself stiffly and waited. Then its wings fluttered and it again flittered about the room and then out the window to the porch, out to the front lawn and then high up, over the trees and then out of sight. In spite of himself, Elias felt he had saved the day. Abe looked up at him. Elias thought back for a moment to the dragonflies from their picnics out on the pond. He scooped up his son, gave him a manly kiss and brought him over to Simon and placed the boy on his shoulders.

"Enough," Elias said. "Greta," he shouted, "get me another plate."

The seeds of Elias' morose demeanor and cynical outlook had always been present. Sure he had mixed feelings, but overall, he resented his Jewish heritage. It was simply a yoke which cut into his profitability. He had converted to another religion for practical reasons. Belief in God had, of course, nothing to do with it.

What had God ever done for Elias? Hadn't he done it all on his own? It was his vision and his personality that had attracted the capital necessary to run not only a machine works and airplane factory, but also an automobile dealership. His brain, his sweat, his strategic planning. God was a figment, a childish crutch which the weak and the unrealistic used to deal with their petty foibles, their fear of death and their way to explain away their failures and own weakness of character which led the masses to embrace tribalism and plebian thinking at best, and racial hatred at worst.

Success was based on steady purpose, sacrifice, boldness, yet conservative management of personal resources, canniness in the marketplace, denial of daily pleasure in favor of grinding out the necessary hourly and weekly application of oneself, and most importantly, the ability to be accepted by the those in power, by such men as Count Zeppelin and General von Molke, Christian men who could get him contracts for airship engines, parts for tanks, and prototypes for new fighter planes.

Elias had entered a prestigious aviation coalition which included that young genius of design, Anthony Fokker, who had manufacturing plants in Germany, Spain, Holland, Hungry and the United States, Hugo Junkers, the second largest airplane manufacturer in Germany, Eric Rumpler, who built his own Rumpler plane in Berlin and Saac Schumann, who was designing helicopters in Frankfort.

It was the Kaiser's intent, as he had done with the wireless stations, to coordinate all aeroplane factories and design facilities into one Lufthansa, but Junkers and Fokker, at least for now, had successfully thwarted this entreaty. This disunion enabled MB Airways to also maintain autonomous status.

In a special meeting with Alex Von Billendorf, personal aid to Kaiser Wilhelm, Junkers, representing his own company, and Simon Maxwell, representing MB Airways, explained that creating a total monopoly would destroy the spirit of competition.

"To lose autonomy at this juncture," Junkers argued, "is to give in to mediocrity. Let Rumpler set his own design apparatus. If he wants to go in with

Fokker, fine," Junkers continued. "But, for the love of God, in this business you need men of daring and initiative."

Von Bullendorf turned to Simon. "And you are of a similar mind?"

"We all work for the Fatherland," Simon said. "But without a measure of independence, I don't believe I would have the free hand I would need to continue my research and experimentation. If I have to explain everything to each division, I'll lose six weeks or more just showing the others my point of view."

Elias had sat silently in the background. If Simon carried this off, they would be able to maintain autonomy against great pressure. With Junkers' support and Simon's great technical knowledge, it looked like they could win this position. Now it would be just a matter of waiting to see if the Kaiser would go for it.

SPRING 1914

It had been four years since Simon and Iris' wedding. Even though the world was in turmoil now that the heir to the thrown of Austro-Hungary had been assassinated, Iris had insisted upon living as if the outside world made no difference. She invited her father and his wife Rebecca, Elias, Debora, Tante Ella and Abe to their modest home for dinner.

Having connected the living and dining room with a long tabletop specially made for the occasion, Simon was able to seat everyone comfortably. Debora had brought dessert, and Roberé von Rosensweig, perhaps as a way to show up his son-in-law's older brother, had purchased a case of champagne.

Elias felt he had been one-upped and did not appreciate it. But more than that, he simply could not allow himself to stand by and listen to Iris' argument for neutrality. "If General von Moltke says we have to support Austria, then we have to support Austria. That's all there is to it," Elias pontificated. Germany was a great nation. Like France and England, it too deserved its "place in the sun."

"I am only quoting Mr. Angel," Iris had rebutted, referring to the British author's famous book *The Grand Illusion,* which anyone who was anyone had by now read. "War is obsolete. It creates false industries and destroys international trade. And that is what the planet desires. Commerce is the bedrock of a stable world economy."

Simon was awed by her vociferous counterattack.

"Idealistic tripe," Elias concluded. "War coalesces industry. If Germany attacks Serbia, as I expect we will, this will mean tremendous business for all concerned. The Fatherland has an army 800,000 strong, a submarine fleet, airships to drop bombs on the urban centers of our enemies, and in part because of your husband's very doing, a new air force capable of protecting our borders."

"Hermann's enlisting in the air corps," Roberé offered.

"Father, he is headstrong and foolhardy," Iris said, adding, "and so stupidly vain."

"I thought he was in the infantry," Elias humphed.

"Göring's been studying at the Freiberg Air Training School," said Roberé. "It was Simon's suggestion."

"And what about his mother, Madam Göring?" Debora inquired.

"Fanny's broken with von Eppenstein. Now she will most certainly leave his Veldenstein castle."

"Hermann will not be happy," Rebecca lamented.

"Why is that?" asked Iris.

"He's never faced reality, you know. He simply assumed von Eppenstein had actually *given* the castle to his momma. I remember when we were children, he was a very selfish boy, he would never share his toys and thought that my toys were his, even though they were girls' dolls. He always referred to the castle as 'mommy's palace'."

"Where will she go?"

"I'm sure we can find a place for her," Roberé answered Debora.

"I'm tempted to join flight school myself." Simon stunned the room into silence.

"I'll hear none of that, Simon," Elias retorted. "If we go to war, your presence in the plant will become ever more important."

"And I imagine you will compensate him if his workload increases?"

Roberé's breach of protocol was too much for Elias, and he started to get up to leave.

"Oh, simmer down," Roberé continued. "Your wife prepared a great dessert. There's always time to talk business and war next week. And maybe Germany will not get involved. Then all this huffing will be for naught."

"You don't know von Molke," Simon said.

MIT

The shuttle from New York to Logan took only about an hour, but during that short hop, Rudy gained a lifetime of information about something he knew much too little about, Facebook. Rudy was part of that older generation that just never really caught on. Sure, he had a page, and yes, he used it occasionally. But in general, he found it a royal pain, odd notices to him on email, announcements of the birthdays of tangential friends -- email was plenty efficient for him. There was something intrusive about Facebook. It seemed to strip you of your individuality and treated you like Pavlov's dogs, prodding you to step back into its world in disingenuous and innocuous ways. So when Rudy saw a college gal sitting next to him checking out her page, as a reporter, he decided to inquire.

Crystal was young and fresh with light blonde hair, clear eyes and an innocent expression. Except for earrings, she wore no jewelry, and no makeup, just a perky off-white dress, slightly low-cut blouse and a plain brown sweater. Although her appearance was understated, what set her apart, aside from a pair of cranberry-colored jellies, was a bright zebra-striped pocketbook big enough to hold her laptop, a bubble-gum green Mac. The plane was still on the tarmac and she was still logged onto her Facebook page.

"Oh yes," Crystal said, her eyes blinking, "I guess you could say I'm addicted. I check my page three, four times a day."

"How many friends do you have?" Rudy asked.

"About 1200. That's about the norm for the people I know."

"Aside from the obvious, what advantages do you see?"

"Oh, tons. Let me see. If people travel, you can see their pictures. You can get in touch with old friends. You can meet like-minded people."

"People with the same interests?"

As they talked, the plane started to move and a request came over the loudspeaker to shut off all cell phones and Internet connections. Crystal continued to talk as she got off-line.

"Yes," she said, "interest groups, announcements for meetings. It's great, really essential, if you're working at school or looking for a job."

"Why's that?"

"Jobs are posted all the time on Facebook. It's just simply the norm. This way, companies can connect to hundreds of people simultaneously. And you can connect to a group of friends instantly."

"Why not just call?"

"This is faster. Say you're giving a party, or setting up a meeting, or organizing a dance. Anything. You just send out a mass announcement and it turns into a thread where everyone linked can talk to each other, like a mini chat room. It's just a great tool for communication. Sometimes I use it more than text messaging."

"I think the thing that amazes me," Rudy said, "is how this new technology literally facilitated revolutions throughout northern Africa."

"Yeah, that's cool," Crystal said. "So, you're really a reporter?"

"For Modern Times."

"The magazine, huh? What'r you working on?"

"A story about computer hacking. That's really why I'm asking these questions."

"Cool."

"Ever have any problems with Facebook?"

"Not me personally," Crystal said, seeming to clam up.

"Well, do you see any dangers?"

"Really? You want me to answer that?"

"Yes."

"Well, I'm not too hip on the stalking."

"What do you mean," Rudy said.

"You have your profile out there. And if you're dumb enough to put a goofy or racy picture on your website, you know, like in your underwear, a company could see it, ruin your chances for getting a job, or your could attract a parasite. Weird people, or dinks from high school you finally got rid of are always trying to latch back into your life."

"Any other dangers?"

"Well, I've seen bullies on Facebook and just outright creeps. I don't know if this is a danger, but it is addictive. You can get bombarded by unwanted friends, read all this crap you really didn't want to know about someone, you know, TMI, your pictures could be photoshopped to make you look gross, you can get bombarded by spam and people can set up fraudulent sites and pretend they are someone else."

"What do you mean?" ·

"Jeeze, it was about two months ago. I get a notice from one of my friends Hailey. She said she lost her wallet in London and could I wire her some money. I didn't even know how to wire money. Turns out it was all a scam. She was in Europe, but she never sent that message out. What was that about! And then there's Farmville."

"Farmville? What's that?"

"Oh, a stupid game. And everyone is always bothering you to play Farmville. Then you get all these pop-up windows and dumb advertisements."

"This is so interesting, Crystal. So what is your overall impression?"

"Can't live without it. I can be connected to all my friends, I mean my real friends all the time. Even now, as soon as they let me log back on, I know I will never be alone."

"That's very powerful, Crystal," Rudy said. "Do you mind if I quote you on that?"

"Sure," the girl replied, her eyes now glowing. "How do you spell your name? I want to let everyone know."

"Oh, come on, Crystal," Rudy tried, "you're going to kill my exclusive. You've got to give me a week or two to get the story out."

"A week or two! That's a frigging lifetime, Mister... Rudy. What is your last name, again?"

"Styne, Rudy Styne." He handed Crystal a business card and got her to sign a release.

Fifty-five minutes later the plane touched down. Crystal turned to smile as she deplaned, and within thirty minutes, Rudy was in Cambridge. Since he was early, he decided to visit Harvard Square. There, he caught sight of a man that seemed remarkably familiar entering one of the bookshops. The guy seemed to glance back and with that feeling of déjà vu, Rudy felt he were looking in a mirror. He shook off a chill. This was one too many coincidences for this reporter. He was going to confront this look alike and end this bullshit once and for all. It was one thing to run into his double at an airport on his way to Germany. That could be brushed off as a chance encounter. But here, in Boston, so soon after, this was too much. He was being tailed.

Running to the bookshop, Rudy entered. There, at the end of an aisle he could see the man browsing through some novels. Rudy felt his heart pound as he braced himself for the confrontation. The man turned with book in hand. "Oh, my

God," Rudy gasped, his face flushed full red. The guy didn't look anything like him at all. "I'm sorry," Rudy mustered.

"Excuse me?" the man asked questioningly.

"Sorry," Rudy repeated, "Would you know the best way to MIT?"

Gad, what an idiot I am! Rudy thought as he weaved his way to MIT. Entering campus, he walked along the Charles River and gazed at a crew team gliding by as he tried to get his mind back on track. Soon, he reached the lane that led to the Information Technology building. Ashley LaPolla was not in her office. A geek in ripped blue jeans so skimpy that they revealed his jockey shorts directed Rudy to the computer lab. Since his name was on a visitor's list, he was allowed in.

Dr. Ashley LaPolla was dressed much like her students. She wore a pair of tasteful pedal pushers short enough to be a smidge provocative, the right amount of eye makeup that gave her the hint of an Egyptian look, a white top revealing a little cleavage and an over shirt that resembled a leopard skin. Her pageboy styled brown hair was tinted at the top with blonde highlights with the hint along one side of psychedelic maroon. She wore large silver hoop earrings that almost reached her shoulder and three shiny silver bracelets with the two thinner ones on her left wrist. For rings, she had one on her ring finger for each hand. Neither resembled a wedding band. Although he knew her age, she was 34, if he had to guess, he would have thought mid-twenties. Hip would be the best way to describe her.

She sat on a desk with her legs dangling, talking leisurely to seven students who all had their laptops open. They were discussing artificial intelligence, what some people call the singularity, that magic cross-over point when an intelligent machine becomes a true thinking entity.

A gal in a paisley halter-top and a bright pin of a red rose in her hair raised her hand.

"Yes, Kaitlin, you have a thought?" Ashley called on the girl in such a way to also let Rudy know that she was aware of his presence and to keep his ears tuned.

The girl took a while to lower her hand. Perhaps she wanted the class to notice that each fingernail was painted a different psychedelic color. "If and when the computer becomes aware of its own mortality," the student said keeping her hand in sight.

"Very good, Kaitlin. But how can we ever get a computer to truly comprehend the idea of death, let alone its own death?"

"By pulling its plug," one of the male students called out.

"Not so, Gregg," Ashley said. "And why is that?"

No one seemed to have an answer.

"Because you can always plug the machine back in," Rudy offered.

"Exactly, Mr. Styne. Class, this is the reporter I was telling you about, Rudy Styne from *Modern Times*. He's here because he thinks he has a scoop."

That got their attention.

"Am I right, Mr. Styne?" She looked him squarely in the eye.

Dr. LaPolla had caught Rudy off guard, as he had not planned to spring "The Question" on her until that night, having hoped they would have dinner together.

"Mr. Styne has flown all the way up here from the Big Apple to see if I am Code Breaker Morant. Am I right?"

The class turned in unison. Rudy felt as if his fly was open, but he thought now was not the time to check. The best defense, he thought... and so he plunged right in. "You've never made any secret of your interest in cracking, Dr. LaPolla."

"Hacking," she corrected.

"Okay, but either way, it is well known that as a graduate student right here at MIT, you accessed the records at Harvard and changed all the computer geeks' grades to C's and D's."

"One of my better days," Ashley LaPolla said as the students broke into laughter accompanied by a couple of "Hoo yahs!"

"And you have also made no secret of your infatuation with that Aussie actor Bryan Brown...."

"Who stars in Breaker Morant!" Kaitlin burst out loud.

Dr. LaPolla looked at her and Kaitlin found herself lowering her head.

"Of course, Mr. Styne. I don't know if I should admit this to the kids," she grinned at her small class, "but, for some reason, I've always found Bry Brown to be the bees' knees."

"The bees' knees?" A nerd in the back with a red and yellow baseball hat half cocked and skewed called out.

"The cat's meow?" Dr. LaPolla tried and looked at the student.

"Her heart-throb, dufas!" the guy sitting next to the nerd said.

"Oh, you gotta thing for him," the nerd concluded.

"Well, who do *you* have a thing for?" Dr. LaPolla asked.

"Paris Hilton," he admitted, causing his classmates to break out into laughter.

"So, you're denying you are Code Breaker Morant?" Rudy said.

"Mr. Styne, let me ask you a question."

"All right."

"If you were a master hacker trying to hide your identity, and if you remember my college prank, I left a website hyperlink at the bottom of the hack where a full copy of the original grades could be found, why would you, as this great hacker, choose a few key elements which would so easily identify yourself?"

"For the same reason you did it in college."

"But you know as well as I, Code Breaker Morant has done a number of stunningly illegal things which could result in his arrest. The thing I did in college was out of a rivalry between two computer classes here in Cambridge. I knew I'd get a little heat, but there was really no damage. It was a college prank between rival colleges, and because of that, it achieved everything I hoped it would, and more."

"That article in *Newsweek* on you?" the nerd in the back with the hat said.

"If you must know, yes," Ashley said. "You also realize that Harvard ended up thanking me because I showed them that their website had a hole in it that led right to the root program that posted their grades. Keep in mind that I did not change their official grades, only the posted grades the kids got on line. That was the beauty of it and we all had a good laugh. CBM has a sinister streak, even if some of his hacks, particularly in the last few years and months, has been to essentially alert a fragile system."

Rudy had been outsmarted. If she was Code Breaker Morant, she had him. He didn't see any way to uncover the truth, at least in this setting. One way or another, he definitely wanted to interview her to at least get more of her take on who she thought CBM was, and if she had any insights on who NTroodr might be.

"If you are not Code Breaker Morant," Rudy found himself winging it, "then why would this hacker make it seem as if it were you?"

"Anyone?" Dr. LaPolla asked the class.

"Camouflage," Kaitlin suggested.

"Very good," Dr. LaPolla said. "Anyone else, Wilfred? She directed her question to the nerd in the cap.

"Disinformation, the cracker's stock and trade." He spoke definitively. "Just so you know, doc," the nerd continued, "Jamie and I nixed you as CBM six weeks ago." He nodded to an athletically built clean-cut looking fellow he was sitting next to. This fellow had a tattoo of an anchor on his wrist, a buzz cut and a boyish grin.

"Why was that?" Ashley directed her question to Jamie.

"Because the last major cyberattack by this guy brought down the computer lab and it took us nearly two weeks to get it back up and running," Jamie said.

Wilfred cut back in. "That was when you were in the midst of running the World Congress in Bern. The timing was just too insane."

"Well, I don't know if that is proof," Rudy offered.

"You're missing the point," Wilfred rebutted. "And you cut me off. That crack cost this lab vital time and resources. But you also seem naïve when it comes to compiling a profile of CBM."

"What are you saying?" Rudy was scribbling notes as the conversation continued.

"CBM seems to be after two things. 1) to control the Internet and thereby assert his power. Dr. LaPolla is the opposite of a control freak. She does everything she can to get us to express who we really are."

"I have to repeat, young man. That's not proof."

"I know, Mr. Styne. But you didn't let me get to number 2."

"I hope you are not going to do Number 2 right here?" Kaitlin said. That broke everyone up.

"Very funny," Wilfred cut back.

"What's your second point?" Dr. LaPolla asked.

"We already said it," Wilfred said. "Misdirection, disinformation. Dr. LaPolla's been set up for the very reasons you cited. The real cracker needs a fall guy, and who better than an MIT computer teacher who hacked in college who has this nutty thing for some corny actor like Bryan Brown. And you totally fell for it." The nerd literally pointed to Rudy who shrunk at the accusation.

"Hey," Dr. LaPolla said.

Wilfred stood up to address the class. "Is he corny or what?"

"Corny," the class shouted in unison.

"Betts," Ashley called on one of the more quiet kids who sat there kind of slunk down off to the side.

"Yes."

"Do you even know who Bryan Brown is?"

"Like duh!" she said. The class laughed. Betts smiled for a point scored.

"Tell me one movie he's been in."

"That Aussie throwback with Mel Gibson."

"A title please."

"*Roadrunner*."

"You mean *Mad Max*?" Dr. LaPolla asked.

"Yeah, *Mad Max*," Betts said.

"Well, he was never in *Mad Max*."

"Hey, Betts, babe," Pool Stick chimed, "the hunk who was in that old flick *Gorillas in the Mist*."

It seemed as if a light went on in Betts brain. "Oh, that guy. I love that movie."

"Yeah, that guy," Dr. LaPolla said. She spoke in such a way as to expect Betts to consider whether or not Bryan Brown was a dish or not.

"I guess he's cool. The kind of cute one with that swagger and awesome smile who was in that Hugh Jackmen movie *Australia*, right?"

"Exactly!" Dr. LaPolla said.

"We figure," a tall lanky kid, mostly elbows and knees, who sat up in the front next to Kaitlin took over, "that the real CBM met Dr. LaPolla at some conference and has a thing for her. It is our guess that such a person would be male, a loner and, obviously, a huge computer geek. But probably doesn't have a Ph.D."

"Why is that?" Rudy asked.

"Because, if he had a Ph.D. and were a professor, he wouldn't need to be a cracker. In short, he's jealous of Dr. LaPolla."

"Boy, Pool Stick, I have to say, I'm impressed," Dr. LaPolla said.

"She became perfect bait for you, Mr. Styne," Wilfred concluded.

"Maybe," Rudy said. "You guys ever read The Purloined Letter?"

The class sat silently until Kaitlin spoke. "The Poe story?"

"Yes," Rudy said.

"You're saying that Dr. LaPolla is hiding in plain sight?"

"I'm just saying, one way or another, she's gotta be linked to CBM. Is that fair, Dr. LaPolla?" Rudy turned the question back to the professor.

"Then, I'm still not in the clear?" Dr. LaPolla asked.

"You've definitely made some good points," Rudy had to agree. "So, who do you think it is?"

"Someone who craves power."

"And if he uses some kind of proxy software like Freegate or Calhoon, he can never be traced?"

Dead silence permeated the room. Rudy had struck a nerve.

"How would you know about Calhoon?" Dr. LaPolla asked warily.

"It's a third tier derivative of Haystack. Leaving TOR in the dust, it's just a much more efficient onion site that enables the undernet. Everybody knows that," Rudy tried, referring to the more well-known IP address protection software that had been featured in *Rolling Stone* and *The Washington Post*.

"Everybody doesn't know that," the professor said as the class continued to sit in contemplative silence.

"Look," Rudy turned the tables, "this is what I do for a living. I just spent an hour at Harvard, and you wouldn't believe what I picked up," Rudy lied. "Let me ask you a question. Is Calhoon all that it's cracked up to be?"

"Do you mean that it can, without any doubt, conceal a hacker's Internet protocol address?"

"Yes, Professor, that's exactly what I'm asking." Rudy hoped he was masking his realization that he might have blown Dickie's cover.

"Let's just say this," Dr. Lapolla summed up, "every keystroke leaves a trace."

It was ten of the hour. As Dr. LaPolla spoke, the students began to pack their things and file out of the class. Some nodded to Rudy as they left. Wilfred made it a point to shake his hand.

"Why don't we finish this over dinner," Ashley said to Rudy. "I want to find out more about this Harvard guy you grilled."

"Sure," Rudy said.

"My place?"

"Fine."

"Good. I have a meeting with the dean and a few other things to do. Say seven?"

"Seven it is," Rudy said. "I'm looking forward to it. Should I bring wine?"

"That'd be great," Ashley said as she reached out to affectionately squeeze Rudy's elbow. It was an unusual display and, for a brief instant, it threw him.

Dr. LaPolla turned to go away. Rudy used the opportunity to shoot her another question. "And you'll tell me who CBM is?"

Giving him a half smile, she turned and continued walking backwards. "I'll tell you this," she said, "it's not your loser friend from Sausalito." She continued whirling until her body was back in synch with her movement forward.

"How did you know about him?" Rudy ran up to her.

"Dickie! You gotta be kidding. He's the biggest joke in the field." She opened a door to enter the dean's outer office.

"Why is that?" Rudy slipped in one more question.

"Because he's got nothing better to do than to sit on his money and peep. See you tonight." She closed the door with an expression that seemed to add, "You think you are so smart, but you're not."

Rudy left the building with a sense of anticipation and of being flattered. Yes, this was a business meeting and no, he had no amorous plans, but Ashley was highly attractive and, he would have to say, flirtatious. As he exited and made his way to the river, Rudy had the sense of being followed. He turned, it was Wilfred.

"Mr. Styne." Wilfred turned his hat backwards.

"It's Wilfred, isn't it?"

"Yes."

"What can I do for you?"

"Really it's what I can do for you."'

"What do you mean?" Rudy asked.

"LaPolla, you think she's a piece, don't you?"

"I think she's pretty, of course. But just so you know, Wilfred, I'm a happily married man. My meeting with your professor is purely business."

"I'm just trying to warn you," Wilfred said.

"Warn me about what?"

"What a two-faced viper she really is."

"What are you talking about?" Rudy said. "All I saw was you singing her praises."

I'm just trying to protect my grades, Mr. Styne. Call me a hypocrite if you like, but I'll tell you a story and you tell me if I'm right. Okay?"

"Okay."

"I had Professor LaPolla for a teacher last year as well. It was a programming course."

"Yes," said Rudy.

"Well, she was really coming on to me, creepily holding my arm when we met, all smiley."

"Yeah, so?"

"So, I was working on a paper on how to write a software program to diagnose a time management chart for a small company. I had written the first draft and she tore it to shreds, gave me a D, so I tossed it. I did get a B in the course because I aced the final."

"So what's your beef?" Rudy couldn't figure out where Wilfred was going.

"That conference in Bern she headed up."

"Yes?" Rudy said.

"Well, look at this." Wilfred took out a program of the conference. There under Ashley LaPolla's name was the title of her article. *Time Management Flow Chart Programs for Political Campaigns.* "That bitch created a software package to sell to politicians so they could maximize their labor force."

"Did you confront her?"

"Of course I did. She denied everything and tried to talk me into her being my mentor when I go on for my doctorate. She's a double-dealing snake, and I'd be careful if I were you."

Rudy looked at Wilfred for a minute to try to get a better read on him. "Thanks," the reporter said and shook his hand.

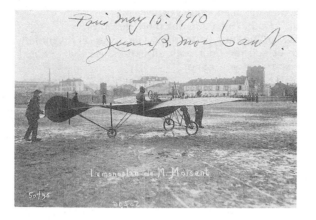

One of the many unusual aeroplanes that competed in the air races, circa 1910.

THE MONITOR

NTroodr sat in his lair, one hand gently stroking the black cat that sat in his lap while his other hand played with his mouse. He had to hand it to himself. Providing free iPhones to the computer labs of MIT, Harvard, Stanford and the other top computer schools had been a stroke of genius. He had initially considered gifts for the top hundred schools, but then realized the amount of data received would be overwhelming. The top ten was good enough, and really, at this moment, he was only interested in one, MIT, and one class in particular, Dr. Ashley LaPolla's.

She had gotten close, closer than she knew. Yes, he was aware of Rudy Styne as well. That guy didn't know shit from Shinola. He was a throwaway runt. But LaPolla was a geek of a whole different order. Unable to install bugs on any of her computers, or any that entered her lab, they all had the best anti-virus software, NTroodr came up with another idea. He targeted their cell phones. By imbedding a command that unleashed listening capability in their iPhones, he had all the access he needed. He began caressing the tail of his feline with the sheer thought of it.

The sound wasn't always perfect, but between the iPhones of Pool Stick, Gregg, Wilfred, Jamie, Betts and Kaitlin, he had the class in fucking stereo. LaPolla had been clever. She swept her room and her equipment before every class, but this iPhone audio system worked even when the device was in sleep mode. If she wasn't Code Breaker Morant, then who was? One way or another, it ultimately didn't matter as long as she didn't uncover HIM. He had to control the damage before the journalist even got a whiff. Ultimately, Styne hadn't a real clue as to what was truly possible, harnessing thousands of computers simultaneously to do his bidding, but NTroodr also knew, the reporter wasn't a dummy either. If Ashley LaPolla conveyed what he feared she might, well, that could be enough to increase the possibility of his exposure at a geometric rate. He had chosen well in using the girl as opposed to Pool Stick or Wilfred. He had been a college guy himself. Guys would care less if their dirty computer secrets were revealed to the world. But a girl in a man's world, it had worked like a charm. He could decide later her ultimate fate. Keeping her on the hook, and not just for sexcapades but also for murder, could pay benefits for years to come.

After freshening up in his room, Rudy left his hotel early. He decided to walk to Ashley LaPolla's home. He had her directions. It was in the heart of Cambridge in the old part of town where there were still cobblestone streets, the feel of the 1700's and the American Revolution.

It had stopped raining shortly before he left for their rendezvous. The streets were still wet. Rudy focused on the sound of his footsteps as he beat the pavement. As he passed the campus he saw a female student in a by rain jacket half jog, and then turn rapidly towards the dorms. As she passed under the streetlamp, Rudy noticed the girl's right hand. It had different colored nail polish on every finger. He was going to call out to see if it was Kaitlin, but maybe all the girls had that style? Rudy stopped at a liquor store, bought a bottle of Ruffino's Chianti, and continued on to Ashley's place, just eight more blocks away.

As he walked, he thought once again to her quick display of understated physical affection, but also of Wilfred's comments that she could be two-faced. The transference of her vibe during her brief pinch on his arm, he couldn't help it, set his mind awhirl. Now he knew why Dickie had a crush on her. Did she really know what Dickie had done? He'd simply have to maintain the lie that he had interviewed an unnamed source at Harvard. *Yes,* Rudy thought, *that seems foolproof.*

Rudy found his face flushing. At her entranceway, he read a placard that said Babson House, 1794. It was made mostly of red brick and had recently been restored to pristine condition. It stood next to a church which had been converted to a residence. Rudy wondered who would be lucky enough to have a church as a home. He turned his gaze back to Dr. LaPolla's front door and knocked.

There was no answer and the door was slightly ajar. That was odd. The hair on his arms were raised, his senses sharpened. He wanted to call out, but a certain fear overtook him. Quietly, he pushed the door open and stepped inside. As he waited, listening, he gently placed the bag with the wine bottle along the side wall. There was no sound whatever except for the hum of a computer, which was giving off a ghostly glow in a room to his left.

It was the staircase, however, that interested him. Cautiously, he tiptoed up. A shorthaired cat that resembled a spotted jaguar scooted down the steps through his legs, almost tripping him, and without wavering, slipped out of the house. Damn it, he thought, he should have shut the door. He stopped and continued listening. Again, he heard not a sound.

This was crazy, and he knew it, to continue up into essentially a stranger's house just because the door was open, but he felt compelled.

At the top of the stairs was a hallway that had to the left, a banister which overlooked the living room. To the right was what looked like two bedrooms and at the far end, a bathroom. He approached the first room. The door was ajar. It was a guest bedroom, neat and unused. He continued to the second bedroom which was larger.

Rudy was aware that he would be vulnerable if he simply approached the room in the normal fashion, but on he went. Adrenaline was pumping through his veins; his heart was pounding.

THE GREAT WAR

Spring 1914: Germany's entrance into the war was swift. The assassination of Archduke Ferdinand in June of 1914, by yet another Serbian fanatic, was but a pretext for the Kaiser to execute his expansion plans in military fashion. Austria had attacked Serbia in retribution. Thinking the Czar would back off from supporting his historical ally, the Kaiser joined in against the Slavs, but Russia surprised them by coming to Serbia's defense.

Knowing that France was aligned with Russia, and wanting to buttress his annexation of Alsace Lorraine, the Kaiser moved decisively. Combining forces with Turkey, Germany quickly gained control over Luxembourg, but to the east there was much more difficulty. Enmeshed in Russia and repelled by the Serbs, the Germans continued their bold two-front assault by storming through Belgium to infiltrate France. By mid-summer, England was well into the fracas, their western front inside French territories. From now on, trench warfare would dominate on land where dreaded poison gas would be used, and a new, complicated battle would be fought in the air.

Having taken early advantage, the Kaiser was dismayed when his cousins in England joined against him on the side of Belgium and France. Wilhelm had little choice other than to launch his submarine fleet to try and sink the British navy and any cargo ships that might supply them with armaments. At the same time, he met with the Zeppelin concern and stepped up production of their great airships so that he could bomb London and keep the Brits off balance.

The advent of the wireless added yet another dimension to this new kind of war. Having set up transatlantic wireless plants on the Eastern Shore of America through Telefunken, the Kaiser learned from his fifth column that the half-British inventor, Guglielmo Marconi, was sailing to America on the Lusitania which was also known to be ferrying arms. Unflinchingly, the Kaiser gave the go ahead to attack the luxury vessel on its return leg.

Rivaling the tragedy of the Titanic which occurred three years earlier, the sinking of the Lusitania was seen as a great victory to the German people. Although 1500 civilians were killed, and Marconi escaped by riding incognito aboard another ship, the Kaiser was pleased that a subversive shipment of American arms to England had been thwarted.

"How many German lives have we thus saved!" Wilhelm announced to the cheering masses.

Trying to regain the high ground, Winston Churchill rashly urged his country to set up a base in the Dardanelles at Gallipoli, the gateway to Istanbul and the Black Sea. This led to total disaster, over 40,000 British, French and Australian soldiers slaughtered with twice that many wounded. But the Brits also sent a fleet of aeroplanes to France to take on the German *Jastas*.

During the first few months, flying crafts on both sides were primitive, used mainly for reconnaissance. If the pilots were armed at all, it would be with pistol! The real terror came from the Zeppelins that could hover high above the Baltic and North Sea, scout ship movements, and drop bombs onto enemy lands.

The first blitzkrieg came in February of 1915. Zeppelins heavily armed, and at this stage of the war, nearly invincible, left their docks from Austria and Germany before dawn to drop their deadly cargo onto Great Yarmouth and Kings Lynn in England. In the first year alone, the Germans dropped nearly 40 tons of bombs, leveling buildings in London and wounding or killing over 600 civilians. It was the terror more than anything that the Brits feared, so they set out to destroy the great Zeppelins in their sheds which were housed in Düsseldorf and Cologne in Germany and Friedrichshafen along Lake Constance in Austria where Elias and Simon had met the Count nearly a decade before.

It would be four long months before the first flying Zeppelin was successfully destroyed by the Allies. This watershed feat was achieved by a reconnaissance Morane-Saulnier monoplane, or MS3, flown by Flight Sub-Lieutenant Reginald Warenford. Although Zeppelins were heavily armed with machine guns, and this one opened fire, Warenford moved evasively and continued to climb to reach what was known as the eagle's nest. From there, freezing in his open cockpit, he reached over, wiped the frost from his goggles and then let the drop-bomb go. A direct hit! The Zeppelin exploded in a terrific eruption of hydrogen gas and their own armaments. The concussion could be felt and seen for miles around.

The heat shockwave was so intense that it sent Warenford's plane into a tailspin and he crash-landed behind enemy lines. Evading ground fire, Warenford repaired his plane and returned to England triumphant. Awarded the Victoria's Cross, the young pilot died just three weeks later in a flight accident. Nonetheless, Warenford's success put the writing on the wall. Zeppelin's were slow and dangerous to fly. But this did not stop the Germans who countered by increasing their flying altitude from one to nearly two miles into the sky. With a fleet of about 100, literally thousands of these great behemoth flights continued. But still, there was Warenford's spectacular triumph, which portended not only the brisk evolution of the aeroplane, but also its role from a mostly passive reconnaissance instrument, to a vicious killing machine.

"Come here, sonny."

Little Abe recognized the postman, so he stepped from behind one of the big rhododendron plants. "Hi ya," he said.

"Can you give this to your father?" The postman leaned over and handed Abe a bright crisp envelope embossed with official markings. "This is a very important communiqué, so I want to make sure I can trust you."

"I can be entrusted, sir," the eight-year-old replied. In his small firm hands, he grabbed the envelope and raced up the long walkway. The postman saw Debora at the doorway and waved hello. She waved in return.

"Now, this looks important," Tante Ella said, eying the envelope. Debora placed it ceremoniously in the center of Elias' desk. After lunch, the two ladies retired to Elias' study to catch the afternoon light.

"It's from the Kaiser," Abe said, staring at the envelope with serious consternation.

"Now, how do you know that?" Tante Ella asked.

"Because I recognize his seal." Abe ran off, but returned quickly with a crude drawing of the double eagle seal, which he had sketched just a few days before. "The postman told me that all the big *mochers* were getting these letters," Inserting his father's monocle, and stepping into a pair of Elias' large slippers, Abe took on the air of a wise elderly statesman. "It seems there is to be a big meeting in Berlin."

"And how do you know that?" his mother asked.

"Because that is where our Father Wilhelm lives," Abe replied, a sense of satisfaction to his conclusion.

Her hand to her mouth conspiratorially, Tante Ella whispered so that Abe could hear, "He looks like a *gantseh mocher* himself!" With his papa's monocle and slippers still on, he wig-waggled out of the room, causing the two ladies to burst into laughter.

Caught up in a manic burst of patriotism, Elias felt rejuvenated. With von Rosensweig, and a dozen other converts and Jewish industrialists, MB Machineworks formed a combine to meet with the Kaiser so that expansion plans for military production could be facilitated.

"I will need more steel, rubber, oil production and gun powder," Kaiser Wilhelm blared. Baron Rothchild, Jonas Sohne and six other bankers assured the Kaiser that the financing for this increase in production would be there. Ignaz Petchek, who owned six iron ore mines in Alsace Lorraine and three corresponding steel plants in Poland, Germany and the Sudetenland, stepped up production. Isadore Simson converted his machine factories to weapons production, Robert Fessen provided solvents and oil refinery equipment, Wagenberg and Sohne agreed to produce army uniforms for minimal profit, and Maxwell and his competitor Shoenfeld, coordinated efforts to produce engines for automobiles, tanks and airships.

In fact, fully 15% of the major German manufacturers were Jewish, or converts including Walther Rathenau, owner of Allegemeine Elekricitats Gassellschaft, the General Electric of Germany. The Hinrichsen brothers were the best cobblers in the land. They would be making boots. Goldschmidt, Seligman, Behr and Erlich provided tools, tank parts, cots and spiked helmets; Heinrich Briegen got contracts for field glasses and monocles; Kopcke produced medicinal supplies; von Rosensweig, speedometers and measuring devices; Tomkins and Wolfe imported coffee and chocolate for the troops; Brudheim and Janonitzer brokered farm produce and livestock; Rosenthal manufactured a less expensive porcelain for kitchen facilities and Rimberg, Vanderwalde, Zanetti and Holtzer supplied chemicals, precision instruments, maps and technical advice. The Kaiser was pleased.

THE EARLY WAR

"Iris, I can't argue with you on this. We are at war. Joining the Luftwaffe is the most patriotic thing I can do."

"So you can kill Frenchmen and Brits, Simon? It's madness."

"Consider the alternative."

"The alternative is that you live and see other idiots die. Let's leave this country, Simon. The Kaiser's lost his sanity. Do you really think Germany can sustain a victory over France, England *and* Russia?"

"We've already taken Belgium and Luxembourg and a good part of France. Krupp's got a field gun that can deliver a cannon ball 100 kilometers away. With that kind of fire power, I think we've got a good chance."

"Of destroying Paris?"

"That's just to intimidate them. The Kaiser doesn't want Paris destroyed. We are a powerful nation Iris, and I want to support the cause."

"You see Brits and the French as your enemy?"

"You cannot talk like that. Wars are fought. Citizens must support their side. We manufacture aeroplanes and parts for Zeppelin's great airships. I fly aeroplanes. I would be derelict of my duty if I turned away from this. Hermann's already finished flight school."

"Sure, Göring actually considers the French as subhuman. But you, Simon. You were just in Paris three, four years ago and you're friends with half of East Church, Tom Sopwith not excluded."

"And we will be friends again. After this war is over. I can't argue you this. A pilot is what I am. A fighter pilot is what I will be. Do I have your blessing?"

"I'll try, Simon," Iris said, fighting back tears.

"May I come in?" Elias entered Simon's home. This was a rare event indeed. He startled Iris, but in a positive way, when he gripped his brother on both shoulders. "Look, Simon. I understand your willingness to support the Kaiser. Maxwell Industries is committed to the war effort. But you can go in as a trainer of pilots. Why be so frivolous with your life? With your expertise, you could train men *how* to fly. It's more befitting a man of your standing in the airline industry, and you can correct the wrongs that could ensue if inferior teachers are placed in charge."

Iris was torn in opposite directions. She resented Elias for taking advantage of his brother, and yet there he was trying to keep her husband out of the battle completely. She walked over to the big house to sit on the Maxwell porch to watch the sun set with Tante Ella. "What should I do, aunt?" she confided. Ella was busy knitting mittens for the soldier's relief fund. "If I side with Elias, I will be betraying my husband, but he will stay alive. Maybe the war will be over quickly. And, if I side with Simon he may do more than be a flight instructor. Once there, what's to stop him from joining in?"

"Elias will talk to the high command," Tante Ella reasoned. "They are well aware of the necessity for producing quality parts. And if Elias lets it be known that Simon is his master mechanic, and thus key to the war effort, why should they risk sending him out? There is certainly no shortage of foolhardy young men to go die for the Kaiser and the Fatherland.

"And, this way," she continued, "you will keep your promise to support Simon's greatest dream, to put on a uniform and defend the land. Ultimately, Iris, I don't think you have a choice."

"I could leave him," Iris shot back.

"And what good would that do?"

"Tante Ella, I'm not sure what love is anymore when he tortures me this way, every day wondering if he will live or die. It is me that may die of simple heartache."

"You and 100,000 other wives and mothers," Ella murmured loud enough for Iris to hear.

Simon packed his bags and headed to the German Army Air Service located in Johannisthal, 15 kilometers south of Berlin. Due to his expertise, he was quickly put on as instructor for both the maintenance crew and for teaching pilots. His breadth of knowledge and connection to MB Machineworks immediately placed him in a position of authority, particularly when he taught Max Immelman's mechanic how to tighten the guide wires that controlled lifting capability of the wings.

There he met Lieutenant Wilhelm Frankl, a fellow Jew from Hamburg, and his old friend Hermann Göring who was flying reconnaissance missions with flight instructor Bruno Loerzer. They had met at a hospital, after each had been shot down, Loerzer with a flesh wound in the shoulder, Göring shot in the thigh.

Older than many at age 24 and a natural flyer, Loerzer rose quickly to the rank of Lieutenant. By March of 1915, Loerzer and his protégé, Göring, had flown over twenty missions in reconnaissance. Early in the war, these planes were mostly two-seaters, and they were barely armed. Fighter planes came in later, first as a way to protect the unarmed reconnaissance planes, and then as ends in themselves. Most often, Loerzer was the pilot, Göring the photographer. Flying low, initially solo, and several months later accompanied by a plane armed with a machine gunner, Loerzer and Göring would photograph the location of trenches, supply routes, the placement of big guns and enemy troop movements.

The key to their success was to land near a photo processing lab, get the plates developed and either hand deliver, or send by Morse code, the tactical information they had retrieved. On a good day they would get back into the sky and give feedback to the Artillery Division so that their Krupp cannons could be recalibrated. In this way Krupp's explosions would do the most damage. Both Göring and Loerzer were awarded the Iron Cross for bravery in battle, although it would be another year before either of them flew solo or took down an enemy ship.

Frankl, one of the first fighter pilots to protect reconnaissance missions, started by flying Voisins but soon switched to a Fokker. He had over a dozen kills before 1916. One of the early Great War heroes, Frankl's cache of medals included the Iron Cross, the Knight's Cross and, by mid-1916, the coveted *Pour le Merite*, Germany's highest honor, an award first achieved by *Jag I Staffelführers* Boelke and Immelman. Frankl became the third Ace.

A long way from becoming an ace himself, Göring begrudgingly admired Frankl, even if he was a Jew.

Frankl decided to rub it in. "Did you know Immelman is also Jewish." Frankl sat at the dinner table draped in his medals. They were at a new airfield at a farm the military had taken over, just twenty kilometers from the French border.

"You'd never know it," Simon commented. "He speaks with an odd accent."

"Total horseshit, Wilhelm," Göring shot back.

"Tell that to his pecker," Frankl joked.

"He's British by birth," *Staffelführer* Loerzer joined the conversation.

"Born in South Africa," Göring said. "My father knew his family, and they were *not* Jewish," he lied. The families had never met. "We did a lot of trade with the Brits. Through Johannesburg." Göring never missed a chance to let everyone know his father had been Governor of German South West Africa.

"Max was going to be a doctor," Frankl said.

"That's when he renounced his British citizenship to become a German," Göring responded. "But frankly, Frankl, and you can ignore the alliteration, I don't care if he's a pygmy, as long as he can continue to shoot down the enemy and teach us his Immelman roll."

"I've already had a lesson," Simon surprised the group. "Anyone for a run?"

"I'm in," Loerzer said.

"Me too," Frankl chimed.

"All right, Simon, let's see you display your twirling derriere," Göring replied speaking with an affected French accent. Grabbing his goggles, he led the crew to the airfield.

"The wind can play a big role," Simon said, "but, you know Max also takes the torque of the propeller into account, the sun, of course, and if you're in a Fokker, its tendency to stall at a specific angle in the climb." Simon scratched a diagram out in the sand with a stick and then led them to the planes. Grabbing a Rumpler, Frankl hopped into the back seat. Loerzer and Göring took a two-seater Albatross. When their planes were at three hundred meters, Simon motioned for Loerzer to bear down on him as if he were to shoot, so they simulated a dogfight, zipping along at great speeds through the valley and over a hamlet a few clicks north of Madgeburg. Just as Loerzer caught up, Simon put his plane into a roll, banking towards the sun and looping back, coming upon the surprised Loerzer broadside. Simon then slowed the plane down to pull behind the Albatross, and chased Loerzer for a while until he tried the move. Then Frankl surprised the lot of them by wing-walking and switching positions with Simon. Göring wasn't going to let those "weasily Jews" get the better of him, so he too wing-walked and switched places with Loerzer and then they went through the procedure again.

"That was fantastic," Göring exclaimed upon landing. "Now we'll have to try it with a Frenchman. Hah!" He slapped Simon on the back and asked if he'd join him for a drink.

"As long as it's not Guynemer," Frankl said, referring to France's greatest Ace. Due to Frankl's rank and success, Göring was left speechless. The French were killing them, and everybody knew it.

While taking time to write Iris a letter, Simon thought back to the first months of the war when dogfights were more like barks with no bite, really just attempts by one side to scare off the planes of the other side. Some pilots packed a pistol, but the thought of shooting a fellow pilot was, in those early days, unheard of. Many of the original pilots knew each other from international aerial meets. Then planes began to use drop bombs, and once the Brits successfully shot down two Zeps, those innocent days simply vanished. Virtually overnight, the rules of engagement changed. The Kaiser had commissioned the construction of 60 more aeroplanes and 25 additional airships. With the great capacity of the airships to carry weight, it was the Kaiser's hope to reduce London to rubble. He would show his first cousin, England's king, just who the dominant force was.

True enough, the Londoners were terrified by the nightly raids, but by the same token, many of the Zeppelin flyers were also frightened. It was well known that hydrogen, which filled the airships, was highly explosive, and the accounts of a fiery downing of one of Zeppelin's monsters was enough to cause even the bravest to question his sanity.

Aeroplanes were becoming more and more adept as a method of attack. They still couldn't gain altitude like the new Zeps, but once the machine guns were mounted, they became a more effective mechanism for destroying troops. Sure, Zeppelins could hit stationary targets like major buildings, bridges and train stations, but Fokker, Junkers, Rumpler, Heinkel and Maxwell bi-planes were where the action was.

Where Fokker tended to copy the French Bleriot and later, the MS-1 designed by two other Frenchmen, Morane and Saulnier, Heinkel put together the ever popular and more versatile Albatross. Because of his expertise, Simon, to the great relief of his brother, did in fact, gain the prestigious job of training other pilots. Along with such brilliant tacticians as Oswald Boelke, who would train Manfred von Richthofen, Simon taught some of the best flyers the world had ever seen.

From Boelke, in particular, he learned the five rules of air combat: fly in groups with the sun to your back, never go into combat unless you have the advantage, attack with surprise and get out swiftly before any tables could be turned. "That's only four, Oswald," Simon commented.

"Count again, Simon," Boelke said, looking over Simon's notes. "You combined two of them in the first sentence."

"Oh," Simon nodded.

There were two leading aces of the day, Oswald Boelke who practiced what he preached by soon amassing an astonishing 40 kills, and Max Immelman, whose Immelman turns (a combination of a loop and a roll), and ability to dive from the sun as if he appeared from nowhere, was so legendary, that the German *Order of Merit*, the highest medal a fighter pilot could achieve, was essentially renamed by the Allies "The Blue Max" in Immelman's honor. In order to attain that distinction, a pilot had to down ten planes and have each verified. Then he became an "Ace." In these early days, Boelke and Immelman each were the "Ace of Aces."

Sure, there was glory, but the death of someone you knew became almost a weekly event. At that time, there wasn't so much the fear that the camps would be bombed or raided. The high command made it a priority to hide and shift the campsites and landing strips. It was just the continuing dread that the next death would be that of a close buddy.

Simon sat with pad and pen by a coal heater stove and sipped a cup of tea. He was working on an idea on how to retract the landing gear when the great duo entered the barracks and flopped themselves down on the two beds nearest to the heater. They were lamenting the casualty rate that the German air force was suffering.

"I just don't understand how we could lose so many planes," Immelman said.

"I've seen the French fly and they are no better than us. Just this week, we lost Druleman and Wintgens."

"You can add Mulzer to the list." Loerzer entered the room with the bad news.

"Not Mulzer," Simon said. "He'd just been knighted."

"According to the *oberleutenant*, a wing simply broke in a goddamned training accident."

"I want to see the plane," Simon said. "What was it?"

"An Albatross," Boelke said. "I was out in that very plane just last week!"

"Jesus Christ Almighty," Immelman said. "So it had nothing to do with the French."

"That was Mulzer," Boelke shot back angrily. "Druleman was lost in a dogfight near Nachtigal, and Wintgens was hit by the Stork." He was referring to Guynemer's elite French squadron.

"What's going on?" Immelman threw up his hands.

"We think it's their gun placement," Simon said pensively.

"That's what I heard." Boelke slammed the table with a hand and got up. "We're stuck mainly with two-man planes, where we are forced to shoot out the back, or solo planes where the gun is really hampered by the propeller."

"Amen to that," said Immelman.

"The French don't seem to be flying two-man planes anymore," Boelke reflected.

"That can only mean that their machine-guns point forward!" Immelman proclaimed. "But how can that be? They'd be shooting off their own propellers."

"Not if they were protected somehow," Simon suggested.

The first plane taken out in the Great War had been a British Spad shot down by ground troops in August of 1914. So the Brits retaliated in 1915 by mounting machine guns, first on a Sopwith Camel, where they were able to rifle unarmed German reconnaissance planes. With this new advantage, Captain Archibald Coastwain took down a Junkers, a Maxwell and two Fokker biplanes in a single day. German pilots came back enraged and demanded each manufacturer to install machine guns on their own planes.

Simon was given leave to return home and plan with Elias on how best to integrate this new design change. Besides weight distribution and other aerodynamic problems, there was also the timing issue. Early experiments had machine guns actually stripping their own propellers, so at first, these armaments were mounted out the back. This meant the everyday fighter plane had a pilot facing forwards and a gunner facing to the side or to the back.

Iris was in pieces. She had tried to keep herself calm, but she was beside herself with fear and anxiety. "We've tried to comfort her," Debora told Simon, "but it is to no avail. One day she threatens suicide, and another day divorce. I simply don't know what to tell you."

Simon found his wife at her mother's estate. She was sitting at the back porch throwing seeds and breadcrumbs to a flock of sparrows and two or three squirrels. She barely looked up when he approached.

"I'm dying here, Simon," she said, her eyes still focused on the pond. "You and this insane war. This is killing me. Do you know I lost two cousins on the Lusitania. It will be any day before the Americans come into this, and then what am I to do? How could this country sink a pleasure ship? And please don't tell me it was because they were also carrying arms. At least the sinking of the Titanic we could blame on God or Nature, but this. I'm just disgusted with – with men, and with you.

"The problem is," and she turned to face Simon for the first time, "I see *us* as the enemy. We started this war. We stormed Belgium, Belgium for the love of God! We use poison gas, we drop bombs over London and shoot cannon balls the size of automobiles a distance of eighty kilometers onto Paris streets, and for what? To what end, Simon? So that the Kaiser can own France? I cannot support this war. I'm fading fast. Why are you home?"

Simon realized that all hope for them had just disappeared like the bird seed that was gobbled up by the hungry sparrows. If he were to tell her the truth, that it was to install machine guns onto the Maxwell bi-planes, she'd leave him in a heartbeat, and yet that was why he had returned. "It's not too late for you," he finally said.

"For me? What are you talking about, Simon?"

He looked away. "Then it's true?" she said.

"Yes," he said quietly.

"Machine guns onto Maxwell planes to shoot down the very men you were calling your comrades just two years ago! What about us, our life together, our dreams? Are you going to throw all that down the drain to support a deranged monarch who chooses murder and mindless expansionism over reason and commerce?"

Simon knew Iris was right. He looked her squarely in the eyes and saw his life evaporate. How could he quit now when his country was dependent on his very expertise?

"You're intoxicated with it, aren't you?"

"Iris," he hesitated. "I'm damned if I leave, a traitor to my country, and to all that we have built, and damned in your eyes if I stay. But at least, if I stay, I will be supporting my family and the Fatherland."

He ended with that magic word, and it went through her heart like a dagger. She collapsed at that moment, wilting in such a way that her head slammed down onto the unforgiving wooden porch.

The doctor said she had a concussion and may have suffered brain damage. Only time would tell. Simon put the world on hold, he had an excuse that could last weeks, and spent the time sitting by her bedside, waiting for her to recover. When she was in deep sleep, he would steal over to the plant to confer with the mechanics and engineers on how best to mount the guns. The goal was to avoid pointing them out the back or the side, but the biggest problem remained the propeller. If the target moved dead center, the pilot ran the risk of destroying his own craft. Already eleven planes, five German, four British and two French, had crashed because the bullets from their own guns clipped off their own propellers.

Shooting out the front was surely the answer. That was the premise that led Simon to design what he called the doorstop mount which was simply a stopper that prevented a gun from crossing over the path of the propeller. It meant that German pilots could now shoot forward, or, more accurately semi-forward, just not straight ahead. The enemy could easily exploit this by trying to cross in front of the plane to confound the gun turrets, and Simon tried to accommodate this

potential tactic, but he saw no easy solution, and then he would have to drop all to
return to his house, and wait for his wife to come around.

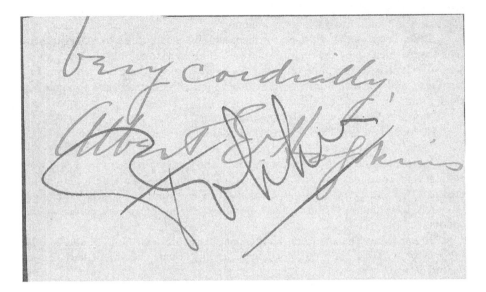

**When Anthony Fokker signs his name, he typically obliterates the
signature of the person requesting the autograph in the process!**

FOKKER'S ADVANCE

Over the next several weeks, Boelke's *Jagdstaffel* or hunting squadron lost four more pilots, all shot down by the well-known French pilot Roland Garros. Everyone knew Garros because he had been the first to fly the Mediterranean. That had been in 1913, just a year before the great Munich to Cairo to Munich race. Working with Saulnier on a Moraine-Saulnier single-seater monoplane, Garros had Saulnier place the machine gun in front of the pilot and then constructed steel wedges to protect the propeller by deflecting wayward bullets. In this manner, by shooting through this new protected propeller he easily took down two-seater German planes where the gunner sat in the back, or single seaters, where Garros could brazenly take the enemy head on.

Confused by these series of losses, Boelke came back from a mission and began to take it out on Simon. His reasons were irrational and Simon was at a loss of how to defend himself. "He must have a design advantage," Simon finally shouted.

"What did you say?!" Boelke continued to tear into him.

Loerzer stepped in between them. "Oscar," he said, "Maxwell is right. This has nothing to do with flying skills."

"Are you saying I don't know how to teach my men!"

"No, Oscar, you are not listening. One of those arrogant Frenchmen is shooting through the front of the plane."

"That's horseshit and you know it. No one can do that. That would be like walking on water!"

Just two weeks later, on April 18, 1915, Garros's fuel tank was hit by ground fire. Forced down behind enemy lines, he lacked the time to torch his plane before he was captured, and thus his firing mechanism was revealed. So the French advantage was short-lived.

Simon shot off a wire to Elias suggesting he experiment with front-mounted machine guns and propeller guards, but Elias was reluctant to proceed without his head mechanic present. With Simon stuck on the front lines, the Kaiser gave the plane to Anthony Fokker, and it was he who studied the gun-mount carefully. But Fokker also went one better. He explored a little known Swiss patent for a synchronization mechanism to augment the contraption.

With this new development, Elias petitioned the Kaiser again, and Simon was given leave once more. When the train pulled into Kempten, a messenger was waiting. Scrawled in Elias' tight script were the words, "Come at once. F. to meet us at 2."

"What does 'F' stand for?" Simon asked.

"I've no idea, sir."

Reflecting on the difficulties he was having with Iris, Simon tried to contain his sobs while they motored along. As they approached the plant, a Fokker plane overhead caught his eye. Beside himself, he shouted, "It's Fokker!"

Leaping from the car, he watched with Elias as Fokker circled the factory. Directly behind the propeller, Simon saw a prominent machine gun.

"Is he insane? The minute he shoots that thing, he's going to tear his propeller to bits!" Simon exclaimed. Elias replied without words. He just nodded and smiled wryly.

Fokker circled the factory, then swooped down to a target area Elias had set up by a clearing a good distance past the end of the runway. *Rat-a-tat-tat-tat-tat-tat*. The shooting machine ripped apart a platoon of dummy soldiers made out of plywood. Simon looked at Elias completely dumbfounded.

Fokker waved down to the two of them and signaled for a second go-around. After the burst of fire, the secret began to dawn in Simon's mind.

"I don't understand it either," Elias said. "But, somehow, his bullets go through the propeller in a perfect way so as not to hit them. This puzzle did not seem solvable, but obviously, he's got it figured out."

"Obviously," Simon said, a clear gleam of recognition now entering his brow. "It's the propeller itself that is firing the weapon!"

"I'm not sure I understand," Elias said contemplating.

Fokker circled back, landed and taxied over to where the Maxwell brothers stood.

"Brilliant, Anthony!" Simon ran over. "Absolutely brilliant!"

Fokker approached. Ripping off his goggles, he put his arm around Simon, and he shook hands with Elias. He had a Top Secret patent agreement which explained that no matter how fast the propeller rotated, the bullets would only shoot in the spaces between each propeller.

Elias looked on, still trying to put it all together, a bit of envy in his eye, but he was happy to make the deal to manufacture Fokker's synchronization method, and quickly signed the agreement. "This should make you a rich man," he said.

"I really don't want to make my living this way," Fokker replied. "But those Brits need to be given a lesson!"

"How long before they catch on?" Elias asked.

"Not long enough. And I don't think they will be paying any royalties when they do," Fokker joked.

"Hah!" Elias guffawed in spite of the seriousness of the situation. "Well at least you'll make royalties from me!"

"Junkers will go ape-shit he didn't think this up himself!" Simon remarked.

"And you," Fokker smiled.

"Anthony, you deserve all the accolades. Congratulations once again!"

"You will take care of Iris while I am gone?" Simon asked Elias.

"Of course. Just take care of yourself. Remember, you are a teacher and manufacturer. You are too important to the war effort…"

"You mean to your factory?"

"Yes, this factory… to risk your life. Hundreds, if not thousands of people are depending on your expertise."

"All right, big brother. I get the message."

With the start of 1916, now armed with Fokker synchronized Spandau machine guns, the Germans again took command of the skies and their kill rate went up accordingly. During this short but devastating period known as the

Fokker Scourge, Max Immelman led the pack with 13 kills, followed by Oswald Boelke with nine. But Boelke was a quick study, and by April, they were tied with 15 apiece, their successes daily fodder for the front page of the German newspapers.

Immelman liked to patrol over the town of Lille. An ancient hamlet with palaces and marshlands strategically placed on the border between France and Belgium, he would often fly over his favorite castle on his way back to *Jagdstaffel*. Because of this habit, he was soon dubbed the "Eagle of Lille." Equivalent flying aces for the Allies included Guynemer and Fonk for France and Mannock, Bishop and McCudden for England.

Simon returned to the front lines and continued his work as a flight instructor. With grand design, Boelke and Immelman were on a rip. Their kill numbers went up threefold, and their fame skyrocketed. Göring had not soloed yet, and was just aching to join the fray. It would be several more months before he would get his chance. And when he finally did, his plane was shot down over German airspace, fortuitously near a field hospital as Göring had only been grazed. A German family nearby took him in and cared for his wounds. The lady of the house turned out to be Jewish. In general, Göring was socially anti-Semitic like a large number of the Christian population. But individual Jews, like his godfather's niece, Iris, the Maxwells, and now this old lady, they were in a different category in his head.

Still on crutches, he returned to flight school to be near the action. It would take six more weeks for him to recover, and he used a good deal of the time to taunt Simon into joining the action.

"The Jews are good for business and profiting from war, but I've yet to see a Jew risk his life on the front lines."

"That's such horseshit, Hermann. What about Frankl? He's already working on his second dozen."

"All right, I'll give you Frankl. He's a helluva pilot."

"And Immelman?"

"The Blue Max." Göring was using the British nickname for the most daring and creative of all the pilots, French, Brit or German. We've already discussed this, Simon. I don't accept that he's a Jew."

"Well tell that to his grandfather, who runs a synagogue in Capetown where he was born," Simon said.

"I decide who is Jewish," Göring stammered. "And I can tell you, Max Immelman is not Jewish."

"And what about Schwartzsein, Coldbrunner and Eisenberg."

"Simon, for every Jew you name, I could name ten who are sitting on the sidelines."

"Allow the Jew full citizenship and then let's count the numbers."

Krause interrupted, running in excitedly. He was talking about the latest upcommer, although a new pilot, there already was something about him that seemed to put him in a league all his own. "Manfred Richthofen got two Vickers last week, and the word is, he's added a Nieuport and a Sopwith on this last run."

"How did Udet do?" Göring asked plaintively.

"A Nieuport and maybe a Bristol."

"I don't understand you," Göring motioned back to Simon. "How you can just sit on the sidelines and let all this happen? I've got to get back to the doctor and have him re-assess. I feel like I'm more likely to die here of boredom than out in the skies with my comrades."

"Is that nail polish you are wearing?"

"It's lacquer to protect my nails. Now stop changing the subject, Simon. We've got the edge now and we're simply going to need you."

Iris came by the Maxwell estate to read the latest letter from Simon. The entire country was in mourning with the death of their greatest pilot, Max Immelman, who lost his propeller during a dogfight in June of 1916. Immelman's death was a crushing blow to the German morale as he had achieved nearly the status of a demi-god. Fearing the loss of another great, the German high command pulled Boelke from the front and sent him on a propaganda tour throughout Austro-Hungary, occupied Serbia and Turkey.

Except for the few unavoidable sorties Simon had to take when Boelke was on leave, he had been good about staying behind the lines to train pilots. But Hermann Göring was gnawing on his nerves. Hermann had already shot down six of the enemy including two Sopwiths, a Nieuport and a Bleriot, and after he returned, yet again triumphant, he would swagger around the camp as if he were the reincarnation of God Almighty. True, no one could keep up with Richthofen whose kill rate was fast approaching that of Boelke's, but it was Hermann who had the ability to make a person feel as if he were a coward if he too were not in on the hunt. At dinner Göring would call Simon "teacher" in such a way as to make the word sound like a curse. Simon was finding it harder to stay out of the game.

"Ah, don't listen to him," Baron Richthofen said as he directed his mechanic to paste on his fuselage another impression of an enemy aircraft.

"That's easy for you to say now that your score has topped The Blue Max," Simon responded.

"With all that blood-splatter on your craft I don't see how anybody could prove you've surpassed the Blue Max," Göring kidded. He was referring to the color of Richthofen's plane, which was bright red.

And so it happened from that time onward, every time Richthofen returned with another kill, his comrades would chant, "Red."

Once these nick-names were kicked about, at another dinner, Göring became petulant requesting one for himself.

"How about Vain-Glorious Göring."

"Very funny, Simon," Hermann said.

"Come on, Vain," the Red Baron jumped in. "Let's finish that game of Chess I had started with Immelman."

Göring could not tell if this was a sadistic joke or true.

DOGFIGHT

In early autumn, the unthinkable happened. Simon explained in his letter. Iris read it aloud before the entire family. They all sat around her in Elias' study, the sun peering through the southeastern windows.

Boelke had already achieved twice as many victories as Immelman had, yet his style was nearly diametrically opposite to that of his acrobatic partner. With geometric precision, he took out his targets, one by one, day by day, so much so that we thought him invincible. It was a beautiful September day. The sky was clear and deep blue. Just a few puffed white clouds. Boelke had taken his "cubs," on a skirmish against British Major Lanoe Hawker's legendary 24 Squadron.

Boelke's pilots included Erwin Böhme, a college educated engineer who had traveled as far as Africa, and a baron, Manfred von Richthofen, who is fast becoming one of the top pilots in the fleet.

Flying like a small flock of birds in a wedge, Boelke took the lead in his favorite Fokker Eindecker, von Richthofen in an Albatross tri-plane was to his right and Böhme, in another Fokker, was tandem on the left. They began their attack like clockwork against two DeHavilland scouts. Richthofen peeled right quickly to take on Lieutenant Alfred McKay, while Boelke and Böhme attacked a captain to the left, a Canadian, Arthur Knight. In the heat of battle, McKay swooped back, Richthofen on his tail. To avoid collision, Boelke and Böhme broke rank in a maneuver designed for just such a situation, but Böhme's plane scraped the undercarriage of one of Boelke's wings, and down he went. The second of Germany's greatest flyers now too is gone. Even the British pilots were in awe of our Ace of Aces. From what we understand, one of them returned to the crash site to drop a wreath in Boelke's honor.

"What does irony mean?" Abe asked.

"It means that your papa wanted Simon to be smart by becoming a flight instructor instead of a fighter pilot, and then Boelke dies by being hit by one of his own students," Iris said. "How many kills did he have, Abe?"

"Forty!"

"My God, forty dead Brits and Frenchmen. Where was I?"

"Boelke's death."

"Yes, thanks, Abe. I think the message is, no one is safe in the aeroplane business." Iris shot a scowl in Elias' direction. "But let me go on." She turned her attention back to the letter, reading:

Hermann Göring sends his regards. He is flying in Jasta 26 under the able command of Oberleutnant Bruno Loerzer.

Boelke had been itching to return to the front lines, but before he did, he took time out to write a eulogy for Immelman, truly the greatest pilot I have ever seen.

"Is that ironic, papa because he was taken down?"

"Yes, son. Iris, please go on."

Immelman's eulogy was so long, Iris continued to read, *that Boelke reworked it into a training manual, Air Fighting Tactics, which has become required reading for all new pilots. He dedicated the book to Max Immelman.*

I think of you every day, please give my regards to the family and tell Elias that our equipment is working admirably.

> *All my love,*
> *Simon*

Iris looked up. "That's it," she said, tears flowing. "I'm sorry, I have to go."

"Why was she crying, momma?" Abe said.

"She misses Simon, my little one," Debora said as she walked Elias out to the porch. "She could be pregnant," she whispered out of Abe's earshot.

"You think so?" Elias looked down at his wife impressed with her intuitive skills.

"Don't say anything."

"One way or another, we'll know soon enough."

Debora gave her husband one of her looks.

"All right, all right," Elias complied. "I won't say anything."

Even though Boelke and Immelman were gone, the Luftwaffe still had the design edge due to Fokker's machine gun invention. Thus, the young pilots remained primed to get into the action while time was still on their side. They knew, though they never said it, that it might only be a matter of weeks. That was one of the reasons Göring was so pushy. He wanted to rake up as many kills as he could while the window was still open. A number of pilots thought Göring fudged the numbers, but he was still a charmer, so no one took him on, and his kill count continued to climb.

Although hundreds of airmen were dying, over 300 alone during one month in what became known as Bloody April of 1917, the Germans were still taking down three aircraft for every one they lost. Part of Simon ached to join the squadron, to become a true member of what became known as von Richthofen's elite *Jasta*. However, he had the respect of his students and of the Baron because he was producing good fliers, and he was still friends with Göring even though he had barely been in battle, so over all, he faced each day with a clean conscience.

In November, *Staffelführer* Richthofen sauntered over. Always accompanied by an entourage of young pilots and willing women when he was off base, the Red Baron had become the most famous person in Germany.

"Come to Christmas dinner, Maxie," the Baron said nonchalantly.

Grinning, Göring gave Simon the thumbs up sign. "Maxie, I like it," Göring said, heavily accenting the last syllable.

"All right, all right," Simon said.

AWRY

Rudy entered Ashley's bedroom. She lay on the bed in an awkward position, her hands to her neck, frozen in a death grip, her eyes still open. She seemed to show sorrow as well as fear. Her death had not been instantaneous. He approached her body. Rudy knew he would have to call 911, but every minute alone before the cops arrived would give him an edge. Lying beside Ashley was both a suicide note and a syringe. He dared not touch the note and so read it from a distance. She talked of her shame of being Code Breaker Morant and her fear that now that she had now been found out by a New York reporter, her career at MIT was over.

He didn't believe the note for a moment. There was no way she had committed suicide. Rudy ran down to her computer. The machine was still on, but now it was sitting in sleep mode. Using a napkin, he tapped it to life and moved the mouse to try and read the hard drive. It had been wiped clean. He called Dickie.

"She's dead! Are you fucking nuts!?" Dickie was shouting. "You gotta call the cops this instance."

"I know," Rudy said. "But if I can lift the hard drive, maybe I could get its contents retrieved. I'm asking you how to do it."

"It's too late. You're screwed," Dickie said.

"Suppose I hadn't discovered the body yet," Rudy countered.

"That's one hell of a stretch, Rudy. Can you locate a screwdriver? Why not just take the whole machine?"

Rudy considered that option, it was a sizable computer, but that's when he heard the sirens. "Dickie, they're coming. I want you to stay on the line with me. I've gotta still be on the phone when they find me."

"Sure, man. You hauling ass?"

"Yes," Rudy shoved the phone in his pocket and searched the back for a way out. There was, indeed, a back door and it was locked. Using a Kleenex, he turned the lock, opened the door and slid out. He would have to hop a back fence to avoid being seen. The sirens were getting louder. Rudy stepped on a picnic table, hoisted himself over and flew through a neighbor's backyard, ending up on the street directly behind Ashley's. When he got to the sidewalk, he put the phone to his ear. "You there?" he said.

"Still here, man. You gotta plan?"

"I had a date with her. I'm just going to continue on. If they track my calls, they'll locate this one and you tell them you were briefing me on questions to ask as if Dr. LaPolla were a master hacker. By the way, what would I ask?"

Dickie told him. Rudy turned one more corner in time to see the police cars scream to a halt in front of Ashley's home. "The cops are here. I'll call you later," Rudy said.

"Forget it, man," Dickie said. "I'm outta here. If she got killed like you said, we could all be in danger."

"You mean you're splitting town?"

"I'm splitting country, old buddy. We're going to have to use throw-aways from now on. Expect some instructions through snail." And then Dickie hung up.

Rudy approached the house, which was already being cordoned off. "What's going on?" he said to the first officer he could get to.

"Just move along, buddy. This is not your business."

"But I have a date with Dr. LaPolla for seven," Rudy said. "Is she okay?"

"Let's see some ID." The officer grabbed Rudy's wallet and gave it look-see. "Hey, Mike!" he called out to an older man. "This here's a reporter for *Modern Times*. Says he had a date with Dr. LaPolla for seven p.m."

A senior officer with short grey hair and a wrinkled brow came over to check Rudy over. "Would you mind coming down to the station to answer a few questions?"

"Not at all, but what's the story?" Rudy read his nameplate, "Officer Payne."

"It's not good."

"Can I get a look see so the press will have representation?"

"Nice try, Mr. Styne, Grab a seat." Payne opened the passenger door of a squad car. They were at the precinct in less than ten minutes.

Rudy was led down the hall to an interview room. It was a sterile space, not even a picture on the wall. Just a metal table bolted to the floor and four chairs, two on each side. A dark window lay to the right. Rudy assumed it was for observation.

"Take a seat," Payne said.

"Am I a suspect?"

"Should you be?"

"Of course not."

"All right, then," Payne began, "what do you make of it?"

What Rudy really made of it was he wanted to get to campus ASAP to grab Kaitlin and also Wilfred, if he could, and get the lowdown. He decided not to tell them everything. At the same time, Ashley had just been murdered and so he also wanted the killer, or as he suspected, killers, brought to justice. "Officer Payne, I think I was involved."

Officer Payne considered the statement. "Do you mind if I turn this on?" He pointed to a recording device.

"Not at all," Rudy replied. "I mean, I think it may very well have been my coming here to Boston to interview Dr. LaPolla that prompted her death."

"How so?"

"Look, Mike, can I call you Mike?"

"Sure, Mr. Styne, you can call me Mike."

"It is possible that Dr. LaPolla's death could be unrelated to my meeting with her, but the odds are unlikely. I'm on the trail of NTroodr."

"N who?"

"Trooder, a play on words for intruder. The 'Oh Shit' cracker."

"That guy?! Come on, that was a bullshit prank," Officer Payne said.

"You call the ability to infect nearly 3% of the world's computers and take them all over simultaneously at the drop of a hat a prank?"

"All right, Styne, you got my ear."

"Good. With all due respect, Mike, this event was merely a pretext, the tip of the proverbial iceberg, and no one knows how big this iceberg is or will be. But it's big."

"What's the point?"

"It has to be power, for sure, absolute power, on a scale almost unimaginable, and that's for starters."

"Whoa!" The impact of Rudy's words had begun to hit home. "So she knew who this cracker was?"

"I don't know if she knew. But my guess is, she was close."

"And who do you think it is?"

"You gotta start with the premise that it's a computer genius. I guess such a person could do all this without going to school, and then, of course, we can't rule out the Russians, the Chinese, or the North Koreans. They are all possibilities. So it could be anybody in the world. But I'll tell you this. Whoever killed Ashley," Rudy realized that he should have called her Dr. LaPolla, but it just slipped out, "that person is not NTroodr."

"Why is that?"

"Several reasons. First off, NTroodr, if he did kill Dr. LaPolla, would obviously have to be in the Boston area at this moment. And as I said, he, or she, could be anywhere on the planet. No, the more likely scenario is that he, I'm going to assume it's a he, already has the ability to control people through blackmail, or, he already had her targeted and it was just a coincidence that I got here on the same day. Either way, you find the assassin, you get a little closer. But odds are there's some type of firewall between the actual killer and the real culprit."

"One more question, Mr. Styne."

"Yes."

"How would this guy gain control over someone?"

"Let me ask you a question," Rudy turned the tables.

"All right, go ahead," Officer Payne said.

"Suppose you knew the exact porn sites that the governor, the two senators and the CEO of a community faith-based organization was frequenting, or the email address and word-for-word correspondence of his or her concubine. What would that be worth?"

Officer Payne raised his eyebrows.

"How about the exact keystrokes of a person's password, their mother's maiden name, their favorite pet, the name of their fifth grade teacher and the bank account and credit card numbers of every one of their accounts. Or the ability to infect their computer with some type of hyperlink that could subliminally purchase some innocuous product, or the ability to simply deduct $5.95 on a random basis from one or more of their credit cards, or better yet, match a deduction with a particular product a person was already purchasing, like an extra charge for an LL Bean shirt or a book at Amazon, and multiply that by 100 million computers. Would that be worth killing for to protect?"

"So, what's your theory?"

"My theory is this. NTroodr was somehow monitoring Dr. LaPolla and maybe also me. One way or another, he knew that a major computer genius with a talent herself for hacking, was onto him. How close, I don't know. But this guy found out and had to have her done. Now, can I go?"

Rudy had said more than he wanted, but still, he had to help, and really wanted to. He just wanted to get at his suspects before the cops did.

Payne stared at Rudy a long time. "I'll be right back." He left the room and walked around into the observation chamber.

"Whadayathink?" he said to an older lady who stood there stoically.

Dr. Oberlain, the police consultant in criminal psychology, was pensive. Dressed in a long grey dress that resembled a suit, long grey haircut to shoulder length and large hoop earrings, Dr. Oberlain looked to be in her mid-60's. "I can't see him as the killer," she finally said. "But I think he knows more than he is telling us...."

Officer Payne cut her off. "Why is that?"

"He wants to get out of here for a reason. My guess is that he has a suspect in mind. The way he hesitated and bit his lip after he explained much of what he really did think. It seems to me," Dr. Oberlain went on, "that he took you as far as he could without giving up the last clue he thinks he has. He's a reporter and he's got a story. That's his first priority. But he also wants to find who killed the lady he called Ashley. He liked her. And it hasn't yet hit him. I think he has some grieving to do."

"So, should I pump him for the suspect?"

"My suggestion is no. Let him go and get a promise from him to keep you in the loop if he uncovers anything else. Give him your card. Gain his confidence. We are really on the same team. He just wants to get there first."

"That's most unconventional, doc."

"He obviously understands that this LaPolla death is much more complicated than a simple murder out of professional jealousy. He did give us a wealth of information because he gave us motive. Let's not forget that. As it is, we should take all this to the feebees ASAP, and also call in our own computer experts to find out what they suspect about this NTroodr. I say, give him some rope and maybe a loose tail and let's see what shakes."

"All right," Officer Payne said. He walked back to the interrogation room. "You can go," he told Rudy. "But I want you to know, we think you know more then you have just told us, and we could keep you here all night to get it out of you. But I conferred with my overseer, and we've decided to trust you to do the right thing."

"And what thing is that?" Rudy asked.

"Keep us in the loop. That a deal?"

"Deal." Rudy reached out to shake Officer Payne's hand.

Rudy left the precinct and called Chessie from his mobile. She didn't answer and he didn't know if she knew yet that LaPolla had been murdered. Not wanting to leave a disconcerting message on the recorder, he simply said, "Chess, I'm fine. If you've seen the news, don't worry, I'm all right. Call me when you get a chance."

Rudy wanted to get back to Cambridge to locate Kaitlin's dorm, but he didn't even know her last name, or Wilfred's, for that matter. Dickie, who probably had the ability to locate that kind of information, had split, and who could blame him, so Rudy was at a loss as to figure out a way to track her down before the next business day when the records office would be open. Assuming he was being tailed, he walked into several bars and then found one to exit out the back. Jumping a couple of fences, he surfaced off Comm Ave. So much had happened since seven, and it wasn't even ten o'clock. And where the hell was Chessie? But he didn't have time to worry about that now. He had to think. And then he remembered the kid in the front of the room with the strange name, Pool Stick. "It's gotta mean he plays pool," Rudy said aloud to himself. Boston at that time of night is like one giant campus. He asked a few college looking guys where the best pool halls were and that's where he went.

The second hall he went to was called Black Balled. A combination bar and pool hall, it had a mixed crowd, all races and definitely a college hang-out. There was a surreal element to the place. Many of the kids had odd hairstyles with psychedelic colors and neck tattoos. Some of the guys even had eye makeup, all a bit remindful to him of that bar scene in *Star Wars*. He asked if anyone knew Pool Stick. One girl ducked when he came into view. It was Betts, from the class. He had lucked out. She started to walk away, but he trotted over and touched her wrist.

"Can I speak to you?"

"What are you some kind of perve? Aren't you a bit old for this?"

"Then you don't know?" Rudy said.

"Know what?" Betts phone must have begun vibrating, because she picked it up to read a text message. She tapped her fingers on the touch screen but the phone went totally blank. "What the fuck?" she said, tapping it again and getting no response. "This piece of shit. I hate the fucking iPhone, always did," and to Rudy's total surprise, she tossed it into a garbage can.

"What are you nuts?" he said. "Here, hold this." He took off the lid of the can, handed it to her and dug into the goop to retrieve it. Grabbing a napkin off the bar, he wiped it clean.

"What's that all about?" he said.

"I had a Blackberry, and I was very happy with it and still own it." She reached into her purse and retrieved her other phone. "But they were handing those out for free, two months calling even paid for, so I took one, we all did, but I never got off on it. You know, everyone's into the iPhone, but it's always been glitchy to me and I can't get the damn speaker system to turn off."

"Did anybody else complain?"

"You kidding? All those guys in the class are Mac freaks. I never got off on the Mac. The damn laptop was a thou more than an HP, and I had always been like totally happy with my Blackberry. I like my fingers to touch real keys when I text. That touch screen stuff -- it's a pain. No way you can type as fast and it's too virtual, if you know what I mean."

"Then, may I keep this?" Rudy looked at the phone, and like she had said, the speaker light was still on, although the rest of the phone was apparently dysfunctional.

"Sure. So what's going on?"

Rudy looked around the room. Strolling past the pool tables, over to where the cue sticks were, he found a small box filled with chalk and emptied it. Shutting the phone off and wrapping it in several napkins, he wiped out the box, put the phone in, and stuck it in his pocket. "Let's sit over there." He pointed to an empty booth away from the action beyond the last pool table.

NTroodr had his hands full. He was not really interested in Betts Valerin. And he was going nuts with trying to deal with all the noise from the bar. He had six other students to monitor along with several professors from MIT that were close colleagues of Ashley LaPolla and also two key counterparts at Harvard. Like Betts had said, her phone *had* always been glitchy and the speaker information came in garbled. But he also didn't like the fact that he had been shut out by her. "Ah, fuck it," he finally reasoned to himself. "I got more important things to think about." He turned his attention to the ones he had the most control over. NTroodr began to think that his perfect crime may not have been so perfect.

"I guess you haven't heard that your professor's been murdered."

"You mean Dr. LaPolla?"

"Yes," Rudy said, "and I'd like to get in touch with everyone from the class. Would you have their phone numbers, email addresses and dorm rooms?"

Betts just sat there. "What happened?"

Rudy was going to say that she had been poisoned, but then he remembered that he supposedly hadn't seen anything. "I don't know," was all he said. "I had a date at her apartment for seven, and when I got there, the place was crawling with cops."

Rudy suddenly realized that if someone called it in from a cell, then that person would have had to have been in the apartment before he was there. It didn't make sense, unless they were trying to frame him. All of this raced through his mind as he tried to somehow also gain Betts' trust.

"Betts, I'll level with you," he said, winging it. "My guess is that one of the students in the class, there were seven of you, may know something that might give us a clue. I'm just asking for your help. They may talk to me, but once the cops get a hold of them, well you know how cops can be. I'm asking you to trust me." Rudy looked into her eyes. "Was any student close to Dr. LaPolla. You know what I mean, closer than any of the others?"

"Wilfred was the closest. We had all been to her house early in the semester. She had a Sunday brunch. But Wilfred had asked her to be his doctoral mentor."

"Even though she screwed him on his management paper?"

"Yeah. He didn't like it, but he also realized that one could go a long way with her as a mentor, and she kind of owed him."

"How about Kaitlin?"

"What about her?"

"Are you friends with her?"

"Not really."

"Why's that?"

"No reason. We just hung in different circles."

"Why'd you want to avoid me when I came over?"

"Like, you're old and you think Dr. LaPolla is bad. The truth is, man, I just don't trust reporters."

Rudy began to see Betts in a different light. Yes, she had been the unassuming one in class, but now that he was closer to her, he noticed how really striking she was as she sat there looking at him, with her left foot on the chair and her face resting on her knee. He doubted she even realized she was sitting that way. Rudy turned his attention to the rest of her appearance. Her shirt, which resembled an untucked pajama top, was subtly quite sexy, much like a very short skirt, low cut in the front, offset by a simple gold heart necklace. With rings on her thumb, first and ring finger, a series bracelets mostly of silver, with one, curiously made out of string, hot pink nail polish on both her finger and toenails, she was wearing sandals, and her hair in a bun with sun glasses propped above her forehead, in some odd way, the whole package lent her a certain air of understated sexy sophistication.

"What do you know about Kaitlin?"

"You're getting creepy, man."

"Betts, you are going to have to grow up. Your teacher's dead. I know it's a shock and it's a shock to me. But I need to speak to all you guys, so if you could tell me what dorms they are in and their full names, I'd greatly appreciate it.

Betts wrote down the one's she knew.

"What about Jamie?" He was the only one missing from the list.

"Don't really know him."

"Why is that?"

"Well, he pretended to hang with Wilfred, but I don't think he really hung with anybody. Lives off campus, I think in Somerset somewheres."

"If you think of anything else, here's my cell number and email address. Betts, don't hesitate. I think you know that I really want to nail the bastard who killed your teacher."

"Yeah," was all she said.

Rudy left the poolroom. As he exited, he made a bet to himself that Betts was giving all her classmates a heads up. Assuming she gave him the right dorm for Kaitlin, he figured he'd be able to corral her when she exited, so he jogged as fast as he could to a location that gave him a full view of Kaitlin's building and waited.

About ten minutes later, he saw Kaitlin exit the main entrance, satchel in hand. Moving at a brisk pace, although the campus was well lit, it was nighttime, so that gave Rudy the edge he needed. Keeping to the shadows, he tailed her to one of the student parking lots. As she approached her car, it squeaked and blinked its lights. He accelerated and grabbed her hand as she tried to get in.

"Hey, what the fuck, man?" she blurted, glaring at him in total astonishment.

Rudy put a raised finger to his lips, whipped out his phone and pointed to it and to her handbag. He moved his finger in a circle to suggest that she silently take her cell phone out of her bag. When she opened it, he directed her to the speakerphone system where she saw, to her horror, that it was on. "Put it in the trunk," he whispered. "Where you off to?"

"Nowhere special," she lied, closing the phone into the trunk.

"Kaitlin, you know she's dead, don't you?"

Kaitlin started to say, "Who?" but she could see, Rudy knew she had been there.

"I didn't kill her," she acquiesced.

"I'm not sure about that," Rudy said. "You hungry?"

"Yeah!"

"How about you take me to a local place and let's sort this thing out."

"Drive or walk?" she said.

"Let's walk. Is there some place close?"

"Yeah." Kaitlin opened up her trunk again, threw her stuff in and shut the trunk. She took them to a small Italian restaurant about halfway between the campus and Dr. LaPolla's house.

"How'd you know it was me?" she said after they had been seated. Both of them ordered spaghetti and meatballs.

"I saw you leave her place a little after six-thirty," Rudy lied.

"You couldn't have."

"Why not?"

"Because I was out of there before six."

"But you were there and you shot her with something, am I right?"

"No, man."

"In the neck. You hit her with a drug in the neck."

"It was only supposed to knock her out," Kaitlin admitted. "They wanted to steal her computer. So I helped. But I didn't kill her, man. She was breathing when I left."

"Did you see who came in after you?"

"Jamie."

"Jamie? You sure?"

"Yeah man, I'm sure."

"How do you know?"

"Because I doubled back and hid. He was wearing a hood but I knew it was him."

"Why would you do this?"

"You can't believe the shit these guys had on me."

"What guys?"

"I don't know. I never met anybody."

"So, how do you know they're plural?"

"Because they had different voices."

"They'd call you?"

"Yeah, all the time, and leave me ominous emails that would literally evaporate shortly after I clicked on them. I even changed computers and they could still get to me. And if I used caller ID, it would look like it was my mother or some friend on the line, but it was them! That was really spooky, I can tell you. Like man, it totally wigged me out."

"What did they or he want you to do?"

"First, I just was spying — reporting back about Professor LaPolla. We had a whole class on what to do to track down cyber thieves. She was working with some agency. She wouldn't tell us. But we all knew she was close to cracking NTroodr. She was pulling your chain, really we all were when you came to class."

"What do you mean?"

"We were a lot further along in denuding this guy than you thought. She told us ahead of time who you were so we changed the topic to AI when you walked in. We really had you, man."

"So what happened with LaPolla?"

"I was given a frigging blow dart. Guy told me it would just knock her unconscious, to give her a shot, get the hell out and they would do the rest. Download her computer, remove the dart, she'd wake up and never be the wiser."

"Wouldn't she know it was you who shot her?"

"Not as I understood it. They told me the drug blocks short term memory and knocks a person out for about an hour."

"How much did they pay you?"

"Ten thou, cash. It's in the trunk of my car now. I can't believe she's dead. Do you know what happened?"

"My guess is that your dart definitely incapacitated her and it may have killed her. Then Jamie came in, finished the job, making it look like suicide. Then he outputted her computer, wiped it and set me up to take the fall."

"So, now what do I do?" Kaitlin said tearfully.

"Let me take you to the police station. I know a cop there. It's the only chance you have. What you did was seriously wrong, but I'm guessing that if you make a deal you may beat this whole thing."

"How's that possible. What I did was.... unforgiveable."

"I can't argue you that, Kaitlin, but I am still going to suggest if you give your statement, they let you go."

"Why would they do that?"

"Because, odds are NTroodr will contact you again, and that will give them the edge they need to actually catch the bastard who really killed your professor."

"Can I call my parents first?"

"No. No one must know. This will be your weight to bear by yourself. Do you understand what I am saying?"

Kaitlin stopped for a moment to really consider this advice. Then she burst into tears. "That this is now my cross to bear alone?"

"Yes. Anybody else knows, with his access, they'd be dead meat. If the cops go for it, you will have to go on with your life as if you are totally innocent."

"Is there anybody I can confide in? I'm not sure I can do this all by myself."

"Officer Payne. He's a good guy. He's the guy I'll set you up with. All right?"

"You sure?"

"It's not like you have a choice," Rudy said, "and one more thing."

"Yeah?"

"How did all you guys get those free iPhones?"

"They were a gift from Spinwebbe."

"The German company?"

"If you say so. All I know is that they told us they were acquiring a new platform called Webnet. It was going to compete with Yahoo and Google and they wanted us to check it out, claimed it contained a video site more powerful than YouTube."

"Ok, let's go."

THE RED BARON

"Richthofen's invited us to his home for Christmas dinner," Simon made a rare phone call to Iris on a land line.

"That's five weeks away, Simon," Iris complained.

"I think I can still get two extra days to come home. You know I have no choice concerning this invitation."

"I may not be here when you arrive." Iris hung up the phone.

"Women?" Hermann Göring overheard some of the conversation.

"Iris," Simon said.

"She's a strong and beautiful lady," Hermann said. "Call her back."

"I can't."

"Oh, come, come. Give me the phone. What's the number?" He dialed, got an operator, and she patched him through.

"Iris, this is Hermann. Simon's never eaten non-Kosher food," he kidded.

"Are you looking out for him," Iris said.

"Actually, I'm making his life miserable."

"You're asking him to go out on a mission? Aren't you."

"Not at all," Hermann lied easily. "We need the best flight instructors to stay alive. It's best for all concerned. Here, Simon wants to tell you that he craves, I mean loves you." Göring handed the phone.

Iris found herself smiling in spite of her anger. This *nudge nudnik* friend of Simon's just knew how to get to her. Who would have ever thought such a momma's boy could become a war hero? The mood changed for the better so Iris decided to share the news.

"Simon," Iris said simply, "I'm pregnant, so keep yourself safe so you will have a family to come home to."

Simon was dumbstruck. On the one hand, he wanted to chastise Iris for keeping such news as this from him, and yet he was also thrilled and found his chest expanding with the knowledge that his seed had taken hold, and that in the not too distant future, there would be a new Maxwell to add to the family.

"Get me a cigar!" Simon told Hermann after hanging up.

"Congratulations," his buddy said, slapping Simon soundly on the backside. Göring was proud, the way he could insinuate himself into another's life. He was vain, there was no doubt about that, but he also had a certain charm in his attempts to exude that air of the carefree gadabout.

Except for the doctor, Iris had kept her pregnancy a secret from everybody. She was only into her third month, and because of her nervous condition and because of the war, she wanted to feel more secure before she let Simon know. But Hermann, as he usually did, had gotten to her, and he helped her lighten the moment. She walked over to the big house and found Tante Ella knitting on the porch.

"Sit," Tante Ella said, patting the seat next to her, her face bathed with the light of the setting sun. Ella wanted to tell Iris that she too had once been pregnant. Some of the family had suspected as much, but except for her husband, she had never told anyone. It was their secret. The life force that she and Stigey had created had given her that sense of wonder, even if only for the few weeks of her pregnancy. She thought back to that primeval feeling that overtook her of feeling like she was contributing to the evolution of the species.

"We had a child once," Tante Ella found herself saying.

"I didn't know," Iris said.

"No one knew, and we lost it before it was born," Ella said. But I do remember the feeling, Iris, the sense that we, I mean me and Stigey, would now really be a part of this world, participating in its change through the creation of our child."

"I'm afraid, Tante," Iris said. "You have picked up and sensed the joy that I feel, but it is a mixed emotion because of this God forsaken war."

"This war can't last forever, my dear," aunt Ella said, "but what can last is a life you can build with Simon and this little one."

"Oh, I hope so," Iris said.

Tante Ella reached over and affectionately patted Iris' stomach. "Through her growth – for I feel it will be a girl – you will set forth a new energy that will help heal this horrible time and bring back that feeling that you used to have when you and Simon were first in love."

"You really think so?"

"I know so," Tante Ella said. "So, have you thought of a name?"

"Yes, aunt, I have. If it's a girl, I want to name her Grace."

"And," speaking with a twinkle in her eye, "if it is a boy?"

"I haven't thought that far, auntie. I'm still too angry at the men."

A series of low puffed clouds passed in front of the setting sun causing shafts of light to beam out from the center like a fan. "Look at that, my child," Tante Ella said. "It looks like God himself, extending his hand over the land to give us his blessing."

"I'm going to pray for peace," Iris said.

"Well, now is a good time, because it seems tonight He might actually hear you." Tante Ella reached over with two hands to hold one of Iris', and together, they sat until darkness fell.

Göring had taken down a Farman just a week earlier and had escaped capture after his plane was shot down off the French border. Now he was feeling invincible, and he taunted Simon once again for staying on the sidelines.

"I get the feeling you enjoy all this killing, Hermann."

"Simon, get out there and take down a few Jikkis and then you'll begin to understand. People are talking. Von Richthofen has suggested you're afraid to fight."

"You know that's not true."

"Well, that's what he thinks. Just because he doesn't say it."

"The commandant won't let me out. I train the best of the lot. You know that. Look at Vöss and Schlegel. They came out of my classes. "

"Three dead this week, Simon. Two from your school. Think about it." Göring gave his violet scarf a tug and whirled his corpulent body. "Feel the surge," he said before exiting the room.

Simon went out for his first run in a *Jasta* led by Lieutenant Loerzer, the flamboyant lady's man who had teamed up with Göring and gotten him a flight commission. It was late spring of 1917. As many of the flyers had feared, the Yanks had now joined the fight.

American war ships had been sunk in the Atlantic and the Mediterranean, but their resources were overwhelming and the Kaiser had misread the will of their President Wilson. He had sent scouts to infiltrate America's eastern seaboard and send back coded messages via Telefunken, Germany's large wireless concern who had towers in New Jersey and Long Island; but Wilson had now seized all transmitting stations, so obtaining data on ship movements became that much harder.

Loezer had patterned his patrol like that of the Red Baron and the late Oswald Boelke, creating a wedge with seven planes. Flying low following tree-tops and dropping into valleys, Loezer used the element of surprise to take out enemy fortresses, strafe troops who ran like scared rats, and attack enemy fighter planes head on. In tight formation, they would then zip up to high altitudes and let prevailing winds take them back to base.

On his second run with them, Simon spotted a Spad below flying due West. Like a hawk on a dive, with permission from the *oberlieutenant*, he left ranks, banked and dove straight for the plane. Spotted earlier than anticipated, the Spad looped right and began a spiral maneuver resembling the Immelman roll. His goal was to hook back and get behind his attacker. Possessed, Simon set the plane into a vertical dive. He thought back to an idyllic day he and Iris had spent having a picnic down by the river with his nephew and Tante Ella. How the great stag and two deer approached and spent several incredible minutes with them.

Not fifty meters from the ground, Simon pulled up on the wheel and changed his descent to a backwards flip, straining every bolt and cable as he executed a full 360°. Upside-down, he found the underbelly of the enemy plane and fired: *Rat-a-tat-tat-tat,* shattering the fuselage and cockpit, blowing the pilot to smithereens, the man's blood splattering as his head exploded.

Unscathed, Simon was welcomed back a hero, praised by the Red Baron, and soon thereafter by the Kaiser himself after downing another Spad and two Bleriots. Göring had said that winning a dogfight was better than sex, the rush of adrenaline, the feeling of absolute power and animal superiority as they shot out bridges, scattered troops and took out tanks. This was war. It was kill or be killed. But many of his friends had died. So many, that like others, Simon rarely formed lasting attachments beyond the original crew he came in with. Underneath, however, he knew the truth. When it came to the Brits, he avoided Sopwiths whenever he could, and in one instance risked an act of treason by letting a pilot live he thought he had recognized from those early days when all countries raced together. By letting this pilot go, in his mind, Simon could somehow justify all the killing, his other acts of sheer violence.

But this new Sopwith was now headed towards a German cavalry brigade. Simon spun back and dove as the British pilot looked around at him in absolute horror. With a big walrus moustache, it looked like Henry Taroon who had been in the "Baby Bristol" during that last race of 1914, one of the fourteen who had completed the entire circuit. Henry Taroon who had identified the functions of a thermal well before most pilots even considered them as anything but a nuisance.

"Simon," Henry shouted, as Simon's machine guns ripped the Camel in two. Simon had tilted the gun to the right in at attempt to avoid the cockpit. But he missed, and Henry was hit.

To Simon's astonishment, Taroon gave Simon a salute as the biplane dropped like a duck hit by a hunter's buckshot. The plane exploded on impact with the ground. Henry Taroon was dead. Simon knew he would never erase that salute from his head.

He got back to base and was heartily congratulated for the victory. "You have another string of kills like this," Göring said, patting him on the back, we're going to have to call you the Hebrew Hawk. Two more, and you'll be an ace."

Ever since Taroon's death, Simon was in a daze. Other pilots began attributing his recent string of kills to his increase in expertise, but Simon knew otherwise, and so he took more risks.

MB Industries was now the fifth largest aircraft manufacturer in Germany behind Junkers, Fokker, Deutsche Flugzeug Werke (DFW) which had been set up by the German government before the war, and Rumpler. Elias' wealth was growing at an exponential rate, and with it, his influence rose comparably. The Kaiser was well known to be an anti-Semite, but he made a number of exceptions, particularly to Jewish men in the armed services, to converts who supported the war effort, and to a New York contingency of Jewish bankers who helped support the Kaiser by sending funds to Berlin to help fight off the Russians. Hell, it was a Jew who developed poison gas, Professor Franz Haber, former associate of Einstein's in Berlin. And then there was Jacob Schiff, the Wall Street banker who had raised tons of money before the Americans had gotten into the war. Yes, the Kaiser did not like Jews, but he had his exceptions.

As Simon made his journey by train to Richthofen's estate in Prussia, he thought about Iris' pregnancy and reflected back to happier times when he and Iris were in the spring of their romance.

"You've never seen a beach before?" Iris' eyes beamed with excitement.

"I've never been to the sea before," Simon admitted. "Sure, we have been to Zion Summer Camp by Lake Frigate, but I'm not sure that counts. I've never seen sand on a shore, nor real waves rolling in from salted water."

"Well, you're simply not going to believe it!"

The duo stepped off the waterbus at Lido Island which was another island just a few miles from uncle Alphonse's place at Murano. And Simon found himself walking hand in hand down a lane of shops. On the right, a new yellow-bricked hotel of Baroque design was being constructed. Two artisans were painting frescoes on the tiled outer wall. They were representations of renaissance Venice, scenes of majestic women in long gowns and men in royal regalia.

At seaside, Simon had the desire to rush upon the sand, but they were still in street attire, and Iris said that their lodging was not far. Taking a right and walking along a roadway, they watched the people in high fashion parade along the sidewalk or ride happily in open horse and carriages along the main road that followed the shoreline.

The Hotel DeBarines came into view. They climbed the marble steps and were greeted by the hotel manager. He gave them a room and sent up a boy with the bags. They grabbed their beach attire and crossed the road to the bath houses which stood in long rows like mini-garages at the edge of the sand.

Iris slipped out of her clothes and switched to a bathing suit. Her naked body was youthful and pulsating with a happy radiance. "Come on, come on," she urged, as she grinned when Simon removed his clothes as well. "No time to wait," she said with a gleam as she reached for the door.

"Hey, wait a minute," Simon grabbed a towel to hide himself.

"I'm just teasing you Simon. But let's go already!"

Her smile was pure and natural. She enjoyed looking at his body. He felt like they were two young horses about to prance the field.

Simon could not believe how hot the sand was. He had to go back and get his shoes as he watched in total amazement Iris walk the beach. "It's mind over matter," she confided.

"I think it's more a factor of weight and inherited characteristics," Simon said.

"You mean I weigh less and you have tender feet?"

"Yes." He watched her beam. Throwing his shoes off by their blanket, he glanced at the hundreds of fellow bathers. So many people enjoying themselves, so many splendid ladies, and he had absolutely no doubt, his was the very best one! He hot-footed it to the shoreline, the water refreshing his overheated feet.

"It's absolutely gorgeous," Iris said as he approached her in the water. He couldn't believe the clarity and greenness. It was as if God himself had created a place just to show off his imagination for his ability to create such aquatic grandeur.

Everything about the gentle refreshing water was kind, he thought as he watched his new bride slice through the small waves.

Pint-sized sailboats glided by. "Someday I hope to return with you and get our own boat," he said.

"So we can sail away and live happily ever after?"

"We will, no matter what."

"I know," she concurred as they kissed.

Simon took a cab from the train station and was let off at the main entrance of von Richthofen's modest castle. Made mostly of stone with an imposing iron gate, there was something foreboding, almost gloomy about the place. Out of the fog, Simon recognized the young flying ace's swagger. He couldn't help but feel he was being set up, but for what, he did not know.

"Thank you for inviting me," Simon said.

"Thank you for coming," Richthofen replied. Simon was about to reach out to shake hands, but his host nodded his head and clicked his heels in such a way as to usurp the need to greet in any other way.

The Red Baron was dressed in a short leather vest covered over with the pelt of a mink draped around his neck as a collar. The eyes of the animal seemed to stare out at Simon as its teeth bit down on the tail to lock the cape in front. As Richthofen turned towards the house, Simon counted eleven mink-tails hanging from the back, the taller ones in the center, the shorter ones, the tails of the cubs.

"Yes," the Baron said, reading Simon's thoughts. "Shot them all, except for the little ones." He turned back and grinned. "Those I got by breaking their necks with my hands." He laughed and then led Simon to the mansion.

"It's kind of you to meet me at the gate," Simon said, not quite sure what to make of the Red Baron's last comments. "I'm sure I could have found the front door myself."

"I wanted you to know how welcome you are here. Eight kills," he added, punching Simon gingerly in the arm. "Two more and you'll be an ace. Göring's worried you'll overtake him."

"I know," Simon said.

"But I came out to meet you at the gate for a very different reason." Richthofen's tone became more serious. "I wanted to speak to you alone without the others."

"So then, what is this about?"

"Your death wish. I've seen it before and I want to know why."

"My death wish?"

"I've seen your maneuvers in the air, Simon. Only a man wishing to die would take those kinds of risks. Göring thinks you're brave, and I've held my tongue. You are an excellent pilot and a worthy flight instructor. But to be frank, all these questions I ask you are based mostly out of self-interest."

"How so?"

"I'm a mathematician. It's really quite simple. The more good men we have in the cockpit, the greater my chances of survival. You know, of course, I'm the Stork's main target, and if you end up getting yourself shot out of the skies, that's simply one less ally I'll have to keep me alive and one less excellent teacher to train my ever-changing support team."

Simon looked closely at the Baron. It was his title and reputation that gave him his cachet. Really, Richthofen was not much more than a lad, just 24-years-old. And for a moment, Simon glimpsed a flicker of fear in the young man's eyes.

"I see," Simon said.

"I'm glad you do."

"So, you don't really care whether I live or die beyond that?"

"What you do after the war, or what you do once you are taken off active duty is of no concern to me."

Simon couldn't tell if he was feigning indifference or simply speaking a simple truth.

"Come." The Red Baron took Simon up to the front entrance. The door was heavily carved of medieval design with a brass lion's head as the handle. Palm on Simon's shoulder, the Baron guided him in. The foyer was lit by a chandelier made from a circular engine from a Belgian aeroplane, one of the very first Richthofen had shot down, which was in May of 1916. Each cylinder head was replaced by an electric bulb shaped in the form of a candle.

"Hermann, Lieutenant. It is good of you to come." Richthofen turned his attention to some of the other guests and left Simon as if they had never spoken.

At the back wall opposite the vestibule there was mounted the head of a boar, it's teeth bared, and beneath it, on either side were the heads of two enormous elk. The Baron's mansion was a taxidermist's heaven, all the hallways and rooms filled with the heads of every animal Richthofen had killed: squirrels, lynx, rabbit, beaver, porcupine, raccoon, moose, antelope, three more boar heads, bear, pheasant, grouse, geese, heron, a mallard duck, a few hawks, two falcons and a Golden eagle. Simon found himself mesmerized by the eyes of a large horned owl that seemed to glare down at him. All-knowing.

A hunter since his youth, Baron von Richthofen now mounted pieces of the wreckage of most of the planes he had downed. He had a machine gun from a Sopwith, engine parts from a bevy of Nieuports and Bristols, the fuselage insignias from two Vickers and other pieces from other planes. Simon entered the main dining room where he gazed upon one of the greatest feasts he had ever seen, including an entire pig, head and all, that was being carved by a scantily clad chef's assistant whose cleavage caught the eye of every pilot in the room. "Is there anything you want?" she said to Simon as she sliced the pig's lips and gave pieces to Richthofen and Göring. Oberleutenant Krüger was off to the side chatting with several trainees

"You're Simon Maxwell?" a young cadet asked.

"Yes," Simon said.

"I was just telling the boys about your company and how the M-B biplane is fast becoming the plane of choice in my squadron."

"And why is that?" one of the more animated cadets chimed in. "Stability of course is a given with all the M-B's, sir. But the oberleutenant is telling us it's the gun turret. More agile than the Eindekker, isn't that what you said, sir?"

"That I did, sport," Krüger said. "It took me out of a jam just three days ago."

"The oberleutenant shot down two Sopwiths in one skirmish," the cadet added.

"Don't forget the Curtiss I got the day before."

"Oh yes, sir, how could I."

Simon nodded to them as they continued their heated conversation. Avoiding the ham, he filled up a plate with cheese and vegetables and then continued his tour, finding himself by a stack of coats in a seat in the Baron's bedroom. He looked over at the lampshades. Both were made from the linens from the wings of two Farman reconnaissance planes.

Aside from framed pictures of the great pilot with dignitaries such as the Kaiser, and also his flying buddies, von Richthofen had also lined the walls with the mounted clothing from some of the pilots he had killed. His *piece de resistance*, in an adjacent sitting room where half-dozen pilots stood around to drink, was a round oak table with a full mounted double-barrel machine gun set in the middle, taken from Major Lanow Hawker's Airco DH-2, who Richthofen shot down in November of 1916. Hawker had been the first British pilot to win the Victoria's Cross, the Brit having earned his medal after taking out a Zeppelin plant early in the war in July 1915. Now he was dead.

Seeing the display hit Simon like cannon fire between the eyes. The other pilots were all in high spirits, but he could not escape the feeling that he was separate from the world of the living. Richthofen had pegged him to the bone. But the way Simon looked at it now, the Red Baron was no more than a glorified assassin, and this is what the masses saw as hero! *"Iris was right. I too am no more than a murderer,"* Simon whispered to himself. Göring tried to wrap a friendly arm around him, but he brushed it off. He exchanged glances with up and comer, Ernst Udet, who seemed to understand, but he hardly knew Udet, so he just tipped a finger to him in a small salute, and Udet returned the gesture. Simon staggered to the door and wandered out. The sky was crystal clear, he contemplated the stars. With the train station was no more than two miles away, he decided to walk it and escape this madness.

"Am I that obvious?"

Simon wheeled. The Baron stood right behind him. "Come, I'll drive you." Clearly, Simon realized, the Baron had read his thoughts. They stepped into a new Mercedes. Even though it was winter, the evening was mild, so the Baron kept the roof off.

"I kill because it is my duty, Baron."

"And I kill for the sport. Is that your point?"

"I'm afraid it is. You simply switched from shooting squirrels, bear and..."

"Owls?"

"Yes, and owls, to killing men. I believe you would have mounted the pilots' heads if you could have gotten away with it."

"Maybe an ear or two," the Baron deadpanned.

Simon gasped.

"I'm just teasing you, Simon. The fact of the matter is, that's what warriors have done for centuries. I'm no different than America's Teddy Roosevelt, who shot elephants, lions and rhinos in Africa, or your Biblical David who neatly slayed Goliath. And, since I've brought up the topic of religion, look at your God, dear Simon."

"My God? Jehovah?"

"Of course, Jehovah. Wasn't it He who brought a plague down on the Egyptians and slew their first born children?"

"That's just myth. Surely you appreciate that?"

"Is it myth, Simon, or does it speak to a higher truth? Man survives because he is predator supreme." The car pulled out from the estate and made its way through a pine forest, the trees glistening with an early evening frost.

"It's very convenient to see me as assassin," the Baron went on, "but what about you, and the hundreds, nay, millions on both sides caught up in this

Armageddon. Would not it be worse if I were inept?... Look, Simon, you either kill efficiently or not at all. You either stay and fight, or you flee to South Africa. There's always the choice, my good man."

The light in the distance grew brighter as the train station came into view. It was obvious to Simon that Hermann had told von Richthofen all about his troubles with Iris. "Here we are," the fighter pilot said simply.

"I can't thank you enough [he paused on the word enough] for inviting me." Simon found himself clicking his heels and saluting Baron Richthofen. Then he turned, and made his way to the train platform.

"We will see each other in hell, my dear brother," the Baron called after him.

SPLIT

Simon found a comfortable seat on the train and watched the landscape pass before him. The beat of the wheels on the track caused his mind to wander and he came upon an ironic thought. He really did believe in hell, but he doubted very much whether the Baron did. Many of his cohorts were cynics or atheists. With millions upon millions killed, mowed down, gassed or bombed, one could understand why God would be abandoned, particularly if a person lost his family, was permanently disabled or blinded, or if he himself had partaken in the slaughter. But Richthofen had always been a hunter, and more than that, he had since youth, reveled in killing. He was proud of each head on his wall, animal, or through the symbol of the plane wreckage, human. It may have been barbaric, but the realization that hit Simon was, it was truthful. And yet, Simon, himself, was a carnivore. To be coldly honest, he enjoyed going to Dieter's Butcher Shop to pick out a big red hunk of cow flank or decapitated chicken, or his favorite, tongue, to take it back for family dinner. He loved meat in all its varied types of preparation, grilled steak, marinated stews, Hungarian goulash, stuffed cabbage, baked chicken, chopped liver. But he had never considered the moral implications. It was Iris who had pointed out that humans were carnivores, so they had no choice. "It is part of Nature's Plan," she would say, "and God's mysterious ways."

Awakening with a start, Simon reviewed in greater depth his argument with Richthofen who simply used the carnivore argument to justify his deeds. "But there must be a distinction between mounting animal heads and mounting downed human aeroplane trophies," Simon had countered.

"Is there? Isn't that a matter of opinion?" The Baron looked back at Simon with an icy coldness that he found frightening. "Or hypocrisy?"

"There must be a difference, or we are no better than snakes."

"Whoever said we were?"

"Baron, you don't really believe that?"

"Of course I do, dear Simon. We are simply more proficient at killing, as Fokker, and now your brother, have proven."

Simon ran the conversation through his mind. He needed to see a wise person, perhaps a rabbi, to gain more understanding on the nature of the moral consequences of war -- or even of eating meat.

Now, the new crop of aces like Ernst Udet, Hermann Göring and Baron von Richthofen, were making their own mark in the newspapers, although some of the old guard were also making news. On April 6th, Lieutenant Frankl, flying in a Fokker bi-plane, shot down three British Sopwiths in less than an hour in the morning, and shot down another enemy plane before nightfall. Here was an unprecedented record, and Simon did his best to needle Göring about it. Somehow, it picked up his failing spirit.

This was brutal sport, but the victors enjoyed a measure of fame unparalleled with any other sphere. Numerous children, and many adults, looked up to these men as heroes, and nine-year-old Abe Maxwell was no exception. Yet for Abe, this would be no passing fad. His collection of autographs and memorabilia on the early aeronauts was detailed and exhaustive. But part of him, and it was a weighty part, hated his uncle for killing Taroon, and he hated himself for these feelings. He cried to his momma, but what could Debora say.

Tante Ella, on the other hand, had an answer. "Believe me," Abe's great aunt said, "Your uncle Simon feels one hundred times worse than you."

"How can that be, aunt? He killed him."

"That's how." Tante Ella looked Abe in the eye and kept her gaze, one eyebrow higher than the other until a new level of comprehension entered into the boy's being.

"Thank you," Debora said.

Iris came to her in-law's house to read yet another Simon letter. Now, her tummy was bulging and Elias realized his wife had been right all along. Tante Ella, of course, had kept the secret, but now, Iris' pregnancy was obvious.

"Congratulations," Debora said, walking over to give Iris a long welcoming hug and also a kiss. Iris reciprocated, but in an odd moment, rested her head on her sister-in-law's shoulder for a beat longer than one would expect.

"I'm afraid," Iris whispered so no one else could hear.

"Sit, sit," Elias interrupted the moment. "Let's hear what my hero brother has to say!"

Abe was still hostile to the thought of his uncle Simon, and he wanted to leave the room, but reluctantly he too took a seat. His eyes were saddened, but also, he did not want to miss hearing the inside scoop. Iris opened up the envelope and began.

It is a very difficult war, not only in the air, but in the trenches. We mourn the death of each pilot that goes down. Just two days after Frankl's great triumph, he was shot down and killed in another dogfight. Everyone knows everyone else. It's like losing a brother, but the ground battles are of a different order entirely. Sixty thousand dead in one day during the Battle of Somme on the first of July. This is a number too incomprehensible for me to fathom. I do, however, feel that I am playing my correct role to our country and look forward to holding you in my arms and seeing the rest of the family as soon as I can get leave.
Your loving husband,
Simon

Before the end of the week, Simon received a wire from Elias. There had been a mishap at the plant, and his expertise was needed to fix one of the presses. Simon showed the wire to the *oberleutenant*, who gave him leave.

The region was in the midst of a cold snap, two snow storms in a row piled as high as five feet in some places. The heater on the train was broken. Passengers bunched together just to keep each other warm.

Simon had a window seat. He let an elderly man poorly dressed sit along his side. He thought of old Mr. Brownell, this memory awakened by the smell of the musty clothes the geezer wore. Simon spent the time staring out at the fleeting landscape. He thought back to the last night he had with Iris in Murano, the night she took him to an observatory where he looked through a telescope for the first time. In one shot, he saw the moons of Jupiter and Saturn's rings! He had trouble believing his senses. Sure, he had seen photos or drawings of Saturn, but out in the Adriatic on a crystal clear night with so many stars sparkling, it became so clear, so very evident, that the planets of this solar system were all close neighbors. It changed his perspective in a hundred ways.

"I told you you'd love it," Iris gleamed.

"I do, dear Iris, but it is you that I adore."

"Oh, I bet you say that to all the girls you take to Venice," she teased.

He looked into her eyes and there he could see reflected starlight. She had opened up to him worlds upon worlds, new and exciting vistas. But now it seemed like a fiction, perhaps from a play or motion picture he had seen, because now it was all too alien for him to accept that it had really been a part of his life, of their life. He reached to his finger and twisted his ring.

The train rattled on through the night. At dawn, as the sun began to peak through the trees, Simon caught sight of a dead wolverine that was frozen solid into a sitting position. Poised as if a sculptor had placed it there, it was clear that the animal had been knocked dead by a previous train in such a way that it was thrown back in a perfect manner. The animal's face was cemented in shock, it's eyes eerily reflecting the sun as it sat surreal-like, as if on a miniature thrown, upper paws extended in almost a regal manner.

"What's wrong at the plant?" Simon demanded, when he arrived in Kempten. The air was biting cold, the slush on the ground now hardened to gritty rivulets of ice. The brothers held onto each other as they stumbled to the waiting car.

"I lied," Elias disclosed, in a voice so low that Gunter could not hear. "It's Iris. She lost the baby and we fear for her sanity. She fell, and again hit her head, but we suspect the injury was self-inflicted."

"Gunter," Elias called up to the front of the car, "let's swing by Simon's home, and we'll pick him up first thing tomorrow morning."

"Yes, sir." Gunter kept his sights on the road, ever vigilant.

Simon's mind went numb with the news, and he had no recollection of even leaving the car or entering the house.

"Her eyes are looking in two directions," Simon confided to Debora the next day. She had walked over early in the morning carrying muffins and coffee in a thermos. "I think she's going mad."

"Can you blame her?"

"I don't know. We are all stuck because of this war, and now," Simon found himself blurting, "maybe even because of her, my baby is dead."

"No!" Debora proclaimed. "This was a miscarriage, plain and simple. Now you take back your words, my brother-in-law. Take them back!"

Shocked by Debora's vehement response, Simon just stood there for a moment. "You're right," he finally said, his body drooping in response. "I don't know what came over me."

"Simon," Debora eased up, "your wife is a special lady. She lives on another plane, and if you want to blame anyone, blame the Kaiser, blame the war for this tragedy. But do not, and I repeat, do not blame your wife. She has enough to deal with."

"I know. I know," Simon agreed. "That was crazy. But I just don't know what to do. I don't know how I can help her."

"Just sit and be with her," Debora said quietly. "Your presence and your silence will be the best medicine."

He nodded agreement.

When Simon walked back upstairs, Iris was finally out of bed, but she staggered when she walked, and her speech was segmented. Two doctors called the head injury permanent, but a third, the one Iris' father took stock in, told Simon that a full recovery *was* possible – as long as Simon did not pilot war planes and did not work on the manufacture of them.

He knew now that Iris had to leave Germany. Her eyes seemed almost normal when he said that, and she thanked him. After studying the map, he set passage for Iris for Capetown, South Africa. For political reasons, he could not risk America. But then she put down her demands. She would only go if he would divorce her.

"Iris, you can't mean that."

"Oh, but I do, sir. Simon is dead to me now." She spoke with her eyes to the floor.

With his hand beneath her chin, he tilted her gaze towards him. Her look was as cold as that of the wolverine he had seen frozen along the tracks, her eyes just about as vacant.

Their last night together was a living nightmare, Iris in their bedroom, Simon on the living room couch. No matter what he did, he could not fall asleep. And it wasn't just Iris. The way his nephew had looked at him when he showed uncle Sye-Sye his scrapbook, the picture of Taroon with the entire Maxwell clan at the Munich Aerial Race. Now a black star next to his name to represent "deceased." Simon tried counting from 100 back to 1. He did it over and over again, but nothing worked. He got up and walked into her room. Iris was lying face up like a princess. He simply got on the bed, pulled a woolen throw over his shoulder and rolled a leg over her. She moaned, reached out with both hands and held his leg. And for that moment, as every night sleeping with her had been, all was right with the world.

He drifted into slumber.

The next morning, Iris described a dream she had. It was about having a crush on a famous man she knew, but could not meet. "I entered a big house," she said. "Not Elias'. There were three steps to get in. I was afraid I would fall back if I went up them, and that's all I remember. Now get out and let me get dressed."

Simon felt as if his heart had been ripped from his chest as he organized final travel arrangements, and then took Iris to the train. She could be routed through Austria to Trieste, and from there she could take a ship down the Adriatic to the Suez Canal where the trip would take her to the east coast of Africa all the way to

Capetown. Her father, Roberé von Rosensweig, had relatives and business associates there. Roberé agreed to take leave from his wife and new baby and accompany Iris all the way. It was a telling moment that revealed a depth to his being few thought possible. When getting visas, Rosensweig simply told officials this was a business trip, intimating that he would probably be able to secure various natural resources for the war effort.

Where one of Iris' eyes embodied the look of love that had sealed her romance with Simon from that magic time when they first met, the other eye was distant and outright cold. Her soon-to-be ex-spouse sensed a meanness of expression, and even revenge from that eye. She was leaving him to punish him even though it was destroying her as well.

"Will you be all right?" he asked lamely as they gently held hands as the train sat at the ready. Simon gazed for the last time at the crinkles of her eyes that never failed to make his heart melt. But above was the furor in her brow. He reached over to hold her shoulders and tried to tune into the ethereal vibe she used to exude so easily. A realm so far beyond war that he stood in awe of it, as if she were a messenger from a higher plane. He felt cheated and trapped, and then he experienced then sensed her schizophrenia which she viciously shifted into him. Her eyes cleared for a moment as the transfer of energy took place. She let his hands go, by throwing them from her, and then she got up to find a new spot on the train. Her father sadly shook Simon's hand good-bye.

"Simon," von Rosensweig said, "I'll look after her and do the best I can."

"I know you will, sir," Simon rotely replied.

The train whistled. Simon had less than 30 seconds to disembark. He envisioned his own abandonment of the war effort, but also his abandonment of his family and Maxwell-Bavarian Industries. And then he realized that if he were to go, it could never work. He would destroy his brother, their company, he would be branded a traitor and be a fugitive for the rest of his life. He also feared if he went, he might still never get her back.

It was over. He turned and jumped off the slowly moving train. He knew he might never see her again. Simon collapsed to his knees as the train disappeared from sight.

Several hours later, he found himself in the heart of Kempten. He had walked over a dozen kilometers in a daze, oblivious to the quick thaw and new rather rapid return of life to the forest. Without Iris, his anchor, the love of his life, he felt like a zombie. Every man that smiled at him in recognition was but another reminder of how he had killed Henry Taroon, let alone the twenty or thirty other soldiers he helped mow down in that last raid in Loerzer's squadron. Bullets ripping into their heads and chests, arteries hit, gobs of red spurting, bodies twitching, Göring's sense of glee. It was blood lust pure and simple. "Did you see them scatter like a scared ant colony?" Göring had said at dinner as he toasted the run. "We only lost one today. What was his name?"

"Schumer."

"Schumer. Let's toast." Göring held his glass high. "Hail Schumer."

Since he was dressed in uniform, with his Iron Cross and other medals in full display, young women and small children kept running up to say hello or reach out to touch him. "Do you know the Red Baron?" one adolescent said. Simon just kept walking. He watched in surrealistic detachment a mother help her daughter pick out cookies at Dieters Grocery. The little girl was well proportioned for her age, a clear face, lovely thin brown hair, excellent young athletic legs.... *A perfect child,* Simon thought, *and I'm a walking dead man.* The more congenial people appeared, the more he saw himself an interloper, a man who did not belong among the living. If his body wasn't dead, it would just be a matter of time. He no longer felt a part of the daily life that everyone else simply took for granted. It was as if the public on the streets and in the shops were moving in slow motion, or that they were part of a dream. They were alive and he was someplace else. Fearful of breaking down in public, he simply continued on and walked out of town.

He found himself along the lane of rhododendrons which led to Elias' house. Unannounced, he entered. Abe was on the floor with Debora, Tante Ella, even Elias. They were pouring over Abe's recreation of the battle of Somme where a million men had been wounded or captured, and a staggering/sobering over a quarter million killed in action. Toothpicks painted brown outlined the trenches, little triangular pieces of paper tinted green depicted mountain ranges, small toy cars and trucks were placed where armored divisions lay, and scores of dried beans colored in blue for the enemy and red for German, Austrian and Turkish soldiers were placed wherever they belonged.

By studying newspapers, Abe was able to keep an accurate tally of the air battles as well, how many planes had been shot down each day, and by which side. Whenever possible, he also listed the name of the pilot, whether he was captured, injured or escaped. Now nearly eleven, he had mapped out all of the armies and air squadrons on a giant map of Europe and the Mediterranean. He even had little boats to simulate what he figured to be the fleets for England, France, the USA and Germany. "You realize," he began, "we cannot win this war."

"There's an editorial in *Deutsche Zeit* that says we should have learned from Napoleon and left Russia alone," Elias slapped the paper. Simon was staring off through a window.

"So, what are you saying?"

"Papa is saying that with a two-front war, it's almost a mathematical certainty that we cannot win," Abe spoke matter-of-factly.

"That's not what Simon meant," Tante Ella said.

"Then what did you mean, uncle Sye-Sye?"

"Your uncle is questioning our very entry into this war," Ella continued, "and on a more personal level, the Maxwell role in the endeavor."

"The Western press sees us as demons," Simon lamented, nodding agreement with Ella. "You cannot fight a war that cannot be won."

"They want total surrender," Elias revealed.

"Is there no way out for us?" Debora asked.

"To the victor goes the spoils," Abe said.

"And do you know what 'the spoils' is?" Simon asked.

"That the winner takes all, mama?" Abe guessed, seeking confirmation from Debora.

"Exactly," Debora said.

"What will that mean for us, papa?" Abe asked Elias.

"Time will tell, son. It's not over yet."

"Not with pilots like Richthofen still out there."

It wasn't what Simon said, so much as the way he said it that triggered alarm bells in the minds of both ladies. They glanced at each other and back to Simon who caught it all.

"You should see his residence." Simon spoke in a hollow voice. "Among the heads of boar, antelope and bear, mounted on his walls, were artifacts from almost every goddamned plane he shot down."

"But that's war, Simon," Elias said.

"War, or slaughter? The very month we put in the Fokker machine guns, Richthofen went out and had 22 kills. That's more dead pilots in a single month than Hermann has had for his whole campaign. You had to see his face. Killing a man is not an easy thing to do, but for the Red Baron, he wore it like glee, practically creaming his pants when a runner brought back another artifact from a downed Spad or Nieuport. 'Look at this,' he swaggered one... I think it was a Tuesday... with part of a prop from a Sopwith Camel in his hand, and this.' And you know what he held up, a grin ear to ear?"

Simon waited for someone to ask, all too stunned to speak, so he waited.

"What, uncle Simon, what?" Abe blurted.

"The goggles of a dead pilot, still splattered with blood. That's what. He slung them over his shoulder like they were the pelt of a mink, and then he strutted out the room whistling a goddamned tune. Excuse my French."

"The French and the Brits have their Aces too. Don't forget that," Elias said.

"Mannock has over 40 kills," Abe said, looking down at his notebook.

"What's he," Elias said.

"A Brit," Simon said. "What's Guynemer have?"

"French?" Debora finally entered the conversation.

"Yes," Abe said. "He's somewheres over 30."

"And Hawker?" Elias asked.

"Richthofen shot him down a few months back," Abe said. "He had only seven victories."

"You say it as if that were something to be embarrassed about, Abe. These victories you talk of mean dead pilots," Tante Ella reprimanded.

"Wasn't it Hawker who hit that Zeppelin plant?" Elias asked.

"That's what the British press said," Simon said. "Now with the Americans coming into this, there's no telling how many more will die."

"Uncle Simon, I still want you to get me the Red Baron's signature. Papa's got me Udet's and Göring."

"I'm sure I can get that for you."

"I showed Udet's photo with his signature to the boys at schule, and suddenly I was the most popular kid in class," Abe beamed.

"Schule, Elias?"

"Don't ask, Simon. It was that or the second divorce in the family."

"We didn't part over religion."

"Are you sure?" Tante Ella blurted.

"And what should I have done, Tante Ella? Let me put it this way. What would you have done?"

"I don't think you have to talk to our aunt in that tone of voice," Elias said.

"I understand," Tante Ella said. "I would have run off with her."

"And what would that have achieved for the reputation of the family, for this company, for service to the Fatherland?" Simon barked.

"We would have survived." Elias said coldly, driving home the point that the company was in his name, not Simon's.

"You say that now. The Kaiser would have abrogated Maxwell Industries within a fortnight."

"Simon is right, the both of you," Debora had heard enough. "Everyone is smarter on Monday morning. Simon did what was best for all. We are at war. Millions have already died, and it wasn't in your nature, Simon, was it? to have left home and country to become a fugitive because Iris was upset with world events."

"I must go." Simon walked over and gave Abe a kiss, ignoring the others, and then he departed.

"What's wrong with uncle Sye-Sye?" Abe said, while repositioning the model planes and troops on the big board to simulate another more recent battle.

"He misses aunt Iris," Elias said.

"It's not just that, my dear boy," Tante Ella said. "You have here this entire set up, but we are talking about real carnage and death. War is horrible and Simon has seen the very worst of it."

"He's had to partake," Debora regretting immediately that she might have revealed too much.

"But he has eight victories already," Abe said. "Just two more, and he becomes an Ace."

"It's not his goal," Tante Ella explained.

"Well, Simon gave me this." Abe reached into his pocket and pulled out the Iron Cross. "There aren't many pilots that have one of these either," he added softly.

Elias looked over at his son, mouth agape. Then he ran out of the house, leaving Debora, Abe and Tante Ella stunned. Although in the prime of his life, Elias was not, one would say, in tip-top shape. It was one area of his life that he had completely neglected. He wasn't sure he could run all the way to his brother's house and the car was in the shop for repairs. Without a second thought, he grabbed Abe's bicycle and hobbled down the road.

Simon stared at his gun for a long time before placing it in his mouth.

"Simon! Simon!"

He heard a faint voice off in the distance. At first he thought it God calling from heaven, or maybe Satan from hell. The faint voice and the fear of hell were two reasons which gave him time for pause.

"Maybe if I live longer I can make up for all the evil I have been a part of," he thought to himself before pulling the trigger.

"Simon! Simon!"

It was not God or Satan. It was his brother. Simon gazed out the window and could not help himself from bursting into laughter. Elias was careening down the hill at breakneck speed, the front wheel all a wobble from the coarseness of the lawn.

"Simon! Simon!" Elias looked up and saw Simon at the window, gun still cocked in his hand. With that, the front wheel hit a small boulder and Elias felt his body go airborne. For just the briefest of split seconds he felt free, and then, instinctively, curled an arm over his head and readied himself to roll at the fall.

Simon came tearing down the stairs. "Elias! Elias!" he ran over and cradled his brother's head in his arms. "Are you all right?"

"I'm not too late?"

"How did you know?"

"I'm your brother, for Christ's sake! What am I going to do with a dead brother?"

"Look at all the extra money you'll have."

"That's not funny. Everything I have is yours, dear brother. I've been greedy and a cheapskate, I know. I never signed the papers. I've taken advantage of you. But also, I have provided. We did build A-1 aircraft, among the best in all of Europe. And if it hadn't been for the war…"

"I can't live without her, Elias. I simply can't."

"Then go."

"But I'll be seen as a traitor."

"We'll work it out. We'll find a way. South Africa has many Germans. It has natural resources. We still have bases in Togo, the Cameroons and parts of Southern Africa. We'll get you a commission. Surely the Kaiser will want to maintain control of what we still have."

"It sounds too crazy."

"Simon, you're a war hero, one of the truly elite. The Iron Cross, my God. You didn't tell us!"

"I'm ashamed. It's for being a murderer. I killed Taroon."

"It was war, Simon. You did your duty. You did the right thing."

"The right thing, hah! I killed a friend. I killed maybe five of the eight I shot down, five men, five flyers in the prime of their lives, and who knows how many troops, dozens, maybe hundreds with Fokker's great improvement.

"And the Red Baron. An appropriate name, Elias. He's nothing more than a mass murderer. If he had the decision to down the plane and give the pilot a chance or kill the pilot, he goes for the pilot every time. I've seen him shoot men in parachutes. Those don't count as 'victories' unless he shot the plane in question, but he's talked about getting some form of partial credit. The Commandant laughs it off, but it's not a joke.

"Germany has made heroes of our best killers. I'm a hero because I murdered good men, our colleagues, for pity's sake! And what really ended all between us...."

"Iris and you?"

"Yes,... It was because she was right. I began on some level to thrive on it, be psyched about the hunt, to be in on the kill, to increase my score, try and overtake Göring, that pompous ass. Do you know he actually wears perfume when he comes back from a sortie, and he takes such glee in painting the name of his kill on the side of his ship, Bleriots, Nieuports, Spads, Sopwith Camels, all destroyed, for what? The only difference between me and someone like Göring or Richthofen is that I didn't mount the heads of my dead pilots or some crap from their planes, on my wall."

"War is war, Simon. We had no choice. We're patriots. Who are we to question high authority? You know how many citizens are behind this war? Everyone who calls himself a German, that's who."

"We deserve to lose."

"Don't say that Simon. Losing would be... well, it would be devastating."

"She will never take me back. I'm a dead man, Elias, a dead man. You hear me? My body may be alive, but my heart is gone. It is over, kaput."

"Listen to me, Simon. You must swear to me that you will do nothing for six weeks. Give me six weeks. Then, if you want to kill yourself," he paused, "we'll discuss it." Again, he caused his brother to smile. "Six weeks?"

"Six weeks, Elias. If I hadn't heard your voice, I'd be dead right now. It was only my fear that it was Satan himself calling me that stopped me in my tracks."

"What are you talking about?"

"Unlike you, dear brother, I fear God. I killed good men. I'm doomed to hell."

"You fought for your country. Surely God, if there is such a thing, can tell the difference between a murderer and a soldier."

"Not if I can't."

"Amuse me. Give me six weeks. Promise me!"

"Your head is bleeding. Can you get up?"

"I think so," Elias started to stand and then collapsed. "I think it's broken."

"Your ankle. I'll get a doctor." Simon got up, and began to walk away.

"You kill yourself, I'll never speak to you again," Elias called after. "And on top of that, I'll never be able to get back to the house."

"I'll call from here and then help you in."

ACES END

Now that the Americans were solidly in the war, there was talk about the new Yankee pilots. The most notable was a man with the youthful name of Eddie Rickenbacker who had chalked up a few quick kills. Richthofen read the reports of his flying skills. Clearly, he was one to be wary of. But then there was Bishop, an astounding Brit who had taken down 25 German planes in just 12 days. He was the one Richthofen really wanted.

In early spring of 1917, flying with a squadron of Nieuports, Bishop led a raid into German territory. Richtohfen's fleet of blood red Albatrosses took them on. They were unprepared. With bull-headed ferocity, Bishop set his sights right for the lead plane, Richthofen's! Barreling and twisting, the Red Baron did his best to elude the Brit, but he couldn't. *Rat-a-tat-tat*, Bishop strafed Richthofen's plane hitting the fuselage and wings. Damaged, but unwounded, Richthofen banked into a cloud and hid until he saw an opening, dove below the forest line and limped back to base.

For France, there was Fonck and Guynemer who each had over thirty kills. And then there was the deadly Proctor from South Africa and the equally dangerous Coppins of Belgium. But Richthofen was still the one to beat. Now, months later, with over 60 victories, he was back at base, busy signing his name on a stack of 200 photographs.

"Hey Baron," Göring kidded, "if the war keeps up another year, you're going to have to build another wing to your castle."

Udet joined the conversation, having just returned from the front. He had shot down an S.E. 5 and a De Havilland. "I've never hunted deer or any other animal for that matter, never killed a beast from the forest." Udet stared off pensively.

"There is no difference, Udet. The hunt is the hunt."

"You know about Guynemer, don't you?" Udet waited for Göring to leave and then spoke privately to the Baron about France's leading ace.

"What about him?" The Red Baron itched to meet him.

"He let me go after my gun jammed."

"That was over a year ago, Ernst. Everyone knows the story how you circled each other for what seemed like hours and then your gun jammed. It's 1918 now, and we're in a whole new game."

"But it haunts me, his chivalry, I mean."

"If you see him, you've got to take him out."

"Something Maxwell said to me stays with me, Baron."

"Who are you talking about? Simon Maxwell?"

"Yes."

"What did he say?"

"All those deaths on our hands. How is it that you sleep so soundly at night? I'm plagued by the nightmares."

"I sleep like a log, Udet, and so should you. We are hunters with our eyes in front, not on the sides of our heads like prey. Life is short, Ernst. It's our destiny.

To kill and not be killed. Death will take us all soon enough. We're up to five sorties a day. You with me or not?"

"Of course."

"Good," the Red Baron said, "because I'm just warming up!"

Baron von Richthofen looked over his Fokker triplane and had the images of two more Sopwith Camel emblems placed with his other victories along the bright red fuselage. This plane had proven its value hundreds of times, but he also had the finest mechanics, and that, of course, was key. All parts must be in tip-top shape. How many men died because of a mere malfunction. That was folly. Proper maintenance was job number one.

In March, Udet flew out for the first time with von Richthofen's Jag. He too was flying a Fokker tri-plane. Moving in their classic V-formation, the Red Baron signaled a dive, and the *Jasta* moved as one, Göring, on special leave from Loerzer's jag, was right behind the Baron, Udet covering the rear. Richthofen banked sharply right, the squadron, tight, following. They opened fire on British ground troop, causing them to scatter like scared rabbits, decimating them. *Rat-a-tat-tat-tat*. Udet, however, pulled up with a sense of horror entering the deepest fiber of his being. He had never shot ground troops before. It tore against his grain. No matter what he did, he could not get Guynemer's heroic gesture out of his mind. What began as almost a sporting competition when the war was in its early stages, just 1,000 days earlier, had now evolved into a brutal game of mass killing. He could practically see the blood dripping from the mouths of Richthofen, Göring and the others. "Simon was right," he thought to himself.

Overhead, he became aware of an R.E.S. reconnaissance plane which was part of the RAF. Dipping around a hill, he gained speed to rise up and meet the ship head on. Two Sopwith camels entered the fray, when out of nowhere, the Red Baron swooped in and took the first out with a dead-on burst as he barreled and banked, and then took out the second. The move was so amazing that the R.E.S. seemed to stall in order to get a look. Unlike Richthofen, who went for the head, Udet aimed for a wing, putting the plane into a death spiral. In a valiant effort to right the craft, the Brit pulled up and crashed landed in a field.

At their base, Göring was frothing with victory. "Did you see those Brits hit the dirt! No wonder they like the word bloody!" he cackled, as he drank another hardy round of brew with the rest of the *Jagdstaffel*. Richthofen gave Udet a pat on the back, impressed with the way he took on a plane head to head. "You should be happy," Manfred said. "That's your 23rd kill."

"I want to see who I hit," Udet said.

"He's at one of our field hospitals," Göring reflected in a more somber tone.

"Go if you must," Richthofen said. "But don't lose sight. I'm placing you second in command."

"What about me?" Göring had the audacity to muster.

"Hermann, you're one of the best wing men we have, but too full of yourself. I need a thinker, like Ernst, not an egomaniac."

The crew guffawed with the Baron's jesting, and Göring capitulated. Taking a yellow scarf, which he kept tucked in his inside shirt, he twirled it around his neck in an overly ostentatious manner, thereby gaining nods of approval from most of the crew.

"That's why I called you in to begin with," the Baron said to Udet upon Göring's flamboyant exit.

Udet borrowed a horse and rode to the hospital to visit the wounded pilot. His name was Lieutenant CR Massdorp, from Canada. Unfortunately, Massdorp died before Udet got there. "May I have this?" he asked the head doctor, referring to Massdorp's air corps medal. I want to mail it to his home town in Ontario."

"Of course," said the doctor. "Let's pray for victory soon."

The Spring of 1918 was starting out exquisitely for the Red Baron. One day in March, he bagged two Bristols and two pilots, and then only a week later to the day, he knocked out a Spad and a Nieuport. All tolled, within a month, Richthofen had killed a captain, three lieutenants, two pilots of unknown rank and also a major. Göring and the other pilots were giddy in celebration as German soldiers wrenched the emblem of the fuselage of the Nieuport that had carried the major and shipped it to Richthofen's estate.

Six weeks, he had to wait, six weeks. Every day, every minute took hours. Iris was not coming back and Simon knew in his gut, he simply could not return to the front lines. He also would not go AWOL. Elias coaxed Simon into returning to work. Once again Elias contacted the Kaiser to gain permission to keep Simon on staff. He would come to Simon's house at 6:30 AM, help get him dressed and drive him personally to the shop, bring him to the big house for dinner every night, and walk him back to his house at night. At the same time, Elias wired South Africa with the hope that Iris would relent and send word that she and Simon had a chance. But Simon wasn't sure he could hold on. And then finally, word from South Africa. Elias ripped open the sealed wire, "Taroon" was all it said. It was signed with an I. What was Elias to do? He couldn't bring this wire to Simon. He asked Debora. "You must tell him the truth," she said. "What other choice is there?"

"How could she be so cruel?" Elias asked.

"She's hurt and mad. I know it's not his fault, Elias, but Simon has dashed all her hopes."

"This might really kill him," Elias said.

"Do you want me to come with you?"

"No, but if he does himself in, I'll go down to South America and kill her myself."

"Elias, don't even think that. You want to be mad at someone, be mad at your beloved Kaiser. Iris was right, this is total madness and it's all on his shoulders, not ours. Have Simon join us for dinner. Maybe he should move in for a while."

"That's a perfect idea. Let's see what he says."

Reluctantly, Elias drove somberly over to Simon's house, the telegram hidden in his pocket. "Simon," Elias called out. No answer. He knocked, entered, called out again and walked upstairs. Still no answer, an eerie silence pervaded the hallway. Elias entered the bedroom. Simon's body lay askew, his hand dangling off the bed, draped almost to the floor, his pistol beneath it. Blood everywhere. Elias pulled the pillow off Simon's chest. He had shot himself in the heart. An odd calmness took over, and so he sat there for a time, his hand resting affectionately on Simon's forehead. His brother's suicide note lay on a desk across the room. Elias walked over and read, *I leave all my earthly possessions to the family of Henry Taroon. Sorry, Elias. Please say my good-byes. Simon.*

The elder brother took a match to the note, placed it in a brass Luftwaffe ashtray and watched it burn to cinder. Then he removed a bottle of scotch from a bottom draw and took a long deep swig. At the bottom of the draw were French postcards of naked women. He shook his head, looked back at his brother's body and contemplated. He burnt them as well.

Wrapping the body in the sheets and two blankets and protecting the head with another blanket, Elias dragged the corpse down the stairs, pulled his automobile to the porch and pushed the body into the passenger side. Exhausted, he rested before picking up the phone. He directed Tante Ella to come to Simon's house with Debora. They arrived and began the process of washing away all traces of blood.

Elias drove out to a field at the outskirts of their estate. He propped Simon by a large oak tree which overlooked the river and waited, pistol in hand. Morning turned to dusk. Weary, Elias started to fall asleep when out of the corner of his eye, something flitted past, hovered, darted about the tree and then landed on his knee. It was a dining needle. It had iridescent lavender eyes, a glowing red patch on its body and two sets of shimmering wings where rainbows could be seen. The dragonfly rotated its head nearly 180° to look Elias dead in the eye. A tear began its descent down his cheek as he sat and contemplated the tragic irony and idiocy of the moment.

Three deer emerged from the forest, two young bucks and a doe. They approached this friendly man they had known since they were fawns. Elias walked calmly toward them, but the fear in his eyes gave up the game. They bolted, but he was quicker. He raised the gun and shot the larger buck behind the front shoulder. The animal shook off the sting and continued unabated until suddenly it stumbled, tried to get up and then fell to the ground. Sickened, Elias walked over to deliver the coup de grace. *Boom!* A third shot was fired low into the woods. Elias positioned the gun under the animal's hoof in such a way as to simulate the absurd possibility that the animal had somehow shot Simon as he sat with a knife to prepare his kill.

As Elias continued to arrange the site, he heard a rumble in the forest and saw one of the other two deer peering at him from the brush. Some unsaid energy was transferred between them and he wanted to apologize. As it turned, and ran off, the weight of the event suddenly hit him. He had never killed an animal before and he was stricken with sense of pain the likes of which he had never felt before. He tried to brush it off, and wipe away a tear, but then another one came and another. Sobbing uncontrollably, he realized that he was crying moreso for himself than for Simon. But he couldn't stop and then found that he was also grieving for his father and for the early death of a mother he barely remembered, for his son, Abe, who would never see his uncle again and for his wife and his aunt, and for Iris.

"Oh, Simon," Elias said, "How could you do this?"

For the briefest of moments, he felt he could sense Simon's presence sitting in the tree like a cat or a raccoon, but he brushed the vision off. "Grow up," he told himself. Wiping his tears and looking around to make sure no one saw him, Elias dusted himself off, re-tied his tie and made his way back to the roadster.

The funeral was held at gravesite. Due to the difficulty to be able to travel to the burial ground in Austria, Elias created a cemetery not far from where Simon's body had been found. Rabbi Sinschwartz read the eulogy. "Yeah, though I walk through the valley of the shadow of death, I shall fear no evil for thou art with me. They rod and thy staff they comfort me."

As the rabbi talked, Elias found himself looking out to the river where a group of swans floated by. Off in the distance, a faint slow flapping could be felt and heard augmented by an occasional syncopated *Honk!* Five geese flying in V-formation circled the gravesite. The mourners looked up. Their flutter increased as they tilted their bodies back. With heads and beaks up, they landed as one, and waddled over to take their place next to Abe. They stood silently by as the rabbi continued.

"Let us be grateful for the time we have had with Simon here on earth. He was a man of unusual talents, a wizard in the machine shop, a soldier and pilot, a patriot, a man of religion and a family man. Rather than grieve for Simon's loss, let us have gratitude, gratitude that we all knew and loved such an inspiring individual. The poet wrote, 'What is essential can never die.' And so, we can find comfort that Simon is no longer burdened by the ravages of this ugly ugly world war, rather, he has now taken refuge in a place far above the clouds that is much safer. He lies in peace, and God is now Simon's inheritance."

A single aeroplane flew low overhead dropping white carnations to end the ceremony. Elias had Debora send a note to Iris, and he also notified the military that Simon had died in a hunting accident on March 7, 1918.

"Anyone going to the Maxwell funeral?" Richthofen asked, changing the mood of the beer hall.

"Jews bury their dead in 24 hours," Göring said.

"I should send a note."

"Yes, Baron, you should." Göring stared at his drink. "He was weak, like most Jews."

"Don't underestimate him, Hermann. You too may find the love of your life some day."

"Yeah, someone to lacquer his toes when he gets too fat to reach them," one of the pilots said in jest.

"I'll be lucky if I survive the war," Richthofen interrupted the mood once again.

"Why talk like this, Baron? You are the greatest fighter pilot the world has ever seen."

"Better than Immelman?"

"You're alive. What better measure is there?"

The Red Baron lifted his glass. "Let's drink to Simon Maxwell and Max Immelman."

"Maxwell and Immelman," the men shouted.

"And Boelke," Göring added.

"And Boelke," the men echoed.

"And to our dead cohorts on the other side." It was Udet, having just returned from a sortie.

"Udet! Udet!" the men shouted. "How'd it go?" Richthofen asked.

"We lost Böhme."

The group was stunned with the death of yet another ace, in part because he had received the *Pour le Merite* just two days earlier. Every man in the room was forced to reflect on the irony of losing a fighter who was responsible for killing their greatest teacher, Oswald Boelke.

"To dead pilots everywhere," Udet raised his glass.

April 21, 1918 was turning out to be a routine day, not even any sightings. The Baron waved Udet and the rest of the crew off and took his time going back to base. He looked over the landscape and noticed a herd of deer trot along a ridge. He'd have to remember that spot. He bet there were bear there as well.

High overhead, beyond earshot and eyesight, Captain Roy Brown was cruising the sky in his biplane Sopwith Camel. Below him he spotted the bright red tri-plane. Had he known it was Richthofen, he may have high-tailed it. He certainly would not have been as calm as he was when he dove and hit the enemy warplane dead center, tearing a deadly burst from one end of the fuselage to the other. He watched it land mostly in tact and then flew back to base.

Taking his Albatross down behind enemy lines, the Red Baron bled to death before his aircraft was discovered. Allied soldiers dragged his body before cameras for the international press. Their jubilation was oddly tempered by the palpable reverence they had for this Ace of Aces, even if he was an enemy, so they held a funeral for Manfred von Richthofen with full military honors. With the Red Baron's death came a corresponding crush in the will of the German people. Udet, who was second in command with 23 kills advanced to *Jag Staffelführer*. He rallied his squadron quickly, and out they went for another sortie. Enemy planes seemed to roll and barrel at them from every angle. Out-gunned, the Jag scattered, but not before Udet was shot out of the sky. It was now up to Göring to lead them back home.

"With Udet gone, what will we do now?" one of the pilots pined.

Göring smacked the soldier across the face. "This is war, man. What did you think?" Hermann had done his best, but back in his room, he fell apart. Even the Red Baron had been in awe of Udet's acrobatic skills. Udet was in another league; Göring was simply not ready to lead a full squadron. He could fake it if he had to, but those kinds of flying skills that the real Ace of Aces had were simply beyond his capabilities, and at this juncture, there really was nobody else.

The following morning, to the utter astonishment of all, Udet sauntered into the dining hall unscathed. Miraculously, he had parachuted to safety and landed near a German encampment, and so was quickly able to get a ride back to base. Udet was fairly short, but he seemed to grow about a foot that day. It was one of those moments when a man becomes legend. Udet used that energy to turn things around. Although the Americans had broken through the lines and were now just 30 kilometers from the German border, Udet saw this as opportunity.

"Their fresh, and crowded together. And they will pay for Richthofen's death!" Udet cried.

Over the next several months, Udet became a man possessed. Without abandon, he strafed enemy troops, shot reconnaissance balloons and tripled his score to an astonishing 62 kills. He was now second in total next to von Richthofen who, although deceased, still led the world with 80. Udet was followed by Lowenhardt whose tally was 53, but he died when his parachute wouldn't open. Vöss with 48 victories, was killed in a battle against seven enemy craft. Loerzer, Göring's overseer, was in the top tier with 44 downed craft. Like Udet and Göring, Loerzer and very few of the other early pilots would beat the odds and see this war through alive.

On the Allies side leading fighter pilots included Fonck and Guynemer with 75 and 54 victories respectively for France; Bishop, Collishaw, Mannock and McCudden with 72, 62, 61 and 57 for Great Britain; Willy Coppens of Belgium with 37; and Eddie Rickenbacker with 23 downed craft for the United States. These were the Ace of Aces, respected on both sides both during and after the war. Although Guynemer, Mannock and McCudden would not live to see victory day, something about what they did in this first major conflict of the 20th century simply put them in class by themselves. After the war, it was not uncommon for the survivors to seek each other out, swap autographed photos and meet periodically at air shows. These were the elite.

When the Allies finally won, they demanded, through the Treaty of Versailles, nothing less than a total humiliating surrender of the Fatherland, and worse, payment of a war debt to the victors that ran to the tens of billions. And when the Allies stormed into Germany, the Kaiser fled, leaving a new government castrated. Forced to capitulate, they were simply barred altogether from the building of *any* kind of mechanical craft. That meant no submarines, no tanks, no machine guns or cannons, no aeroplanes with motors in them, and thus, no commercial aircraft. To the proud German people, this treaty was the final death blow.

Fokker, Junkers, DFW and Elias Maxwell were forced to shut down operations. Since Junkers had an international presence, he was soon able to produce planes in other countries, but still he took a tremendous financial hit.

Back in Kempten, Abe was reading the Torah and learning to speak and comprehend Hebrew. He conferred with the rabbi often about his uncle's death and about what Simon had said about killing in war. Even Elias seemed to have a religious awakening in the face of that tragedy.

Every Sabbath, Elias couldn't help himself, he would go down to the river and sit beside his brother's grave. Oftentimes taking with him a pair of clippers to tend the grave's garden, sometimes, Debora or Abe would accompany him. But mostly, he went alone. Still a convert on the outside, he had, none-the-less, agreed for Abe to be Bar Mitzvahed. There would be a modest celebration as Elias had done his best to keep the event under wraps. He did not want his gentile business colleagues finding out. Of course, the other converts knew, but they, like Elias, would keep this little secret.

"My uncle saw himself as a murderer. That is what I overheard papa tell my momma shortly after he found uncle Simon's body. If my uncle killed pilots in battle, does that make him a murderer?" Abe asked the rabbi.

The rabbi peered down over half-moon reading glasses and scratched his beard in contemplation. Abe sat quietly studying the rabbi's black robes, black fedora which he wore in place of a yarmulke and white silk prayer shawl, the end of which the rabbi held in his other hand. "The rules in war are different," the rabbi finally spoke. "It is the duty of a soldier to obey the state's commands," The rabbi paused once again, stood up, circled the office and took his seat once again. "No," he concluded, "your uncle was a great war hero. He was not a murderer."

"But will he go to hell for killing other humans?"

"The Jew does not believe in heaven and hell, Abe."

"That's not what I read."

The rabbi was shocked by the boy's response. "What have you read?"

"This." Abe handed the rabbi a book on Cabala.

"Who gave you this?"

"Tante Ella."

"Do you know how old a person is supposed to be before he studies Cabala?"

"Two score years."

"And how old are you."

"Point six-five score year."

"So, how long do you have to wait to read this book?"

"But it's too late, rabbi. I read it. The book talks about eternity and transmigration of souls. If we go back to God at death, isn't that some form of heaven?"

"The important thing, my little one, is not what happens to you at death, but what you do while you are alive. Now, let's get back to your passage for entrance into manhood."

"But I want to know where my uncle is."

"If I answer you honestly, will you get back to your study?"

"Yes," Abe said, now confident he would find out the truth.

"The absolute truth is, my little one, I don't know. I believe this is not something a man can ever know. It is beyond human knowledge. But I will say this. If there is a heaven, and if there is a hell," the rabbi added as to completely answer the tyke's question, "then in all sincerity, I think your uncle Simon will be in heaven. Is that a fair answer?"

Abe looked at the wizened teacher. He saw truth and was satisfied.

The Treaty of Versailles, reduced Germany to third world status and made it a debtor nation. Nevertheless, it was also a blessing for some people. Builders had to rebuild, bankers had to shuffle great sums of money and new heroes had to become manifest.

DOPPELGÄNGER

The last plane left Boston for New York at midnight. But it was past two a.m. when Rudy finally left the precinct.

Officer Payne's first instinct was to put the little bitch in the slammer. But he came around, as Rudy knew he would, and let Kaitlin go.

They would target Jamie and pin it all on him, assuming they could catch him. Kaitlin would remain free, go back to school and simply continue on, but she would wear a wire. If Rudy was right and Officer Payne agreed, NTroodr would try to use her again. And when he did, they would be that much closer to nailing him.

Rudy was too hepped up to go to sleep. Since there were no more flights out of Boston that night, he decided to rent a car and drive it. If he figured it right, it was four or five hours away, he'd be home in time for breakfast.

Now that she was married, Chessie didn't like Rudy flying off without her, even if it was just his job. If she hadn't been pregnant, maybe she would have gone with him. She had been a freelance photographer. But her back ached from the weight of her pregnancy. She thought back to how miffed she was when she first learned she was pregnant to essentially the opposite feeling now of real satisfaction. Something deep within her told Chessie that she was on the right path, that by bringing this new child into the world, her life would gain a greater depth of meaning.

Chessie had spent the first thirty years not really thinking about potential motherhood. In fact, after that breakup with Mike, Chess had pretty much given up the idea of settling down and raising a family. And then this happened so quickly. It really did take her several months to adjust, but at the same time, something else had changed, it was a primal sense that everything was right with her marriage and even with the world at large. Contentment. That's what she felt, contentment even with the size of her bulging stomach and the size of her swelling breasts, contentment with the occasional kicks she felt and contentment with her man, Rudy Styne.

But why hadn't he called? Rudy always called around dinner time, no matter where he was. It was just one of those things he did, factoring in the time difference no matter where he was on the globe, timing his call to catch her before she really settled in for her meal. The call was nearly two hours past due.

A strange shiver overtook her, a certain sense of foreboding. But she brushed it off. So he didn't call. Big deal.

Ding-dong!

Chessie looked at the clock. It was nearly eight P.M. That's an odd time for the doorbell she thought. Chessie walked to the front. Without a peephole, she had no choice and just opened the door.

"Rudy," she said, "you scared the crap out of me. How come you're home so early? And why didn't you call?"

Chessie reached out to give Rudy a playful slap on the shoulder. "You look terrible," she said, noticing the wrinkles and even grey hair she had never seen before. "And where did you get those clothes?"

"Mrs. Styne, I am Rolf Linzman. I didn't mean to alarm you," the man continued in his distinct German accent.

"Very funny, kiddo. Now, give me a kiss and get those clothes off. *Mach schnell!* Put something on I can recognize you in!" Chessie paused to consider the face. Nodding approvingly, she continued, "Good make-up job. You really almost had me."

Chessie leaned her head back to get a better look and then continued. "You look worn. And your accent sounds as phony as a three-dollar bill. I'm sure Rolf Linzman speaks a whole lot better than that. God, you look ancient. How was Boston?"

"Maybe I should come back at another time," Rolf said, turning to go. "I am truly sorry." Rolf looked one more time deep into Chessie's eyes, turned and began his walk back towards his car.

Chessie just stood there and watched him. "Come on, Rudy. Enough is enough. Rudeeee," she called, and then ran out and grabbed the man's shoulder. After another moment of consideration, the reality of it all began to dawn. "You really are him, aren't you?"

"Yes," Rolf said.

"I can't believe it." Moving closer, she found herself giving him a cordial kiss on the cheek. Their eyes locked again.

"Let me touch you," Chessie reached out to give Rolf a hug. He stood there somewhat stiffly as she wrapped her arms around him, placed her cheek against his shoulder and through the hug, began to read him. Although he looked exactly like Rudy, down to every detail of his face, he was definitely much older and his vibe was very different. It was the hug more than anything else that convinced her that it was Linzman. Once more, she leaned her head back to size him up. "I'm sorry Mr. Linzman. Please come in." Chessie dragged him back towards the door. "Make yourself at home."

Rolf gave Chessie a hand back up the stairs and they entered.

"May I take your coat?"

"Yes," Rolf said, handing it to her. "Again, I apologize, Mrs. Styne, for not alerting you or calling ahead."

"Nonsense!" Chessie said. "And call me Chessie. If you call me Mrs. Styne one more time, I'm going to feel like Rudy's mother!" Chessie couldn't help it, but she found herself staring. It was just too startling, sitting there glaring at the man she was in love with, yet at the same time, knowing it wasn't him. Seeing Rudy's face so much older added to the complexity of her ability to process the situation. "I'm sorry," Chessie explained, "you are going to have to allow me to stare a bit more. My eyes see my husband, but my brain is telling me something very different. You really are his doppelgänger."

"The evil twin?" Rolf suggested.

"No," Chessie countered. "That's not what I meant at all."

Four a.m. Rudy was wide awake, out on the highway. Not a soul on the road except for a few trucks. He would use this time to think. It was too easy if Heinz Gruuban was behind all this. Having sized up the man on his trip to Munich, he didn't think he was. But anything was possible. Maybe Gruuban thought the iPhones would never be linked to nefarious activity. Rudy had Bett's phone. He would have his technical guy look at it. To be safe, he removed the battery. Maybe the circuits could give them a clue.

The time flew by. He scooted over the Throgs Neck Bridge, took the Long Island Expressway to his exit at Cedar Swamp Road, found his lane and parked the car at his house. It wasn't quite seven a.m. He noticed the rental out in front.

The breakfast room was lit. There was a man sitting with Chessie. The guy looked just like him! *What the hell was this all about?* This had to be his look-alike, Rolf Linzman, son of Gunter Linzman, the man he had met in Germany.

"Hello, Rudy," Rolf said in a voice that, except for the accent, sounded like his. "Your wife was kind enough to let me sleep in the guest room last night. I hope you don't mind."

Begrudgingly, Rudy went over and shook Rolf's hand. The connection was electric as each man looked at the other with what seemed like similar, yet at the same time opposite thoughts.

Rudy broke off the moment by letting go. "Chess," he said, "do you mind if I speak to you for a moment?"

"Will you excuse us?" Chessie said.

"Of course." Rolf returned to his chair at the kitchen table and sipped his coffee.

Rudy took Chessie into a far-away bedroom.

"I gotta tell you, Hon," Chess said excitedly, "when this guy knocked at the door, I was thrown for a frigging loop. At first I thought it was you, because it *was* you, but of course it couldn't be you. He's much older, and it took me forever to process it. I couldn't separate the two of you. It was just so far out. He looks so much like you, it's like it *is* you, but with grey hair and a German accent."

"Do you know what I have been through?"

"Did you even listen to a word I said?"

"Yes, Chess. It's freaky. But you knew where I was."

"You went to interview a professor at MIT."

"So you don't know she's been murdered?"

"Murdered?! What are you talking about?!"

"Dead, as in dead as a doornail," Rudy said. "We were to meet for dinner, but when I got there, I found her on the bed, her eyes glassed open. And then I heard the police sirens, and I had to get out and circle back. I'll have to tell you all about it." Rudy paused and then switched gears. "Why didn't you answer your phone when I called last night? You were having dinner with *him*, weren't you?"

"Yes, and you should call him by his name, Rolf. He's got to be your brother, Rudy. You guys are identical."

"And you couldn't pick up?"

"I didn't want to be rude."

"Rude! It was ten o'clock at night. Don't you think I'd be worried?"

"I'm sorry, Rudy. I turned down the ringer. I didn't hear it. I just figured you'd be here by the morning, like you said."

"Let me ask you this, Chess. Don't you think it odd that this man, my supposed brother, who is connected to Gunter Linzman, my possible father, and business associate, Heinz Gruuban, the mega-Internet mogul, is here the very night the lady I was interviewing who was investigating these guys, was killed?"

"What are you saying?"

"He could be involved, Chess. Wake up! That guy in there could be NTroodr for all I know. It could've been my freaking double who planned this whole thing. Before we go back, what did you guys talk about?"

"Nothing much, Rudy. He didn't want to talk shop, he said. We were just killing time, waiting for you."

"I just hope that's not all he was killing."

"What's that supposed to mean!" Chessie snapped.

Avoiding a direct answer, Rudy grabbed Chessie's hand, said under his breath a quick, "I'm sorry," and brought her back to the kitchen.

"Can I make you something?" she said to Rudy.

"Whatever you guys are having," Rudy really was hungry.

"Ham and eggs and home fries?"

"Perfect." Rudy turned back to Rolf. "Before we begin," Rudy said, placing a finger to his lips, he scribbled on a piece of paper: *Can I see your cell phone?*

Rolf removed it. Yes, it was an iPhone and yes, the speaker system was on. Rudy led Rolf to another room and placed the iPhone by a speaker and popped in a DVD of a lecture Rudy had given on journalism in the New Age and they walked back to the kitchen.

"Where to begin?" he began.

Rudy and Rolf talked for the next eight hours straight. They talked about their respective childhoods, life in America versus life in Germany, growing up in the early-1960's verses growing up in the mid-70's, Rudy grilled Rolf about his father, and his heritage. Somewhat evasive, Rolf instead, ragged on his mother, how she didn't love him, how he felt like an outsider. Rudy never experienced those thoughts. They were operating from two different plains, Rudy was quite happy with his upbringing, Rolf, resentful. Although both appeared interested in figuring out how they could indeed, be brothers, Rudy seemed more determined, whereas Rolf was more interested in preserving the empire that his father had built.

"The past is the past," Rolf spat, exuding an edgy and perhaps even dangerous vibe. Rudy thought he'd just ask Rolf outright.

"Where'd you get that phone?"

"Heinz Gruuban gave it to me," Rolf replied. "He said he had obtained a large shipment of iPhones from Apple. It could have been a thousand or more. They were trying to entice him to use their product line with the cell phone company he was creating in association with Webnet, and I know he gave tons of them away to various universities."

"Like MIT?"

"Sure, and Harvard, but also major schools in Europe. The idea was to hook the student elite onto our platform, because I'm working with Gruuban to link up Webnet to a satellite system we are about to launch. And we too are working on a co-production deal with Apple."

"So you don't really know where those phones came from?"

"I guess not. I always thought they came right from Apple."

"You know Dr. LaPolla's been murdered?"

"Who's she?"

Rudy could tell Rolf didn't really know.

"How about NTroodr. Do you know who he is?"

"I'm afraid I don't." Rolf said. "That fucker's been on my tail for near on a year. I can't shake him." With his German accent, the word sounded almost like "fokker."

"How long have you had that phone?"

"Three—four months."

"And he's hacked your computer?"

"Yes. And frankly, I'm in a tight spot with what he knows."

"So what do you know about you and me?"

"I don't. That's why I'm here. Now, I've told you a little about my father, now I want to know about yours." Rolf seemed too eager.

"I never met my father. My mother told me he died when I was an infant. I always accepted it until uncle Abe showed up at the wedding and I found out my blood type didn't match my mother's."

"I never thought my mother was my mother either," Rolf said. "My father's got to be your kin, however."

"It would seem so," Rudy said. "But I just can't figure how your father could be my father if Abe Maxwell is my grandfather."

"Maxwell!" Rolf scorned.

"Yes, Abe Maxwell. My mother always told me he was my uncle, but he told Chessie the link was more direct."

"I remember Simon Maxwell, when I was a boy," Rolf reflected.

"You knew him?"

"No. It was a name on a tombstone on the property."

"You mean in Kempten, out at the old Motorworks?"

"Yes," Rolf said.

"That's Abe's uncle," Chessie recalled. "Remember that guy in Venice? He told us about Simon's wedding and he gave us a picture."

"That's right," Rudy said. "I'll have to dig it up."

"Let me get a paper," Chessie said, "And sort this thing out. I think Gunter is the father of both of you. You guys look too much alike to form any other conclusion." Chessie started a family tree.

"We are missing Abe's father and Abe's grandfather," Chessie remarked.

"You mean," Rolf said, "we would both have the same mother and the same father? That's not possible."

"How else can you explain it?" Chessie asked.

"That would mean that my father's been having a 15 or 20 year affair with someone other than my mother."

"Abe's daughter," Rudy said. "You know he's suing your father for ownership of MB Airways."

"That's a bullshit suit. We deal with nutcase suits like that two, three times a year."

"Yes," Chessie said, "but how many nutcases have the name Maxwell painted on your smoke stacks at the Kempten plant?"

"But that plant's been closed over thirty years, " Rolf said.

"Abe's old enough to have owned the company before the war," Chessie reasoned.

"He's really that old?" Rolf asked.

"Mid-nineties, my mother figures," Rudy said. "He could even be older."

"He can't really have a legitimate claim on a company he hasn't seen in over 50 years."

"What if the Nazis stole it from him?" Rudy countered. "Then he'd have a claim."

"Oh, so that's your game. You want to steal my company. I came to you in peace. But you Jews are all alike," Rolf spit. "I'm sorry, Chessie. You were very kind but I can't abide by shysters." Rolf grabbed his jacket and stormed out of the house.

Rudy took off after him.

"Let him go," Chessie said.

Rudy ignored her. Running down the walk, he grabbed Rolf's collar, just as he was getting into his car.

"Mr. Linzman," Rudy began, "first of all I could care less about your company or you, even if we are related. I'm on the trail of a master hacker and a murderer. And that's NTroodr. That's my interest. I never even knew I had any connection to you up until a couple of weeks ago. So you keep that in mind when you use your phone and broadcast whatever we said to the very man I'm after."

Rudy grabbed Rolf's car keys, leaving his German double stranded, as he stormed back into the house. Rolf stood there agape until Rudy returned. He tossed the keys and the phone into Rolf's car.

"Rolf," Rudy said with a phony sincerity to his voice, pointing to the phone, "I'm glad you brought us that pet kangaroo. I'll be sure to tell Phil to ride the elephant when we get to the cage. We'll see you in the Bronx."

"I'll try and capture the snowy egret," Rolf played along. There was a reluctance to the handshake, but at least they did clasp hands, and then Rudy turned his back and walked away.

"What was that all about?" Chessie asked.

"I thought I'd give NTroodr something to chew on."

"You think Rolf is NTroodr?"

"No, but he is connected in some way, and when I figure that out, a big head is going to roll."

It was the following morning. Chessie checked her Blackberry for any messages. There was one from Mike about an upcoming Sotheby's auction of 19th century paintings, and Mike was asking if Chessie could attend. There were several paintings he thought were underpriced and he needed someone there to physically compete.

"He's giving me a half million to play with."

"You think that's enough?" Rudy said.

"He's given me a list, and if I do it right, I think I can pick up about three paintings."

"In this day and age," Rudy said, "that sounds like a steal."

"That's what we're hoping for," Chessie grinned.

NTroodr sat at his multi-screen control center with his octopus of remote mouses and continued to monitor his flock. Once he had figured out that Rolf's iPhone was sending him an old speech Rudy Styne had given on economic theory, it made NTroodr more curious. Nevertheless, he knew he had picked up some code words when the phone was removed, and so he wrote down "pet kangaroo," "ride the elephant," and "snowy egret," and did his best to figure out what it all meant. And then he got a better idea.

Having hacked Chessie's Blackberry, he saw the information about the upcoming Southeby's auction, which was trivial, but he used the entrée to play awhile longer until he was able to activate her microphone. Using voice recognition software, he converted her conversation with her husband to text so he didn't have to listen in real time, and then later, at a more opportune moment, he'd look it over as he continued to monitor his many other minions. Some of the conversation was inaudible, and that was to be expected, but what follows is the meat of what he obtained.

"What's wrong, Rudy? You seem troubled."

"Well, wouldn't you be if you'd just seen a gal murdered and less than twenty-four hours later, your exact double shows up at your door. Only the guy is ten or twenty years older than you, and up until a couple of weeks ago, you never even knew he existed."

"That's not what I'm talking about, and you know it."

"I know, Chess, I know. But it's all related. What's happened is that these events have made me question what I'm doing, who I am, what this is all about. What's the point of it all?"

"The point, Rudy, for you -- for us – is to live our lives, so we can bring this new child that I'm carrying, up into this world and help this new being develop into who he or she will want to become."

As NTroodr read, he found himself playing an imaginary violin. He turned the page and continued reading.

"But on some level, Chess, that's exactly what I'm talking about."

"I'm not following," Chessie said.

"Well, put yourself in my place. You've had this vision of who you were for your whole life, your entire childhood, adolescence, college years, adulthood, the whole nine yards. And, suddenly, you find out that everything you ever knew about yourself was a total lie."

"That's not so," Chessie declared.

"What do you mean? Of course it is."

"You grew up with a mother who loved you, who still loves you. That's not something to be taken lightly. Does it really matter whether she's biologically related to you?"

"Of course it matters, Chess. Because I thought I was a normal kid. And now, I find out I've got an asshole for a brother to deal with that I never even knew existed. You were here. You saw him."

"He's not as bad as you make him out to be, Rudy. I spent an entire night with him."

Rudy gave her a look.

"Don't even say it, Rudy. You know what I mean."

"I know," he said, passing by the obvious joke. "But you still miss the point."

"And what point is that?"

"I don't know who I am!"

"Oh, that's bullshit, Rudy. You sound like a broken record."

"It's not like you're even listening to me," Rudy rebutted.

"Oh, so suddenly you're concerned about a heritage you never gave a second thought about up until this moment?"

"What do you mean?"

"Did you ever once try and find out about your mother's heritage, her parents and grandparents, where they came from, really, who your dead British father was, what his background was, where he came from?"

"No, but...."

"No, but! That's what you have to say!" Chessie bit into him. "Rudy, all of a sudden you now care about something long dead and past, something you have no control over, something that can never change. So, why the new interest? You were never interested before."

"That's the point, Chess."

"What's the point?"

"Now, I am."

"You am what?"

"I'm interested. Suddenly, now I want to know my past. I want to find out where I'm from, who I am, who my family was, what Abe's real story is, how Mr. Linzman fits in. I can't explain it other than to say, if I don't find out, I will feel that I could never be at peace with myself."

"You mean, you want to know who your so-called 'real' mother is?"

"Is that so terrible?"

"But, at what cost, Rudy? You realize what you are going to do to the lady who brought you into this world, who cared for you day and night your entire life. Who still cares for you. You want to rattle all that, for what? a ghost that has played no role whatever in your life? Or because you're a journalist, to fill in a few gaps, to write a good story?"

"That's hitting below the belt, Chessie. I'm trying to be open with you. I tell her I need to know the truth, and now you're making me feel worse."

"You mean to locate your biological mother?"

"Yes."

"And you think digging out a past that was buried a half-century ago is worth it? For what, Rudy? For what end?!"

Rudy didn't even know how to respond to Chessie's grilling. All he could do was look at her, and he didn't like what he saw. It seemed that up until that moment, whenever he looked into her eyes, something inside him would melt. But, now, now, he saw defiance, anger, perhaps, even a touch of fear in her eyes. And that's when it occurred to him that maybe she was just trying to defend her family, to not rattle the cage. And so he relented and reached over to give his wife a kiss, but she turned away.

"I can't shut my eyes to this, Chess. I've got to try."

Chess looked back at her man and something in her gave a little. "Just don't forget what you've got, kiddo."

Rudy turned towards the door. He felt the need to get out, before things got worse. To take a walk, to clear his head. He reached for the doorknob.

"Where you going?"

Rudy turned back and their eyes met again.

"How about a hug?" she said.

Rudy was no idiot. He reached out to his one and only and she, in return, wrapped her arms around him and hugged tight. "I'm sorry buddieo," she whispered. "Just do your thing."

"Thanks," he said.

1918

Gunter had borrowed his master's automobile to drop off his son, Gunter II, at the Christian Academy where the boy was attending school. And then he drove back to the mansion to pick Elias up.

"Can I come, papa?" little Abe asked.

Not quite sure what to do, Elias said yes and let Abe sit in-between he and Linzman as they made their way to the local quarry to finalize arrangements for Simon's headstone. In particular, he wanted to discuss with the sculptor exactly what he wanted put on it.

As per usual, Abe was holding one of his favorite toys, a precise scaled-down model of a Maxwell biplane, one that was used in the war with toy machine guns mounted on each wing.

"Would it be all right if I borrowed this for a few weeks?" Elias asked his son.

"You want to put this on uncle Simon's gravestone?" Abe intuited.

"Not exactly, Abe. I want the sculptor to replicate the plane above uncle Simon's name."

"Are you going to include the machine guns, papa?"

"Of course not, my little one. Without the guns."

"I think he'd like that papa," Abe said.

"Yes, my little one."

Abe looked over at the driver. Gunter nodded in agreement and then turned the roadster into the quarry. Elias continued, "I think he'd like that very much."

242   *Marc J. Seifer*

ENNUI

Rudy awoke with the next day with an overarching feeling of dissatisfaction. Ashley LaPolla was dead and he had not solved the crime. Sure he had gotten close, but that was not good enough. He found himself cursing while preparing breakfast when all he did was drop a butter knife onto the floor.

"Rudy," Chessie said, "you have to give yourself a break. You can't blame yourself for the professor's death." Chessie reached down, picked up the utensil and placed it in the sink.

"But I feel like I failed," Rudy admitted, "and worse than that, I was completely off base."

"What are you talking about?"

Rudy looked at her cell phone as they exchanged glances. He opened the back door so they could continue their conversation outside, away from all technology. Taking their cups of coffee, they walked around to the front, found a seat on the porch and continued their conversation.

"Code Breaker Morant," he said. "I accused Ashley of being that notorious hacker when, in fact, all I did was play the fool. I did *exactly* what the real Morant wanted me to do, accuse the patsy. I'm such an idiot, and now, because of that, she's dead."

"You followed a reasonable lead." Chessie sipped her coffee and continued. "That doesn't make you the fool, it makes you an investigative reporter."

"How can you say that?"

"Well, where did this Morant guy come up with Ashley LaPolla's name in the first place?"

"What are you saying?"

"Clearly, he didn't pick her out of a hat, and you certainly weren't the first to notice the connection between the name, the movie Breaker Morant and her infatuation with Bryan Brown. One way or another, it's a clue and you pursued it."

"But as soon as I targeted her, she got killed."

"You don't know that." Chessie put down her cup and stood up to continue her point. "This NTroodr had to have seen her as a threat long before you came onto the scene."

"What makes you say that?"

"Remember, she was on TV."

"Yes, but so were a number of hacker experts."

"Rudy, you can't keep blaming yourself."

"But she's dead, Chess, dead. And I can't help but feel that I played a key role."

"I don't see that at all."

"What are you saying?"

"I'm talking about the MO."

"MO?"

"Yes, Rudy, how could you expect a computer hacker to turn to violence, let alone murder."

"You're saying that computer nerds and violence don't mix?"

"That's exactly what I'm saying."

"You gotta point, Chess. That kind of decision, to kill another human being, doesn't really seem to fit the kind of person who spends their days hacking."

"Exactly."

"But that only means I have to re-think the kind of person I'm really dealing with."

"It also means you have to double your guard."

"Yeah, and on top of that, I feel I've put Dickie in jeopardy as well."

"Old Dickie can look out for himself, Rudy. I'm more concerned with your relationship with Rolf. If he's your brother.....' Chessie just left the sentence dangling.

"Then I've got go confront my mother?"

"We already went over that. It's uncle Abe I'm talking about."

"You mean grandpa Abe?"

"Yes, grandpa. Why don't you call him? With all of this intrigue, surely he can explain himself before I give birth."

"I'd be happy to, but I really have no idea how to reach him." Rudy got up and led Chessie back into the house.

"Why don't you leave a message with uncle Hoxie. I'll bet you anything Abe will be in contact with him," Chessie said.

Three days later, Rudy heard a familiar German accent on the phone. It was 7:10 am. He turned off Good Morning America and grabbed a pen and paper in case he had to take notes. "Rudy, I'm up to my eyeballs in legal strategies," Abe confessed.

"With who?" Rudy asked.

"Your wayward father, that's who," Abe pulled no punches.

"About M-B Airways?" Rudy doodled the acronym in a variety of styles on the page.

"Yes, Maxwell-Bavarian Airways."

"And he is my real father? Gunter Linzman?" Rudy asked for clarification, but waited for what seemed like a very long pause.

"In a manner of speaking," Abe finally answered cryptically.

"What does that mean?!" Rudy practically shouted, clearly annoyed. "And are you, in a manner of speaking, my grandfather?"

"Rudy, my boy, you know the term 'Let sleeping dogs lie'?"

"Of course."

"Then you need to trust me. Life can sometimes be complex, moreso than you can imagine."

"I don't understand. These are simple questions, Abe."

"And I will give you simple answers. But I've dedicated a lot of thought to this, and I've decided that the best course of action is to..."

"Wait until the bris?" Rudy interrupted.

"Exactly, my boy, and at that time, I'll be in touch."

With that, Abe hung up leaving Rudy dumbstruck.

"So, he's not going to talk until the baby is born," Chessie said after hearing of the conversation. "Then let's just let it drop for now and live our life. I'm going to work at home today. Go back to your office, get back in the grind. It's not good for you to overthink this."

"I wanted to wrap this up," Rudy confessed.

"We've waited this long, surely we can wait a little longer."

"But I'm champing at the bit."

"Sometimes questions remain," Chessie said. "Such is life."

"That may be," Rudy countered. "But I don't have to like it."

"Well, here's something you can like." Chessie approached, draped her arms over Rudy's shoulders and touched her lips to his.

The vibe was electric, but still, Rudy pulled his head back. "I admit that was very nice, but it doesn't solve anything."

"Maybe not," Chessie said, her eyes gleaming, "but a prelude is a prelude."

"Hmmmm," Rudy said, looking into his mate's eyes, considering his options.

THE RUDY STYNE QUADRILOGY
A Brief Overview

Readers were first introduced to Rudy Styne in Book I, *Rasputin's Nephew*, the prequel to *Doppelgänger*. In this first story, Rudy mistakes a dream for reality and then finds aspects of the dream accurately predicting the future. With a green light from Captain Whitmore to explore the field of parapsychology, Rudy enters the complex and dicey world of the paranormal. There he encounters Eurasian operatives who have had their brains rewired to make them psychokinetic. Not only are they murdering Western psychophysicists who are researching the neurophysiology of psychic phenomena, they are also planning on kidnapping a superpsychic so they could harness his brain for nefarious purposes.

Book III, *Crystal Night* is the sequel to Book II, this present book, *Doppelgänger*, and should be read after reading Book II. In *Crystal Night*, the back story continues to follow the Maxwell family saga as they try to maintain their prestigious MB Airways through the rise of Nazi power and the second world war. In the modern tale Rudy's journey continues as he searches to find a master hacker and at the same time works to uncover the truth to his origins. Here is a sneak preview:

☆
CRYSTAL NIGHT

It had taken Gunter Linzman nearly twenty years to ice this merger. He could feel his grandfather's blood streaming through his veins as he thought back to how they had wrestled MB Airways from Lufthansa, salvaged it through the horror of World War II and its aftermath. The struggles he had endured, dealing as a youth with the likes of Hermann Göring, visiting concentration camps to save the love of his life, honoring her legacy and then blocking it all to help lead his beaten country out from defeat. And now five decades later, Germany was once again a world power, with key positions on every continent, now also controlling a sizeable chunk of the American market through Bertelsmann, which dominated the publishing industry with their ownership of Random House, Doubleday, Bantam and Knopf, car manufacturing through Daimler Chrysler, BMW, Volkswagen and Mercedes Benz, telecommunications through T-Mobile, the pharmaceutical market through Bayer, control of cement manufacturing, tire and rubber, overnight mail delivery through DHL, and the *coup de grace*, ownership of the iconic New York Stock Exchange. Now, they owned Wall Street too.

But Gunter Linzman III had topped even that. Through his personal efforts, he alone had moved German domination into the American aerospace and satellite industry, for he now controlled Rockwell Marlen Aeronautics & Advanced Technology Corporation. Known in the biz as R-MAT, this leader in air and space had been the pride of the industry starting as far back as the 1930's when Rick Marlen and Bobby Rockwell formed their legendary partnership by cornering the market in transatlantic aircraft design. And then, two generations later they won every major contract for NASA when America beat the Russians in the space-race. As had been the plan, the 4th Reich was no longer a myth. Pan-Aryan supremacy had not only been achieved throughout 21st century Europe, Africa, Asia and the Middle East, but now in the New World as well.

Gunter Linzman suggested to R-MAT's CEO, Vance Fitzgerald, that they sign their merger agreement in front of cameras in the greatest metropolis in the world. He thought about the lookout platform on the Empire State Building, but that was too obvious. The Hotel Pierre would do just fine. Lawyers had finally completed the details, and this was a done deal. Fitzgerald would need some stroking. Gunter's publicity man would take care of most of the outlets, Fox TV, *The Wall Street Journal*, *The New York Times*, the other TV stations. But Gunter would call *Modern Times Magazine* himself. He was patched directly through to Captain Dean Whitmore, editor-in-chief.

As Linzman talked, the captain looked over his crew. Sally-Ann was typing away, working diligently, as she always did on the new story he had assigned her, but Mort and Bill were hovering again. How did those guys ever get any work done? Whitmore thought to himself as he tried to concentrate on the phone conversation.

"Mr. Linzman, can you hold a second." The captain put down the phone and marched into the newsroom. "Mort, Bill...."

"Yes, boss," they said in unison.

"You're fired."

"Sorry, sir," each said, as they made their way sheepishly back to their respective pods.

"Thanks, captain," Sally-Ann said.

"You're welcome!" the captain winked as he gave those two reporters a half-frown, half-smile and returned to his glassed-in office.

"Sorry, Mr. Linzman, please go on."

"It's Mr. Rudy Styne, Mr. Whitmore. That's the man I want to give my story to. Am I overstepping my bounds?" the German asked in his natural foreign accent.

"Not at all," the captain replied. "Mr. Styne should be in any moment. Wait! Here he is." The captain put down the phone and called out, "Rudy, get in here." He pointed to the phone and mouthed 'Linzman.' Rudy turned around to walk out. "One minute," Whitmore said again into the phone and lit out after Rudy.

"Rudy," Whitmore had caught up to him, "that's Gunter Linzman on the phone. He just bought Rockwell Marlen in one of the biggest aviation mergers in the nation's history. With Rockwell's link to our top-secret defense system, this puts a German concern in an incredibly powerful position that is simply unprecedented. And he wants to give *you* an exclusive."

"Gunter," Rudy said. "I thought it was Rolf." Rudy went to his desk and pressed the appropriate button.

"Rudy," Mr. Linzman said, excitement in his voice, "I've got a big meeting tomorrow. *The* big meeting. How about if we get together tonight for that dinner we missed in Munich. We could kind of celebrate."

"You know your son is in town?"

"No, as far as I knew, Rolf's in Qawatar trying to straighten out that mess there." Gunter was referring to the Mid-eastern coup Rudy had read about on his recent plane ride.

"Why don't you call him? If he hasn't left yet, maybe he should be there as well. You don't mind if I bring my wife?"

"Not at all. Her name is Chessie, isn't it?"

"Yes," Rudy said, surprised that Mr. Linzman would go so far as to learn her name.

"I'd like to meet her. And see if that photographer I had dinner with in Munich can come, too."

"Kim?"

"Yes, lovely girl. We might as well get a few photos."

"And, how about if I bring my mother?" Rudy asked, testing the waters.

"Is she out of the hospital? I apologize for not asking."

"Yes, it was just food poisoning. We had a scare, that's for sure, but she's fine."

"What's her name again?"

"Gladys Styne."

"Gladys, yes, Gladys. Sure, bring her. I'll book the Winston Room for seven, is that okay?" Gunter used the American idiom.

"Seven it is," Rudy said. Then he dialed Chessie.

"You're really going to ask your mother?" Chessie asked.

"I know she is still a little weak. But how else will I ever know if she and the old man had a thing?" Rudy got his car, picked Chessie up at her office, and drove back out to the Island. After dropping Chessie off, he drove out to his mother's place, the house he had spent his entire youth in.

"How are you doing?" Rudy asked when he got in.

"Come here and give your mother a kiss," Gladys said. Rudy complied.

"Mom, we're invited to dinner tonight with Mr. Gunter Linzman."

"That's nice, dear."

It was clear to Rudy, the name seemed not to ring any deep bells.

"That's the man you were supposed to see when you were meeting with that Heinz something…"

"Gruuban," Rudy inserted.

"Yes," Gladys continued, "when you were in Munich. He owns…"

"Spinnwebe."

"Yes, that German Internet company. I know, Rudy, but I've been sick," Rudy's mother explained.

"I know, mom. And do you know who Gunter Linzman is?"

"Not really, hon. He owns an airline, doesn't he?"

"MB Airways. mom. You're invited if you would like to come."

"I'm still not quite up to snuff, Rudy, but thank you for asking."

"I met his son just a few days ago," Rudy said.

"I know, Chessie told me."

"When was that?"

"Yesterday, the day before. I don't know. Why?"

"No reason. Did you know that Gunter Linzman's son looks exactly like me?"

"Exactly?" Gladys asked questioningly.

"Well, certainly much older, but still, like my double." He handed her a photo of Rolf. "It's eerie, that's why I want you to come."

Rudy's mother eyed the picture intently, and as she did, Rudy could see her mind travel off to a place far away. "You think Linzman's your father?" she finally said, handing Rudy back the picture.

"I don't know what to think anymore. I can't get a straight answer from you."

Gladys looked at her son for a long time, an expression of deep compassion emanating from her eyes. "If I give you a straight answer, will you let it rest?" Rudy nodded.

Gladys breathed out slowly and then she began.

☆

CRYSTAL NIGHT by Marc Seifer
A Rudy Styne book

Available online and at bookstores everywhere!

ACKNOWLEDGEMENTS

Doppelgänger and its sequel *Crystal Night* began in the mid-1990's as I scratched out preliminary notes which followed a few central ideas. The first was linked to an experience of mine stemming from the late 1960's when I actually did run into my double. If I tell you the story, you have to promise that it can't leave the room. Is it a deal? Okay, then.

One of my good friends, who Dickie is loosely based on, could be a real schmuck. In those days, if a big movie came out, lines could stretch around a block and oftentimes viewers would have to stand on line for a full two hours because there were not enough seats to hold everybody for the showing. One of the biggest films of that year was *Butch Cassidy and the Sundance Kid* starring, of course, Paul Newman and Robert Redford. My friend suggested that we try and catch the 9 o'clock show. This was in downtown New York City.

However, when we got there, the line literally was around the block which meant we would have to stand on line for two hours and see the film at 11. We bought our tickets, but instead of moving towards the end of the line, my friend said, "Come'n." And with that, he entered the theater while the 7 o'clock film was still in progress. But instead of trying to get into the movie, he led us into a downstairs bathroom. The idea was, as soon as the 7 o'clock let out, we would sneak in.

Inside the bathroom were two other young lads, and one of them was my *doppelgänger*. We were the same height, we both had a moustache, we were about the same size, we also both had our hair tied back, and as far as I was concerned, he looked just like me. I said to the guy, "Hey, we look alike." He didn't agree. So I took him to the mirror and we looked together at our image. My friend agreed as did his friend, but my *doppelgänger* wouldn't capitulate.

As it turned out, these two guys were on a double date, and their girlfriends, like them, were hiding in the girls' bathroom waiting. So I said, "I tell you what, when the movie lets out, how about we swap coats and let's see how long it takes your girlfriend to figure out it's not you."

Unfortunately, although the guy looked just like me, our personalities were very different and he wouldn't go along with the idea. Thus, we never got to do the experiment.

Through my adolescence and early adulthood I had dated three different girls who were identical twins. In one instance, I had met one of the girls at the beach and then tried to pick her up at a dance. It turned out to be her sister and she was the one I went out with.

Another theme in this book has to do with the idea of adoption. I have had many students through the years who have been adopted who have sought their birth parents. Some of the stories were heart warming, other stories really tore at your heart. In one instance, a girl was able to track down her biological father. She knocked on the door of the man's house and a young fellow who turned out to be her half-brother answered. He implored her not to make further contact and she reluctantly agreed.

I was not adopted, but fashioned a story which centered around the possibility that the lady who raised the protagonist was potentially not the biological mother. If indeed, this were the case, how would the child react? That is the dilemma facing Rudy.

The saga of the Maxwell family continues in *Crystal Night*, the sequel to this book. The idea simply was this: suppose the Nazis stole a Jewish company and then 50 years later one of the original owners wanted it back? This premise set me on a quest to find a company which would fit my needs. After contacting the Simon Wiesenthal Center, they were kind enough to send me a list of over 900 Jewish companies from Hamburg that were stolen by the Nazis. After looking through the list I settled on an automobile manufacturing plant and since the story started a little after the turn of the century, it made sense to morph the concern into an airline.

This decision helped the plot in many ways and also set me on a journey to learn as much as I possibly could about the early history of flight, from a European perspective. In particular, books about the World War I flying aces helped immeasurably, particularly biographies of the Red Baron, Ernst Udet, Hermann Göring and Georges Guynemer. Another key book was the amazing and truly enlightening autobiography of Theodor von Karmen, a genius of aerodynamics who built a wind tunnel at Göttingen and counseled such individuals as David Hilbert and Albert Einstein. I refer the reader to the bibliography for a more detailed accounting of my sources.

In terms of people to thank, in particular, I would like to thank my mother, Thelma Imber Seifer, who read most of the manuscript as it was being written, Lynn Sevigny and Eli Helman for their artistry and in the last days of the project, Pat Mullaney, who typed out the last hundred or so pages as they were written in the Spring of 2009. Other people to thank include Holocaust survivors Felix Klein and Bruno Bettelheim, also Rabbi Ballon, Stanley Krippner, John White, Uri Geller, Kerry Tyson, Ron Kresch, Sandy Neuschatz, Geoff Gardner, Richard Vangermeersch, Lucille and Paul Adler, Elliott Shriftman, Adam Kay, Nelson DeMille, Bob Leuci, Lee Smolovitch, Devin Keithley, Ella and Harry Adler for their stories of the Holocaust, Bentley Davis Seifer from which the boy Abe Maxwell was partially based on, and my brother Bruce Seifer and sister, Meri Keithley. Lastly, I would like to thank my wife and life partner, Lois Mary Pazienza, the inspiration for Chessie, Rudy's wife.

Marc J. Seifer, Ph.D.
Narragansett, RI

BIBLIOGRAPHY

Bekker, Claus. *The Luftwaffe War Diaries*. London: Corgi, 1967.

Bettelheim, Bruno. *The Informed Heart*. New York: Penguin, 1988.

Bojohr, Frank. *Arisierung in Hamburg*. Hamburg: Hans Christian Verlag, 1997.

Calabresi, Massimo. The War on Secrecy. *Time,* 12/13/2010, pp. 30-37.

Chernow, Ron. *The Warburgs*. New York: Random House, 1993.

Chesnoff, Richard. *Pack of Thieves*. New York: Anchor, 1999.

De Berniers, Louis. *Captain Corelli's Mandolin*. New York: Vintage, 1995.

Deighton, Len. *Winter*. New York: Ballentine Books, 1987.

DK Travel Books. *Venice*. London: 1997.

Dobson, William. Needles in a Haystack. *Newsweek,* 8/16/2010, pp. 38-41.

Dodd, Christopher, with Bloom, Larry. *Letters From Nuremberg*. New York: Crown, 2007.

Fonk, René. *Ace of Aces*. New York: Ace Books, 1967.

Gibbons, Floyd. *The Red Knight of Germany: The Story of Baron von Richthofen*. New York: Doubleday & Page, 1927.

Google. Numerous searches for main characters.

Griffith, Renata. Interview of her memory of her family, Fuchs-Bucher, sent on the Ship of Fools, 2001.

Grossman, Lev. The Men Who Stole the World. *Time,* 12/6/2010, pp. 54-59.

Grossman, Lev, & Newton-Small. The Deep Web. *Time,* 11/11/2013, pp. 26-33.

Gurney, Gene. *Flying Aces of WWI*. New York: Scholastic Books, 1965.

Gutman, Israel (Ed.). *Encyclopedia of the Holocaust*. NY: Macmillan, 1990.

Herlin, Hans. *Udet: A Man's Life*. London: MacDonald, 1960.

Hilberg, Paul. *The Destruction of the European Jews*. Chicago: Quadrangle Books, 1961.

Holmes, F.L. Hands Krebs: *The Foundation of a Scientific Life*. New York: Oxford University Press, 1991.

Hoffman, Peter. *Stauffenberg: A Family History*. Great Britain. Cambridge University Press, 1995.

Hunter, Jack. *The Blue Max*. New York: Bantam, 1966.

Irving, David. *Göring: A Biography*. New York: Avon, 1989.

Irving, David. *Rise & Fall of the Luftwaffe*. Boston: Little Brown, 1973.

Klemperer, Victor. *I Will Bear Witness: A Diary of the Nazi Years: 1933-1941*. New York: Random House, 2000.

Korda, Michael. *Worldy Goods*. New York: Bantam, 1983.

Krebs, Hans, with Schmid, Roswitha. *Otto Warburg: Cell Biologist & Eccentric*. Oxford: Clarendon Press, 1981.

Lee, Asher. *Goering: Air Leader*. New York: Hippocrene Books, 1972.

Loftus, John, & Aarons, Mark. *Secret War Against the Jews*. New York: St. Martin's Press, 1994.

Maltais, Michelle. Iran: Super Cyber Attack Launched From U.S. *Los Angeles Times*, 6/2/2012.

Manchester, William. *The Arms of Krupp: 1587-1968*. NY: Bantam Books, 1970.

McCracken, Harry. Where Everybody Knows Your Name. *Time*, 3/26/2012, p. 18.

Meir, Golda. *My Life*. New York. G.P. Putnam & Sons, 1975.

Messerschmidt, Willy. *Air Plane Design*. London: Century Books, 1975.

Miami Herald. "German Government Pledged 5 Billion for Slave & Forced Labor," March 3, 2001.

Nemirovsky, Irene. *Suite Francaise*. New York: Knopf, 2006.

Rich, Nathaniel. The Most Dangerous Man in Cyberspace. *Rolling Stone*, 9/2/2010, pp. 70-73, 88-89.

Roth, Cecil (ed.). *Jewish Encyclopedia*. New York: New American Library, 1985.

Schleunes, K.A. *The Twisted Road to Auschwitz*. Urbana, IL: University of Illinois Press, 1970.

Seifer, Marc. Personal trips to Amsterdam, Bavaria, Brussels, Haifa, Innsbruck, Jerusalem, Locust Valley, Lucerne, Luxembourg, Manhattan, Monteriggioni, Neuschweinstein, Newark, Paris, Venice, Verona.

Simon Weisenthal Center, List of Jewish companies taken over by the Nazis in Hamburg, 2002.

Six and a half million passwords from Linkedin posted on hacker website. *Providence Journal*, 6/8/2012, p. B1.

Stoll, Clifford. *The Cookoo's Egg*. New York: Pocket, 2005.

Sutton, Nina. *Bruno Bettelheim: A Life & Legacy*. New York: Basic Books, 1996.

Symons, Alan. *Jewish Contribution to the 20ᵗʰ Century*. London: Polo. 1997.

Shirer, William. *The Rise & Fall of the Third Reich*. New York: Simon & Schuster, 1960.

Treadwell, Terry, & Wood, Alan. *German Knights of the Air: 1914-1918*. London: Brassey's, 1997.

Udet, Ernst. *Ace of the Iron Cross*. New York: Doubleday, 1970.

Von Karmen, Theodore, & Edson, Lee. *The Wind & Beyond*. Boston: Little Brown, 1967.

Vassiltchikov, Marie "Missie." *Berlin Diaries: 1940-45*. London: Methuen Publishers, 1987.

Wikepedia. Numerous searches for main characters.

Wilson, Robert. *A Small Death in Lisbon*. New York: Berkley Books, 2002.

Marc Seifer in Novi Sad, Serbia at book signing of his Tesla biography.

BIOGRAPHY: Marc J. Seifer, Ph.D. is the author of the **RUDY STYNE QUADRILOGY:** I. *Rasputin's Nephew*, II. *Doppelgänger*, III. *Crystal Night* and IV. *Fate Line*; *FRAMED! Murder, Corruption & a Death Sentence in Florida* (true courtroom thriller); *Where Does Mind End?* (psychology textbook); *Transcending the Speed of Light: Quantum Physics & Consciousness* and *The Definitive Book of Handwriting Analysis.* His acclaimed biography *WIZARD: The Life & Times of Nikola Tesla* is "HIGHLY RECOMMENDED" by the American Association for the Advancement of Science. Starring in the 5-part mini-series **THE TESLA FILES**, wth appearances on PBS The American Experience, The History Channel, AP International TV, NPR's To the Best of Our Knowledge and All Things Considered, The Morning Show, Canberra Australia, the BBC and Coast to Coast Radio, Dr. Seifer has also appeared in *Scientific American, Nature, MIT's Technology Review, Publisher's Weekly, The Historian, The Journal of Psychohistory, Cerebrum, Wired, Glamour, Cosmopolitan, The Washington Post, The Economist, The Wall Street Journal, Investor's Daily* and *The New York Times*. A handwriting expert and also an expert on inventor Nikola Tesla, he has lectured at West Point Military Academy, Brandeis University, CCNY, Long Island University, Cranbrook Retreat, NY Public Library, The Open Center in New York, Oxford and Cambridge Universities in England, for the Serbian Academy of Sciences in Belgrade, in association with the US State Department in Zagreb Croatia, at the University of Vancouver Canada, in Jerusalem Israel and at the United Nations. His works have been translated into ten languages. He is a retired teacher of psychology from Roger Williams University, Bristol, Rhode Island.